D0251803

continued . . .

Shop Till You Drop

"Fans of Janet Evanovich and Parnell Hall will appreciate Viets's humor." —*South Florida Sun-Sentinel*

"Elaine Viets's debut is a live wire. . . . Helen Hawthorne takes Florida by storm. Shop no further—this is the one." —Tim Dorsey

"I loved this book. With a stubborn . . . heroine, a wonderful South Florida setting, and a cast of more-or-less lethal bimbos, *Shop Till You Drop* provides tons of fun. Six-toed cats, expensive clothes, sexy guys on motorcycles—this book has it all." —Charlaine Harris

"Fresh, funny, and fiendishly constructed, *Shop Till You Drop* gleefully skewers cosmetic surgery, ultra-exclusive clothing boutiques, cheating ex-husbands, and the Florida dating game, as attractive newcomer Helen Hawthorne takes on the first of her deliciously awful dead-end jobs. . . . A bright start to an exciting new series. This one is hard to beat." —Parnell Hall, author of the Puzzle Lady crossword puzzle mysteries

"A smashing success [that] contains wit [and] local color. . . . The heroine is a delightful mix of grit, determination, and stubbornness. . . . Electrifying." —*Midwest Book Review*

Also by Elaine Viets

HIGH HEELS
ARE MURDER

JOSIE MARCUS, MYSTERY SHOPPER

Elaine Viets

A SIGNET BOOK

SIGNET
Published by New American Library, a division of
Penguin Group (USA) Inc., 375 Hudson Street,
New York, New York 10014, USA
Penguin Group (Canada), 90 Eglinton Avenue East, Suite 700, Toronto,
Ontario M4P 2Y3, Canada (a division of Pearson Penguin Canada Inc.)
Penguin Books Ltd., 80 Strand, London WC2R 0RL, England
Penguin Ireland, 25 St. Stephen's Green, Dublin 2,
Ireland (a division of Penguin Books Ltd.)
Penguin Group (Australia), 250 Camberwell Road, Camberwell, Victoria 3124,
Australia (a division of Pearson Australia Group Pty. Ltd.)
Penguin Books India Pvt. Ltd., 11 Community Centre, Panchsheel Park,
New Delhi - 110 017, India
Penguin Group (NZ), cnr Airborne and Rosedale Roads, Albany,
Auckland 1310, New Zealand (a division of Pearson New Zealand Ltd.)
Penguin Books (South Africa) (Pty.) Ltd., 24 Sturdee Avenue,
Rosebank, Johannesburg 2196, South Africa

Penguin Books Ltd., Registered Offices:
80 Strand, London WC2R 0RL, England

First published by Signet, an imprint of New American Library,
a division of Penguin Group (USA) Inc.

First Printing, November 2006
10 9 8 7 6 5 4 3 2 1

For my sole sisters

Acknowledgments

For *Dying in Style*, the first book in this series, Josie and I received the key to the city of Maplewood. We were honored. The key is framed and hangs in my office. Maplewood is indeed the right home for Josie.

Many people helped with this book. I hope I haven't left anyone out. Thanks to my St. Louis experts: Jinny Gender, Karen Grace and Janet Smith. St. Louis public librarian Anne Watts did extensive research on various subjects, including gambling in Missouri. Jennifer Snethen took photographs of Maplewood to remind me that it is a storybook city.

Thanks also to Valerie Cannata, Colby Cox, and Susan Carlson, and to Kay Gordy, who knows all about two-year-olds.

I also want to thank Emma, my expert on nine-year-olds. She used to be one last year. Emma gave me deep background on what it's like to be nine years old. I wish I could use her real name, but the world is a dangerous place these days for little girls.

As always, thanks and love to my husband, Don Crinklaw, for his extraordinary help and patience. It's not easy to live with a writer, but he manages.

My agent, David Hendin, is still the best.

Special thanks to my editor, Kara Cesare, who devoted long hours to editing and guiding this project, to copy editor Jan McInroy and the Signet production staff, and to publicist Julie Samara.

Many booksellers help keep this series alive. I wish I had room to thank them all. Thanks to Joanne Sinchuk and John Spera at South Florida's largest mystery bookstore, Murder on the Beach, in Delray Beach, Florida. Thanks to Pam Marshall at the Hollywood Barnes & Noble, and to Susan Boyd in Plantation and Helen La-Forge at Fort Lauderdale. Thanks also to Mary Alice Gorman and Richard Goldman, to Barbara Peters at Poisoned Pen, to Bonnie and Joe at Black Orchid in New York, and David and McKenna at Murder by the Book in Houston. Kim, Jamey, Jim, and the gang maintain a book shrine for my novels at the Waldenbooks in Pompano Beach.

Special thanks to the law enforcement men and women who answered countless questions on police procedure. Some of my police and medical sources have to remain nameless, but I want to thank them all the same. Particular thanks to Detective R. C. White, Fort Lauderdale Police Department (retired). Any mistakes are mine, not theirs.

Thanks to the librarians at the Broward County Library and the St. Louis Public Library who researched my questions, no matter how strange, and always answered with straight faces.

Thanks to public relations expert Jack Klobnak, to Patti Nunn, and to my bookseller friend, Carole Wantz, who can sell swimsuits in Siberia in January.

Chapter 1

"Josie, please, can I come in?" Josh was kissing her neck and her right ear.

Josie Marcus kissed him back. There was a deep silence, broken only by heavy breathing. "Sorry, Josh. It's a school night," she panted. "I have to be in by ten."

Josh unbuttoned the tiny pearl buttons on her shirt, then kissed the tops of her breasts. "I'll be very quiet," he said.

More silence. More kissing. More panting.

"My mother's upstairs," Josie said breathlessly. "She's got ears like a bat."

"Come to my place," Josh said. "There are no old bats. Just a big bed with fresh sheets and some very nice wine." He flicked open the front closure on her bra and said, "Oh my God."

Josie was glad the porch light was out. Her knees were weak. That must be why she was clinging to Josh. "I can't," she whispered frantically. "There's my daughter, Amelia. I have to be home for her." Josie refastened her bra.

"How about my car?" Josh said, kissing her again.

"It's parked under a streetlight," she gasped. When he kissed her that way, she could hardly stand up.

"We'll have the windows steamed up in no time," Josh said.

Josie almost said yes. Then she saw the curtains twitch at the house next door. Now she felt hot, but it was the heat of anger.

"I can't," she said. "Mrs. Mueller will see us."

"Who," he said between kisses, "is Mrs. Mueller?"

"The neighborhood gossip. She'll tell Mom and my life will be hell."

"Josie, how old are you?" Josh said.

"Thirty-one."

"Why are we making out like horny teenagers on your front porch?"

"Aren't you glad I make you feel young?" Josie pulled away and buttoned her blouse.

"That's not how I feel," Josh said. "I may never be able to straighten up again. We're too old for this."

"No, we're exactly the right age," Josie said. "If we were teenagers, we'd be boffing like crazy. Only adults have these problems."

"Josie, please let me in."

"Josh, I really want to, but I can't." Josie tucked in her blouse. "We should have thought of this earlier."

"Are you kidding? It's all I've thought about tonight. But I wanted to take you to dinner like a gentleman instead of just jumping your bones. Look where it got me."

Josie laughed. Josh didn't. "Who the hell is this Mrs. Mueller and why is she so important?" he asked.

Josie studied him in the starlight. Josh was four years younger, smart and sizzling. Her friends wouldn't believe she was telling him no. Josh had a sensitive poet's face, a dangerous walk, and expert hands. He wanted to be a sci-fi writer, but right now, Josh was the best barista in Maplewood, producing sensational espressos and cappuccinos on his gleaming machine. When Josh was with Josie, he pulled out all the stops.

She kissed his nimble fingers and tried to explain the constraints on her life. "Mrs. Mueller rules the neighborhood," Josie said. "She's convinced I'm a slut, and I haven't done anything but wear a couple of trampy outfits for my job. If I go to your car, she'll have proof. She might even take pictures. She'll tell my mother, who is also my landlord and my babysitter and therefore has absolute power. It's a Sunday night. I have work tomorrow and Amelia has school. If I let you inside, we'll wake up Mom and I'll never hear the end of it. Even if we don't wake up Mom, Mrs. Mueller will be standing by with a stopwatch. She'll watch the shadows on the window shades and listen for the bedsprings."

"She sounds obsessed," Josh said.

"Mrs. Mueller has had this thing about me ever since I was fifteen. She caught me smoking behind her garage and ratted me out to Mom. I got even by putting a bag of dog doo on her porch and setting fire to it. Mrs. Mueller stamped it out."

Josh burst out laughing. "Mrs. Mueller fell for the flaming-dog-doo-of-death trick?"

"You may think it's funny, but she never forgave me. My name is mud. No, it's worse than mud."

"Why do you care what she thinks?" Josh kissed her so hard, her last few wits nearly fled.

"I don't," Josie said. "But Mrs. Mueller runs all the major church committees and clubs in the neighborhood. She rules Mom's social life. Mom thinks the sun rises and sets on that awful woman. To make it worse, Mrs. Mueller has this perfect daughter named Cheryl. She keeps rubbing Cheryl's achievements in my mother's face until Mom can hardly hold her head up.

"Josh, you're single, so it's hard to understand. If it was just me, I wouldn't care, but Maplewood is like a small town. Gossip about me will hurt my mother and my daughter."

"I do understand," he said. "I just don't like it."

"Amelia has a sleepover soon. Maybe we can be together then," Josie said.

Josh kissed her again. They stood hand in hand on Josie's front porch, looking at the clear November night. The old sycamore trees rustled and the houses creaked in the warm wind. It was one of St. Louis's famous freaky weather switches. The night was a springlike sixty-five degrees when there should have been frost.

"Look," he said. "A falling star. Make a wish."

Josie saw the curtains twitch again.

"I wish Mrs. Mueller would get hers," Josie said. "I

wish she'd be so embarrassed she couldn't hold her head up in Maplewood—no, the whole St. Louis area. I wish she'd fall so low, she'd have to look up to me."

Josie got her wish. Every word would come true.

And she would regret them all.

Chapter 2

Mel held Josie's right foot, slowly rubbing her arch with his thumb. His stroking fingers inched toward her toes. Josie tried not to flinch.

"Pink nail polish is so feminine," Mel said softly.

"Thank you," Josie said.

Yuck, she thought. I can't yank my foot away from this pervert. I have to pretend to like this. I have a job to do. Some job—having my foot fondled by a freak. If my mother knew, she'd hit the roof. What if my daughter found out?

How is Amelia going to know? Josie's sneaky side said. Are you going to tell her? God forbid your daughter should do this for a living.

Mel had stripped the pointy red Prada heel from Josie's other foot and examined it closely. Was he looking at the stitching or sniffing her shoe? Josie's stomach lurched.

Mel stopped stroking her stockinged foot and set it gently on his sloping footstool. She buried it in the soft padding. If only it was Josh massaging her foot. If only Josie wasn't in the Soft Shoe, the exclusive retro shoe shop in St. Louis.

The Soft Shoe was a perfect copy of a 1950s women's shoe store, with powder pink decor and salespeople who sat on old-fashioned slanted footstools, slipped off your shoes, then brought you stacks of styles to try on. The store was a shoe lover's dream.

Mel was its nightmare. He gave Josie the creeps, and she couldn't say why. He was slender and well dressed in a beautifully tailored gray suit. Maybe it was the pink carnation in his buttonhole. It made him look like an old-style gigolo. Mel wore too much cologne and his carefully cut hair was a little oily. That was it. Mel was oily. His manners, his hair, even his manicured hands were slightly oily, and he kept rubbing them.

"I see that you have an appreciation for quality," Mel said. "Prada is well made. Sexy, too. Plenty of toe cleavage, which men adore. Smart women know that."

Many smart women didn't know—or care—about toe cleavage, the hollow between the big toe and the second digit. But Mel's hand grew moist as his eyes drifted toward the tiny valley between her toes. Josie wished she was wearing her grandmother's black lace-up Enna Jetticks, which would conceal her feet completely. Except they might really excite Mel.

"You're looking for a high heel?" Mel smiled. All the man needed was a pencil-thin mustache.

"Yes," Josie said. "Something special." She smiled back. She hoped she looked winsome, and not like her feet hurt.

"I know all the styles that please men and make women feel pretty," Mel said.

Mel was the Soft Shoe's top seller nationwide. But the company suspected Mel might love shoes a little too much. Management was in dangerous territory. If they falsely accused Mel, he could sue Soft Shoe. Plus, the company would lose its best salesman. But if Mel really was a foot fetishist and the company let him prey on customers, there would be a nasty scandal—and more lawsuits. That's why Soft Shoe had hired Josie's company, Suttin Services, to mystery-shop the St. Louis store and target Mel.

Josie's boss, Harry, gave her the Soft Shoe assignment this way: "The company wants you to ask for a salesman named Mel," he said. "He's really into ladies' feet, if you know what I mean."

"You want me to investigate a pervert?" Josie had said.

"He's not dangerous, Josie," Harry had told her. "The

worst he'll do is give you a foot massage. Might feel good on your tired tootsies. Listen, this Mel may not even be what they think he is. The company is a little suspicious, that's all. He's a shoe salesman who's a little too interested in women's shoes."

"Is he a foot or a shoe fetishist?"

"Both, I think," Harry said. "At least they've had complaints about both. How the hell would I know? I'm no freak."

Josie thought that subject could be debated, but not now.

"Look. They've had a couple of complaints from lady customers and they don't know how seriously to take them. Women can be crazy, you know what I mean?"

Josie had not called her boss on his sexist remark. Harry was hopeless. Besides, Josie got a bonus for special assignments and mystery shopping paid little enough. But now that Mel was sitting on his sloping pink stool, oozing over her foot, Josie wondered if the extra money was worth it.

"You wait here," Mel said. "I'll be right back."

Mel had an odd crouching walk as he ducked through the pink curtains into the back room. So far, I have nothing suspicious for my report, Josie thought. What can I say? He held my foot a little longer than usual? He rubbed my arch in a suggestive manner? I'll sound like a nutcase. All I have is my feeling that something is off about Mel.

Still, other women must have felt the same way, or Josie wouldn't be here. She would have to try on shoes until she knew for sure. She owed it to her sole sisters, as well as to the company.

Josie couldn't bring her mystery-shopping questionnaire into the store, but she knew the questions by heart. Right now, Mel had a perfect score. Had he greeted her warmly when she entered the store? Had he introduced himself in a positive manner and mentioned the store name? Had he waited on her promptly? Had he offered to bring out the high-fashion stock? Yes, yes and yes.

Here he was now, carrying shoe boxes stacked up to

his chin. The Big Bopper sang on the retro sound track about Chantilly lace and a pretty face. Josie's mother had danced to that tune when she was young.

"I have a sassy pair of open-toed Bruno Maglis." Mel took off the shoe box lid with a flourish.

Josie studied the shoes. They were cute. If she could afford nearly three bills for shoes, she'd buy them. At least she was being paid to try them on.

"I like them," she said. "But I have on the wrong stockings. Mine have reinforced toes."

"Where did women get this idea that men don't like reinforced toes?" Mel said as he slipped the shoes on Josie. Sweat had popped out on his forehead, although it wasn't warm in the store. He wiped it with a silk pocket square.

"Some of us men long for the good old days, when women wore stockings with reinforced heels *and* toes," Mel said. "Unfortunately, panty hose have taken over everything. They're so orthopedic. Women have lost their affection for high heels. Why don't women wear heels anymore, like they did in the fifties and sixties?"

"Because they hurt," Josie said. She had to walk miles through the malls in heels for her mystery shopping. Spikes were torture.

"But heels do such nice things for the calf and leg. I'd think women would endure a little discomfort to look attractive," Mel said.

"Hobbling is unattractive," Josie said, and wondered if she'd blown her cover with her anti-heel remark. "I'll take the Bruno Maglis."

"May I show you a Kenneth Cole D'Orsay pump?" Mel was practically on his knees begging as he brought out the turquoise shoe with the open sides.

"Sure."

Mel slipped the pair on her feet. Josie stood up and took a few steps to the long mirror. The open-sided shoe was sexy, no doubt about it. Her legs looked terrific.

"Adorable," Mel said. "I'll be right back." He disappeared behind the pink curtains again, with that strange crouch.

Josie sighed. She was going to be here all day, with

nothing to show for it but mauled feet. If Mel was misbe-
having, she hadn't caught him at it.

Mel returned a few minutes later with another precari-
ous pile of shoe boxes. "I have a gorgeous little sling-
back with a stiletto heel," he said. "And an absolutely
precious ankle-wrap sandal."

Mel opened the boxes like a courtier showing jewels
to his queen. Josie tried them all on, wishing she was
wearing them for Josh instead of Mel. After nearly an
hour, she was knee-deep in a welter of rejected shoes. All
she could say in her report was that Mel had spent more
time than usual with her, and that it wasn't wasted time
for him. She was buying three pairs of shoes—nearly a
thousand dollars' worth of stock—or so he thought.

Damn. I'll have to come back here for another visit,
Josie thought. Maybe then I'll figure out why Mel both-
ers me. There's something wrong about that man. I wish
I could see it.

"You don't want to take these old shoes with you."
Mel indicated her red heels.

I do, Josie thought. Because I'm returning everything
I bought here today to another Soft Shoe, in Plaza Frontenac. Josie wouldn't get to keep those gorgeous shoes.
Returning recently purchased items to yet another store
was one of mystery shopping's less glamorous assignments. But it was an effective way to test customer
service.

"Actually, I do want them," Josie said.

Mel looked sad. So did her resale-shop Pradas. Were
they really so down-at-heels? Funny how shoes that
seemed attractive when she walked into a store looked
worn and dusty when she bought new ones.

"Then let me clean them for you," Mel said.

At least I'll get a free shoeshine, Josie thought. I can
keep that.

Before she could say anything, Mel had her shoes in
one hand and was heading for the pink curtains with
that odd crouching walk. He reminded her of Josh on
her front porch last night.

Suddenly, Josie knew what the salesman was going to
do to her innocent Pradas. She ran toward the back

room, flung open the pink curtains and caught Mel, crouching like a teenage boy behind stacks of shoe boxes.

"Unhand that shoe, you heel!" she thundered and ripped her still-pure Prada from his grasp.

Josie had him. After her report, Mel would never molest another pump.

Chapter 3

"So you caught him red-handed with your shoe," Harry said.

Josie's boss grinned like a whacked-out weasel. He wanted Josie to repeat the story over and over. The man creeped her out almost as much as Mel.

"Tell me about this toe cleavage again," Harry said.

"Please," Josie said. "I'm trying to forget. The details are in my report. You read it. I rescued my shoe from a fate worse than death."

Harry laughed. It was a wild, honking sound, like the mating cry of a Discovery Channel beast. Josie hoped something large, smelly and in love wouldn't come galloping through his office door at Suttin Services.

"Have a seat," Harry said, when his laughter finally choked off.

Josie plopped into the beat-up wooden chair opposite his desk. It wobbled dangerously, then tilted to one side. Harry liked to keep his mystery shoppers off balance. She wondered if he'd sawed one chair leg shorter.

"Did you really call Mel a heel?" Harry said. "Where did you get that word? Nobody freaking talks like that. What century are you in?"

"The Soft Shoe was so retro, it seemed to belong," Josie said. "Buddy Holly and the Big Bopper were playing on the sound track. The store was this ladylike powder pink. It just popped into my mind. Besides, what would you call Mel?"

"An asshole," Harry said. A small landslide of yellowing paper slid down the north face of his desk.

"Classy," Josie said.

"Hey, if the shoe fits," Harry said. "I read about guys like him, but I didn't think they really existed."

Most people wouldn't think Harry was real, either. He looked like a troll in a fairy tale—a Grimm fairy tale. Like his name, he was hairy. He had hair on his head, in his ears and in his nose. The joints of his fingers sprouted hairs like weeds in sidewalk cracks. He was also fat.

Harry was on the Atkins diet, but he'd never be a poster boy for the plan. He ignored most of its guidelines, except the one about eating meat. Harry always had a roast something in one hand when Josie saw him at Suttin Services. Phone conversations came with chomping and slurping sounds that were worse than the visuals.

Today, Harry snacked on a turkey leg. It glistened as he talked. Grease smeared his fingers and glossed his rubbery lips. While he stuffed his face, Harry drooled over an Omaha Steaks catalog the way another man would look at a *Playboy* centerfold. The Omaha headline seemed almost pornographic: BOLD AND BEEFY BONELESS STRIP SIRLOINS.

"Look at these beauties," Harry said. "Man, if I could get my hands on meat like that, the weight would roll off me."

Josie studied the luscious, dripping meat. It seemed to throb on the page. "Holy cow. Four eight-ounce steaks for sixty-seven dollars," she said.

"Hey, it's less than you'd pay in a restaurant," Harry said through a mouthful of masticated turkey. "How about this? Four eight-ounce prime ribs for seventy-three dollars. Four of those babies, medium rare. Man, that's living. You want class? Here's stuffed filet mignons with blue cheese, shiitake mushrooms and—"

"Harry, you wanted to see me?" Josie said.

"Yeah. I wanted to say, 'Good work.' You got your bonus." Harry handed Josie an envelope. His smile was slippery with satisfaction and turkey grease. She'd solved the Soft Shoe problem in one visit.

Josie knew better than to trust Harry. He'd sold her out before. "Thanks," she said, dropping the envelope in her purse.

"Of course, we'll keep your name confidential." Slurp. Chomp. He stripped five inches of flesh from the turkey leg.

"You still have to shop the other three Soft Shoe stores, but Mel is history," Harry said. "He's fired. They gave him his walking papers this afternoon."

"Good. He deserved it." Sometimes Josie felt guilty when she knew her bad report would get some underpaid employee in trouble. But not this time.

Harry went back to salivating over his catalog, and Josie knew she was dismissed.

She was glad to be out of Harry's dusty, stuffy office and into the crisp November day. Josie picked her way through the potholes on the Suttin lot, found her anonymous gray Honda and settled into the butt-sprung seat.

"The envelope, please," Josie said, and ripped open her bonus. Inside was a crisp fifty-dollar bill. Very nice.

Josie wished she could tell her mother about her triumph. She wished Jane would be proud of her. But her mother would be horrified at the way Josie caught Mel the foot fondler. It would only confirm Jane's opinion that Josie had ruined her life.

In Jane's world, young women did not spy on slimy shoe salesmen. In fact, they didn't work at all, unless they volunteered for a committee for a worthy cause. Jane, alas, had lost that life of genteel luxury when her husband walked out on her. She worked long, dull years at a bank to put Josie through school. Jane's plans for her clever daughter included a college degree, a house in the suburbs, a lawyer-doctor husband, and a country club membership. Josie was supposed to resume Jane's interrupted life.

Josie destroyed those hopes the night she lit a hundred candles and fixed a pitcher of margaritas for Amelia's father. She wound up pregnant and he wound up in jail.

But, Lord, what a night, Josie thought. At least I ruined myself in style. Josie didn't believe that night was a mistake. She liked her life as a mystery shopper. She loved her freedom and her daughter with equal fierceness.

If only Mom could see that I'm happier the way I am, Josie thought. If only Mom would be proud of me. But that was never going to happen.

Josie gave her mother credit. Jane worshiped respectability, but she had stood by her pregnant, unmarried daughter. She adored her granddaughter, Amelia. She helped Josie with emergency babysitting. She let her and Amelia live on the first floor of Jane's two-family flat at reduced rent. But she never quite forgave her daughter. Occasionally, Jane's resentment at her ruined plans would flare up, like an attack of rheumatism.

Only one woman could appreciate Josie's special moment with Mel—her best friend. Alyce Bohannon lived in the Estates at Wood Winds with a lawyer husband who worked late, a fat-cheeked toddler, and a living room that belonged in *Architectural Digest.* Alyce had everything Josie should have had, except excitement.

Alyce went along on some of Josie's mystery-shopper assignments because she was bored with her perfect life—an irony Josie's mother never saw.

Josie called her friend on her cell phone. "You won't believe what happened today," she said.

"I'm sure I won't," Alyce said. "Are you hungry? Have you had lunch?"

"I watched Harry dismember a turkey leg," Josie said. "I lost my appetite."

"That man is disgusting," Alyce said. "You need to eat properly. I'll make us a nice salad, pop in some fresh rolls, and open a bottle of wine. Come out and tell me everything."

Alyce lived in far West County, one of the newest and richest parts of the metro area. Not long ago, her subdivision had been woods and farms. Josie drove the winding back roads to the Estates at Wood Winds, dodging the long, skinny tree branches that clutched at her car. Something small and gray with a pink hairless tail ran in front of her Honda. Josie slammed on her brakes, heart pounding. Did she hit the creature? There was no small squished corpse on the road. No bloody thump on the bumper. Josie sighed with relief and restarted her car.

Alyce loved to tell Josie about the charming wildlife she'd seen near her home—baby fawns, brown cotton-tailed bunnies, rollicking raccoons. Josie never saw any of these Disney animals. To her, the woods were a lonely place with gray, ratlike creatures and trees with branches like dead claws. They made her think of serial killers, shallow graves, and horror movies.

I'm a city kid, she thought. I need concrete under my feet.

The bored guard at the Estates at Wood Winds waved Josie through the gate. She pulled into the double drive of Alyce's Tudor mansion. Even the half-timbered garage had mullioned windows. Josie gave the three-knock signal on the side door.

"Come in!" Alyce met her at the door with a glass of white wine. "Drink," she commanded, handing Josie a fat, cold glass. "And sit."

Josie obeyed. She was always slightly stunned by the perfection of Alyce's home. In Josie's city flat, the floors sloped and sagged, the plaster walls had cracks, and the woodwork was thick with old paint.

Alyce's home glowed with newness. Everything was fresh, clean and shiny. The kitchen was paneled with luscious linenfold oak and hung with copper pots. The air was perfumed with baking rolls and fresh coffee. Alyce stood at a granite-topped cooking island the size of Bermuda, slicing strawberries for the salad.

Josie pulled up a wrought-iron chair. She knew better than to ask if she could help. Josie couldn't operate most of the Williams-Sonoma appliances in Alyce's kitchen. She hadn't even heard of half of them. Josie thought the stainless-steel mandoline was a musical instrument, not a fancy French chopper. She'd never seen a breading tray before. She'd managed to live without the Carrara marble mortar and beech pestle that Alyce swore were "indispensable for crushing herbs and spices." The canned spices Josie bought at the supermarket seemed pretty well pulverized.

The kitchen was Alyce's personal heaven and she was its golden-haired goddess. Alyce didn't walk. She floated, as if on a cloud. She was six inches taller than Josie and generously built, but she had an unearthly, gliding walk. Even her fine silky blond hair seemed to float.

"So tell me what happened," Alyce said.

She arranged two mounds of spinach salad loaded with goat cheese, caramelized onions, walnuts and strawberries on cobalt blue plates. The rolls were hot. The wine was cold. Josie nibbled, sipped and talked about how she bagged Mel.

When she finished, Alyce said, "Josie, that story sends chills down my spine. I don't even want to think about that creepy guy. I bought shoes at that store. I wonder if he waited on me?"

"I think you'd remember," Josie said.

"Thank God you caught him," Alyce said. "But how can you wear those Prada heels after what Mel tried to do to them?"

"I haven't much choice," Josie said. "They're part of my Fashion Victim disguise."

"Aren't you afraid Mel will come after you?" Alyce said. "You got him fired. He has to be furious."

"Harry says he'll keep my name and address confidential," Josie said.

"Hah. We know how quickly your boss sold you out last time there was trouble," Alyce said.

"Harry is a spineless rat," Josie said. "But I'm not worried about a shoe salesman. Besides, it's over." She glanced at her watch. "It's also two o'clock. I'd better pick up Amelia at school. Thanks for giving me some graciousness in a grungy day."

"I appreciate the excitement," Alyce said. She sounded wistful, but Josie knew Alyce wouldn't live in a world without garlic peelers.

Josie made it back to Clarkson Road without any critters throwing themselves under her car. She had half an hour to get to the Barrington School for Boys and Girls. Josie had one thing in common with her mother. She wanted the best for her daughter. In this case, the best was the Barrington School. Amelia was a scholarship student.

Josie waited in the long driveway until her car pulled in front of the school and the principal called, "Amelia Marcus." Amelia came running out the school door, her straight black hair flying out behind her. Her shoestrings were undone, but Josie wasn't sure if that was the current style or her kid was a slob. She liked to watch her daughter move. She had her father's physical confidence and his bright intelligence. Amelia had inherited everything but his facility for languages, and Josie was glad of that. If Nate hadn't been so good at Spanish, he might not be in prison.

Amelia plopped onto the car seat and dragged her backpack in after her.

"So what did you do at work today, Mom?" she asked. Her lapses into adult conversation amused Josie, but she always answered them seriously.

"I shopped Soft Shoe. Spent the day trying on designer shoes," Josie said.

"Sweet," Amelia said. It was her favorite word of approval. "Did you get to keep any?"

"No, I had to give them all back." Josie steered the car down the school's long driveway.

"Bummer," Amelia said.

"For sure," Josie said. "Especially the open-toed Bruno Maglis."

All the way home to Maplewood, they talked about shoe shopping. As their car turned off Manchester Road onto their street, Amelia rolled down the window and waved frantically at a slender man in his vigorous early seventies. He was tall and slightly stooped, with a long nose and a handsome head of gray hair. "There's Grandma's boyfriend, Jimmy," Amelia said.

"That's Mr. Ryent to you, Amelia. Grandma says he's just a friend."

"I saw them kissing on the front porch the other night," Amelia said.

Did you now? Josie thought. That information might come in handy later. She wondered if her nosy neighbor,

Mrs. Mueller, watched her mother, too. Then Josie remembered she was supposed to be the parent.

"Why weren't you in bed, young lady, instead of spying on your grandmother?"

"I wasn't spying. They woke me up," Amelia said. "They were talking and laughing real loud. I looked out the window and saw them. Mr. Ryent said Grandma had skin like a rose, but she's all wrinkled, Mom."

"There are different kinds of beauty, Amelia," Josie said. "The beauty of a mature woman is special, and so is the man who can appreciate it. It's nice that Mr. Ryent is so romantic."

"He asked her to go bowling with him. Said he had two good balls. Grandma thought that was funny. Why is that funny, Mom?" Amelia said.

"I don't know," Josie said, biting the inside of her cheek to keep from laughing. "I'm not a bowler." Well, that much was true.

As she parked in front of their flat, Josie saw the curtains twitching at Mrs. Mueller's house and absent-mindedly waved.

Mrs. Mueller did not wave back.

Chapter 4

"Mrs. Mueller's daughter, Cheryl, came to visit her mother today," Jane said.

Josie braced herself. She knew what was coming—another Perfect Cheryl Report. Jane got this look of dazed envy when she talked about Cheryl, as if she were recounting the adventures of a saint or a superhero. According to her mother, Cheryl was both.

Josie had endured the Perfect Cheryl Reports since age seven. That's when she and Jane had moved to Maplewood.

Josie was the new kid in a strange neighborhood. She felt lost. She was starting a new school at midyear and didn't know anyone. Their big, bright house in Ladue, which had so many rooms Josie couldn't count them, was gone. Now Josie and her mother lived upstairs in a creaky five-room flat. An old woman who smelled of mothballs and played the TV too loud lived in the downstairs apartment, but they couldn't complain about the noise because she paid the rent on time. Josie's mother cried every night, when she thought Josie was asleep. Josie's dad had moved to Chicago with his new wife. He never called, not even on her birthday.

Cheryl was seven, just like Josie. She lived in the biggest house in the new neighborhood. It was a three-story redbrick with a white wraparound porch. Josie knew that Cheryl was one of the cool kids. Even after a day at school, Cheryl's ruffled pink blouse was unwrinkled. Her white-blond hair was straight as a model's in *Seventeen*.

Josie's plain brown hair stuck out in six directions, her

shirttail had slid out of her pants, and her socks had rolled down into her shoes. She pulled them up and walked across the lawn to greet Cheryl.

"Hi, I'm your new neighbor, Josie Marcus." She stuck out her hand, the way Jane had taught her.

"So?" Cheryl said. She stared at Josie's hand until it seemed small and shriveled. Then Cheryl turned her back and slammed her front door. Their relationship went downhill from there.

Jane never understood why Josie couldn't make friends with nice Cheryl Mueller next door. "She'd be such a good influence," her mother would say, and launch into yet another Perfect Cheryl Report.

Josie learned not to complain. "You're jealous," her mother would say. Josie knew it was true. But that didn't stop her from praying that Cheryl would stop being perfect, just for a moment. Please, God, let Cheryl get yelled at by a teacher, get a zit, have a bad-hair day.

It never happened.

In grade school, Cheryl was a Girl Scout who collected a sash full of merit badges. Josie collected detentions and time-outs.

In high school, both were honor students, but Cheryl was class valedictorian with a perfect 4.0. She was also head of the Drama Club, editor of the school paper and had the lead in the school musical. She was a cheerleader, when girls still thought it was an honor to root for the boys. Josie played soccer in the days before young women got big scholarship money for sports.

Worse, Cheryl had real breasts when Josie was still stuffing socks in her bra.

Both went to the prom. Cheryl was prom queen and wore a shimmering blue strapless gown that made her look like a starlet. Josie wore black and looked like a streetwalker.

In college Cheryl was elected to the student council. Josie won the intramural beer-drinking contest, women's division. The Party Hearty loving cup was not displayed on her mother's mantel.

Cheryl got engaged about the same time that Josie got pregnant. Josie knew it wasn't the baby that made her throw up every morning. Her nausea was caused by listening to the details of Cheryl's wedding. Just the mention of Alençon lace still made her queasy.

Now Josie braced herself for yet another Perfect Cheryl Report. She knew it would ruin a perfectly good corn-bread-and-chili supper. She secretly hoped Amelia would interrupt the report, even though Josie had told her daughter a thousand times that was rude. But Amelia was busy crumbling crackers and mixing them into her chili. The one time Josie wanted the kid to misbehave, Amelia wouldn't.

"Cheryl brought her mother a lovely bouquet of stargazer lilies," Jane said. "Lilies are so rich-looking, don't you think?"

Josie stuffed her mouth with corn bread so she couldn't answer. Jane didn't seem to expect her to.

"Cheryl baked her mother an English tea cake from a special low-fat, low-carb recipe. It was absolutely delicious. You'd never guess it had eighty-eight calories per slice. Cheryl offered to give you the recipe, but I said it was a waste of time. You can't cook like Cheryl."

Josie gulped her chili, which she'd made herself. This dinner was going to give her heartburn.

"It was so nice of her to invite me, too. We had real leaf tea," Jane said. "Cheryl refuses to use tea bags. She made Earl Grey, which I usually like for breakfast, but it was perfect with the cake."

Of course it was perfect, Josie thought. Everything Cheryl did was perfect. But Josie knew if she made a sarcastic remark, she'd get a lecture along with the report.

"Cheryl brought the cutest sugar cubes," Jane said. "Each one was decorated with a tiny pink rose. When you put the cubes in the hot tea, the sugar melted and the rose floated on the top. It was so elegant."

Josie ate while Jane raved on about Cheryl. Josie had thought her chili would be a special treat on a cool November night. Dinner had smelled delicious when Josie first dished it out. Now it tasted odd. Josie knew where the bitter taste came from. The more Jane talked about Cheryl, the more Josie felt like a failure. She was being childish, but Josie couldn't help it. Cheryl had been a mean little kid. She grew up into a spoiled snob. Why couldn't Jane see that?

Because Cheryl had the life that Josie's mom wanted for herself—and her daughter.

Jane could never get into bragging matches with Mrs. Mueller. Today was a fine example. After Perfect Cheryl treated her mother to a tea party worthy of Buckingham Palace, what could Jane say? "My daughter busted a shoe salesman who wanted a close personal relationship with her Prada"?

Josie couldn't tell her mother most of what happened at Soft Shoe. The details would send Jane shrieking upstairs with a headache. All Josie could say was that she'd mystery-shopped it. An upscale store was a safe subject.

"I've heard about that place. Cheryl shops there," Jane said.

That gives it the final stamp of approval, Josie thought nastily.

"Cheryl bought the most beautiful Bruno Maglis there," Jane said.

"The open-toed mules?" Josie said. "They cost two hundred fifty dollars."

"Imagine paying that for a pair of shoes." Jane said it with the wistful wonder normally used for movie stars who wore couture. Josie's mom bought her shoes on sale at Marshalls. Josie didn't think Jane had paid more than twenty-five dollars for footwear since her father left them.

Poor Jane. Mystery shopping wasn't anything for a mother to brag about. Josie's pay was lousy. The job seemed glamorous, but trudging through stores rating service was hard work, and occasionally downright demeaning. But mystery shopping gave Josie something more precious than money—time. She could work on a flexible schedule. Josie could take Amelia to school in the morning and pick her up each afternoon. Although her daughter showed signs that she'd soon turn into a sulky teenager, for some reason she liked to talk to her mother in the car. Josie wouldn't trade those quirky conversations for a six-figure salary.

Amelia wasn't ashamed to be seen with her mother, at least for now. Mystery shopping gave Josie time for unplanned expeditions to the zoo while Amelia still enjoyed her company. At night, she helped Amelia with her homework. These were luxuries many working moms didn't have. They were caught in the guilt trap of long days at work and not enough time at home.

"Two hundred fifty dollars was my whole week's salary when you were in grade school," Jane said, startling Josie out of her reverie. "Imagine spending it on a single pair of shoes."

Josie thought of her mother's bunioned feet in her black flats, and felt a rush of guilt and love. Jane was only sixty-eight, but she looked work-worn and tired.

Would she have aged as well as her dieted and face-lifted Ladue neighbors if Jane hadn't had to bring up a young daughter by herself? Jane had seen the photos of her mother as a young woman. She was softly pretty, with big brown eyes and curly brown hair. Could Jane have remarried another lawyer or doctor and had the life she'd craved? Josie had dated enough men to know how a small child could kill a budding romance.

Her resentment over the Perfect Cheryl Report vanished. Josie put down her chili spoon and went to her mother's chair. "GBH, Mom," she said. That was the family code for Great Big Hug. Jane tensed at first, then hugged her daughter. As Josie folded her mother in her arms, she saw Jane's thinning gray hair.

I turned most of those hairs gray, Josie thought, and kissed her mother's head. You don't truly understand your mother until you are one.

Josie sat down again and gave Jane an edited version of her visit to Soft Shoe. "You would have loved the store, Mom," she said. "The decor, the music, everything. The salesman even had a pink carnation in his buttonhole. It was so nineteen fifties."

"Those were civilized times," Jane said. "A man who wears a suit and a boutonniere is different from the salespersons you normally encounter."

"That's for sure," Josie said fervently.

Jane looked at her daughter sharply. Josie was glad when Amelia interrupted them.

"Did you go to the Soft Shoe at Plaza Venetia? They

have a Dry Ice store there," Amelia said. "Can we go?"
She had cracker crumbs everywhere, even in her hair.

"You want to go shopping again?" Josie said.

Now that she'd turned nine, Amelia was interested in
shopping. That made Josie uneasy. Josie worked as a
mystery shopper, a job she hoped her daughter would
never have. Jane was a shopaholic, addicted to the
Home Shopping Network. A few months ago, Josie had
found her mother's closets stuffed with unopened boxes
of jewelry, cosmetics and exercise equipment. Jane was
seeing a counselor now, and there were fewer visits from
the UPS man, but Josie worried that her daughter had
inherited a twisted shopping gene.

"Can we, Mom, can we?" Amelia begged.

"What do you need from the mall?" Josie said.

"I don't *need* anything. All the girls at school go to
Dry Ice. Please, Mom."

"I'll think about it," Josie said.

Amelia was shrewd enough to shut up.

Once the Perfect Cheryl Report ended, Josie waited
for the kicker. She wanted to see if Mrs. Mueller had
ratted her out to Jane. But her mother never mentioned
her romantic interlude with Josh on the front porch.
That was a relief.

The next morning, Josie set off for work wearing her
yard-sale Escada suit and her rescued red heels. The
whole outfit cost less than thirty dollars, but Josie
thought it was a success. She could pass as a trophy wife
with a chest full of implants and a purse full of plastic
at the upscale malls.

Mrs. Mueller's curtains twitched as Josie hurried to
her car. That nosy old woman was hiding behind the
white lace. Josie hoped she was making notes on her
outfit. The needle-toed shoes would kill her feet, but at
least Mrs. Mueller would consider her properly dressed.
When Josie wore a tube top and short shorts for one
down-market shopping assignment, Mrs. M complained
that Josie made the neighborhood look bad.

Amelia herded her mother to the car like an anxious
sheepdog. "Hurry, Mom. We're going to be late," she said.

They almost escaped. But Stan the Man Next Door, their neighbor on the other side, ran toward their car.

"It's your boyfriend." Amelia sniggered, with the casual cruelty of the young. Stan never missed an opportunity to talk to Josie.

"I don't have time for this," Josie muttered as she fired up the engine. But it was too late. Stan was blocking her exit. She had to either talk to Stan or run him down. The second choice was tempting, but it would make her even later.

Stan was wearing a limp short-sleeved shirt that was gray with age. One side sagged from the weight of a pocket protector. His powder blue necktie was snagged polyester. Stan dressed like a pensioner of eighty instead of a thirty-five-year-old man.

"Josie," he said. "Your porch light is out. That's not safe. Do you want me to get a new bulb and change it for you?"

Josie blushed. She'd unscrewed the porch light the night of her date with Josh, so they'd have some privacy from the permanent neighborhood watch. One twist and the bulb would be back in action.

"Thanks, Stan," she said. "I'll fix it tonight. I appreciate you looking out for me."

She hoped he hadn't looked out when she'd been making out with Josh. She knew Stan was in love with her and made excuses to repair things at her place. Josie could never love a man who wore a pocket protector. It was shallow and she knew it, but that didn't change her mind.

"He really likes you, Mom," Amelia said seriously as they drove off.

"I really like him," Josie said. "He's a good friend."

"Grandma thinks you should go out with him again," Amelia said. "She thinks you didn't give him a fair try."

"I like Stan, but not as a date," Josie said. Once was enough.

"He's not a hottie," Amelia said. "He's got droopy buns."

"Amelia! Where did you get that talk?" Josie said.

"Zoe says her older sister, Celine, bun-watches at the mall. She won't let Zoe go with her because she's too young. Celine says some boys have hot buns and some don't."

Zoe was the bane of Josie's existence. The kid was nine going on thirty-nine, and destined for the Future Sluts of America. But Josie had to admit the bun-watching bit was pretty funny.

"Amelia, you shouldn't talk about men like that," Josie said, trying not to giggle. "It makes them into sex objects. Men don't like that treatment any better than we do."

"But it's true. Guys who wear pocket protectors never have good buns," Amelia said.

Josie gave up the fight for men as persons in their own right. She burst out laughing. "At least if you're watching their shirt pockets, you won't be staring at their behinds."

"Josh has sweet buns," Amelia said.

"That's quite enough," Josie said, as she turned into the driveway of the Barrington School.

But her daughter was right. Josh had sweet buns, a firm chest and unprotected pockets. Josie was half crazed with longing after their date the other night. She craved him almost as much as her morning coffee at Has Beans. She had time for both before her first stop at the mall.

The coffeehouse customers seemed to come in waves, and right now the tide was out. There was only one older woman at a back table.

Josh whistled when she came in the door. "Nice outfit," he said. "You look like a rich guy's third wife."

"That's exactly how I'm supposed to look," Josie said. "I may seem harmless, but I'm deadly. Fix me an espresso and I'll tell you how I ruined a man's life."

"Fatal attraction," Josh said. "I love it. It's the element of danger that draws me."

He looked around the coffeehouse. The older woman was finishing her decaf and giving them looks as black as her dyed hair. Josh would have to rein it in, or Mrs. Black would report him for sure. He started fixing Josie's espresso.

Josie loved to watch Josh work. His arms were strong and his hands were quick, which led to pleasant thoughts that had nothing to do with coffee. She had a fine back view of Josh in his well-tailored khakis. Buns and coffee. Amelia was right. Definitely sweet.

The black-haired woman slammed her empty cup on the counter and left.

"Finally," Josh said, and vaulted over the counter with one hand. "When do I see you again?" He wrapped his arms around her.

Josie could feel his hard body. She ached for his kiss. But Josh backed away suddenly and said, "Damn, the Vulture is here."

The Vulture could usually be found hunched over the coffeehouse computer. With his sloping, skinny shoulders and long beak of a nose, he looked like a bird of prey. The Vulture bought one cup of coffee, the limit to use the computer, and loaded it with so much sugar the spoon could stand up in the cup. The Vulture hunted for odd scraps on the Internet to put on his blogging site.

Josh went back to the other side of the counter, this time through the service gate. Josie could feel the tension radiating between them.

"So," Josh said in a strained voice, "you were going to tell me how you ruined a man's life. Besides mine, I mean." He lowered his voice. "I may die of frustration."

Josie told him about Mel the foot freak. When she described the salesman crouched behind the shoe boxes with her helpless high heel, Josh laughed so hard he had tears in his eyes.

"Tell me this didn't really happen," he said. "This Mel guy really attacked your shoe?"

"He did and it wasn't funny," Josie said, then burst out laughing. It *was* funny, in a disgusting way. "What kind of person has an affair with a high heel?"

"Oh, I don't know," Josh said. "My mom married a loafer."

Josie groaned.

Five caffeine fiends flooded through the door, jittery as any junkies in need of a fix. Josie knew better than to get in their way. She took her espresso to the coffeehouse couch. She should drink up and leave. She had to work.

"You gotta paper?" a half-decaf, half-regular asked Josh.

Josh reached under the counter for a much-read *City Gazette*. But Josie saw him stop and stare at the front page. Odd. Josh was always a blur of motion behind the counter.

"Here's your paper. Excuse me a minute," Josh said to the half-and-half. He put a chocolate biscotti on a plate and brought it to Josie. "Don't go yet. I may have something to show you."

This should be interesting, Josie thought. She sipped her espresso, munched her biscotti, and fidgeted on the hard coffeehouse couch, but that didn't make the customers leave any faster. It was ten minutes before Josh could see Josie without the crush of coffee hounds.

Finally, the last shaky-handed customer left with his coffee. Josh came over, carrying a creased and wrinkled newspaper. "What was that kinky shoe salesman's name again?" he said.

"Mel," Josie said. She didn't like Josh's worried look. "Mel Poulaine. Why? Is something wrong? Is Mel going to sue Suttin Services because he was fired?"

"No. Mel's not going to bother anyone ever again." Josh stopped and looked at her. "He's dead, Josie."

"He didn't kill himself, did he?" Josie felt sick. Please don't say he committed suicide because I got him fired, she prayed, but Josie was too afraid to say that out loud. I had to report the pervert. Didn't I?

"Somebody else killed him," Josh said. "Mel was murdered."

Chapter 5

OLYMPIA PARK SALESMAN SLAIN, the *St. Louis City Gazette* headline screamed.

Josie saw the picture underneath, gave a small shriek and sloshed her espresso on the coffeehouse couch. Why did the paper use that photo? It was Mel, all right, with that strange oily smile, as if death was some secret pleasure.

The caption said, "Olympia Park resident Melvin Poulaine in happier times, as Soft Shoe salesperson of the year."

"Omigod," Josie said. "That's him, right down to the carnation in his buttonhole."

"He looks like a forties gigolo," Josh said. "What's that on his hair—Crisco?" He looked at Josie. "Are you okay?"

"I'm a little shaky. I don't know a lot of dead people. Mel was awful, but he didn't deserve to die. When was he killed?" Josie grabbed a handful of paper napkins from the dispenser and scrubbed at the thick brown stain on the couch. Her efforts only smeared it around the gray upholstery.

Josh skimmed the article while she scrubbed. "I think he was killed the same day he was fired. You killed him, Josie. You wanted to avenge his assault on your sole."

Josie gripped the paper napkins so tight she squeezed them into a ball. "That's not funny, Josh. I've been mixed up with the police before. What if they come after me again?"

"Did you see that man after you left the store?"

"No," Josie said.

"You can account for your time?"

"I guess so," Josie said. "After I left the shoe store, I went to the office, then I had lunch with my friend Alyce. After that I picked up my daughter at school and spent the evening at home with Mom and Amelia. But nobody else saw me once I was home."

"What about Mrs. Mueller?" Josh said. "She's better than a spy satellite."

Josie laughed with relief. "I never thought I'd be glad to have a nosy neighbor." She went back to rubbing the coffee stain into the couch. Josh gently pried the napkins from her hand, sprayed something from a plastic bottle on the upholstery and made the stain disappear.

"I do magic," he said, kissing her fingers. "Let me get you another espresso." He was up and heading for the counter.

"No! Wait! I don't need more caffeine," Josie said.

"Yes, you do," Josh said. "Your brain cells should be on full alert. This Mel story doesn't make sense. How could a shoe salesman afford to live in Olympia Park? Have you ever been in those houses?"

"I've never even been on the streets," Josie said. "Olympia Park has armed guards everywhere. My mom went to a big party there when she was still married to Dad. She said it made the newer gated communities look like trailer parks."

"I'm surprised they haven't put up a sign: OLYMPIA PARK—EXCLUDING ST. LOUISANS SINCE 1905," Josh said. "Did you know Olympia Park had a written covenant that Irish, Jewish and people of color could not be home-owners? They still have ways to prevent people they don't like from moving in. Ten years ago, the homeowners association refused to sell to Bigtime Barney."

"The used-car salesman with the awful cable TV ads?"

"That's the one. The association bought the house from the owner for the same amount Barney offered him, then held it until they found a suitable buyer. They sold it to a partner in an old-line St. Louis law firm."

"These people don't sound like they'd want a shoe salesman for a neighbor," Josie said.

"Exactly," Josh said. She could hear him clattering around, preparing her espresso. "Bigtime Barney wanted to pay seven mil for the place. Olympia Park houses start at two million dollars. Start."

Josie whistled. "That's a lot of shoes. Does the article say how Mel made his money?"

"Drink this." Josh was back with a double-shot espresso, thick and dark. Josie took a sip and felt a hot zing—unless it came from being so close to Josh. He sat down next to her on the couch. Another zing. Nope, it definitely wasn't the caffeine.

Concentrate, she told herself. Mel's death has you rattled. It must have stirred up some hormones. Josie gathered enough thoughts to ask a semi-intelligent question. "How did a killer get inside a community with guards at the gate?"

"Let's see what it says here." Josh scanned the news story. "Hmm. The housekeeper found the victim."

"Housekeeper?" Josie said. "Mel the shoe salesman had a housekeeper?"

"If you live in a two-million-dollar house, you don't mop your own floors," Josh said.

He cleared his throat and read: " 'The housekeeper, Zinnia Ellis of Maplewood, found the victim, Melvin Aubrey Poulaine, forty-nine, at about nine forty-five Monday evening. Miss Ellis called paramedics, who were unable to revive Poulaine. A police spokesman said Poulaine was apparently struck and killed.' "

"Struck and killed with what?" Josie said.

"That's it. The story doesn't say how he was killed or when. I can't figure out if he died inside or outside of his house. There's no mention of suspects and no quotes from the neighbors about how they saw a one-armed man running into the night. Judging from the number of 'no comments' in this story, it sounds like Mel's neighbors flat-out refused to talk to the reporter. People in Olympia Park keep a low profile. You rarely read anything about them in the newspaper, not even in the society pages."

"What else would you expect of Olympia?" Josie said. "Gods don't talk to mortals. Does the article say if Mel had any family—an ex-wife, maybe, or children?"

Josh studied the story. "His only surviving relative seems to be an aunt in Long Beach, California. There's nothing else about his family. Don't you wonder where Mel got the money to live the way he did?"

"You bet," Josie said. "If Mel had money, why was he working in a shopping mall? I wouldn't traipse around the malls if I didn't have to. He probably made minimum wage plus commission. That won't get you in the gate at Olympia Park. I don't think he could make that kind of money legally."

"Mel doesn't strike me as a cocaine cowboy or a hit man," Josh said.

Josie giggled. The caffeine had her keyed up. It couldn't be because Josh was sitting so close to her. He was surprisingly muscular. She'd discovered that on her front porch. Hard in all the right— Get a grip, she told herself. Mooning around like a lovesick teenager won't help you when the cops show up on your porch asking questions. And don't kid yourself—they will talk to you.

"Maybe Mel was into blackmail," Josie said. "But he'd still need millions. Can you make that much money blackmailing people?"

"It would have to be something really big," Josh said. "Big enough to get him killed."

Josie finished her espresso.

"Can I get you another one?" Josh said.

"No, I'd be awake until next Thursday," Josie said. "I'm not going to worry anymore about Mel. He's not my problem. He's not a problem for Soft Shoe, either. The company must be relieved he's dead, especially if they had complaints from customers. They can't sue a dead man."

"Maybe the company put out a contract on him," Josh said.

"Nah," Josie said. "They're not killers. They use too much pink."

Josh laughed. Josie looked around the coffeehouse and realized it was empty. So did Josh. The air around them was suddenly charged. Josie noticed everything about him—his blond hair, his cool goatee with the soul patch, his strong shoulders and long legs.

Josh took Josie in his arms and groaned. "I can't stand this," he said. "When do I get to see you alone?" He gave her small, feathery kisses along her neck.

"The weekend after next," Josie said. "Amelia has her first sleepover. It's her best friend Emma's birthday party."

"Cool," Josh said. He undid her top blouse button. She sighed and unbuttoned his top two shirt buttons. What a great chest that man had.

"It's a big deal for Amelia," she said, breathing faster. "Some of her classmates have been doing sleepovers since they were in kindergarten. This is her first one. I know Emma's mother and I can trust her to lay down the law, so I said yes. Amelia is all excited."

"Me, too," Josh said, and kissed her hard.

"You certainly are," Josie said, and reached for his belt.

The door banged open. Josie jumped. A skinny woman in a beige raincoat marched up to the counter. "Is this a coffeehouse or a whorehouse?" she said loudly.

Josie blushed and pulled away from Josh. She quickly buttoned her blouse.

"I'll be right there," Josh said. He whispered, "Martha is a jerk. She's also a lawyer, so that's probably redundant. Martha is back for her third double espresso. She's wired like the scoreboard at Busch Stadium."

"I'd better go," Josie said.

"Don't," he said. It was a plea. "Martha will be gone in a minute. Here, read the Mel story." He handed her the battered front page. It had been folded more times than an old road map.

Josie read the story twice and didn't learn another thing. The few facts seemed to slide out of her head. Only the picture of the grinning Mel stayed with her. Two days ago, he'd been swanning around the poshly pink shoe store. Now he was in a morgue drawer.

The coffeehouse door slammed shut. Martha was gone. They were alone again. But now Josie was acutely aware of the store's big plate-glass windows and the constant stream of coffee lovers. It was too public here. She wandered over to the counter.

"I gave Martha a free coffee and calmed her down," he said. "The decaf is going bitter. I need to brew some more. Two extra-large decafs will be coming here in about five minutes."

Josh poured the coffee in the half-full pot down the sink, then busied himself with changing the filter and spooning in fresh-ground coffee.

"Did I ever tell you I dated a girl from Olympia Park?" he asked.

"When was this?" Josie said.

"The summer I turned sixteen. I met her at the Clayton swimming pool. Muffy—"

"Get out of town. She wasn't named Muffy," Josie interrupted.

"I swear," Josh said. "She looked like a Muffy, too. Anyway, I was sitting in her living room, which looked like a museum, trying to make conversation. Muffy's father was there in this big old wing chair, treating me like something his darling dragged in from the Dumpster. He even wrinkled his nose as if I smelled bad. I was so nervous. 'I like your house,' I blurted. 'I've never seen one with a marble carport.'

"Muffy said in this snotty voice, 'It's a portico, not a carport.' I felt like an idiot.

"Muffy was shipped off to Europe until school started so she wouldn't associate with the riffraff anymore."

Josh laughed, but Josie could tell his blunder still hurt after all these years.

"Her loss," Josie said. "She had money, but you have talent, Josh. I read your novel. I don't usually like science fiction, but I couldn't put it down. Those robot slaves were unforgettable. And their Rubicon masters— they were amazing."

"Thanks for reading it," Josh said. His smile lit the dark intelligence in his eyes. "I made most of the revisions you suggested. You've got a real eye for editing, Josie. The final manuscript is nearly finished."

"So what's your plan?" Josie said.

"I thought I'd hold up a bank for enough money to take my book to New York," Josh said.

"But seriously," Josie said.

"Seriously, I need to find some money fast if I'm going to get anywhere. I can't keep sending query letters from St. Louis. New York thinks this city is nowhere. An agent actually asked me if I had a horse. I couldn't believe it. I said it was hard to keep one in my second-floor apartment."

"You wouldn't want anyone that dumb for your agent," Josie said.

"No," Josh said, "but I have to find a good one. I want to set up some appointments, then spend a week in New York. I've had some nibbles from a couple of big agencies, but I need to interview the agents in person. I have to get enough money for the trip. My credit cards are maxed out."

Josie remembered their dinner the other night. We probably ate his plane ticket, she thought. "Josh, I have two hundred dollars in my savings account. You can have it."

"I can't take your money," he said.

"You should. You have real talent. I believe in your work. Consider it an investment. I'm not giving you money. I'm buying Josh futures." Josie flashed briefly on a future that was a bigger fantasy than anything Josh could create. She saw him as a best-selling author in a book-lined study. She was his personal editor. Their Manhattan apartment—

One look at Josh's face and her fantasy shriveled and died. It was set in a stubborn mask. "I haven't sunk so low that I'd take money off a working mom," he said. "I have to solve this myself."

"Will the store let you work extra hours?" Josie said.

"No. Has Beans is cutting me back five hours, so I'm only working thirty-five hours a week. That means I'm no longer a full-time employee and they don't have to pay my health insurance."

"Josh! That's awful. What will you do? Get a second job?"

Josh laughed bitterly. His hands shook as he poured

the water, and it splashed over the coffee machine. "Two shit jobs add up to more shit, not more money. My book is good, Josie, really good. Even you think so, and you don't like science fiction. It could make me a fortune if I find the right publisher. I know it could."

"I'm really sorry," Josie said.

"I'll think of something," Josh said. But he banged the glass coffeepot down so hard on the burner Josie was afraid it might break.

Chapter 6

"Perhaps Madame would be more comfortable shopping at Wal-Mart." The salesclerk looked down his long, thin nose at Josie, as if she were a cockroach on his jewelry counter.

Josie's eyes widened in surprise. Did he really say that? Obviously, the man didn't know she was a mystery shopper.

"I asked to look at your gold-filled hearts," Josie said. "Are you going to show them to me or not?"

"If you wish," he said, in a tone that made it clear he didn't wish it.

Josie knew the man's game. He only wanted to sell expensive rings and watches. He wouldn't get much commission on the store's small items, so they weren't worth his time. She bet he regularly chased off those customers.

Josie smiled sweetly. This jewelry job was a break from her Soft Shoe work. She would enjoy nailing this guy. How many other customers had he insulted? No wonder the store's sales were slipping. This was what her job was all about—protecting innocent shoppers. No one deserved this treatment.

How did he know she wasn't a trophy wife? She sneaked a peek at herself in the store mirrors. She thought she looked pretty damn good in her pinched-toed Pradas and garage-sale Escada. Her hair was perfect. Then she saw her chipped nails. Of course, rich women didn't do their own housework. He'd spotted the giveaway. But this time, he'd outsmarted himself.

Wal-Mart indeed, she thought. He'd be lucky if he got

a job stocking shelves there when she finished with him. Josie left the store with hurt feelings and sore feet. When she hobbled back to her car, she saw a new ding and a scrape on the right fender. Someone had hit it with a shopping cart. Josie sighed. Another hazard of mystery shopping.

She checked her watch. If she hurried, she could pick up Amelia at the Barrington School on time. At least the traffic was cooperating today. She made it to the school with five minutes to spare.

She could tell by the way Amelia slung her backpack into the car and flopped on the seat that her daughter was going to be a pain in the neck. Josie was in no mood for it.

They were barely to the end of the school drive before Amelia started in. "I want to go to the mall," she whined.

Josie ground her teeth. In the parenting magazines, supermoms used sensitive questions to gently probe the real reason for their child's unhappiness. But Josie was short on supermom patience this afternoon. She hated whining. When Amelia was moody, her jaw had a stubborn, bulldog thrust that echoed Jane's. Her grandmother, the shopaholic. Josie was not going to raise a mall rat.

"What do you need?" Josie said. She realized she was going forty in a school zone and slowed the car. Speeding would only add a ticket to this rotten day.

"I want to get a present from Dry Ice for Emma's birthday," Amelia said.

Dry Ice was the latest little-girl craze. There wasn't a useful item in the store. That was part of its charm. It had outrageous purses, clothes, bedding and fake-fur lamps. Josie remembered the absolutely essential junk she had to have at Amelia's age. She'd desperately wanted a Trivial Pursuit game and one of the hot new CD players. She didn't get them. Josie wasn't allowed to rip her jeans like everyone else did after *Flashdance*. Jane wouldn't even let her see the movie. Was her own daughter's childhood going to be another series of don'ts?

Amelia must have felt Josie's mood shift. "Please, Mom. I'll even use my own money," she pleaded. The ultimate nine-year-old sacrifice. Thanks to cash gifts from her grandmother on her birthday, Christmas, even Groundhog Day, the kid had more walking-around money than Josie did.

"I have to get Emma's present from Dry Ice," Amelia said. She sounded desperate. "It's important, Mom."

Josie knew it was. As a child, she'd shown up at too many birthday parties with off-brand Barbie dolls that Jane bought on sale. Josie's mother had forgotten what it was like to be a kid. "Those dolls look just like the real thing," Jane would say. "Children can't tell the difference."

But they could. Josie could remember the birthday girl's curled lip when she unwrapped Josie's gift. There was dead silence, until the girl's mother prompted, "What do you say, Tara?"

Tara's grudging "Thank you" was worse than an outright insult. Josie still felt the sting of shame twenty-two years later. Her daughter was never going to feel that way. Josie wasn't a supermom, but she understood that much.

"What do you want to get Emma?" Josie said.

"Dry Ice has this laptop cosmetic kit. It's sweet, Mom. Looks just like a laptop computer, except instead of keys it has sixty-six colors of lip gloss and eye shadow. The applicators are in the mouse pad. Emma will love it."

"I'm sure," Josie said. "But her mother won't. You girls are not allowed to wear makeup."

Amelia stuck out her lower lip. "Zoe does."

Josie mashed her molars together again. Zoe's mother had had her brains sucked out during her last liposuction. Zoe's mother thought it was okay for her nine-year-old daughter to wear eyeliner and belly shirts. She let Zoe play laser tag, which Josie thought was way too dangerous for kids that age.

"Zoe gets to do everything. I don't get to do anything," Amelia said. The whine was back, worse than ever.

"If Zoe got to jump off the Poplar Street bridge, would you follow her?" Josie said. Omigod, I sound like my mother, she thought.

"Oh, Mooom," Amelia said. "That's not fun."

Her whine would make any mom hit the margaritas. Give me strength, oh, Lord, Josie prayed. She's not even a teenager yet.

"We'll go to Dry Ice, but you're not getting Emma a makeup kit," Josie said. "How about a gift card? Then Emma can buy what she wants."

The sunshine fairy must have waved her wand over Amelia. Josie's daughter suddenly became all smiles. Her jutting chin was tucked back. Her lower lip retracted into a tender curve. The cinnamon sprinkle of freckles reappeared on her nose.

"Sweet," Amelia said. "Cards are good. Thirty-five dollars?"

"Thirty, and that's my final offer."

"Sold," Amelia said.

Josie realized she'd been suckered into paying for Emma's gift. The fat wad of cash in Amelia's sock drawer would remain untouched. Oh, well. Josie had her Soft Shoe bonus. She could afford the gift card. She'd planned to take Josh to dinner with that cash, but now it didn't seem right to eat, drink, and be merry with money earned by getting a future murdered man fired.

As Josie's car turned into their Maplewood street, the late-afternoon sun was smiling, too. It warmed the old brick houses to a mellow red and turned the broad lawns seed-catalog green. Jane's flower garden glowed with the deep, rich colors of fall: dark reds, golds and oranges.

Two boys in baggy shorts skateboarded in the street, leaping a homemade wooden ramp. A small girl rode her pink bicycle on the sidewalk. A fat old man waddled along beside his fat old dog.

Stan the Man Next Door was giving his lawn a final mowing before winter set in. He waved. Josie and Amelia waved back.

Now he was a good neighbor, Josie thought. Too bad

Mrs. Mueller, who lived on the other side, couldn't be as nice as Stan.

The curtains twitched at Mrs. M's house, but Josie ignored them.

Amelia grabbed her backpack and raced up the sidewalk, crying, "Grandma!"

Jane was waiting at Josie's front door, arms folded stiffly over her chest. Oh, oh. A bad sign. From the rigid way her mother stood, Josie knew something was wrong. Jane barely unbent to hug Amelia.

"I need to talk to you," Jane said to Josie. "Alone." There was a light breeze, but Jane's sprayed helmet of gray hair didn't move.

"Amelia, go to your room, please," Josie said.

The changeling child was back. "Oh, Mom," Amelia said. "I haven't done anything."

"I didn't say you did. Your grandmother and I need to have a grown-up talk. It's okay if you want to listen to 101 The River."

Amelia flounced into her room, then turned up her favorite radio station until the walls vibrated. Good. At least Amelia wouldn't eavesdrop on their conversation.

"Want a soda, Mom?" Josie asked. "I've got some cold ones in the icebox."

"It's a refrigerator, Josie," her mother said. "Iceboxes went out in the thirties."

"True St. Louisans never call it a refrigerator," Josie said. She took an ice tray out and ran water over it to loosen the cubes. "What do you want, Mom?"

"I want you to listen to me," Jane said. "Sit down. You're making me nervous."

"What's wrong, Mom?" It's Mrs. Mueller, Josie thought. She complained about Josh and me. The old biddy was waiting for the right opportunity. After a Perfect Cheryl Report, I'll look like an even bigger loser, groping my too young boyfriend on the porch.

"It's Mrs. Mueller," Jane said. Her face had that clamped-down look.

I knew it, Josie thought.

"She wants to ask you for a favor," Jane said.

"She what?" Josie said. Her voice rose to a near-shriek.

"I knew you'd act that way." Jane thrust out her bull-dog jaw, prepared for a fight.

Josie gave her one. She'd had to put up with a snotty clerk and a cranky kid. A mom with a chip on her shoulder was the last straw. "You're right," Josie said. "Mrs. Mueller has made my life hell since I was fifteen, and now she wants me to do her a favor. Well, she can do me a favor. She can get a life and quit watching mine."

"That was all a long time ago, Josie. She's—" Her mother hesitated. "She's in a position to help me. Mrs. Mueller can make me the Maplewood chair of the St. Louis Flower Guild."

Jane hung her head, as if she was ashamed for Josie to see how much she wanted this honor. Now that she was retired, Jane tried to recapture a little of the genteel life she'd lost years ago. She could never afford to move back to her beloved Ladue. But she did have time for the worthy causes she loved. Jane had long coveted the Maplewood flower chair, but it always went to someone richer and better connected.

"Mrs. Mueller says she can swing the votes if you'll help her," Jane said.

That old woman had the political instincts of a Washington lobbyist. She'd offered the one bribe Josie could never refuse. She couldn't turn down the thing her mother wanted most. Mrs. Mueller was diabolical.

Josie looked at Jane, small, stooped and work-worn, and felt a stab of pity. "GBH, Mom," she said. She pushed back her chair and held out her arms.

"You'll do it?" Jane said.

The hope Josie saw lighting her mother's face made Jane seem ten years younger.

"Yes, Mom, I'll do it." She hugged Jane's tense, tired body. Josie would swallow her pride and work with Mrs. Mueller to keep that light in her mother's face. "What does she want?"

"Did you know a salesman named Mel at Soft Shoe? The one who got himself murdered?" Jane said.

Bits of Josie's brain felt like they were cracking off

and sliding down her spine. What did Mel the foot fondler have to do with the straitlaced Mrs. Mueller? That woman would turn catatonic if she ever spied on Mel.

Jane must have thought Josie couldn't place Mel. "He was tall and had dark hair. He always wore a pink flower in his buttonhole."

Josie couldn't tell her mother she'd caught Mel molesting her Prada. "I mystery-shopped his store at Plaza Venetia. He waited on me."

"Did you get him fired?" her mother said.

"That's confidential," Josie said.

"He's dead," her mother said. "You're not a priest or a lawyer. It won't go any further than Mrs. Mueller and myself. But it's important. We need to know."

What the heck. The police probably knew already, Josie thought. It wouldn't be any secret now. "Yes, I gave Mel a bad report. He was dismissed the day he died."

"What did he do to get himself fired?"

"Uh," Josie said. Could she really tell her mother this? She looked at Jane's liver-spotted hands and thinning hair and thought about Mel's dirty little backroom deeds.

"Josie, I'm sixty-eight years old," her mother said. "I was a married woman. I had a child. You don't have to protect me. Young people think they discovered sex, but we had to know about it to get you here."

She's right, Josie thought. I'm being condescending. "Mel liked women's feet a little too much."

"Humpf," her mother said. "Well, that might help."

"Help how?" Josie said. She was completely lost.

"Cheryl is in trouble," Jane said. "The police think she killed Mel."

Chapter 7

"Perfect Cheryl killed Mel the perv? I don't believe it." Josie choked on her soda, and a geyser of laughter erupted. She couldn't stop it.

"I'm glad you agree," her mother said. Those four words should have been issued with a frost warning. "Except *we* don't find it funny."

We. That must be the royal Mrs. Mueller and Jane. Josie's mother sat regally at the kitchen table, a queen prepared to banish a rebel.

That's me, Josie thought. I'll be in the doghouse unless I get myself under control. She tamped her laughter back inside and tried to listen with a straight face. In her head, she heard a little kid's singsong voice: "Cheryl isn't perfect. Cheryl isn't perfect. Nah. Nah. Nah." Josie was gleeful and ashamed, all at once.

"We're sure it's a mistake," Jane said. "Cheryl shopped for shoes at that store, but she would never do the disgusting things those policemen were saying."

"What disgusting things?" Josie said. "What could Cheryl possibly do that would interest the police?" Or anyone else, she thought nastily.

"I'm trying to tell you," Jane said. "But you keep interrupting."

"I'll be quiet as a mouse," Josie said. But an evil little snicker escaped her. She couldn't help it. She'd endured twenty-four years of Perfect Cheryl Reports. It was almost worth it for this moment. Cheryl definitely had both feet in deep doo-doo. Josie had a mental image of

Cheryl daintily stepping in something brown and squishy. It would coordinate perfectly with her outfit.

Josie giggled. Her hands itched for her cell phone. If only Alyce could hear this.

"Take a drink and get control of yourself," her mother said.

Josie was afraid to swallow her soda. She might snort it out her nose if she started laughing again. The police said Perfect Cheryl and Mel the Pervert were doing disgusting things. Considering Mel's proclivities, that could give new meaning to "round heels." Josie saw Cheryl handcuffed to a pink chair while Mel tickled her toes with his carnation. She started giggling again. Maybe Cheryl used the carnation to perk up his—

"Josie!" Jane fixed her daughter with a heart-stopping glare. "Are you quite finished laughing at that poor girl?"

Shame wiped away Josie's smirk. She was behaving worse than Amelia. She expected Jane to send her to her room without supper. Josie hung her head, unable to look her mother in the eye.

"If you're able to control yourself, perhaps we can have a serious discussion," Jane said.

Josie managed a nod. She was afraid to say anything. She felt decades of giggles struggling to get out. They could erupt any moment.

Her mother seemed satisfied that Josie was subdued into seriousness. Jane folded her hands, leaned forward, and began talking in a whisper, as if the news was too horrible to say at full volume.

"Mrs. Mueller was at Cheryl and Tom's house yesterday, watching Ben, the baby. Such a darling child. Do you know he's slept through the night almost since birth? Cheryl had a committee meeting. She's such a good mother. She doesn't like to leave her baby with a sitter."

Mom can't keep from giving a Perfect Cheryl Report, even at a time like this, Josie thought. But then the report took a sudden, delightful detour.

"Before Cheryl could go to the meeting, two homicide

detectives showed up at her front door," Jane said. "The whole neighborhood could see what they were. They didn't try to hide it."

Being a homicide detective is nothing to be ashamed of, Josie wanted to say. But she knew better than to interrupt.

"The detectives insisted on seeing Cheryl. She explained that she had an important committee meeting. The detectives said she could talk to them there or they could talk downtown. They were quite nasty. They treated that poor girl like a criminal."

Jane paused dramatically, waiting for Josie to come to Cheryl's defense. Josie still didn't trust herself to comment.

"Well, naturally, Cheryl invited them in," Jane said. "What else could she do? But she didn't offer them any coffee. They'd acted like such bullies, they didn't deserve it."

That showed them, Josie thought.

"Those two detectives talked to Cheryl in her living room for almost an hour. Mrs. Mueller stayed with Ben, but she could hear the conversation."

I bet, Josie thought. Mrs. M probably had her ear glued to the wall.

"Mrs. Mueller said it was degrading. The things those detectives said! They claimed Cheryl's car had been at that Mel person's house the night of his murder. They told her an eyewitness saw it at Mel's. Of course, that couldn't be right. They asked Cheryl why she was at Mel's house. Cheryl is a married woman. She'd never go to an unmarried man's house alone."

"Oh, come on, Mom," Josie said. "Even Mrs. Mueller can't believe there's something wrong with a grown woman going to a man's house without a chaperone. What century is this?"

"Maybe it isn't something you worry about," her mother said. "But Cheryl guards her good name. Mrs. Mueller always says you can't be too careful. People have dirty minds."

"You mean Mrs. Mueller does," Josie said.

"I'm talking about the police." Jane's voice was building in outrage. "They wanted to know the nature of her relationship with that Mel person. They actually said 'relationship.' Mrs. Mueller thought they were implying that Cheryl had sex with Mel."

"Eeuuw," Josie said. She couldn't help it. She thought of Mel's oily hands on the snobbish Cheryl and shuddered. As much as she wanted to believe the worst of Cheryl, Josie couldn't see her in bed with Mel. She couldn't see any woman sleeping with him, except maybe a pro for pay.

"That's not possible, Mom," Josie said. "It's just not."

"I knew you'd defend a fellow woman," her mother said. "Really, one look at Cheryl and her lovely home, and I don't know how those detectives had the nerve to ask that question."

Josie agreed with her mother. "It does sound far-fetched."

"The accusations didn't stop there," her mother said. "Next, they asked if Cheryl knew anything about Mel's interest in kinky sex." Jane lowered her voice and looked around the kitchen, in case Amelia was lurking nearby. She was reassured by the blasting music coming from the kid's room.

"The detectives said this Mel had an unnatural thing for women's feet and shoes."

Maybe Mel had asked Cheryl to tiptoe through his tulips, and she'd killed him, Josie thought. Nah, that didn't make sense. A princess like Cheryl would know how to stomp a worm like Mel. Killing him would be a waste of her energy. Cheryl would shrivel him with a single look.

This whole situation was too weird. "The cops are crazy, Mom. Cheryl wouldn't have anything to do with Mel. I could hardly stand being around him for an hour at Soft Shoe. Mel gave me the creeps. He fondled my foot when he waited on me."

"Josie Marcus, why did you let that man touch you that way?" Jane said. "You should have walked right out of there."

"I didn't let him, Mom. I busted him in the course of an investigation. I got him fired. Now, do you want me to help, or do you want to criticize me for something I didn't do?"

Jane turned unexpectedly contrite. "I'm sorry, Josie," she said. "You're right, of course."

I am? There's a switch. Josie was loving this. First, the mighty Mrs. Mueller begged for her help. Now, her mother was apologizing. Best of all, Perfect Cheryl had an Achilles heel. Oops. Careful. No foot puns. The giggles might come back.

Josie concentrated on watching the ice melt in her glass while her mother recounted Cheryl's ordeal.

"The police asked Cheryl for her fingerprints. Can you imagine? Cheryl knew her rights. She's a smart girl. Graduated at the top of her college class."

Unlike me, Josie thought.

"Cheryl told those detectives no. Then they wanted to know if they could take a look around her house. Cheryl stood up to them. She asked them to leave unless they had a warrant."

"Good for her," Josie said. "Did the police actually ask if she'd killed Mel?"

"Well, they didn't come out and say it in so many words," Jane said. "But they certainly acted like they thought she was guilty. Why else would they want her fingerprints?"

"Maybe for elimination purposes?" Josie said. She had learned about the police and fingerprints the hard way.

"Then why say they had a witness placing her at the murder scene?"

"Did the police say how Mel was killed?" Josie asked. "No."

"It has to be a mistake," Josie said. "Cheryl looks like a lot of rich, skinny West County blondes. Their eyewitness mixed her up with someone else."

Jane bristled momentarily at this description of Perfect Cheryl, but she kept blessedly quiet.

"Cheryl drives a black SUV," Josie said. "There are herds of them in her neighborhood. I'm sure it will be straightened out shortly."

But not before I can rake in more brownie points, she thought.

"The police wanted to search her home like a common criminal's," Jane wailed. "And they said terrible things about her. She's a young mother with a child. This could ruin her reputation."

"Mom, I'm sorry Cheryl's been dragged into this." Josie wasn't sorry. She was enjoying the situation immensely. "But I don't see how I can help. She needs a good lawyer."

"No," her mother said. "She needs you. Mrs. Mueller thought you would know all about what goes on at that store because you're a shopping professional."

A shopping professional? Was this the same woman who'd called Josie a slut when she went mystery-shopping in a tube top?

"Mrs. Mueller wants you to talk with Cheryl. Have coffee and a chat with her. That's all."

"Why?" Josie asked.

"Cheryl might tell you something that she wouldn't say to her mother." That admission must have hurt the proud Mrs. Mueller, who thought she knew everything.

"You might learn something that could explain how this horrible mistake happened," Josie's mother said. "Then it will all be over and their lives can go back to normal."

Josie heard something else in those sentences—Mrs. Mueller's fear that her darling daughter might be up to something. Not murder, perhaps. Maybe Perfect Cheryl had been having a little extracurricular fun with someone's husband and didn't have an alibi she could claim.

"Cheryl and I aren't exactly friends, Mom," Josie said. "She won't tell me anything. She won't say two civil words to me. Even Mrs. Mueller must know we can't stand each other."

Jane dismissed their dislike with a shrug. "That was kid's stuff, Josie. You're both grown women now. It's time to put your childish feuds aside. You have so much in common."

Right. Both our mothers worship Cheryl.

"That's all you have to do, Josie," Jane said. "Just talk to Cheryl. Help her, and Mrs. Mueller will make me Maplewood chair of the St. Louis Flower Guild. Please, Josie, will you do that for me?"

Jane was begging. She wanted that chair so badly, and Josie, the loser daughter who got pregnant and dropped out of college, could make her mother's dream come true.

At last, Josie thought. I can make it up to Mom for the trouble I've caused. She helped me when I needed it most. She stood by me. Mom is always there when I need a sitter or someone to pick up Amelia at school. So what if she lied and told Mrs. Mueller that I was a widow? She has to hold up her head in the neighborhood.

Josie could finally make her mother proud. It would be so easy. Josie wouldn't argue with whatever goddess handed her this favor. She'd take it and run.

"Sure, Mom. I'll do it tomorrow on my lunch hour." Josie would stop by for a talk with Cheryl. They'd have real tea with floating sugar roses, compare notes on Mel's foot massages, and that would be it. Case closed.

"Thank you." Her mother's voice trembled slightly. Were those tears in Jane's eyes? "I appreciate this, dear, and Mrs. Mueller does, too. I know she can be a difficult woman, but she has a good heart—and so do you. I'll tell her you're going to help Cheryl."

Jane hugged her daughter, then ran out the door and across the yard to give Mrs. Mueller the good news. Josie stared after her mother, stunned by the swift reversal of her fortunes. Half an hour ago, she was the daughter who couldn't do anything right. Now she was her mother's golden girl. She owed it all to Mel the foot man.

Did the cops really think Mel was parking his boots under Cheryl's bed? Josie tried to picture sex with the slippery shoe salesman. The guy was so oily, he'd squirt out of the sheets. Now there was a picture.

Josie could feel the giggles rising up. This time there would be no stopping them. She had to act fast. Josie slammed the heavy wooden front door shut and bolted

it just as a tiny titter escaped her. Then a loud laugh.
Then a great big guffaw.

Josie leaned against the door and howled until the
tears ran down her cheeks. It was mean. She knew it,
but she couldn't stop. All these years she'd waited for
Perfect Cheryl to slip. Now, it had finally happened. Except this wasn't a slip. It was a pratfall. The cops thought
Perfect Cheryl was a shady lady and a stone killer. Mrs.
Mueller and her mother thought Josie was a savior.

The shoe was definitely on the other foot.

Chapter 8

Josie yawned her way into the kitchen to nuke her morning coffee. Amelia was at the kitchen table, washed, dressed, and eating breakfast. Amazing. There would be no "you're going to be late for school" hassle this morning.

Why should there be? Josie thought, as she poured last night's leftover coffee into a mug. I'm perfect. I have a perfect daughter. And a perfect working day. I'll be mystery-shopping bookstores, which means I can dress like a normal woman and wear comfortable loafers.

Josie threw a red wig and a black sweater into her tote. Some clever clerks spotted mystery shoppers and spread the word to the other stores in the chain. It helped to have a change of hair and clothes.

According to the thermometer at the back door, it was sixty degrees, a welcome surprise for November. More perfection.

Josie took a sip of her reheated coffee. Yuck. It was bitter. But she'd stop by Has Beans for the perfect brew after she dropped Amelia at school. She'd also see Josh. A little sugar with her coffee.

Josie and Amelia left for the Barrington School with time to spare. Josie waved to Stan the Man Next Door as she climbed into the car. Mrs. Mueller's curtains did not twitch.

On the way to school, Amelia talked about her friend's party plans. "Emma is having a chocolate-and-vanilla cake with purple icing for her birthday, Mom."

This party was clearly the event of the Barrington social season.

"Purple is Emma's favorite color," Amelia said. "If it's nice out, her dad is going to cook hot dogs and burgers. She's going to have a helium gas tank for purple balloons, a popcorn machine like in the movies, and DVDs on the big-screen projector in the theater room.

"But mostly we're going to play games. Emma has her own personal playhouse. It has a game room with three pinball machines, an original Ms. Pac-Man, an air hockey table, and a foosball table."

"Wow," Josie said. "Her parents are renting all those games for the party?"

"No, Mom," Amelia said. "Emma *has* all those games. By the way, I won't need that gift card."

"You're not going to give her a birthday present?" Josie asked.

"Rich kids like Emma don't want you to bring them presents," Amelia said, as if she were giving a sociology lecture.

"But you've brought other girls Dry Ice gift cards."

"There's rich and there's rich," Amelia said. "We're all bringing school supplies, but we're not giving them to Emma. They'll go to poor kids."

Like you, Josie thought. Her daughter showed no envy of her rich friend. How did I have such a good child?

"How did you find out the right thing to bring to the party?" Josie asked.

"I asked Emma," Amelia said. "She's my friend."

"She really is your friend, Amelia. That's what friends do. They keep you from embarrassing yourself. You're lucky."

Amelia shrugged. "Emma's sweet."

I'm living in a greeting card, Josie thought, as she kissed her daughter good-bye.

Josie saw Josh's car in the lot at Has Beans. He was working this morning. Josie expected nothing less in her perfect world. By the time she opened the coffeehouse door, her steaming espresso was on the counter.

That's when Josie's cell phone rang. "Come home right away," her mother said.

"What's wrong, Mom? Are you okay? Is anything wrong with Amelia?"

"There's an Olympia Park homicide detective here. She wants to talk to you."

"What about, Mom?"

"She won't say. Just come home." Jane sounded frightened. "Please."

"Okay, Mom, I'll be right there," Josie said. "I'm right around the corner."

"Something wrong?" Josh said, as she snapped her phone shut.

"It's Mom." Josie started to add, "There's a homicide detective at my house," but decided that was a romance killer. "She has an uninvited guest."

"Do you need me to chase him off?" Josh said.

Josie laughed. "Her. Thanks, Josh, but I don't need a bodyguard. This is a nuisance, not a serious problem."

Josh poured her espresso into a go-cup. Josie raced out the door with barely a backward wave. Olympia Park, she thought. Must be Mel the dead salesman. She was home in two minutes.

Jane was in Josie's living room, wringing her hands and looking worried. "The detective is in the kitchen," she whispered. "She didn't want coffee, but I gave her a glass of water."

"Thanks, Mom. Why don't you go upstairs?" Josie said. "I'll call you as soon as she leaves."

"Are you sure?" Jane said.

Josie was sure her mom would be more of a hindrance than a help. "I'll be fine. It looks better this way."

Homicide Detective Kate Causeman looked like the girl next door—in a bad neighborhood, since she was carrying a gun. She had long, curly blond hair, tied back to keep perps from pulling it. Her tailored beige suit and flat lace-up shoes were smart but no-nonsense.

"This is just a routine interview," the detective said.

She smiled, but Josie watched her eyes. The girl next door had twin blue lasers.

"We're trying to reconstruct Melvin Poulaine's last

day," Detective Causeman said. "I understand that you mystery-shopped his store."

Josie could do girl-next-door pretty well herself. She smiled back, took a seat and said, "Yes, that's right."

"It was your report that led to his firing?"

"Yes," Josie said. "But that happened after I left the store. Terminating Mr. Poulaine was a Soft Shoe management decision."

"When you surprised him in the back room, what did he say?" Was that a smile lurking at the corners of Detective Causeman's mouth?

"He didn't say anything. I yelled at him to let go of my shoe." Josie could not bring herself to say she'd called Mel a heel. It sounded too ridiculous. "I left and faxed my report to Suttin Services an hour later. I didn't have any further contact with Mr. Poulaine."

"What did you and Mr. Poulaine talk about when he waited on you?" the detective said.

"We discussed shoe styles," Josie said.

"Did he say what he planned to do later in the day?"

"No," Josie said.

"Did he mention any problems with anyone?" Detective Causeman asked.

"No."

"Did he have any money issues?"

"No."

"What was the state of his mind?"

Warped, Josie thought. "He seemed fine," she said.

"Did he have boyfriend or girlfriend issues?" Detective Causeman asked.

He wanted to elope with my shoe, Josie thought. "We didn't talk about anything personal," she said.

"Was he suicidal? Homicidal?" the detective asked.

"I tried on shoes for an hour. It's the only time I met the man. I don't know anything about him," Josie said.

But I'd better find out fast, she thought.

"Thanks for the water," Detective Causeman said.

Josie noticed she didn't drink any. She showed the detective to the door and leaned against the hall wall. Josie felt like she'd been slammed in the stomach. Suddenly, Mel and Cheryl didn't seem so funny. Mel was really dead. Cheryl was really in trouble. A homicide investigation had a way of reaching out and ruining all the lives it touched—and Josie's was within its cold grasp.

Mrs. Mueller was right to be worried about Cheryl. She knew her daughter could go to prison. But Josie bet Cheryl was still sheltered by her invincible ignorance. The problem with people like Cheryl was they didn't know they were in trouble until it was too late. Nothing bad had ever happened to them. They felt entitled to their fabulous luck.

Josie had seen this on a smaller scale at the malls, when store security pulled in well-heeled shoplifters. The light-fingered rich didn't believe those SHOPLIFTERS WILL BE PROSECUTED signs were meant for them.

"I can pay for it," they would say, as if that solved everything. But it didn't. They never understood that the stores wanted to make an example of them, to scare away other rich folks getting five-finger discounts. Even as they were being hauled off to jail, they still thought they could talk their way out of the mess. Only the humiliation of a strip search convinced them.

Josie did not like Cheryl. She wouldn't mind if the cops scared her a little. But the woman didn't deserve to go to prison. Her little boy needed his mother. And Josie's mother needed her committee.

Josie had to act fast. She ran upstairs to tell her mother that everything was all right.

But it wasn't. The day had changed. An icy wind whipped gray clouds across a lead sky. Brown leaves crackled like bones underfoot as she marched to her car.

There was no time to waste. Josie could shop the bookstores later. She had to see Cheryl now. Mrs. Mueller's perfect daughter might be too smug to understand how much trouble she was in, but Josie knew. Maybe she could convince Cheryl. At the very least, Josie might learn something that could keep Cheryl from going to jail. Mrs. Mueller was right. Josie did have good mall contacts. A security guard or someone at a nearby store might have seen someone following or threatening Mel.

Josie had to see Cheryl before the police showed up at her house again.

Josie hit the highway hard, heading for the West County suburb of Ballwin. Her mother was not going to lose her dream committee chair.

Josie was on a mission. She had to save the woman she hated to help the woman she loved.

Chapter 9

Cheryl and Tom's big beige two-story house had spindly trees in the yard and too many Pella windows. Cheryl answered the door wearing a camel pantsuit two shades darker than her caramel hair.

"Hi, I'm Josie Marcus." She extended her hand. "Your mom asked me to stop by and see how you were doing."

Cheryl's handshake was limp as old celery. "Come in," she said. Her smile was brittle.

She doesn't want me here, Josie thought. Well, we're even. I don't want to be here, either. But Cheryl doesn't understand she's in trouble. I do.

Josie nearly went snow-blind in the living room. Everything was white—the rugs, the couch, the lampshades, the marble-and-wrought-iron coffee table. It was a show room, designed to impress visitors. Pale seascapes chilled the walls. Josie sneaked a peek at the closest one. It was signed.

Cheryl firmly steered her out of the room. Josie was not important enough to sit on that frigid furniture. The dining room was as dark as the living room was light. It featured mahogany furniture and murky landscapes. On the table was a silk flower arrangement. The bowl looked old.

"Pretty flower bowl," Josie said.

"It was Mommy's," Cheryl said. "She gave it to me." Mommy?

A lighted china cabinet filled with ghostly Lladro figurines covered one wall. The top of Cheryl's wedding cake was displayed on a shelf like a trophy. The tiny bride and groom were garlanded by silk flowers. Josie knew from her mother's Perfect Cheryl Report that the little couple were "real bisque china."

Josie followed Cheryl down a narrow hall and caught a glimpse of another dark room. More landscapes in heavy gold frames. A few lonesome paperbacks and dull textbooks huddled together in a nearly empty bookcase. Josie figured the other shelves would be filled later. With its dark wood, green leather and glass-shaded banker's lamps, the room looked like a gentlemen's club. Was it a lair for the husband or a place to hold the overflow of networking parties?

The kitchen was as big as Josie's flat. The shiny stainless-steel appliances had the warmth of an autopsy room. The counters had none of the clutter of a real cook. This was a place to microwave. French doors led to a patio with a gas grill. Josie bet most of the summertime cooking went on out there.

They bypassed the kitchen's lonely splendor for the family room. This was where Tom and Cheryl really lived, Josie thought. The floor was cluttered with magazines and toys. A scrapbook was open on a card table, surrounded by shoe boxes crammed with photos. A Danielle Steel paperback and an afghan were flung on the couch.

Josie was sure the monster La-Z-Boy belonged to Tom. *Wall Street Journal*s were piled untidily next to it. Cheryl moved a stack of children's books and a jelly doughnut with one bite out of it from a chair. Josie sat down gingerly, hoping she missed the oozing jelly.

"Would you like some coffee?" Cheryl said.

"That would be nice," Josie said. "May I use your rest room?"

"Better use the one upstairs," Cheryl said. "Ben jammed a toy and heaven knows what else in the downstairs toilet. The plumber is supposed to come today to fix it."

"Sounds expensive," Josie said.

"It's not as bad as when Ben shoved a peanut-butter sandwich in the VCR," Cheryl said. "They don't call this age the terrible twos for nothing."

"Been there, done that," Josie said.

She followed the framed photos of Cheryl and Tom up the stairs. The first photos showed Tom in his wedding finery. He had thick dark hair, broad shoulders, and the smile of a man who'd won the grand prize. Cheryl was a picture-book bride, but she smiled for an unseen audience, not her new husband.

In each photo, Tom's hair grew progressively thinner and his body pudgier. By the time baby Ben was born, Tom was fat and his hair was thin. His smile had turned tentative, as if he wasn't as sure of his prize. But Cheryl never changed, and she never smiled for Tom.

The photos of baby Ben with a two-candle birthday cake brought Josie to the top of the stairs. The bucks stopped here, she thought. The upper rooms were nearly empty. No one saw them. Nothing brightened the beige walls, not even family photos. Cheap miniblinds covered the windows. Pricey wallpaper and window treatments would come after the downstairs show rooms were furnished.

I am so full of venom, if I bite myself, I'll die, Josie thought. What is wrong with me?

But she knew. This was the life she was supposed to have. She'd rejected her own accountant and lighted china cabinet for a wild romance, a child out of wedlock, and a flat in Maplewood with her mother.

And I'm glad, she thought defiantly. But Josie couldn't resist a short tour. The master bedroom was a mess. The king bed, in a rather battered modern style, was probably from Tom's bachelor days. The dresser was heaped with perfume, earrings, hairy brushes and crumpled tissues.

The walk-in closet looked like a jumble sale. Josie saw piles of unironed shirts, unhung skirts, abandoned scrunchies and scarves. Socks were tossed like confetti. There were enough designer shoes to start a store. They're all my size, Josie thought. If I slip a pair into my purse, Cheryl will never miss them. She eyed some sexy black Jimmy Choos.

Her larcenous thoughts finally shamed Josie into leaving. She used the cluttered bathroom and hurried back down the stairs. Cheryl had coffee on a tray and cookies on a pretty plate. Sugar and cream were served in her wedding china. This display isn't for me, Josie thought. It's to show off her nice things.

"Your mom asked me to talk with you. She thought I might be able to help you," Josie said.

"Oh, yes, you're that shopper person," Cheryl said. "The one next door who lives with her mother. You're not married, right?"

Josie had been put in her place.

"I am a mystery shopper," Josie said. "I shopped the Soft Shoe store the day Mel was murdered."

"Really?" Cheryl looked at Josie's comfortable loafers. "I would have never guessed."

Keep your temper, Josie told herself. Remember your mother. She wants to be Maplewood flower chair.

"Is there anything I can tell you about Mel?" Josie said. "Your mom is worried sick after the police interviewed you." Take that, Ms. Perfect.

"I'm sure it was just a misunderstanding," Cheryl said. "Mothers worry too much. You know how it is." She gave a we-girls smile.

"Actually, I think your mother is right," Josie said. "And I don't usually agree with your mom." She smiled back. "You've never been in trouble before. I'm not sure you realize how serious your situation is."

"I'm well aware of what's happening. More than you are," Cheryl said. She held the silver sugar tongs as if she wanted to snip off Josie's nose. Instead, she grabbed a sugar cube.

"There was a rumor that Mel was into women's feet," Josie said.

Cheryl squeezed the sugar cube until it disintegrated. "Not mine," she said. "I wouldn't stand for that."

Josie almost laughed, then realized Cheryl had no sense of humor. She wasn't making a deliberate pun. "There were complaints about Mel and some of the women customers."

"What do you mean, complaints?" Cheryl's voice grew hard.

"Look, Cheryl, it wasn't my idea to come here," Josie said. "Your mother thought I could help you because I know the shoe store and I've had some dealings with Mel—and they weren't pleasant."

"I don't need your help." Cheryl stood up. "I don't want you here. I have no idea how Mel wound up dead at the bottom of his staircase. There's nothing someone like you can do for me. If there's a problem—and there isn't—my husband will get me the best lawyer in West County. Now, if you don't mind, I have an errand to run before the plumber gets here. I have to leave."

"Fine," Josie said. "I'm outta here."

Josie watched Cheryl stomp out of the room, leaving her to find her own way through the perfectly decorated house.

That's it, she thought. I've done my duty. I talked with Cheryl. Fat lot of good it did, but I don't care if she acts like a spoiled brat. Mom will get her committee chair, and I can get out of here.

Josie found her purse in the clutter of magazines and toys, and checked her jeans for jelly doughnut juice. The rooms where Cheryl actually lived were night-and-day different from the show rooms, she thought, as she picked her way through the dusted and polished perfection at the front of the house. The ice-white living room felt ten degrees cooler than the rest of the house.

The doorbell rang, and Josie heard Cheryl erupt into curses. "Son of a bitch," she said. "That damned plumber was supposed to call first. He's two hours early. I'll ream his ass."

Whoa, Josie thought. Wish Mom could hear this. Mrs. Mueller's little girl has quite a mouth. She poked her head around the living room doorway and saw Cheryl march toward the front door, anger in every step.

Through the front window, Josie caught a glimpse of the two people on the doorstep. This must be some ritzy neighborhood, she thought. The plumber and his assistant were in suits. Cheryl flung open the door, then turned whiter than her living room. Something was wrong.

One of the suits flashed a badge. He was about her age, Josie figured, with an open face and little ears like knobs. Standing next to him was the curly-haired detective who'd been at her house that morning.

Holy shit, Josie thought, stepping back into the shadowy living room. I can't let Detective Causeman see me here. She'll think I'm mixed up with Cheryl.

Josie ducked into the bathroom with the plugged toilet, rummaged in her purse, then pulled on the black sweater and red wig. She added hot-pink lipstick and checked herself in the mirror. Not bad. Even Jane would have trouble recognizing her in that getup. The newly transformed Josie peeked around the corner. She wanted to watch this show.

Cheryl was confronting the two detectives. She barred her door, refusing to let them in. Josie gave her top points for tailoring. The curly blond detective's suit sagged at the knees. Cheryl's had creases as sharp as her tongue.

"What are you doing here? I told you not to come back." Cheryl's voice had an ugly edge. That temper thing again.

Bad move, Josie thought. Always be polite to cops. They have ways of getting even. But Cheryl, who'd never been in trouble, didn't know that.

The knob-eared detective stayed super-polite, which Josie thought was a bad sign. She heard something slightly off in his voice. She was enough of an actress herself to recognize a performance.

"We'd like you to accompany us to headquarters to answer some questions about the murder of Melvin Poulaine," he said smoothly. Detective Kate Causeman said nothing.

"Get out of my way," Cheryl said. She tried to leave, but the knob-eared detective didn't move. Cheryl couldn't get out her own front door.

"I'm not going with you. I'm calling my lawyer." Cheryl spit out the words like a Mob princess.

The detective stood silent as a pin-striped rock. His lips were smiling, but his eyes were cold. Cheryl didn't see this dangerous sign. She tried to walk past him, but he blocked her exit. She pushed him out of her way and either stumbled or deliberately kicked him.

"Did you see that?" he asked his partner in mock surprise.

"I certainly did," Detective Causeman said. The curly-haired detective sounded as stagy as Detective Knob Ears. "I believe Mrs. Malmy has assaulted a police officer."

"Well, then," Knob Ears said, "we'll have to arrest her—and fingerprint her."

It was a setup, Josie thought, and silly, spoiled Cheryl stepped into it. The detectives were going to get her fingerprints one way or the other.

The two detectives clamped their hands down on her arms. Detective Knob Ears said, "Cheryl Malmy, you have the right to remain silent . . ."

Cheryl wasn't silent. She was stunned with shock. Josie could practically read her mind. Nothing like this had ever happened to her. The world always did what Cheryl wanted.

Now it had turned on her. Perfect Cheryl had a new set of bracelets.

She was led from her home in handcuffs.

Chapter 10

The *snick!* of the handcuffs unleashed something in Cheryl. Suddenly, she came to life. She fired orders at Josie, still standing in the shadows in her red wig.

"Get my baby, Ben," she said. "He's at the sitter's. The number is by the phone. Tell Bonnie I said you could pick him up. The code words are 'baby blue.' Call my mother. Take the baby to her. She'll watch him. Have her call the lawyer. Take care of Ben."

This last was said as the detectives were leading Cheryl away. Josie was relieved that Cheryl never said her name or noticed her new hair color. She even forgave her for not saying "please" as she rudely issued orders.

Josie sprinted for the kitchen and tore the babysitter's number from a list by the kitchen phone. With any luck, the detectives would think the redheaded Josie was a neighbor, a harmless suburban woman.

Josie slid quietly out the side door. The cops were escorting Cheryl into their car with exaggerated courtesy. Detective Causeman held her hand over the doorframe, so the handcuffed Cheryl wouldn't bump her head as she got into the car. Cheryl must be seething, but this time she was smart enough to keep her mouth shut. No neighbors came out to watch the show. Cheryl still had a little luck left.

Josie hoped her own luck held and Detective Causeman didn't recognize her. She strolled down the street away from Cheryl's house, as if she lived in the neighborhood. She kept going until she saw the detectives' car pull out of Cheryl's drive. Then Josie doubled back and slipped into her own car, grateful it looked so anonymous. She was shaking when she sat down.

Deep breaths. Deep breaths. Josie wanted to run. She wanted to roar through the subdivision streets at ninety miles an hour. Go slow, she told herself. Don't call attention to yourself. It took superhuman effort to keep her car at the subdivision's sedate twenty-five-miles-an-hour speed limit, but Josie did it.

She drove for nearly a mile before she pulled over in a strip mall and punched the sitter's number on her cell phone. Her hands fumbled with the buttons and she couldn't complete the call. Josie took another deep breath. This time, she dialed the number.

"Hello, Bonnie?" Josie said.

"That's me!" Bonnie had the smiley voice of so many professional child care workers.

"I'm Josie Marcus. Cheryl asked me to pick up Ben and take him to her mother's. She said to tell you the code is baby blue. That's okay? Good. Where do you live?"

Josie wrote down Bonnie's directions. She didn't trust her memory right now. The babysitter's voice was high-pitched, like a cartoon character. Josie could hear a Baby Einstein video and toddler shrieks in the background.

"Thanks," Josie said. "I can be there in ten minutes."

Josie speed-dialed the call to her mother. "Hello, Mom. It's me. I went to see Cheryl. Yes, the house is lovely, but that's not why I'm calling. The police arrested Cheryl. I said they arrested Cheryl. Not for murder. For assaulting a police officer. Yes, I was at the right house. It was definitely Cheryl. I didn't make a mistake, Mom. I heard them read Cheryl her rights."

Jane still refused to believe Josie. She wasn't talking so much as making protesting noises.

"What did she do? She was rude, Mom. What do you mean, they don't arrest people for being rude. She tried to push around a homicide detective. I think she made him angry. His partner is the curly-haired blonde who was at our house today, Detective Causeman. Yes, I'm glad you were nice to her, Mom. Look, I have to go. They're taking Cheryl to the Olympia Park police station.

"Cheryl needs a lawyer. Can you tell Mrs. Mueller that? Also, tell her I'm picking up the baby at the sitter's and I'll bring him straight to her house. Yes, Mom, I'll drive slowly with a baby in the car.

"No, Mom, that's all I know right now. I'll be home as soon as I can.

"What? You're proud of me because I put aside my animosity to help a family in trouble? Thanks, Mom. GBH to you, too."

Josie shut the phone.

Well, how about that? Her mother was proud of her. Josie felt aglow. The sun appeared through the slate gray clouds for just a moment, a surreal lemon light.

Josie thought about the scene with Cheryl, when she'd snapped orders at Josie. She had worried about her child first and last, like any good mother. She'd also wanted her own mom. But she'd never mentioned her loving husband, Tom.

Then she thought back to her earlier conversation with Cheryl. "I have no idea how Mel wound up dead at the bottom of his staircase," Cheryl had said.

How did she know that? It wasn't in the newspaper. Did the police tell her? Detective Causeman never told Josie how Mel died. Did she tell Cheryl? Or was Cheryl at Mel's house the night he was killed? Did she see him lying dead at the foot of the stairs? Did she send him there? Josie had learned something from her encounter with Cheryl after all, but it wouldn't make her mother happy. It put another ding in Cheryl's perfect facade.

Bonnie the babysitter lived in the low-rent part of Ballwin, in an old subdivision with small, slightly run-down ranch houses. Bonnie's was mint green. The yard was filled with orange plastic toys.

Bonnie was a large, smiling woman in painter's overalls. Josie didn't think those were paint streaks down her front. Her door opened with the cheery jingle of sleigh bells. The tiny living room was as clean as a woman with kids could keep it, and completely overrun with children. A little girl solemnly balanced blocks on the floor. A boy tried to take them away from her. She swatted him on the head and resumed building her block tower.

Two more boys bounced on the plaid couch, watching Baby Einstein and pointing excitedly at the video's stuffed cows and trains.

"Choo-choo," howled the boy who turned out to be Ben. He was a rosy little guy with chubby cheeks and an air of serious purpose. Josie loved his clothes—miniature jeans and a red-checked flannel shirt. The baby lumberjack look.

"So you're taking him to Grandma's?" Bonnie said.

"Nana," Ben shrieked.

"Cheryl asked me to drop him off at her mom's in Maplewood," Josie said. She didn't mention Cheryl's arrest. "She gave me the code."

"We worked that out," Bonnie said. "It changes every day. Cheryl gets stuck in meetings a lot. If she can't get free by three thirty, she calls me and sends someone to pick up Ben. The person doing the pickup has to have the code. It's a safety precaution."

"Does Ben stay here often?"

"Four or five days a week. Cheryl usually drops him off between ten and eleven in the morning, then picks him up by four. I'm almost his second mom. For a while Ben even called me Mommy, which ticked off his mother. I told her it was a phase, but she didn't believe me. He got over it. She did, too. Do you have a baby car seat?"

"No," Josie said.

"I'd better lend you one," Bonnie said. "That will be thirty-five dollars for the babysitting and a twenty-dollar deposit for the car seat." Her cheerful voice had a bit of an edge. Inside that motherly figure was an adding machine.

Josie gulped. She was doing a fifty-five-dollar favor for a woman who'd thrown her out of her house. But she looked at Ben's guileless blue eyes. I'm not doing this for Cheryl, she thought. It's for the baby.

"Will you take a check?" Josie said.

"Oh, yeah. If it bounces, I'll beat it out of Cheryl." Bonnie smiled, but Josie thought she might do that.

Ben wasn't shy around strangers. He put his chubby arms around Josie's neck when she carried him to her car. He was a solid little fellow with silky white-blond hair. Bonnie helped get him into the car seat. Ben settled without fuss, looking around quietly and gnawing on a toy. He was such a good boy, Josie thought.

She drove slower than usual, not just for Ben's safety but because she felt so disconnected. First, there was Cheryl's house with the perfect show rooms and the chaotic interior. Now there was Ben, who was at the sitter's four or five times a week—so often he called the woman Mommy.

Wasn't Cheryl supposed to be a full-time mother? Didn't Grandma Mueller run over for an afternoon so the child wouldn't have to be with a sitter? Why was Ben practically living at Bonnie's house? Not that he was in bad hands. The boy looked clean, contented and well cared for—but not by his mother.

By two o'clock, Josie had delivered Ben to a teary-eyed Mrs. Mueller. Josie felt sorry for the old trouble-maker. She seemed smaller, slightly shrunken. Her chins wobbled when she talked. Her iron gray hair was flattened on one side. Mrs. Mueller must have been napping, and she hadn't bothered to fix her hair. That had never happened before, either. Josie's world was reeling.

"I appreciate this," Mrs. Mueller said. Those words alone sent shock waves through Josie's system. "I know we haven't been friends in the past, but you've helped my daughter and grandson. I'll never forget this. I'll do everything I can for you."

"Just make sure my mom is Maplewood chair of the Flower Guild," Josie said. "It's important to her."

"That I can do."

"Uh, it was fifty-five dollars for the babysitting and the child seat," Josie said. "I have the seat in my car. You may need it."

"No, no, I have my own," Mrs. Mueller said. "Can I bring the money over later? I don't have the cash on me and I'm waiting for Cheryl's lawyer to call back, so I can't run to the bank."

"Of course," Josie said.

She staggered off Mrs. Mueller's porch, literally thrown off balance by all the changes. Perfect Cheryl had pushed a cop and gotten herself arrested. Mrs. Mueller, the terror of Josie's teenage years, was in hock to her for fifty-five bucks. Mrs. M's curtains no longer twitched when Josie left the house. They never would again. Jane's errant daughter could entertain the Cardinals baseball team, and her nosy neighbor wouldn't care.

Mrs. Mueller had been watching the wrong daughter.

Chapter 11

Randy the bookseller had an engaging grin and hair like an unmowed lawn. "Anything else I can get you, miss?"

"Miss." Josie liked that. She was getting ma'amed more often these days. Too bad there was no way to rate Randy for that on her mystery-shopping report.

Randy patted Josie's trade paperback Steinbeck. "*East of Eden* is such a cool book," he said. "I love Steinbeck. He still has something to say, you know? I'm reading *Sweet Thursday* now. There's this great line where Mack takes a drink. Steinbeck says he 'beered his dry mouth and throat.'"

"That is good," Josie said. Please, Randy, remember your bookstore questions, she prayed silently.

"That will be fourteen ninety-one," Randy said. "Hope you like the book as much as I did."

Randy had failed. Most stores would consider him an asset, Josie thought. He was smart, courteous and helpful. But he got so caught up in selling his books, he forgot the Bookstable spiel.

Josie heard the bookseller at the next register reciting it like a well-trained parrot. "Do you belong to our Bookstable Bookarama Bonus Club? For only thirty dollars, you get bodacious discounts on books, music and coffee."

The woman customer snapped, "You ask me that every time I come in here, and I give you the same answer. No!"

Josie suspected most customers hated the canned pitches. But the bosses in Bookstable's Atlanta headquarters insisted on them. Now Josie would have to take points off Randy's evaluation. She felt bad, but she couldn't lie on her mystery-shopper report, no matter how much she liked someone. It was part of her code.

She left the store with her Steinbeck book, shoulders slumped. She had a job to do, but she didn't always like it. Maybe if Randy got a bad report, he'd find a job at a place that appreciated him, she told herself. Right. And maybe my boss, Harry, will give me a ten-thousand-dollar raise.

In the parking lot, Josie filled out her report. She was tired. That was it. It was only one thirty in the afternoon. Josie had had a month's excitement packed into one morning, but she still had to do her mystery shopping. This was her final bookstore report. She deserved a coffee break at Has Beans before she picked up Amelia at school.

It seemed light-years since she'd been in Has Beans this morning. Josh had her double espresso waiting for her then. He had another one now, with a chocolate-chip biscotti on the side.

"How's your mom?" he asked.

"Mom?" Josie said, then realized that was three crises ago when she'd sprinted out of the coffeehouse to rescue her mother from the homicide detective. "Boy, have I got news for you."

"Spill," Josh said. "While I clean up the spills on the counter. My district manager is due in ten minutes." He brandished a spray bottle.

"I like to watch men clean," Josie said.

"I don't do windows," he said.

"I wouldn't ask you to do anything I wouldn't do," Josie said.

Josh leaped across the counter in a single fluid motion, like the hero in a pirate movie. He took her in his arms and said, "What exactly won't you do?"

Practically nothing, Josie thought, if you keep holding me like that. "I left the list at home," she said. "What happens if your boss catches us like this?"

"He'll kill me," he said. "But I'll die happy."

He kissed her soundly, then leaped back over the

counter. Josie felt pleasantly dazed. If this was a preview of their date, this man was definitely worth waiting for.

While Josh scrubbed the coffee stains with intense precision, Josie told him about Cheryl's arrest.

"You're right," he said. "It was a setup. The cops wanted her fingerprints. They couldn't find them in any official records. The only other way they could get her prints would be a court order—and if they got the wrong judge that could be difficult. So the detectives had to arrest her for another reason.

"My guess is they'd already sized her up as someone with a temper. They figured she'd take the bait and try to push around a cop. If that didn't work, they'd stop her on some trumped-up traffic charge. They might even arrest her for littering. One way or another, if the cops want you, they'll get you."

"How do you know this?" Josie said.

"The hard way." Before Josh could say any more, a tall man in a black Has Beans shirt appeared at the door.

"The boss," Josh whispered. In a louder voice he said, "Can I give you a refill on that coffee, ma'am?"

"No, thanks. I have to go," Josie said.

Josh's hint that he'd been in trouble with the police worried her all the way to the Barrington School. He was the first man she'd been interested in since her fling with Amelia's father. She'd made a bad choice then. Was she doing it again?

Josie picked up her daughter, who started in with her annoying ass game. Amelia, like most other nine-year-olds in her class, was fascinated with cuss words. She knew better than to say the f-word, the b-word, or even the s-word. They were completely off-limits, punishable by revoking computer and phone privileges, even grounding. But the a-word offered intriguing possibilities.

Zoe, the annoying midget adult in Amelia's class, had invented the ass game. The idea was to see how many times a kid could get by with using "ass" legally around her parents. Words that had "ass" in them also counted, but not as much as the actual a-word. Josie hated the ass game, but at least it kept Amelia searching the dictionary. Tonight, Josie was in no mood. She ended the game after one try.

"Justin said Hilary was sitting on all her assets," Amelia said. She hit the first syllable hard.

"That's enough," Josie said. "I don't want to hear you talk like that again."

"Like what? It's in the dictionary," Amelia said.

" 'Sitting on her assets' has a double meaning," Josie said. "I don't want you to say that about any woman, ever. It's demeaning."

Amelia stuck out her lower lip. Josie sighed. She wished she could sound as wise as the people in the parenting magazines.

Dinner was fast and sullen. Amelia dropped silverware and slammed plates on the table. Homework wasn't much better. Amelia had to memorize the Gettysburg Address. She stumbled over the same section again and again.

"But, in a larger sense, we cannot dedicate—we cannot consecrate—we cannot hollow" she said, in a singsong voice.

"It's 'hallow'," Josie said for the umpteenth time. "It means we cannot make it sacred."

"It's stupid," Amelia said.

"It is not," Josie said. "It's one of the greatest speeches of all time. It's also the shortest. It's about honoring the people who died before us, so that we can live in freedom. It's about—"

Josie realized her speech was longer than Lincoln's. Amelia looked tired. "It's about eight thirty," she finished and stroked her daughter's glossy dark hair. "Why don't we call it a night? We'll go over it again in the morning."

Amelia raced down the hall to her room, her phone, and her computer, grateful to be free. Josie flopped on the couch and closed her eyes. The next thing she knew, the doorbell was ringing, loudly, insistently. Josie jumped up and shook herself like a sleepy pup. What time was it?

The wall clock said nine thirty, late for visitors in this

neighborhood. Something must be wrong. She cautiously peered out the peephole on the front door.

Mrs. Mueller was standing on Josie's porch, looking like her old formidable self. Her hair was once more sprayed into submission, her back was straight, and her chins were firm.

Josie opened the door cautiously. The great Mrs. Mueller never went to anyone's house on this street. Important committee meetings were held at her home. She swept into Josie's living room and chose the best chair as her throne.

"Mrs. Mueller," Josie said in surprise. "I'll go get Mom."

"No, I need to talk to you," Mrs. Mueller said. "Sit down."

Josie sat in her own living room on the second-best chair. "Can I get you some coffee or a soda?"

"No," Mrs. Mueller said. There was a long silence.

Josie finally said, "What can I do for you?"

"It's Cheryl. She's in trouble." Most mothers would burst into tears at those words. But Mrs. Mueller had subdued countless unruly boards of directors. Her eyes were drier than Arizona.

"The police arrested her, as you know. Cheryl's attorney said it was a sneaky way to get her fingerprints. They got a search warrant for her house, too. The police are trying to pin a murder on my little girl."

Josie blinked. She would have voted Mrs. M least likely to say those words.

"Do you know why?" Josie asked.

"Not officially. But my nephew George is a police officer in Richmond Heights. He called in some favors and got a little information. It's not good, Josie. It's just not good."

"I don't even know how Mel died," Josie said. "I haven't seen anything about it in the paper."

"George says when the police arrived, they first thought Mel Poulaine had been drinking and was killed in a fall down his stairs. Then they realized he'd been murdered. Something about the blood-spatter patterns being too high. Someone hit him on the head and tried to make it look like an accident."

"The police think it was Cheryl?" Josie said.

"Yes. The police have a witness who saw her in that Mel person's house the night he was murdered. They found Cheryl's fingerprints on a wineglass. There are just smudges on the other glass. It has traces of some kind of drug in it. They're saying Cheryl bashed in Mel's head and tried to make it look like he died of a fall."

Josie winced, but said nothing.

"The police took some of Cheryl's clothes and shoes, but they didn't find any blood on them."

"What was the murder weapon?" Josie said.

"The warrant said it was 'a heavy, rounded object, possibly a paperweight.' The housekeeper told the police there's a heavy blue Tiffany paperweight missing from a hall table. They searched Cheryl's house, but they didn't find it."

"So there's no murder weapon or bloody clothes connected to Cheryl. What do they have?" Josie said.

"Nothing else. Cheryl admits she was in Mel's house. She says she was a good customer and he invited her for a cocktail. She had one drink and left. Mel was alive and well when she left."

Mrs. Mueller said that last part a little too quickly. Josie was pretty sure that Mrs. M ranked unchaperoned drinking right after murder in her personal list of sins. Josie didn't mention Cheryl's little slip about Mel lying at the foot of the staircase. She'd save that if she had another talk with Cheryl.

Josie was surrounded by another long silence. "There's more, isn't there?"

Mrs. Mueller heaved a great sigh. "The police found forty-eight thousand dollars in Cheryl's closet."

"She kept that much cash in her closet? Where?"

"In her shoe boxes," Mrs. Mueller said.

That explained all the shoes on the floor, Josie thought.

"Cheryl won't tell me where she got the cash, but the police found the dead man's fingerprints on the boxes and the paper bands around the money."

"Are Mel's prints on the money itself?"

"I don't think so. My nephew George says you don't usually get prints off money. It's handled by so many people, it's one big smear of body oils. But it doesn't look good with that Mel person's prints on the money bands."

"Why would Mel give Cheryl money?" Josie said.

"I don't know. Maybe she was holding it for him, keeping it safe. You must help me find out why," Mrs. Mueller said. "I'm sure there's a reasonable explanation."

Josie knew there was no explanation that any mother would want to hear.

"Cheryl won't talk to me or her lawyer," Mrs. Mueller said. "I can't help her until she does."

Josie wanted to say, "What about her husband?" but she knew the answer. How could Cheryl tell Tom she'd been drinking with another man while he'd been working late? She didn't even ask for him when she was being arrested.

"I'd like to help, Mrs. Mueller, but Cheryl won't talk to me, either. She threw me out of her house today."

"I know," Mrs. Mueller said. "She says she doesn't want anyone's help, but that is when my girl needs it most. I know you can help her, Josie. You're the same age. You grew up next door. You were school chums."

"We weren't real close," Josie said. We hated each other's guts, she thought.

"Cheryl's back home now," Mrs. Mueller said. "You don't have to talk to her. I want you to follow her for the next three days. Find out where she goes. Find me a reason. I'll pay you a hundred dollars a day, plus expenses."

It is true, Josie thought. You do turn into what you hate. I'm going to be a spy, just like Mrs. Mueller.

"Why don't you have your nephew George do this? He's a policeman," Josie said.

"Cheryl knows George too well. You have all those disguises for your work. She'll never spot you. Half the time I don't recognize you when you come out of your house dressed the way you do. Besides, there are some things I don't want my family to know. George's mother never liked Cheryl."

"But—" Josie said.

"Your mother will pick up Amelia at school for you. You won't have to worry about that."

"But—"

"You can call in sick for three days, can't you? It may take less time. You may only have to follow Cheryl for two days. Or one. Just one. I'll cover your salary for the days you aren't at work, so you don't miss any income."

"But—"

"I'll make your mother Altar Society chair as well as Maplewood chair of the St. Louis Flower Guild."

That's why I'm doing this, Josie thought. Not for Cheryl or Mrs. Mueller, but for Mom. The Altar Society chair would make Jane one of the three most powerful church ladies in the parish.

"Deal," Josie said. "But here's my condition: You have to answer my questions. I won't spread your information around the neighborhood, but I need straight answers if I'm going to get anywhere."

"All right," Mrs. Mueller said. Josie could see the woman grit her teeth. Mrs. M was not used to taking orders.

"Did the police arrest Cheryl for Mel's murder?"

"Not yet," Mrs. Mueller said. "They arrested her for pushing the detective and accidentally stepping on his foot. Her lawyer says once a jury gets a look at my little Cheryl and that great big detective, they'll laugh the case out of court. The charge is totally bogus."

Josie gulped. It was almost worth taking the case to hear Mrs. M say "totally bogus." She wasn't sure Cheryl would be found innocent, either. A jury of women would know sweet Cheryl was tougher than titanium.

"Cheryl is being charged with misdemeanor battery," Mrs. Mueller said. "They booked her, photographed her and took her fingerprints. The police read Cheryl the Miranda warning and told her not to leave town."

"Next question: Do you know your daughter uses a babysitter at least four days a week?" Josie asked.

"That's not possible," Mrs. Mueller said. "Cheryl is a

stay-at-home mom. That's the agreement she and Tom had. He would earn enough for two and she would be a full-time mother."

"That may have been the deal, but she isn't keeping it," Josie said.

"I don't believe it," Mrs. Mueller said.

"I picked up your grandson at the sitter's house, remember?" Mrs. Mueller shook her head, but her eyes were trapped. She didn't want to believe it.

"Cheryl has a code arrangement with the sitter," Josie said. "It changes daily. If she's going to be late, she calls a friend, gives her the code and has her pick up the baby. Do you know this friend?"

"No, I don't. My Cheryl is a popular girl," Mrs. Mueller said. "She has so many friends. I can't believe any of this."

But Josie could hear the doubt in Mrs. Mueller's denial. This time, she did believe it. Her faith in Cheryl—and her own pride—were crumbling. Her face had developed seams and sags. She had lipstick on her teeth.

"What is Cheryl's relationship with her husband?" Josie asked.

"Tom is a good provider."

"But how is he as a husband?" Josie said.

"He never plays around, unlike some young men."

This didn't sound like the romance of the century. "Does he love her?" Josie said.

"Of course. Tom is a hard worker. That's how he shows his love. He has a position at one of the biggest CPA firms in St. Louis. He has only the best clients in Ladue, Warson Woods, Olympia Park, Clayton and Frontenac. He leaves for his office at six every morning and rarely gets home before seven or eight at night. During income tax season, Cheryl hardly sees him at all. You expect an ambitious man to build his career."

"Is your daughter lonely?" Josie said.

"Cheryl understands. She has her committees and activities," Mrs. Mueller said.

"Do Cheryl and Tom have money troubles?" Josie said.

"Of course not. Did you see their house?"

"It's beautiful," Josie said. "But it must be expensive to maintain. The upstairs is nearly bare."

"They're furnishing it right, buying only the best. That's what I advised Cheryl. Don't settle for second best in men or furniture. It's too hard to get new ones."

Poor Tom. He was no better than a china cabinet.

"Can I talk to her husband?"

"Absolutely not. Tom has enough problems right now. I don't want him bothered."

Especially by any awkward questions I might ask. Mrs. Mueller would want to keep the perfect son-in-law in the dark about Cheryl's possible marital slips.

"One last question," Josie said. "How did the police find out Cheryl was at Mel's? What made them go after her fingerprints? Was she involved in another crime, something minor, like shoplifting?"

"Certainly not!" Mrs. Mueller looked like she might have a stroke. A button popped on her blouse.

"It was a neighbor of that terrible Mel's," she said bitterly. "Some old woman in Olympia Park. She kept a diary of visitors to that house. She wrote down Cheryl's license-plate number, description, and the time she entered and left that awful Mel's house. The police say Cheryl was there during the time he died."

"What time was that?" Josie said.

"Between seven and nine that night. Apparently, the old biddy had nothing better to do than spy on that Mel's house, day and night. She's nothing but a common snoop."

"Imagine that," Josie said.

Chapter 12

Alyce groaned. "This is better than sex," she said. "This is a food orgy."

"Spoken like a married woman," Josie said.

"Hah, as a single woman you can have any man you want," Alyce said. "I'm limited to one. A good one, don't get me wrong, but a different man would be nice once in a while."

"Sex would be nice once in a while," Josie said. "I'm not a single woman. I'm a single mother. I can't have strange men waking up in my bed. What kind of example would that be for my daughter?"

"Could be a good one. Wish my mom had been a free spirit," Alyce said wistfully. "I might be leading a more interesting life."

"Alyce, you are perfect the way you are," Josie said. "I can't imagine you any other way."

She smiled at her big blond friend with the floaty hair. "Besides, this is my whine. I'm trying to explain the trials of single motherhood. It's okay for you to wake up with a man in your bed. It's good for family values and all that. If I have a man stay overnight when Amelia is home, I'm a slut."

"Can't you leave her with your mother?" Alyce asked.

"Not when Mom's living upstairs. I can hear my mother snoring through the furnace vents. What do you think she'd hear? I'm celibate as a nun."

Alyce stared at her and Josie remembered the scene on her front porch with Josh. "Okay, it's not that bad.

But it's easier for me to invade Canada than spend the night with a man."

"And it's definitely overdue. You're getting testy," Alyce said. "When is that hot-looking Josh spending the night?"

Josie blushed. "I have a date with Josh next Saturday night. Amelia has a party at her best friend Emma's house. She'll be gone overnight."

Josie didn't want to talk anymore about her nearly nonexistent sex life, even if she had started the discussion. "Eat your lunch, or it won't be better than anything, much less sex."

"Okay, what do we have here?" Alyce said. She rubbed her manicured hands together in anticipation, then glided around Josie's kitchen table, admiring the bulging boxes and bags. Josie was proud of her lunch layout. She'd even stuck a single red rose in a Fitz's Root Beer bottle. Presentation was everything.

"This is my all–St. Louis lunch," Josie said. "It's my payback for all those lovely brunches you give me." She pointed to an open pizza box, rich with grease and red sauce.

"That's an Imo's pizza," she said. "St. Louis thin crust, topped with pepperoni, mushrooms and Provel cheese."

"You gotta love that orange cheese," Alyce said. "Can't find it anywhere else but St. Louis. What are those brown lumps and that cup of yellow gunk?"

"Pretzel sandwiches from Gus' Pretzels. Bratwurst wrapped in soft pretzel dough. I got the honey mustard dip, too."

"And what's that?" Alyce pointed to a puffy, pointed brown oblong.

"A Gus' specialty pretzel. It's shaped like a Rams football."

"Oh, yeah, now I see it," Alyce said.

"Gus' also has wedding pretzels, birthday pretzels and First Communion pretzels," Josie said.

"I'm afraid to ask what a First Communion pretzel is," Alyce said.

"It's made in the shape of a cross," Josie said.

"Isn't that sacrilegious?"

"Absolutely not. A Gus' pretzel is a sacred St. Louis institution."

Josie continued her tabletop tour. "Over here, we have dessert. Those are Dad's Cookies—Scotch oatmeal. The hard ones that don't dissolve when you dunk them in coffee. That's Ted Drewes Frozen Custard in the yellow-and-green cups. And to drink, Schlafly Pilsner and Fitz's Root Beer, both made in St. Louis."

Josie plunked the bottles on the table. Her meal seemed a little casual, even with the flower. It certainly didn't look like Alyce's carefully planned confections served on crystal and china. Maybe I should have put the food on real plates, Josie thought. But I don't have any pretty wedding china. Besides, I don't have to wash paper plates.

Alyce didn't seem put off by the spread's lack of style. She picked up a pretzel brat, pulled off a piece of orange pizza with stringy cheese, and plopped them on a paper plate.

"There's not a healthy thing on this table," Alyce said. "I'm sick of salads with low-fat dressing, tired of taste-free low-carb bread, bored with root vegetables, seeds and berries. Life is a banquet. Eat and enjoy."

Josie felt better. Alyce always said the right thing. It was one of the reasons they were friends. They'd met a couple of years ago on a multi-community Clean Up the County committee. Josie had volunteered in a fit of civic responsibility. After two endless, useless meetings, she would have quit if she hadn't been sitting next to Alyce. The big blonde's barbed remarks about the do-nothing board and her "let's quit talking and do something" attitude made Josie realize they were sisters, despite their economic differences. They managed to help clean up a large section of Manchester Road and remain good friends.

Josie started packing her own plate. "I can't tell a garlic press from a bench press, but I know my calories, cholesterol and grease."

The two women sat side by side in reverent silence, broken only by respectful smacking. They quickly demolished the pizza and the pretzel brats, then slurped down the beer while they pulled salty, doughy pieces off the Rams football pretzel. Somehow, they managed to save room for the Ted Drewes dessert.

Alyce scooped up creamy frozen custard with a Dad's cookie. "Did you ever notice how the old St. Louis businesses have real people's names?" she said. "There really was a Gus who made pretzels, a Ted Drewes who sold frozen custard, and a Dad who dunked cookies. Real people make real food here."

"Yeah," Josie said. "Real fattening food." She was feeling guilty now that the lunch was almost gone. Her table looked like it had been attacked by marauding bears. "I'd better remove the evidence before Mom gets home or I'll get another heart-healthy lecture."

"Why hide it? Your mother will see the pizza boxes and frozen-custard cartons when she takes out her garbage," Alyce said.

"Nope. I'm dumping this junk in Mrs. Mueller's trash."

"So what's going on with your nosy neighbor and her not-so-perfect daughter?" Alyce said.

"That's why I invited you here for lunch," Josie said. "Mrs. Mueller made me an offer I can't refuse. We're going to become busybodies. Want to do surveillance with me for the next three days?"

Josie told Alyce about Mrs. Mueller's visit. Alyce listened carefully, her intelligent blue eyes sizing up Josie, hearing what she wasn't saying as much as what she was.

"How are you going to follow Cheryl?" Alyce said, when Josie had finished. "She knows you."

"Only as a brunette. I have a closet full of wigs and disguises."

"What about your car? Won't Cheryl recognize it?"

"Nobody ever notices my car. I can't even find it half the time," Josie said.

"Don't underestimate that little witch," Alyce said. "Cheryl isn't stupid. She's been getting by with all sorts of shenanigans for years. If she's doing something wrong now, she's going to be extra cautious. We'd better take my SUV. She hasn't seen it."

"Then you'll do it?" Josie said.

"I can't wait to find out what she's up to," Alyce said. "It will make my day."

"I tell you, Alyce, I never believed in karma until I found out Mrs. Mueller's daughter was caught by the local busybody," Josie said.

Alyce laughed and chomped the last cookie. "There is a God and she is just," she said.

At ten o'clock the next morning, Josie and Alyce were parked down the street from Cheryl's house in Alyce's massive SUV. The sky had that gray, bleak look that threatened snow—or suicide.

Alyce was shivering so bad her teeth chattered. "It's never this cold in the movies," she said, pulling her coat tighter around her. "I'm sorry I can't keep the engine running."

"I can see my breath in here," Josie said. "I need some coffee."

"Then you'd need a bathroom," Alyce said.

"You never see that in the movies, either," Josie said. "Private eyes don't have kidneys. How do I look?"

"Your own mother wouldn't recognize you in that black wig and red lipstick." Alyce hadn't bothered with a disguise for the first day, since Cheryl didn't know her.

"Her house is the one with the Pella windows and the white pillars, right?" Alyce said.

"That's it. The prefab Tara," Josie said. Being without coffee made her mean.

"It's everything I expected," Alyce said. "Small yard, big garage. Bad feng shui. I bet their car is leased."

"You should see that house inside," Josie said. "All for show downstairs, nearly bare upstairs."

"Typical," Alyce said. "Did she have a humongous lighted china cabinet in the dining room?"

"Yes. How did you know?"

"Probably following mama's advice: You always get your living-room furniture. You can buy a good bedroom set later. But you have to spend the money on a good dining-room set with a china cabinet before the children come, or you'll never see it. I heard that from my mother and Cheryl probably heard it from hers. One of my friends had to resort to a weekend of oral sex before she nailed that china cabinet. It's the symbol of the good provider."

"That explains the wedding cake topper on the shelf," Josie said. "Let me give you the rest of the verbal tour. The kitchen is gourmet, although I don't think she really cooks."

"I always think when they call a kitchen gourmet, it means you could eat it—or maybe it could eat you," Alyce said. "What's wrong with me? I sound like I have fangs and I don't even know these people. I'm sure they're likable."

"Not Cheryl," Josie said.

"But she's never done anything to me and she sets my teeth on edge. Cheryl and Tom are just trying to get a couple of rungs up the social ladder. They're probably making more money than Daddy and she's spending it on that showcase house. In ten years, it will be beautifully furnished and they'll be solid suburban citizens."

"Then they'll own the cars and the house?" Josie said.

"Then they'll be as deeply in debt as the rest of us," Alyce said. "What time is it?"

"Ten twenty-three. I hope someone doesn't call the cops on us," Josie said.

"I'll say I'm collecting for one of my charities," Alyce said. "I threw some paperwork and a collection can in the backseat, just in case."

"You're a natural at this," Josie said.

They watched the usual suburban scenes. Repair people arrived. A woman jogged by with a sports stroller. A man ran down the street, belly bouncing above his designer sweats, comb-over flopping in the cold wind.

"I bet he was good-looking ten years ago," Alyce said. "Suburban life takes its toll on men, too. You're lucky to be dating a writer like Josh. He won't settle for the safe life."

"That's what worries me," Josie said. "From some remarks he's made lately, I think he walks too close to the wild side. He knows too much about how the police work."

"That's what makes him sexy," Alyce said. "I don't

like naive men and neither do you. You can bet Stan the Man Next Door doesn't know a thing about the cops. Would you rather spend your nights comparing paper towel prices with him?"

"Isn't there anything in between?" Josie said.

Before Alyce could answer, Cheryl's garage door rumbled up. Josie could see her strapping baby Ben into his car seat. There was no sign that Cheryl had been hauled off to jail the day before. Her caramel hair was in a perfect chignon. Her camel pants were impeccable. Cheryl backed her black SUV out of the garage.

"Here we go," Alyce said, and started her engine.

"Finally, you can turn on the heater," Josie said.

They were a mile from Cheryl's house when Josie said, "She's heading for the sitter's. Follow her, but don't turn into the subdivision. We'll be too easy to spot. We can wait in the mini-mart lot. She'll be back at the subdivision entrance in ten minutes."

Josie's predictions were correct. After Cheryl dropped Ben at the sitter's, she headed for Highway 40. But she didn't get off at any of the expected exits.

"I think she's driving downtown," Josie said.

"I wonder where?" Alyce said. Proper West County women did not drive alone into downtown St. Louis. They considered it too dangerous. Some bragged about how many years it had been since they'd been "in the city."

"No, wait! She missed the last Missouri exit," Josie said. "She's going into Illinois."

"Illinois? What's there?" Alyce said.

If West County women rarely visited the city, they never went to Illinois. They regarded it as one long stretch of industrial polluters, strip joints, and sin spots.

"She's turning off into East St. Louis," Josie said.

"Omigod," Alyce said. She was genuinely shocked. "What on earth is she doing there?"

Alyce would vacation in Baghdad before she went to East St. Louis.

"She's turning in to the Royal Duchess casino," Josie said.

Chapter 13

The Royal Duchess looked like a riverboat made of plywood.

"Some Duchess," Josie said. "This is a floating Wal-Mart. Isn't that the Casino Queen over there?"

"Sure is," Alyce said. "Makes the Duchess look like the Bellagio. The Duchess spent all her money on the parking lot. It's lit up like Las Vegas."

"At least something looks like Vegas," Josie said.

Josie had flown to Las Vegas with Amelia's father in a private plane. They'd had a wildly romantic weekend in an outrageous purple velvet suite with a four-poster bed. Josie had drunk champagne and won five hundred dollars at roulette. That was when she still took chances.

The Duchess did not look like a place for champagne or romance. The parking lot lights were so bright, even the gray November day seemed sunny.

"At least I feel safe here," Josie said. "This place has more security than a federal prison."

"This is a prison, too," Alyce said. "It's full of losers."

Josie was surprised by Alyce's bitterness. Maybe she was against legalized gambling. Josie wanted to ask her, but Alyce was struggling to track Cheryl's SUV through the endless parking lot. Cheryl drove erratically up and down the aisles, sometimes speeding, other times stopping for no reason. Suddenly, she whipped into valet parking.

"Do you want valet parking, too?" Alyce asked.

"No. We'll need to move quickly," Josie said. "We

can't wait for some kid to bring the car if we're chasing Cheryl."

"Fine. The valets always change my radio buttons," Alyce said. "Most car parkers don't listen to NPR."

Josie and Alyce followed Cheryl into the casino. Cheryl moved with the sureness of someone who felt at home. Josie stumbled, blinked and tried to adjust to the lights. They were dim and flashing, all at the same time. She heard the constant sound of money clinking and jingling, although she didn't see any coins.

"This is like a bad disco," she said to Alyce.

"Including the customers," Alyce said.

A man with lizard skin, a high black-dyed pompadour, and a purple shirt open to his navel stared at Cheryl's beige perfection and puffed out his flabby chest like an old rooster. His chest was carpeted with gray hair and gold chains.

"Omigod," Josie said. "If Elvis was alive, he'd look like that." Suddenly, she swung around. "Where's Cheryl?"

Their quarry had disappeared into the crowd where three wide halls intersected.

"We've lost her," Alyce said.

They raced through herds of gamblers. Running on the bright confusion of the red-and-orange carpet made Josie dizzy. Bars beckoned. Neon glowed. Lounge acts, dressed like older, fatter versions of Elvis, the Bee Gees, and Frank Sinatra, sang dead men's songs.

"Doesn't anyone alive sing anymore?" Alyce asked.

"Never mind the state of casino music," Josie said. "We have to find Cheryl."

They ran by hard-faced women in tight jeans, grandmas in sweet pastels, workingmen in baseball caps. There was no sign of Cheryl's understated elegance.

They sprinted by spinning roulette wheels and tense, soundless baccarat tables. No Cheryl. They could see high-stakes poker players roped off behind velvet barriers. Cheryl wasn't sitting with that select group.

"Wait! That's her," Alyce said. "She's playing the dollar slots." Josie skidded to a stop.

Cheryl was enthroned on a padded black leather chair, pushing a bill into a slot machine. A baby spot highlighted her hair, turning it brassy gold.

"I thought you had to be at least seventy years old to play the slots," Josie said. "Cheryl's too young. Where's her plastic coin bucket?"

"Boy, are you out of it," Alyce said. "Casinos don't have buckets. Slots don't give out tokens anymore. They have tickets. Casinos don't have slot machine attendants, either. Now they're called luck ambassadors."

"You're making this up," Josie said.

"Jake and I went to a casino—Harrah's, I think—with some lawyers from his office. I lost a hundred dollars. I'm an expert."

Josie stood back on the garish carpet and surveyed the scene. "I think we can watch Cheryl from the nickel slots and she won't see us. Have a seat."

Alyce plopped down. "This padded chair feels good."

Josie stuck a dollar bill into a $10,000 jackpot nickel slot machine. "Where's the handle on this thing?" she said.

"You don't pull slot machines anymore," Alyce said. "You press a button."

Lights blinked, lemons and cherries spun, and finally two lemons and a cherry came up.

The machine went dark. Game over.

"That's it? I lost a whole buck in two seconds?" Josie said. "It gulped down my dollar and I didn't even get any pulsing lights or ringing bells. Why not put a gun to my head and empty my wallet? I can't believe people get addicted to this. I've had more excitement buying a train ticket."

"People don't get addicted to losing," Alyce said. "They get hooked on winning. You're lucky. If you'd won the grand jackpot, you'd be back here every day trying to duplicate that high."

Josie didn't feel lucky. She kicked the machine. A luck ambassador started toward her. "We'd better sit in the penny slots. I'll be bankrupt in an hour at this rate."

"You find us two good seats," Alyce said. "I'll stroll by Cheryl and see how much she's spending."

Josie tried out several penny slot machines until she got two with an angled view of Cheryl's slot. Cheryl didn't notice Josie. She didn't notice anything but her relentless machine. She fed it bill after bill, as if she were chained to a ravenous robot. The slot machine gave her nothing, but Cheryl never stopped shoving money into it.

Alyce glided back from her reconnaissance tour of Cheryl's site, slightly breathless, blond hair floating every which way. "Cheryl's gambling with ten-dollar bills. She lost fifty dollars while I was there. Fifty! She's going through money like Kleenex in the cold season."

Josie started keeping track of the bills Cheryl pushed into the machine. She played her own penny slot just enough to keep the luck ambassador away. The only thing Josie won was two free plays. Both tries were losers.

It was a joyless way to spend a day. The casino had no clocks, no windows, only the ruthless machines and the corrosive cries of greed and disappointment. There was no glamour, either. The room looked like a beer dive. The luck ambassadors wore saggy jeans and polyester shirts.

Josie wanted to run outside into the cold, fresh air. Alyce shifted restlessly in her chair. If there had been a kitchen nearby, she would have whipped up a soufflé to pass the time.

"There's no reason for both of us to sit here the whole time," Josie said. "We can take breaks as long as we stay close by."

Josie bought a surprisingly good grilled chicken sandwich at a casino restaurant. Alyce went for lemon meringue pie. They gulped coffee, Mountain Dew and Diet Coke to stay awake. Time moved like a walker in a nursing home.

Cheryl never left her slot machine, not for food, drink, or the rest room. Unlike other gamblers, she made no desperate runs to ATMs along the walls. Her camel leather purse seemed to have an endless supply of ten-spots.

Cheryl won and lost with an equal lack of emotion.

She was down some five hundred dollars after the first hour. Then she had a winning streak and gained more than two hundred dollars. Her machine rattled and rang with programmed animation, but Cheryl's expression never changed. She threw all her winnings and more back into her hungry little machine.

As the day limped on, Josie felt like someone had drained her blood. "This is boring," she whispered to Alyce. "I've lost twenty bucks in the penny slots. Do you think I can put my losses on Mrs. Mueller's expense account?"

"What time is it?" Alyce asked.

"Two fifty-five," Josie said. "Cheryl has dropped seven hundred bucks in three hours."

"My Lord," Alyce said.

Promptly at three o'clock, Cheryl rose from her chair, drifted through the casino like a sleepwalker and handed her ticket to the valet. Josie and Alyce jogged to their SUV, then followed Cheryl to the highway.

"Those were awesome losses. I've never known anyone to gamble away that kind of money," Josie said. "Even the poker players at the VFW hall never lose more than a hundred bucks a night."

"Do slot machines count as gambling?" Alyce said.

"How can she afford to drop that kind of money? I've seen her house," Josie said. "Seven hundred bucks would fill those empty shelves downstairs with decorator books, or buy new wallpaper for the upstairs."

"Here's something else I don't get," Alyce said. "Why drive to East St. Louis when there are newer and better casinos close to her home?"

Cheryl's SUV headed steadily west into the rich suburbs. Soon she was driving in a pack of pricey cars, blending back into her perfect life. By four o'clock, Cheryl turned into the babysitter's subdivision. Josie and Alyce cruised by and saw Cheryl carry a smiling Ben to her SUV. His chubby arms were wrapped around his mother.

"We don't need to follow her any farther," Josie said. "Cheryl's going home."

"Me, too," Alyce said. "I want to hug my husband

and child. I want to take a long shower and get that neon glare out of my eyes. What a horrible afternoon."

"I guess you won't be going with me tomorrow," Josie said. "I don't blame you."

"Are you kidding? I wouldn't miss it," Alyce said.

Alyce dropped Josie off at her car. Josie drove home in silence. What was she going to tell Mrs. Mueller? Should she say her daughter had a gambling problem?

I'm blowing this all out of proportion, Josie thought. Cheryl went to a casino one day. She lost a little money. Okay, she lost a lot of money, but that doesn't make her an addict.

But she seemed so at home there, a voice whispered. She's done this before.

So what? Maybe Cheryl went to casinos to blow off steam. Being perfect had to be a burden. The casino was an escape, the last place where her mother and her neighbors would look for her. Was it more acceptable to spend seven hundred bucks for shoes or for the slots?

Josie couldn't answer that question.

But she did know one thing: It was too soon to tell Mrs. Mueller.

The old woman came out on her porch when Josie arrived at her own flat. Mrs. Mueller looked like trouble. Her dress was the same iron gray as her hair. It could have been a prison matron's uniform, except for the black silk rose on her bosom.

"Come inside," Mrs. Mueller said. "I want to talk to you."

Now that she was Josie's employer, Mrs. Mueller was issuing orders, not asking favors. Josie followed, mostly out of curiosity. She hadn't been inside her neighbor's house since she was fifteen and her mother made her apologize for the flaming dog doo.

The house had changed very little. The living room was still twice the size of Josie's and carpeted in pale green. The carpet was protected by plastic runners. The runners were covered with throw rugs. There were more pictures of Cheryl on the mantel than Josie remembered, plus new photos of Tom and baby Ben.

Those were the only major differences. The lampshades still had their original cellophane covers. The curtains were a welter of draped, looped and pleated fabric. The pale green couch still had those slippery plastic slipcovers, installed at great expense when Cheryl reached puberty. They weren't meant to save the couch, but Cheryl's reputation. Any boy who dared make out with Cheryl would slide right off the couch.

"What did you find out?" Mrs. Mueller said.

"Nothing really interesting," Josie said. One look at Mrs. Mueller's determined face, and Josie knew she couldn't mention the casino yet. Mrs. M would drive straight to Ballwin and confront her daughter. That would put Cheryl permanently on her guard.

"Well, did she go to the babysitter's house?" Mrs. Mueller demanded.

"Yes, she dropped off Ben about eleven and drove around. I followed her until four p.m., when she picked him up, but the results are inconclusive. I'll know more tomorrow."

Mrs. Mueller gave Josie a look that made her feel fifteen again. It wasn't a good feeling. "I'm counting on you, Josie. And so is your mother."

Josie heard the threat.

A worried Jane greeted her daughter at her door. She'd picked up Amelia from school, then started dinner. A big pot of stew simmered on Josie's stove. A salad smiled on the kitchen table. Both were welcome surprises, but Josie knew the meal came with a price.

Jane started stirring the stew, mostly for something to do. "Did you find out anything?" She put down the wooden spoon and began wringing her hands, anxious for an answer.

What were the ethics of revealing client information to your mother? Josie wondered. She decided not to say anything. Jane was putty in the wily clubwoman's hands. She might accidentally let something slip to Mrs. Mueller.

"Too early to tell," Josie said.

Amelia was suddenly standing in the kitchen. Josie swore her daughter could dematerialize. The kid winked. She knew her mother was lying.

"You rest up until supper's ready," Jane said, too cheerfully. "You've had a long day."

Josie couldn't rest. She'd been cooped up in the twilight world of the casino. She wanted real air. "Come on, Amelia, let's go for a bike ride," she said.

"It's cold," Amelia said.

"Bundle up and we'll go for frozen custard."

That twisted logic appealed to her daughter. Amelia ran for her coat, shrieking, "I want chocolate."

"You'll ruin your dinner," Jane said.

"We're going to have dessert with dinner," Josie said. "We'll just eat it first. Riding bikes will give us an appetite for stew."

Mother and daughter escaped into the frosty November night. Josie liked riding down her street, peeking into the golden squares of window light, seeing people eat dinner and watch TV. They seemed safe and normal.

Amelia and Josie stopped for tall frozen-custard cones at Mr. Wizard's on Big Bend. Oddly, it did warm them up.

"How was the Gettysburg Address?" Josie asked. She licked the drips off her cone.

"Mom, that's gross," Amelia said. "Use your napkin. I got five out of six."

"Not bad," Josie said. The napkin stuck to her fingers.

"Senator Harry Palmidge is coming to speak to our class about Lincoln," Amelia said.

"You mean your school," Josie said.

"No, Mom, just our class."

"A United States senator is speaking to a bunch of third graders? Your classmates' parents must be major donors."

"Mom, you're so cynical."

"No, I'm a realist. Trust me, Amelia. Senators never spoke to my grade school class in Maplewood."

"Did anyone talk to you?" Amelia said.

"Just the cops, telling us to stay out of jail."

"Did it work?" Amelia grinned.

"I haven't been arrested yet," Josie said.

But the lecture hadn't worked for Cheryl, Josie thought. She'd been arrested for pushing a policeman,

and there might be worse in her future. Josie shivered.
She didn't like what she saw today. The sight of Cheryl,
hypnotized by the slots, scared Josie. It hit too close to
home. She wanted her mom to get her precious flower
chair. Then Josie wanted to go back to the malls where
she belonged.

"Let's go home," she said, suddenly chilled to the
bone. "Grandma will be worried."

After Amelia was in bed, Josie went on the Internet to
read about women gamblers. They had other problems
besides their addiction. Men didn't take them seriously.
Jeez, Josie thought. Even women addicts couldn't get
equal treatment.

One woman in Gamblers Anonymous wrote, "The
men did not know what to do with the women who came
to the meetings. Some were literally chased away after
being hit on or intimidated by the men and made to feel
'less than.' The women were new to the GA program
and their gambling was different. They were told that
bingo, slots, video poker and the lotteries were not
real gambling."

That's exactly what Alyce and I did, Josie thought.
We made jokes about granny gamblers.

The newsletter woman had solved her problem by
starting a Gamblers Anonymous group for women. Men
tended to be action gamblers, she wrote. They bet on
skill games like poker. Women were escape gamblers.
"We play luck games like bingo, the lottery, slots or
video poker machines. We gamble first as recreation,
then as escape from problems."

But what did Cheryl want to escape? Josie thought.
Her mother? Her life? Her husband? Maybe all of the
above.

The newsletter woman was smart and strong. She
knew she had a problem and she got help. Josie found
hundreds of news stories about St. Louisans who weren't
so lucky. They stole fortunes to feed their gambling
habits—and got caught.

A bookkeeper embezzled more than two million dollars. A husband and wife extracted more than a million
dollars from their companies. A brewery employee filed

four hundred thousand dollars in false expense-account reports. Would these people have stayed honest if the casinos never came to town?

The wretched criminal roll call continued. The occupations sounded like a high school career day: A bank vice president. A lawyer. A stockbroker. The director of a children's charity. A church pastor.

Some pilfered a few thousand. Others made off with millions. All the money was lost gambling. Josie wondered what happened to their wives, husbands and children. How did they live with the shame and loss?

She couldn't read any more. She felt sick. In her mind, she saw a chubby blond boy reaching for his mother—and a homemaker shoving bills in a slot machine.

What did Cheryl do to get her gambling money?

Chapter 14

"I know why Cheryl was gambling in Illinois," Alyce said. "At least, I think I do."

Alyce and Josie were back for a second day of surveillance. This time, Alyce's SUV was parked on a hilly street above Cheryl's house, where they had a good view of her garage. It was nine o'clock in the morning. Tom was long gone, but Cheryl hadn't come out yet. Her garage door was shut tight. The paper was still on the lawn.

The whole subdivision had an abandoned look. Except for a plumber's truck, nothing was moving.

"Missouri has stricter gambling laws than Illinois," Alyce said. "You can only lose five hundred dollars every two hours in this state. Most Missouri casinos have two-hour gambling sessions. If gamblers lose five hundred bucks in one throw of the dice, they have to sit out till the next session."

"So you think Cheryl was in Illinois to do some serious gambling," Josie said. "Makes sense. She dropped half a grand in an hour yesterday. If she'd been in Missouri, she would have had to wait sixty minutes before she could lose the other two hundred. What a weird law. Does that wait make any difference?"

"It makes gamblers crazy," Alyce said. "It makes them cross the river and throw away their money in Illinois."

"Well, by gambler's logic, the wait would cost Cheryl money," Josie said. "She would have missed her winning streak. Of course, she lost her winnings, along with another two hundred bucks."

"But that's not how gamblers think," Alyce said. "Are you warm, or is it just me?" She unbuttoned her coat and lowered her window.

"No, it's definitely hot in here," Josie said. "St. Louis weather is perverse. Yesterday it was thirty. Today it's going up to sixty. The sun is already beating down on the windshield. Plus, you're wearing that long black wig. Wigs are always hot. This blond one I have on today itches like crazy."

"This wig is part of an old Halloween witch costume. I didn't want Cheryl to recognize me. How do I look?" Alyce said.

"Uh, different," Josie said.

The black wig made Alyce look older and, well, witchy. Josie would forget about the wig for a few minutes. Then she'd be startled by the spooky black-haired woman beside her. Alyce looked like she told fortunes for a living.

"Different how?" Alyce said.

"You look less Episcopalian," Josie said, scratching delicately under her wig with a pen. "More mysterious."

Alyce laughed. "It's too dark for me, isn't it?"

"You look a little washed out," Josie said. "But Cheryl will never believe you're the blonde from the casino yesterday. Your SUV is a good cover, too. There are at least three like it on this street. But I'm still not sure why Cheryl gambled in Illinois."

"Because of the Missouri loss-limit law," Alyce said. "It's supposed to control problem gambling. It keeps gamblers' losses down to six thousand dollars a day—or forty-two thousand a week—or one hundred sixty-eight thousand dollars a month."

"Some control," Josie said. "I'd be bankrupt in less than a week."

"A lot of high rollers think the loss-limit law cramps their style. Illinois doesn't have as many hassles. The Missouri casinos are screaming bloody murder. They claim they'd make another three hundred million a year if the state got rid of the loss-limit law, and that would generate another sixty-something million in tax money."

"Our esteemed lawmakers will cave in for that kind of money," Josie said.

"Idiots," Alyce said. "They never count the other costs. We'll spend all that money and more catching the crooks created by gambling."

"You won't believe the crime casinos cause," Josie said. "I found a zillion stories about people who embezzled money so they could gamble. Accountants, brokers, church people, lawyers—"

"One of those lawyers was a partner at Jake's firm," Alyce said.

"You're kidding," Josie said.

"I used to talk to him at the Christmas party," Alyce said. "Nice guy. Always showed me pictures of his kids. He took eight hundred thousand dollars from an old woman's trust account—after he used up his home equity, cleaned out his children's college fund, and ran up forty thousand dollars in credit-card debt. He went to prison."

"That's horrible. What happened to his family?" Josie said.

"They lost their house and filed for bankruptcy. His wife, Michelle, is barely hanging on. She's selling real estate."

"The last refuge of an abandoned West County wife," Josie said.

"She's not in West County anymore," Alyce said. "She's living in some awful box by the airport with the kids." The black wig sat on her head like a dark spell. Josie could feel her friend's mood darkening, too. "Michelle used to have a life like mine—charity work, a nice house, a nanny."

"Didn't she know her husband was gambling at the casinos?" Josie said.

"He said he had to work late," Alyce said. "All our husbands work late. He had the credit-card bills sent to his office. Michelle had no clue he was a compulsive gambler until it was too late. She divorced him once she found out, but her credit was ruined."

"Not to mention her life," Josie said.

"You think St. Louis is this big family city," Alyce said. Her pale face was blotchy red with anger. The black wig looked frizzy in the heat. "Actually, we're the eighth-largest gambling market in the country. Gambling is everywhere. But we go around pretending it doesn't—"

They heard the rumble of a garage door. "It's Cheryl," Josie said. She checked her watch. "She's leaving earlier today. It's nine ten."

Mrs. Mueller's daughter was beautifully dressed in a black pantsuit with a nipped-in waist. She had a red scarf draped on one shoulder, a tiny red purse and high heels.

Cheryl buckled Ben into his seat.

"Ten to one she's heading for the sitter," Alyce said.

"No takers," Josie said. "Why doesn't Cheryl have a nanny?"

"She's posing as a dutiful full-time wife and mother," Alyce said. "That's why she has to sneak the kid to the babysitter. I wonder how she hides Bonnie in her household budget?"

Cheryl's SUV made for the sitter's house like it was a magnet, then drove straight to Highway 40. Alyce stayed three cars behind, tracking Cheryl easily through the light traffic. "She's going back to the Royal Duchess," Josie said.

But she didn't. Cheryl took the long, sweeping exit for Interstate 270, then Interstate 70.

"She's heading for the airport," Josie said. But Cheryl took the exit in the opposite direction.

"She's going to Earth City?" Alyce said, disbelief in her voice. "Nobody goes there."

That wasn't exactly true. Nobody from Alyce's crowd—or Cheryl's—went there. Josie often drove that way when she mystery-shopped discount stores and franchises. Now she saw the highway was lined with billboards advertising "the loosest slots" and the big casino shows.

Alyce was right. Josie had seen those signs every week, but she'd never noticed them before. One advertised a casino gospel brunch. FILL YOUR STOMACH, SATISFY YOUR SOUL! it said.

"Gambling may be everywhere, but it really isn't part of St. Louis," Josie said. "It's for the tourists, like the Arch. When's the last time you were at the Arch?"

"When Jake's aunt was in town," Alyce said.

"Your average St. Louisan doesn't go to the casinos, either," Josie said. "They're for people from small towns like Kirksville and Macon, who come to the city for a wild weekend. Most St. Louisans never think about the casinos. If we go once a year, it's a big deal."

"Tell that to Michelle," Alyce said.

The shiny casino complexes rose out of the drab, flat land along the Missouri River, like a neon Oz. Cheryl's SUV turned in their direction.

"Cheryl's going to the boats in the moat," Josie said.

"Another weird phenomenon created by the Missouri laws," Alyce said.

"You know a lot about gambling laws," Josie said.

"I should," Alyce said. "I've listened to my husband Jake complain about them often enough."

Josie didn't think that was the entire reason. Alyce had a "there but for the grace of God" interest in Michelle's miserable story. If Jake switched his late-night stays from work to gambling, Alyce would be selling real estate, too.

"Here's the way Jake explained it to me," Alyce said. "In 1992, the state legalized riverboat gambling on the Missouri and Mississippi rivers. It sounded harmless, old-fashioned, even romantic."

"Gambling on paddle-wheel steamers," Josie said. "Men in brocade vests and string ties, women in hoopskirts and parasols."

"Don't forget the other attraction," Alyce said. "Gambling would be on the river, where nobody would have to look at it. St. Louisans don't like to face our problems. But the casinos started pushing for changes.

"First, the state did away with the cruising requirements. The casinos could be on big anchored barges. No cruising on the river. High rollers liked that. They weren't stuck on a cruise with nothing to do but eat the salmonella special on the buffet.

"Next, the casinos invented boats floating in moats.

They were linked to the river by man-made channels, which technically made them riverboats. The boats in the moats kept a lot of lawyers busy suing each other. In the late 1990s, Missouri voters changed the law so casinos could be in inland basins, a thousand feet from the river's main channel.

"The boats in the moats were legal. Casinos with high-rise hotels were now possible. The plans for the newer casinos have fixed walls and floating gaming floors."

"Waterbed gambling," Josie said.

"They look like regular casinos," Alyce said. "You can't tell the casino floors are actually on water, except they might drop an inch or so when there's a crowd."

They passed Harrah's St. Louis complex. It looked like bits of Vegas abandoned in Missouri. Cheryl turned into the drive for another casino, the Prince's Palace, a massive boat in a moat with a high-rise hotel. The entrance was landscaped with clipped shrubs. The signs were beige marble, like tasteful tombstones.

YOU'RE THE KING AT OUR PALACE, said one.

WELCOME HOME, YOUR MAJESTY, said another.

At nine forty-five in the morning, the parking lot was packed. Once again, Cheryl dropped her ride with a valet. Josie and Alyce hoofed it from a distant lot.

"I'm not going to need a health club while this surveillance lasts," Alyce said, blotting her forehead. Sweat dripped from under her fake dark hair.

Josie gave her wig one last vigorous scratch with a pen. She wouldn't be able to touch it inside the casino. "Is my hair on straight?" she asked.

Alyce nodded yes.

The Prince's Palace looked vaguely Venetian. The inside was more like an expensive resort than a casino—cream paint and beige marble with a touch of gold.

"This looks like Cheryl," Josie said.

They saw her in the special speeded-up high rollers' line. Then Cheryl was swallowed by the elegant vastness. Josie and Alyce were stuck waiting with the commoners.

"We've lost her again," Alyce said.

"Don't worry," Josie said. "We know where to find her."

Josie and Alyce filled out the paperwork for their gaming cards with a young woman who looked like a bank loan officer. "The ten-to-noon session is just starting," she said, with a professional smile.

Cheryl had timed her arrival almost to the minute. By the time Josie and Alyce were finished with their paperwork, Cheryl was playing the ten-dollar slots.

"Look at her pushing money into that machine," Alyce said. "She keeps losing. Why won't she stop?"

"Losing is just as exciting as winning," Josie said.

Watching Cheryl lose had a sick fascination, like watching a car wreck. Josie and Alyce took seats at the nearby nickel slots and dropped some dollars in their machines. Today they weren't worried she would spot them. Cheryl's world had narrowed to her hungry slot.

"She's losing even faster today," Alyce whispered. "I'm guessing she'll hit the five-hundred-dollar limit any moment."

It was nearly twenty minutes before Cheryl gathered up her purse and left the casino.

"She's giving up for the day," Josie said.

By the time they'd hiked to Alyce's SUV and headed toward the entrance, Cheryl had retrieved her vehicle from the valet. She whipped out her cell phone and made a call, then took off for the highway. Josie and Alyce followed at a sedate pace.

"She's going to the airport," Josie said.

"Maybe Tom was on a business trip and she's picking him up," Alyce said.

But Cheryl's SUV turned off before the airport and bumped down a road that had been a major highway years ago before the interstate. Now it was potholed and pitted with struggling businesses.

Her SUV turned into an old motel, a one-story building with peeling white paint. The red trim looked like a disease. A battered neon sign said, FREE LOCAL CALLS! FREE VCR! POOL!

"Whoa," Alyce said. "What's a nice girl like Cheryl doing in a place like this?"

"Three guesses," Josie said.

Alyce parked at the mini-mart next door in a shady spot. They had a good view of the motel lot and a light breeze off the Dumpster.

Cheryl stayed in her SUV. Five minutes later, a blue minivan crunched into the motel lot. A balding man about fifty climbed out. He was sweating heavily and wiping his round face with a white handkerchief. The man had a sober gray suit and a briefcase.

"I think he's taking a meeting," Josie said.

The man went into the motel office, then came out with a key. He opened the mottled pink door to room 117 at the far end. Cheryl joined him, red high heels pattering on the broken sidewalk.

"He isn't exactly the last of the red-hot lovers," Alyce said.

Josie wrote down the balding man's license-plate number. Alyce sat in the mini-mart parking lot, silent with shock.

"I never liked her," Josie said. "But I didn't think she'd stoop to this."

"How can she even go into that room?" Alyce said. "Did you see that TV show where they tested the motel bedspreads? You could see all the semen on the beds."

"I bet the spreads in this motel look like a sperm bank," Josie said.

"Eeuuw," Alyce said.

That killed the conversation for a while. Finally, Josie climbed out of the SUV and went into the mini-mart. She came back with cold water, Mountain Dew, cheese-and-peanut-butter crackers and Hostess cupcakes.

"We might as well sin, too," Josie said.

They munched, watched and waited. Two hours later, the minivan man came out of room 117. Cheryl waited until he pulled out of the lot. Then she was back on the highway. Cheryl turned off at the Prince's Palace entrance.

"Omigod, she's heading for the casino again," Josie said.

"Tell me she's not doing what I think she's doing," Alyce said.

"Turning tricks for cash?" Josie said. "What do you think she was doing with that guy in a hot-sheet motel—looking at his baseball cards?"

"I thought she was having an affair," Alyce said. "I didn't think she was a prostitute."

"Now we know where Cheryl got the forty-eight thousand dollars," Josie said. "I can't tell her mother this."

"I thought you'd enjoy it," Alyce said.

"I thought I would, too," Josie said. "But I don't. I feel awful."

"What are you going to do?"

"Talk to Cheryl," Josie said.

"You wouldn't," Alyce said.

"Watch me," Josie said.

Chapter 15

"You guard the door while I fix myself up," Josie said. "I have to take off this disguise."

"First it's nasty motels, now it's bathroom doors," Alyce said. "Do you do anything that doesn't involve life-threatening bacteria?"

"Oh, come on, Alyce. This bathroom looks like a country club," Josie said.

The casino rest room's creamy paint and marble had the feel of a high-priced spa. A wicker basket held rolled terry towels. The toilets were hidden behind louvered doors, as if they were gateways to palm-fringed patios.

"I don't hug the doors there, either," Alyce said. But she dutifully pressed her body against the door so it couldn't be opened from the other side.

Josie pulled off her blond wig and stuffed it in her purse. She winced at herself in the mirror. Her brown hair was mashed flat, except for a two-inch chunk that stuck out over her ear. Josie worked with a brush and hair spray until it was only a one-inch chunk. Her hair looked unwashed and oily.

"That's it. That's all I can do," Josie said.

"You've got a terminal case of hat hair," Alyce said.

"You should talk, Morticia," Josie said.

Alyce was sweating profusely in her witchy wig. "At least no one will recognize me," she said. "Okay, what's the plan?"

"You hide out in the slots and watch. I'm going to confront Cheryl."

"Then what?" Alyce said.

"If you see security take me away, call your husband, the lawyer," Josie said.

"But—"

"Hey, why can't I open this door?" an angry voice said. "What's going on in there?"

"Sorry, must be stuck," Josie called. She pulled Alyce off the door and yanked on the handle. A stick-thin woman fell into the bathroom. She gave Josie a black look.

Alyce glided off to the nickel slots. Her witch wig did not float like her own blond hair. Josie found Cheryl sitting at her same machine, the one that had swallowed five hundred dollars the last gambling session. She was still losing.

The two hours in the no-tell motel had left no mark on Cheryl. Airbrush out the slot machine and Cheryl could have been in a tea shop. Her trim suit was unwrinkled. Her legs were crossed at the ankle. One manicured finger reached for the slot machine button. Josie blocked its path.

"Why, Cheryl, what a surprise!" Josie used her phoniest suburban-lady voice.

Cheryl stared at Josie as if she was a glob of cellulite. "Nice hair," she said sarcastically. Her eyes were harder than the casino's beige marble.

Josie's heart was pounding with fear. She had to break through Cheryl's hard surface to make her talk, but she didn't know how the woman would react if she pushed. Would Cheryl storm out or scratch out Josie's eyes?

Nope, my eyes are safe, Josie decided. Cheryl would never do anything that would mess up her clothes.

"I never expected to see you here today," Josie said. "But then I never expected to see you at that sleazy motel with that man. You know, Tom's a lot younger and cuter."

"You are making no sense, as usual," Cheryl said. She was beyond marble now. Titanium, maybe.

"Room 117," Josie said. "Blue minivan. License-plate number—"

"Get out of here," Cheryl hissed. "Or I'll call security."

"I don't think so," Josie said. "Tell me why you were in that motel room or I'll tell your mother."

It was the ultimate threat and Cheryl knew it. She collapsed into noisy tears. It was the last reaction Josie had expected—or wanted. Tears could bring the casino security. Maybe that was what clever Cheryl had in mind.

Josie thought the tears were fake, but she dove into her purse for a wad of Kleenex. "There, there," she said, raising her voice slightly. "I hate to bring you bad news about Mother, but I was sure you'd want to know. Let's talk."

She steered Cheryl to the closest coffee shop, one hand clamped on her arm like an arresting officer. Cheryl didn't resist. Hooray for Mrs. Mueller, Josie thought. I should have thought of this sooner. Cheryl is afraid of her mother. But so am I.

Josie saw Alyce's head pop up like a gopher in a hole. Josie shifted her head slightly toward the coffee shop. She chose a table in a deserted corner, then ordered two coffees from the waitress. Cheryl was still sniffling, but the waitress paid no attention. She was probably sick of sob stories.

When the waitress left, Josie said, "Look, Cheryl, I need to know what you were up to at that motel. Your mother is worried sick."

"Are you going to tell her?"

Josie couldn't figure out if Cheryl was angry or frightened. Her perfect face had an odd lack of emotion. She was carefully blotting her eyes. She'd managed to cry without making her eyeliner run.

"It depends on what you tell me," Josie said.

"It's not what you think," Cheryl said. "I didn't have sex with him."

"So you read to the guy from the Gideon Bible and he paid you." It was Josie's turn to be sarcastic. She enjoyed it.

"Almost," Cheryl said. She stopped sniffling. The tears dried up like raindrops after a summer storm. "We watch videos together and he pays me. His wife doesn't like to do that."

"That's all?" Josie asked. "His wife hates movies?"

"Videos," Cheryl corrected. "I think she goes to movies. I swear on my son Ben's life that all I did in that motel room was watch a video."

"Let me get this straight," Josie said. "This guy pays you to watch dirty movies with him, but you don't do anything else?"

"Oh, no. *Pretty Woman* isn't dirty," Cheryl said.

"That's what you watched?"

Cheryl lowered her eyes. She tried to look modest, but her face was too hard. "He's fixated on the movie. He's got a thing about Julia Roberts. His wife is so sick of it, she won't let the video in the house. He pays me to watch it with him. We sat together on the bed."

"Fully clothed?" Josie said.

"Of course," Cheryl said. "I took off my shoes, but that's all."

"I wouldn't worry about keeping that bedspread clean," Josie said. "There's a lot worse on it than mud."

Cheryl shrugged. "Look, it's a little strange, but it's harmless. He gives me two hundred dollars to watch a PG-13 movie with him."

Why can't I find jobs like that? Josie wondered. Of course, I'd have to sit on that motel bedspread.

"You're spying on me for my mother," Cheryl said, and her eyes grew mean. This was the Cheryl that Josie knew and didn't love. "You tell her anything about that motel and I'll sue your ass so bad, I won't ever have to worry about money again."

"Lawsuit threats won't work on me, Cheryl. I don't have any money," Josie said. "You've got a lot more to lose than I do. Even if I believe you were only watching Julia Roberts in that scummy room, nobody else will, including your husband."

Cheryl flushed and said nothing.

"Cheryl, listen. The police aren't stupid. If I can find this out, they probably already know. It's going to come out soon and it will be really embarrassing. Why don't you let me help you?"

"You?" Cheryl said. Her scorn could have melted

steel. "How can a loser like you help me? You didn't take any pictures of me at that motel, did you?"

"Uh," Josie said.

"I thought so," Cheryl said. "Some detective. You can't prove a thing, Sherlock. Go ahead and tell my mother. She won't believe you. No one will. If I catch you following me again, I'll have you arrested for stalking." She tossed her perfect hair and walked back toward the slots.

She's right, Josie thought, as she paid the coffee tab. Mrs. Mueller wouldn't believe where Cheryl spent her day, even if I showed her photos. I need something more to convince her.

Cheryl was back pumping dollars into her favorite slot. The machine clanged and lights flashed overhead. Bells rang. Cheryl had won big, but the game was over for Josie.

She found Alyce lurking in the nickel slots. "Are we leaving now?" Alyce said. "I can't wait to take off this wig. What happened with Cheryl?"

Josie told her as they walked down the wide beige casino carpet and into the oddly warm November sun.

"Do you think she's telling the truth?" Alyce said.

"The truth, but not the whole truth," Josie said. "She's lying about something. We're not getting the full story about what happened at that motel. Mr. Minivan paid her to do something, but I'm not sure what."

"There's no way to check," Alyce said.

"But there is," Josie said. "Cheryl will be at the casino for at least another hour. Let's go back to the motel."

"Yuck," Alyce said. "Another chance to catch a disease."

"I promise you won't have to touch the bedspread," Josie said.

"What if someone I know sees me at that scummy motel?"

"Then they're doing something they shouldn't and they won't be able to say anything," Josie said.

Alyce parked in the mini-mart lot again. She and Josie walked to the sad motel. It looked worse in the harsh afternoon light. The walls were cracked and the window-sills were spongy with rot.

A cart was parked in front of room 117. A thin African American woman was carrying a stack of even thinner towels into the room. The whites of her eyes were deep yellow and her dark skin was grainy.

"Excuse me, ma'am," Josie said. "May I ask you a couple of questions?"

"I ain't testifying in no divorce, no matter how much you give me," the maid said.

"I just want information," Josie said.

"That's what they all say."

"In this case, it's true." Josie handed the woman a twenty and followed her into the room.

The sagging bed was covered with an avocado green spread. The carpet was dirty yellow shag. A picture of a sad-eyed clown was bolted to the wall. Alyce stayed close to the door, ready to run if the dangerously ugly furniture grabbed her.

"I'm sorry, I didn't catch your name," Josie said.

"It ain't no cold," the maid said. "I ain't passing it around. State your business and go."

"This room—117— Did you change the sheets after that couple left?"

The maid shook her head. "Nope. No need. Never used them. Never messed around on the bedspread, either."

"What did they do?" Josie asked.

"I don't know and I don't want to know. They watched that TV. It was warm on top."

She pointed to an ancient Zenith bolted to a stand, then carried her towels into a tiny white-tiled bath. "They used two of these here hand towels for their hands only. Weren't no nastiness on them. There was nothing in the wastebaskets. Used almost a whole box of Kleenex, but they either took those with them or flushed 'em. Didn't unwrap the soap, but that's no surprise. People in a place like this don't use the soap. Don't wanna smell like they've been showering someplace besides home."

"That's all that went on in this room?" Alyce opened her purse and brought out another twenty.

The woman took it and said, "I don't know what happened in here. All I can tell you is it didn't look like much to me. Far as I can tell, the only thing that got hot in this room was the TV."

"Thank you," Josie said.

A red SUV pulled into the lot. Alyce ducked behind the door like a guilty wife until the driver opened room 121.

"Let's get out of here," Alyce said. She almost ran to her SUV. "I guess our Cheryl surveillance is over. We've blown our cover."

"I've blown mine," Josie said. "She doesn't know about you. We still have work to do. Let's wait a few days until Cheryl thinks I've forgotten about her. Then I'll get a new disguise and go back to watching her."

"Are you going mystery shopping in the meantime?" Alyce asked.

"Yes, but I'm also going to keep at this, if I get the okay from Mrs. Mueller. I have an idea how to get more information. The late Mel had a housekeeper. I want to talk to her. I need an introduction to the woman."

"Sorry, I don't know anyone in Olympia Park," Alyce said. "Too rich for my blood."

"The housekeeper lives in Maplewood," Josie said. "That's what it said in the paper. Mrs. Mueller or my mother probably know her. I'll talk to them."

"Are we going home now?" Alyce sounded plaintive.

"It's two thirty," Josie said. "Let's wait in the casino lot and make sure Cheryl comes out at three."

Josie put on her blond wig while Alyce drove back to the Prince's Palace. It was two forty-five when they entered the stately drive. Alyce cruised the parking lot twice, then pulled into a spot where they could see the valet parking. At 3:08, Cheryl came out. She did not look happy. Josie wondered if she'd lost all her video-watching money.

Alyce followed Cheryl's SUV to a supermarket. Cheryl came out, piled an armful of grocery bags in the backseat, then drove to the sitter's house. Finally, Cheryl turned into her subdivision. She was going home with her baby son. It was four thirty in the afternoon.

"The perfect wife and mother heads home after a day at the casino and the hot-sheet motel," Josie said.

Chapter 16

"Dinner's ready, dear," Josie's mother said.

Josie never thought she'd hear those words when she unlocked her front door. Not from her mother, two nights in a row. Jane was a good cook, but she didn't bother logging much time at the stove anymore, especially not for her wayward daughter.

Jane came out of Josie's kitchen wearing a dress and an apron with white ruffles, a combination Josie hadn't seen since her father lived with them. Josie caught the perfume of expensive broiling meat. This meal was far more elaborate than last night's stew.

"Medium-rare filets," Jane said. "And twice-baked potatoes."

"Eeuuw. I don't like blood," Amelia said.

"I know, sweetie," Jane said. "That's why Grandma made you hamburgers. We also have green beans amandine. For dessert, I have a homemade chocolate cake."

I have the Stepford Mom, Josie thought. God help me, I like it.

"Thank you, Mom. This is a nice surprise." Josie kissed her mother on her soft cheek.

"You're doing important work," Jane said. "You need to eat right."

Josie looked into her mother's eyes and saw her hunger. Jane had craved those two committees all her life. Now they were within reach, thanks to Josie. I've got to succeed for Mom's sake, Josie thought. I've failed at so much.

"Now sit down and I'll bring in your dinner," Jane said.

Josie sat. Jane bustled off to the kitchen.

"Is Grandma feeling okay?" Amelia whispered.

"If this is an illness, I don't want a cure," Josie said.

"She's acting weird," Amelia said.

"Being nice to me is not weird," Josie said.

"Yes, it is. Grandma always says you should grow up, get a job at the bank and quit wasting your time mystery shopping," Amelia said. "Now all of a sudden, you're perfect."

"I've always been perfect. She just realized it," Josie said.

"Huh," Amelia said.

Jane came back carrying two plates. Josie's had a medium-rare filet, a twice-baked potato with a luscious cheese topping, and crisp green beans sprinkled with thin-sliced almonds.

"Omigod," Josie said.

"Please, Josie, don't blaspheme at the dinner table," her mother said.

"It was a prayer of thanksgiving," Josie said.

Amelia rolled her eyes, but seemed to relax. This was the grandmother she knew.

Josie shrugged off her mother's sharp words, as she always did. She savored every bite of her dinner. "This filet is exactly the way I like it."

"I think it's important to have things right," her mother said. "For instance, with the Flower Guild, I'm thinking we should change our rules on perennials—"

Josie let her mother talk about the improvements she would make as the Maplewood chair. She enjoyed watching her mother talk, hands sketching grand plans in the air, eyes bright and optimistic. Jane had gone through a rough time not too long ago, locking herself away and ordering hundreds of useless items—from ankle bracelets to frilly dolls—from the Home Shopping Network. This Jane was a different woman: lively, interested in the future, connected to her community.

"And I told the committee, I thought a berm in the garden we maintain on the west corner by St. Philomena's Church would be an interesting addition. Don't you think so, Josie?"

"Right, Mom. I've always thought we needed more berms." What's a berm? she wondered.

Jane put a cup of hot coffee and a chunk of chocolate cake the size of a paving stone in front of Josie.

"What's a berm, Mom?" Amelia asked.

Caught, Josie thought. She was relieved when the phone rang.

"I'll get it," Amelia said, assuming all calls must be for her.

"I'll get it," Jane said, still in Stepford Mom mode. She picked up the phone first.

"Why, Mrs. Mueller, how are you?" Jane said. "What a nice surprise. You want to speak to Josie? She's right here, finishing her dinner. Don't keep her too long or her coffee will get cold."

She handed Josie the phone like a respectful secretary. Mrs. Mueller barked like a demanding boss. "Did you find out anything today?"

"I learned something interesting, but I'm not ready for any firm conclusions yet," Josie said.

"Well, I'm tired of being stalled. What was Cheryl doing all day? I tried to call, but her cell phone was off."

"I can tell you some of it, but you can't mention anything to her yet, or it will ruin the investigation. Do you promise?"

"What is it? What do you know?" Mrs. Mueller said.

"Do you promise?" Josie insisted.

"Yes, yes," Mrs. M said impatiently. "What is it?"

Josie took a deep breath. She remembered Cheryl's warning: "Go ahead and tell my mother. She won't believe you. No one will." Josie could hardly believe it herself. Yet the signs were there, if she wanted to see them: the secret babysitter, the husband who was hardly home, the forty-eight thousand bucks in the shoe boxes.

Here goes, Josie thought. "Cheryl is gambling at the casinos."

Josie heard two gasps, one from Mrs. Mueller and then another. Jane must be listening on the bedroom extension.

"Ridiculous!" Mrs. Mueller said. "Cheryl doesn't gamble."

"I personally saw her lose twelve hundred dollars in two days," Josie said.

No gasp from her mother this time. Either Jane contained her surprise or she was too stunned to react. "You're wrong. It must be someone else. Someone who looks like her." Mrs. Mueller's voice did not sound quite so strong.

"There's no mistake. I followed Cheryl from her home to two different casinos," Josie said. "She used cash to gamble. She plays the slot machines."

"The slots! Those are for old ladies," Mrs. Mueller said.

"They're one of the most profitable forms of gambling. Women like them," Josie said. "Cheryl lost seven hundred dollars on the Royal Duchess."

"My daughter went to East St. Louis!" Mrs. Mueller found that even more shocking than Cheryl's gambling.

"She also went to the Prince's Palace in Maryland Heights. She lost at least five hundred dollars there."

"She'll ruin her family," Mrs. Mueller moaned. "I saw that news story about the housewife who gambled away her house and then killed herself. Tom makes a decent salary, but he can't afford twelve hundred dollars in two days. She'll bankrupt them. Where is she getting that kind of money?"

"I have an idea, but I need a little more time," Josie said. "In the meantime, I'd like your nephew George to check out a license plate for me."

"Anything," Mrs. Mueller said.

Josie gave her the minivan's plate number.

"Does this belong to a man?" Mrs. Mueller said.

"Yes," Josie said. "But there could be a perfectly innocent explanation."

"I hope you're going to keep following Cheryl until you find out what's happening," Mrs. Mueller said. Her tone said, You will if you know what's good for you.

"I wanted to talk to you about that," Josie said. "Cheryl may suspect someone is following her. It's best if I back off on her surveillance for a day or so. If your budget allows it, I want to spend a day investigating from a different angle. Mel had a housekeeper named Zinnia Ellis. She's a Maplewood woman. Do you know her?"

"Zinnia. The name is familiar. Wait. Yes, I know her. She works the church bake sales. Goes to nine o'clock Mass. A very devout woman."

"Good," Josie said. "I want to talk to her. She may know something about Mel and Cheryl."

"I will give you the extra day, if you're really planning on doing something. Or are you just taking my money?"

"So far, I haven't seen any money from you," Josie said. "That includes the fifty-five dollars I advanced for the baby car seat and the sitter. Don't threaten me, Mrs. Mueller, then ask for my help. I'll tell you when I have something."

Josie slammed down the phone. I'm enjoying this way too much, she thought.

"Josie!" her mother said, wringing her hands again. "Is everything okay?"

"It's better than okay, Mom," Josie said.

Jane's shoulders were hunched. She seemed to shrink inside herself. She's so afraid, Josie thought. Is she frightened of that old biddy next door or afraid I'll screw up?

"GBH, Mom," Josie said, giving her mother a hug. Jane seemed so frail, more fragile than Amelia. She was old, tired and disappointed. "It will work out, Mom. I promise."

Amelia stared at the two grown-ups. Both were acting crazy. "I'm going to my room," she said.

The phone rang half an hour later. "That will be Mrs. Mueller with an apology," Josie said smugly.

But it wasn't. Her mother's boyfriend, Jimmy Ryent, was calling.

"Jimmy," Jane said. Josie noticed the color rising in her mother's cheeks and the way she curled her gray hair around her finger. "What am I doing next Saturday night? I'm not sure, Jimmy. Let me check my calendar."

Josie's mom sat there, staring into space. She was making him wait, according to the ancient rules of dating she grew up with. She finally spoke into the phone again. "I just happen to have the evening free. Dinner and a movie? What time?"

A date. Josie's mother was making a date. Mom didn't have to worry about what to do with Amelia. Jimmy could spend the night if he wanted. I'm jealous of a sixty-eight-year-old woman, Josie thought. I should be. She has more of a love life than I do. This is a new low.

A contrite Mrs. Mueller called back at eight o'clock. "Your appointment with Zinnia is set for tomorrow at ten. But you'll have to go to that Mel person's house. The police have released it as a crime scene, and the heirs want Zinnia to supervise the cleanup. You couldn't pay me to walk through that door."

But she would pay Josie.

"Zinnia's left your name with the guard at the Olympia Park gate," Mrs. Mueller said. "Josie, thank you for doing this."

Progress at last. Mrs. Mueller was actually being polite.

Alyce couldn't go with Josie to Olympia Park the next day. She had to take her baby to the pediatrician. Josie missed her friend. As she pulled up to the guard's box, she wondered what Alyce would make of this place. The entry gates were phallic white limestone towers, like something designed by Ludwig of Bavaria. Even before Freud, didn't people know what a penis looked like?

The guards found Josie's name on the list and directed her past a lake with white swans. Peacocks fanned their gaudy tails and screeched in Olympia Park.

Mel's gray-white stone house was even more impressive than the photos in the paper. The arched entrance belonged to a mausoleum. Topiary in pots lined the drive and the doorway.

This was a shoe salesman's house?

Josie parked in the circular drive. The housekeeper met Josie at the door. Josie wasn't sure what a Zinnia would look like, but the name seemed to fit her. She was a sturdy woman of about sixty, with an open, pink face. Zinnia seemed as old-fashioned as her namesake. She had her hair in a neat bun. She wore sensible shoes with thick, square heels. Mel would never get caught in the back room with Zinnia's footwear. Josie liked the woman's hands. They were neat and capable.

Josie stepped inside Mel's mansion and stared. It was the biggest house she'd ever been in, bigger than the Maplewood Library or St. Philomena's Church.

Zinnia seemed used to this reaction. She launched into a tour-guide spiel. "The house was built more than a hundred years ago," she said. "The staircase is heart of oak, built by German artisans brought over for the 1904 World's Fair. The stained-glass window on the landing is ten feet high. It is the work of Louis Comfort Tiffany."

Normally, Josie would have admired the golden-haired maidens dancing in a field of lilies. Now all she saw was their intricately entwined bare feet. The window was a fetishist's delight. The oak staircase led down to a marble floor. If Mel had landed on that, his head would have cracked like an egg.

Zinnia must have followed Josie's eyes to that cold, hard floor. "I found Mr. Mel at the foot of that staircase, poor man. Blood was everywhere. The police took the carpet."

Zinnia pointed high up on the wall near the first landing, where there were faint brownish smears and splotches on the pale wallpaper. "The blood was all the way up there. I've scrubbed and scrubbed, but I can't get it all off. It will have to be repapered. That's what made the police suspicious, you know. The way the blood was so high on that wall. It meant Mr. Mel was standing when he was hit on the head. He wasn't killed by a fall."

"That's dreadful," Josie said. "Do they know what killed him?"

"They won't say. But there's a Tiffany paperweight missing from the hall table. I knew Mr. Mel was dead the moment I saw him. I called for an ambulance just the same. His diamond watch was broken in the fall. It stopped at eight thirty-two.

"I found him at nine forty-five that same night. It was a terrible shock, but I'm glad Mr. Mel wasn't alone all night long."

Zinnia slid open the giant pocket doors and led Josie into a double parlor. The room had enough gold brocade furniture for four or five living rooms, marble busts on columns, and a walk-in fireplace. Over the fireplace was an oil portrait of a blonde with her hair in a thirties style. She wore a slinky satin evening dress and strappy heels. Her even-featured blank young face could easily pass for pretty.

"Mr. Mel's mother," Zinnia said. She smiled for the first time, and Josie saw large yellow teeth.

Josie wondered if that picture gave Mel his lifelong preoccupation with shoes. "Very nice," she said. "You know Mrs. Mueller from church, right?"

"A fine woman," Zinnia said. She stood in the center of the room. She did not offer Josie a seat, nor did she take one. It was not her place.

"Do you know her daughter, Cheryl? The police say your employer had wine with Mrs. Mueller's daughter in this room. They found the glasses in the sink."

"That's what I heard, but I'd gone home for the evening," Zinnia said. "I only came back because I forgot my purse. I'm getting so forgetful. I tried to call Mr. Mel, but he didn't answer his phone. Now I know why, poor man. I couldn't wait until morning. I had to know if my purse was there. I had a hundred dollars in cash in it. I let myself in, and saw my purse right where I'd left it in the hall. Then I saw Mr. Mel. There was no sign of Miss Cheryl."

"Had you seen Cheryl here before:"

"Yes. Several of Mr. Mel's best customers visited him," Zinnia said. "Nice young women, all of them. Well behaved. I wouldn't have worked here if anything funny was going on."

"You don't think he was having an affair with Cheryl?"

"Certainly not." Zinnia's round pink face flushed a deeper shade. "Miss Cheryl sat right here in this parlor, every time I saw her, and behaved like a proper young lady. I didn't listen in on their conversation, but they seemed to be talking business."

"Shoe business?" Josie said.

"Some kind of business. Something about building a bigger customer base and finding the right people. Mr. Mel asked her if she wanted to make another one, and she said she'd have to get a larger percentage of the profits this time."

For someone who didn't listen in, Zinnia heard a lot.

"Any idea what they were talking about?"

"I have no idea. I was busy with my duties. But it would take a dirty mind to make something evil out of that conversation."

"Were Mel and Cheryl arguing or angry?"

"No. There was nothing wrong with that discussion in any way."

"The police think that Mel paid Cheryl for sex."

Zinnia's face flushed with indignation. "I don't believe that, not for a minute. I never saw any of that kind of behavior, and I told them so. I changed Mr. Mel's sheets. I wouldn't stand for any monkey business in this house. Mr. Mel was a good employer, even if I didn't agree with his hobby."

"You mean his fascination with feet?" Josie said.

"Feet, legs, stockings, shoes. He has a whole walk-in closet full of women's shoes. He said it was because of his work. The police took most of them.

"Mr. Mel used to have parties for his friends. I had nothing to do with them. I'd come in the next morning and there would be women's shoes all over the place. Mr. Mel had to clean those up himself. I wouldn't touch them. Sticky, some of them were."

Josie's stomach twisted.

Zinnia kept talking. "Do you know some of those old fools tried to drink champagne out of an open-toed shoe? I said, 'Mr. Mel, there are some things I will not do. Cleaning champagne out of a stranger's shoe is one of them.' He told me there was nothing in the Bible that prevented a man from appreciating a woman's feet. But it still wasn't natural."

"Did the police take anything else besides his shoe collection?" Josie said.

"Oh, yes. His computer. And boxes of magazines, newsletters, photographs, videos and DVDs. I was glad they took those disgusting things out of the house."

Josie really wished Alyce was here. Maybe she could make sense of what Zinnia was saying. On one hand, the housekeeper insisted nothing "funny" was going on and everyone was perfectly behaved. On the other, Mel was giving wild champagne parties for his pals, and Zinnia refused to clean up after them. And Mel had "disgusting" videos.

Did Zinnia have an unspoken agreement with her boss: As long as she didn't see any indiscretions, they didn't exist?

"Those other young women you saw here, do you know their names?" Josie said.

"I certainly do," Zinnia said. "Respectable women, every one of them."

That word again. Zinnia was using it way too often. Was she trying to convince Josie or herself?

"One was an important executive, Paladia Henderson-Harrison. She wore the most beautiful suits. Tailored, they were. Must have cost a fortune. The other was a homemaker, a friend of Cheryl's. She had an old-fashioned English name, like in a mystery. Fiona. That was it. Fiona Christie. She had two children, a boy and a girl. I've seen their pictures."

"One more question," Josie said. "Where did a shoe salesman get the money for a house in Olympia Park?"

"Mr. Mel inherited the house from his mother. But he was a rich man in his own right. Mr. Mel wasn't always a shoe salesman," Zinnia said. "He was on Wall Street for years. That man was a financial wizard. Made a fortune, he did. Enough so he could quit and work his dream job."

"Which was?" Josie said.

"Why, selling shoes."

Chapter 17

"I'll show you Mr. Mel's fantasy room," Zinnia said. "It's where he had his parties."

She led Josie up the grand stairs, moving lightly as a young woman. Josie was puffing by the second landing.

"How high are we going?" Josie hoped she didn't sound like she was gasping for air. It was humiliating to be in worse shape than a woman thirty years older.

"Only to the fifth floor," Zinnia said.

It wasn't five flights of stairs. It was more like ten or fifteen. These stairs had more switchbacks than a mountain road. After the magnificent oak staircase ran out, they took the back stairs. These steps were painted a practical brown and studded with rubber treads.

"You'd think Mr. Mel would put in an elevator," Josie said.

"His mother wouldn't hear of it," Zinnia said. "She thought an elevator was pure laziness. She always said walking was good for your health." Zinnia steamed ahead, living proof of the power of walking. She had muscular calves and well-toned arms, probably from carrying vacuum cleaners up five flights.

"It's cheaper than a StairMaster." Josie wheezed like an asthmatic. She vowed to ride her bike every day. How did she get so out of shape?

"When did Mel's mother die?" Josie said. Probably when she reached the top floor, she thought.

"In 1999, at the age of eighty-two. But Mr. Mel would never disobey her wishes. He hardly changed a thing after she died."

Did he put in the fantasy room before or after Mom climbed the stairway to heaven? Josie was afraid to ask.

The higher they went, the narrower and more twisted the stairs became.

"We're here," Zinnia said, just a little too brightly. The older woman was enjoying Josie's uphill struggle. "It's down this hall."

The hall was painted white, carpeted in beige and lit with brass scones. It looked ordinary, even innocent.

Why was Zinnia showing me Mel's deepest secret? Josie wondered. Did the housekeeper owe Mrs. Mueller a favor? Had she, too, been promised the committee of her dreams? Or was it simply a relief to let another woman into her late employer's weird world? Zinnia must have spent her days at Mr. Mel's searching for dust specks, but overlooking huge problems.

And what was Mel's fantasy? Josie tried to imagine the room's decor. Did Mel go in for fur and smoked mirrors? Black leather and whips? Beds shaped like golden swans?

The double doors at the end of the hall gave no hint of what was behind them.

"This is it." Zinnia threw open the doors with a flourish. Josie expected almost anything except what she saw: a near-perfect copy of the Soft Shoe showroom.

"It's the shoe store," Josie said.

There were the same pink leather chairs for customers, the shoe mirrors, pink padded footstools and pale carpet. The shoe displays were swathed in the same pink tulle, but the little Lucite stands were empty.

"Mr. Mel kept his favorite shoes there," Zinnia said. "The police took them all."

Pink curtains led to what Josie guessed was a storage room. "Did he keep shoes in there?"

"Yes, but the police took them, too."

Josie peeked around the curtains. She saw a few empty shoe boxes and lots of empty shelves.

"He and his friends used to party up here, right?" Josie said. "This is where they drank the champagne?"

"Yes. It was where they were happiest. Sometimes

Mr. Mel brought in young women so the men could play shoe salesman, but I wasn't here for that."

Of course not, Josie thought. You kept your eyes firmly shut to Mr. Mel's games.

"May I ask you a favor?" Josie said. "Could I sit on one of those footstools?"

"Suit yourself," Zinnia said, and shrugged. She stood by the door, arms folded across her chest, back rigid. Mr. Mel's fantasy room made her uncomfortable.

Josie sat. The footstool seemed slightly lower than the one in the Soft Shoe store. Josie realized why: It was a better angle for looking up skirts. Ick. She shifted to a customer chair and put her foot on the stool's pink padded oblong. It felt slightly harder than the one at the store.

"He had these footstools specially made, didn't he?" Josie said.

"Oh, yes. Mr. Mel had particular ideas. Anything else you want to see?"

Josie wanted to see Mel's bedroom and the rest of the house, but she didn't have the nerve to ask. She'd already had more of a tour than she expected. If she pressed too hard, she wouldn't be able to come back when she had serious questions. Josie thought Zinnia might somehow be the key to unlocking Mel and Cheryl's secrets. But she'd have to ease out the information without Zinnia knowing it.

"Thank you, Zinnia," Josie said. "I appreciate your time. I have to go back to work."

"And where's that?" Zinnia said.

"A shoe store," Josie said.

Zinnia sighed softly. "Poor Mr. Mel will be with you in spirit," she said. "He so loved shoe stores. It was a cruel day when he was fired. It was a misunderstanding with some crazy women's libber. The things she said about Mr. Mel were dreadful. I told him it was a mistake and once Soft Shoe realized it, they would take him back in a heartbeat. He was their best salesman."

"I'm sure he loved his work," Josie said.

She set a new three-county downstairs slalom record,

hoping to reach the front door before Zinnia figured out that she was the one who got Mel fired from his beloved job.

Josie waved good-by at the door, and plopped down in her car with relief. She checked her watch. It was ten thirty. She had two Soft Shoe stores to shop that day. A week ago, they would have been plum assignments. Now Josie felt nervous and uneasy. She no longer looked at shoes the same way, thanks to Mel. He'd ruined the carefree innocence of shoe shopping for her. Worse, he'd waited on her, then died that night. Was there a connection? Josie felt like mystery shopping's black widow.

At the first Soft Shoe, a thin, stylish woman brought out the shoes for Josie to try. That was a relief. Male shoe salesmen made her feel skittish.

At the second store, Josie was waited on by an older, white-haired salesman. He was perfectly polite, but when he tried to put a black spike heel on her foot, she rudely grabbed it from his hands and slipped it on herself. She didn't want him touching her. The salesman's eyebrows shot up into his snowy hairline, but he said nothing.

The stores passed their shopping tests with high marks, but Josie was shaking when she left the last Soft Shoe store, at the Galleria. Maybe Mel really was with her in spirit. The stores felt haunted. Josie fled the mall as if his ghost was following her.

I'll do my paperwork later, Josie thought. I need coffee. Oh, heck. Who am I fooling? I need Josh. I hope he's at the coffeehouse on a Saturday afternoon.

He was. Josh looked as hot as ever. His goatee was styled into sharp, neat lines. His hair was newly cut. He was wearing new clothes. Also, cool shoes, although Josie was currently turned off by that topic.

"Just in time," Josh said. "In about fifteen minutes, two rabid cappuccinos will come through that door. Right now, the place is ours." He kissed her soundly.

"Mmmm. I like the service here," Josie said.

"How soon can I see you alone?" he said, kissing her neck and shoulder.

"Next Saturday," she said.

"That's a whole week away. There's no one in the back storage room," he said.

"Is that what you think I am? A backroom quickie?" She pushed him away. Anger flared up, although Josie wasn't sure if she was angry at Josh, Mrs. Mueller or Cheryl. All three were frustrating her.

"Josie, I'm sorry," he said. His kiss was different this time, sweeter, more respectful. "I shouldn't behave that way. You're just so hot. This hurts, you know?"

He looked deep into her eyes. "I'll behave. I promise. What can I get you? Espresso?"

She nodded. I should ask Josh about his problems with the police, she thought. No, I'll wait till he trusts me enough to open up and tell me.

And what if he never does? whispered an evil little voice. She hushed it up by asking, "Want to hear the latest on Mel's murder and not-so-perfect Cheryl?"

It was the one subject that could distract him—and her. When Josie finished her story, Josh handed her a double espresso and said, "Cheryl did it."

"I don't like her," Josie said. "But I can't see her as a killer. She would get blood on her designer outfit."

"She can afford a new one," Josh said. "For the sake of argument, let's say Cheryl didn't kill Mel the shoe molester. Then who did?"

"Some other woman whose toes he molested?" Josie took a sip of espresso and winced. Way too hot.

"That's hardly a motive for murder," Josh said.

Josie remembered how she'd felt when Mel had finished with her foot. She'd wanted to kill him. "It's a good motive," she said. "But no man on the jury would believe it. How about one of Mel's kinky friends?"

"Why would they kill Mel? He was the main access to their favorite fetish," Josh said. "Here's another question we can't answer: Where did Cheryl get the forty-eight thousand dollars?"

"From Mel," Josie said. "His fingerprints were all over the money bands and shoe boxes."

"Then why did she go to the motel with that guy for money?" Josh asked. "Mel couldn't have arranged that meeting. He was dead."

"He could have given her the guy's name beforehand and expected a cut of the money," Josie said.

"So you think Mel was a pimp?"

"I don't know what I think," Josie said. "Zinnia, his housekeeper, says Cheryl was a good shoe customer, period. She says Cheryl was always well behaved and so were the other women who came to Mel's house."

"And you believe her?" Josh said.

"Yes. At least, I believe they didn't do anything while Zinnia was in the house. Ever think that money could be legitimate? Mel worked on Wall Street. Maybe he invested it for Cheryl because she was a good customer. She could buy more shoes if she had her own stash."

"And she kept forty-eight thousand dollars in a shoe box?" Josh said. "The wife of an accountant?"

Josie tried another sip, and nearly cooked her tongue. She was dying for caffeine, but the espresso was still four-alarm hot.

"Just because her husband is careful with money doesn't mean she is," Josie said. "Cheryl and Mel were involved in some kind of business deal. Remember what the housekeeper said? Mel asked Cheryl if she wanted to make another one, and she said she needed a larger percentage of the profits. What do you think that was about?"

"She made a dirty movie," Josh said.

Josie laughed. "Cheryl? A shoe-porn queen? I don't believe it."

"Two weeks ago, you wouldn't have believed she was a gambler," Josh said. "Well, she is. She loses big time. She blew twelve hundred bucks on slot machines in two days."

"You're right. That doesn't seem real," Josie said.

"You saw her go to a motel that rents rooms by the hour," Josh said. "She met a guy there. She admits he paid her two hundred dollars, which she gambled away. Cheryl is a housewife hooker, pure and simple."

"She's not pure and I don't think it's simple," Josie said. "All she did was watch an old movie with the man. That's what Cheryl says and the motel maid backs her up."

"The maid didn't exactly back her up," Josh said.

"The maid said it didn't look like they were having wild sex. Nobody pays you to watch old movies. Otherwise, I'd be a millionaire."

"You look like a million bucks," Josie said. He did look good in his sleek new clothes. Stan the Man Next Door should study Josh's wardrobe. No wash-and-wear shirts and pocket protectors for Josh.

Josh refused to be distracted by compliments. Josie liked that. "Cheryl had forty-eight thousand dollars in cash," he said. "The easiest way to earn that kind of money was as a hooker."

"But Zinnia said Cheryl wasn't one," Josie said.

"The housekeeper is a nice, churchgoing woman. She left Mel's every afternoon. What if Cheryl and her friends came back for his foot-freak parties? Would Zinnia know?"

"She washed Mel's sheets," Josie said. She tried another sip. Still too hot. What did he make it with? Molten lava?

"Um, Josie, I don't know how to say this, but if a guy is doing funny things with shoes he may not need sheets. Besides, a man as rich as Mel could throw out the sheets."

"Shut up!" Josie said. "Let's not go there. Here's another reason why Cheryl wouldn't be at Mel's nighttime parties. She had a husband and a child. If she was MIA from home in the evening, she'd have to cook up some explanation for Tom and get a babysitter for Ben."

"Tom worked late," Josh said. "He might not even know his wife wasn't home. You can check with the sitter and see if she ever watched Ben in the evenings."

"So I could," Josie said. "I could also return that car seat and get my twenty-dollar deposit back. There was another way to get that forty-eight thousand in cash. What if Mel was blackmailing his freaky friends?"

"Why would Mel give the money to Cheryl, unless she was in on the scheme?" Josh said. "She'd still be mixed up in it. The police could say she was blackmailing Mel. No matter how we twist this, everything points toward Cheryl as the killer. You need to find some other suspects."

"Who?" Josie said. She wished she didn't sound like a big owl.

The bell rang and two women, twitchy as heroin addicts, came through the door. "It's the rabid cappuccinos," Josh said. "Gotta go."

"Not until you tell me how to find those other suspects," Josie said.

"Keep watching Cheryl," Josh said. "They'll come to her."

"Why would they do that?" Josie said.

"They have to know if they can get away with murder."

"Can we get some service here?" the skinnier woman said.

Josie left her espresso cooling on the counter.

Chapter 18

"I can't believe we're back watching Cheryl again," Alyce said. "And on a Sunday morning, yet."

"How else can we find out anything about her?" Josie said. "Does your husband mind you doing this today?"

"He's out of town," Alyce said. "He doesn't know and the nanny won't tell."

"I've hit the wall," Josie said. "I couldn't get anything useful from Mel's housekeeper."

"I thought Zinnia gave you some names of Mel's other women customers," Alyce said.

"They're not listed in the phone book," Josie said. "Either that, or I'm spelling them wrong. I'm not a detective, Alyce. If Mrs. Mueller wasn't paying me, I'd be walking the malls this morning. Maybe Josh can help me with an Internet search."

"Oh, come on. You can do your own search," Alyce said.

"Josh is better," Josie said.

"At what?" Alyce said, and grinned.

Josie ignored that question. They both knew the answer. "I suspect Mel was some sort of pimp," Josie said, "but I can't prove it and Cheryl's mother won't believe it unless I find proof. Even if I do, that information sure won't help Cheryl. Besides, if Cheryl was one of Mel's girls, she still had to get home to fix supper for her husband. What kind of hooker is that?"

"A housewife hooker," Alyce said. "It's a tough job. Those other hos have it easy. They get to walk the streets in bunny-fur jackets. They don't have to worry about menu planning, lawn services and committee meetings."

"What's got into you?" Josie said.

"It's this stupid wig," Alyce said. "What if someone recognizes me?"

For today's surveillance, Josie gave Alyce a wig with short, springy brown curls. It was in constant motion, like a million Slinkies.

"Alyce, your own mother wouldn't recognize you," Josie said. "Episcopalians don't have curly hair."

"I'm not worried about Mother. She's dead, so I can't embarrass her. I'm concerned someone from Jake's law firm will see me."

"They might see you, but they won't know you," Josie said. "You look like a Dynel Medusa."

"That's better than a flat-chested Dolly Parton," Alyce said.

Josie's flossy blond wig trailed to the seat of her skintight red velvet jeans. "Maybe I should have gone for Dolly's fake chest instead of her fake hair," Josie said. "But none of my blouses would fit if I had a big chest. At least the wig will keep me warm. This halter top is breezy even when I'm wearing a winter coat."

"Don't complain about the cold to me. Dressing like white trash was your idea," Alyce said.

"This assignment is using up my disguises," Josie said. "And, excuse me, but is that your idea of trashy?"

Alyce was wearing her gardening jeans, old loafers and a T-shirt that said, GO TO BED WITH SOMEONE NEW EVERY NIGHT—READ A GOOD BOOK. She couldn't look trashy if she wanted.

"I tried," Alyce said. The brown wig bobbed and wiggled.

"I succeeded," Josie said. "What does that say about me?"

"Speaking of trashy, here she comes," Alyce said.

Cheryl came out in a splendid camel coat. "How does she get by wearing that color with a baby?" Alyce asked. "I'd be covered in spit-up."

"She doesn't deserve a child as good as Ben," Josie said.

"Let's go," Alyce said, and started up her car.

Cheryl dropped the little boy at the sitter's house, then turned onto the highway. Alyce stayed several car lengths behind, in back of a pickup truck loaded with bedroom furniture.

"Cheryl missed the Earth City turn-off," Josie said. "I hope we're not going to the Royal Duchess again."

The pickup hit a pothole and a mattress bounced out. Alyce deftly swerved around it. Her wig did the wave. "Maybe Cheryl isn't gambling today," she said.

"Maybe this is my real hair," Josie said, running her fingers through the limp blond strands. "Nice driving, by the way."

"Thanks. You need a tattoo to go with that hair," Alyce said.

"I've got one. A barbed wire tat around my bicep."

"Tell me you're joking," Alyce said.

"It's henna," Josie said. "It will come off."

"It took me a week to remove the henna tattoo when we went to the islands," Alyce said. "I almost scrubbed my arm off."

"I'll wear long sleeves until it comes off," Josie said.

"What if it's not off by the time you have your date with Josh?" Alyce said.

"He'll like it." Josie smiled, her thoughts as trashy as her wig.

"Cheryl's turning off at the Riverfront," Alyce said.

"Then she's going to the riverboat casinos on the St. Louis side of the Mississippi," Josie said. "She's playing in Missouri today."

The casinos were anchored near the pure stainless-steel sweep of the Arch. The Mississippi churned under them, brown and powerful.

Alyce's SUV bumped along the old cobblestone streets, rattling their teeth and making Alyce's wig do the hula. They followed Cheryl's SUV into the parking lot for the Lucky Lou paddle-wheel casino.

The Lucky Lou looked like it was made out of cardboard. Bright colors and waving flags added forced gaiety.

"Mark Twain would weep," Alyce said. "The Lucky

Lou is more like a cheap carnival ride than a riverboat. It can't even take you on a cruise. It's not a real boat."

"It will take you for a ride," Josie said. "I wouldn't want to cruise this river in a boat as flimsy as the Lucky Lou. Look at the way that water moves. It's almost muscular."

"I see the Mississippi played by Bruce Willis," Alyce said.

"But with more hair," Josie said.

"Please," Alyce said. "For five whole minutes, I forgot about this wig."

Cheryl walked briskly toward the riverboat ramp.

"She didn't even look around," Josie said. "She knows I busted her. Why isn't she watching for me?"

"She doesn't care," Alyce said. "She feels invincible. She's blinded by her addiction and her arrogance."

"Shhh, we're closing in," Josie whispered. "Cheryl will hear us."

"She wouldn't hear U2 live and in person," Alyce said. "She only hears the siren song of the slots."

Cheryl went through the casino like a woman in a drug dream, oblivious to anyone else. Crowds parted around her, men stared, but Cheryl never noticed. Josie and Alyce filled out their session cards, then followed Cheryl.

"These casinos are all starting to look alike," Alyce said.

"This one has the *Cocktail* bartenders," Josie said.

At the neon-lit bar, Tom Cruise look-alikes juggled bottles and flipped streams of colored liquor, while customers applauded. Josie and Alyce gaped like a couple of hicks at a fair.

"Do you think liquor evaporates when you toss it around like that?" Alyce asked.

"Not as fast as Cheryl evaporates," Josie said. "Where did she go?"

"Where do you think?" Alyce said. "Does she have a magnet in her coat or what?" They tore themselves away from the leaping liquid and found Cheryl sitting at the ten-dollar slots.

"We won't be here long, thanks to Missouri's two-hour sessions," Josie said. "She'll be out of money by noon."

But this was Cheryl's lucky day. The Lucky Lou slots rained dollars on her. Bells rang, coins jingled, lights flashed and a small crowd gathered around Cheryl's slot machine. She ignored everyone and kept feeding it cash. It showered more money on her.

"How much has she won so far?" Alyce said.

"Nearly a thousand dollars. I can't believe it's one o'clock," Josie said. "The only thing duller than watching Cheryl lose is seeing her win. She doesn't even smile."

"She's afraid she'll lose the money," Alyce said.

Cheryl's good luck took a couple of bad hits between two and three o'clock, but at three ten, she won another thousand dollars. At three thirty, Cheryl was still playing. She got out her cell phone and made a call with one hand while playing her machine with the other. She wouldn't break her winning streak even to speed-dial a phone.

"Come on, let's go," Josie said.

"Where?" Alyce said. "You don't know who she called."

"Yes, I do," Josie said. "Cheryl is talking someone into picking up Ben. Bonnie the babysitter said Cheryl called about three thirty if she got stuck in a meeting. She's meeting major money today. She won't leave. Let's head for the sitter's. I want to see Ben's rescuer."

Josie and Alyce were lucky, too. No pickup trucks lost mattresses on the highway. Even the usual traffic slowdown near Brentwood didn't happen.

They were parked on Bonnie's street at 3:54. At 3:57, a dark green SUV pulled into the babysitter's drive. A caramel blonde who looked like a carbon copy of Cheryl got out. She was back five minutes later, carrying a chubby boy in blue OshKosh rompers.

"That's Ben," Josie said. "I'd recognize those fat red cheeks anywhere."

The child squealed in delight. "Poor little guy," Josie said. "Cheryl is one cold woman to leave him for a slot machine."

The caramel blonde hugged Ben, then strapped him into his seat in her SUV. Josie counted two more small heads in the vehicle.

"Think those are her kids?" Josie said.

"Definitely," Alyce said. "She's got MOM written all over her."

Josie and Alyce followed the caramel blonde to a house almost exactly like Cheryl's, right down to the Pella windows and white pillars. The family name was painted on the mailbox in scrolled letters. THE CHRISTIE'S it said.

"I hate misplaced apostrophes," Alyce said. "The Christie's what?"

"House," Josie said. "I think we've found Fiona. According to Zinnia, she's one of the women customers who visited Mel. How do you think Cheryl explains to her husband that their son is at another woman's house?"

"She probably says Ben has a play date," Alyce said. "It's chic. Also important for the child's socialization. Play dates are a big deal in the upper-crust burbs. Even at age two, your child has to play with the right people, little future professionals who will grow up and advance your son's career."

Alyce drove by the Christies' house, turned around in a circle at the end of the street, and drove back. Fiona was holding a baby younger than Ben. A slightly older child was hanging on to her legs. She was carrying and cajoling the three children inside the home.

"Keep on driving. I think we can call it a day," Josie said. "We know what Fiona will be doing for the next few hours."

"How long do you think Cheryl will stay at the Lucky Lou?" Alyce said.

"Until she loses all her money," Josie said.

"How long will she keep this up without her family finding out?" Alyce said.

"Until she bankrupts them," Josie said.

"How much trouble do you think she's in?" Alyce asked.

"A lot," Josie said. "We just don't know what it is."

"Are we going to do this tomorrow?" Alyce said.

"If Mrs. Mueller is still paying me. We learn something different every day."

"We learn something more depressing every day. Josie, tomorrow is the last time I'll watch Cheryl. I don't want to do this anymore. I don't want to see any more of Cheryl's messed-up life."

"I can't stop," Josie said. "It's like some awful reality TV show."

"I'm voting no after tomorrow," Alyce said. "And I refuse to wear this Clarabell the Clown wig again." The curly wig looked like a can of worms.

"You can be yourself," Josie said. "She won't recognize you. Just come with me for one more day. I promise it will be worth your time."

All the traffic that they missed on the ride to the baby-sitter's house was waiting for Josie on the way home. It was nearly five before she turned onto her street. Stan came running out with a small cardboard box while she parked her car.

Oh, no, Josie thought. Please don't give me a gift, Stan. I don't want to have to give it back.

"UPS brought this over yesterday when no one was at your house. I wanted to give it to you," Stan said.

Josie read the label and her heart sank. It was for Jane. Her mother was ordering things from the Home Shopping Network again.

Stan saw the look on her face. "I should have brought it over sooner, shouldn't I?"

"No, Stan. It's nothing you did. Thank you for being a good neighbor."

Poor Mom, Josie thought. Stress could make Jane slip back into her old shopping addiction. Josie would have to find some way to ask her mother. She pulled off the Dolly Parton wig her mother found so embarrassing and shoved it in a shopping bag. No point in adding to Jane's pressures.

Before Josie could unlock her door, she was ambushed by a triumphant Mrs. Mueller.

"Well, you were wrong again," Mrs. M said. "My nephew George checked that license plate for you. It belongs to the pastor of the Hillwood Heights Evangelical Church, the Reverend Zebediah Smithson. It's plain to me that my Cheryl was doing nothing wrong if she was in the company of a church pastor."

"Uh," Josie said. She was too stunned to reply. The church pastor was forking over money to watch movies in a no-tell motel? Where did a man of the cloth get that kind of cash—from the collection plate?

"I assume you've found nothing useful today, either?" Mrs. Mueller's voice was imperious, branding Josie a failure before she ever answered.

"Cheryl was at the Lucky Lou downtown," Josie said.

"I was hoping you could find out something more helpful than that," Mrs. Mueller said.

"Me, too," Josie said.

She walked into her home and felt the approaching thunder of trouble. Something was off. The air was thick with tension.

"I've fixed chicken and dumplings for dinner," her mother said. Jane was nervous, trembly, on the verge of tears. She kept wiping her hands on a kitchen towel, when they were perfectly clean.

"Are you okay, Mom?" Josie said.

"Why wouldn't I be?" Jane said.

"UPS left a package for you with Stan," Josie said.

"It was just a little thing," Jane said. "A kitchen gadget. Only nine ninety-nine."

"Mom," Josie said. "You promised. No more Home Shopping Network."

"I'll make an extra appointment with my counselor," Jane said. "I'm sorry, Josie. I've let you down." She started crying.

"GBH," Josie said, and gathered her sobbing mother into her arms. "You've never let me down, Mom. You've always been there when I needed you. I won't let you down with Mrs. Mueller."

"She says you're not getting anywhere," Jane said.

"I've already found out more than she wanted to know," Josie said. "Don't you worry, Mom, you'll get those committees or I'll burn a pile of dog doo ten feet high in her yard."

Jane laughed and blew her nose. "Wash up, dear. I'll get your dinner."

"Where's Amelia?"

"In her room," Jane said.

Not a good sign. Her daughter was moping, too. She'd spent the day at her best friend Emma's house, and that usually put her in a good mood. But Amelia seemed unnaturally subdued tonight. Her straight hair looked limp and her face was pale.

"What's the matter?" Josie said.

"Nothing," Amelia said.

Josie had learned to read the nothings. A school nothing had a higher pitch to it. This was a personal nothing. It was a flatter sound. "What happened at Emma's?"

Amelia looked surprised. "How did you know?"

"I'm your mother," Josie said. Might as well maintain her omniscience as long as she could.

"Zoe—" Amelia said and stopped.

Josie struggled to tamp down her temper. What now? she wondered. Was the precocious Zoe wearing high heels and a bustier? Smoking cigars? Buying her own car?

"Zoe's sister OD'd," Amelia said.

"She's dead from drugs?" Josie said. She felt like someone had punched her in the gut. "Her sister's sixteen, right?"

Amelia nodded. Two tears slid down her cheeks. "I knew her, Mom. Celine was sweet. She was one of the big kids who said hi to me and didn't treat me like a baby. Celine died."

"What happened?" Josie said.

"Gemma, she's in our class, was at Emma's house, too. She said Celine and her boyfriend were at this club on Washington Avenue and they scored some coke in the alley. It was extra strong or something. Celine started shaking. She fell and hit her head on the bricks in the alley and an ambulance took her away.

"Gemma heard her mom talking on the phone this morning. Gemma's mom said Celine had a seizure and she went into a coma. Gemma's mom said it was a good thing she died, because Zoe's sister would have been a vegetable. Is it good that Celine died?"

"It can be," Josie said, and felt the panic tearing her insides.

Now what do I say? Josie wondered. What words of wisdom can I give Amelia that might save her when she's sixteen?

How do you make your daughter understand there are fates worse than death? How do you tell your child that some impulsive moments can never be changed— like the one that had created her?

How do you know when you are changing your life forever?

If Josie didn't have those answers at thirty-one, how could her daughter know them at age nine?

Chapter 19

Click.

Josie pulled out her camera and snapped Cheryl when she dropped the baby off at Bonnie's house again on Monday morning.

"Why are you doing that?" Alyce said. "Her mother knows she uses a sitter."

"Her husband doesn't," Josie said. "Cheryl gave me the idea. She said I didn't have any photos of her gambling. Now I will."

Click. Click.

Josie photographed Cheryl going into the Prince's Palace.

Click. Click.

Josie captured Cheryl frantically feeding a flashing slot machine. Josie took other pictures, including one of Elvis's guitar mounted on the casino wall.

"Why are you photographing a guitar? Cheryl's nowhere near it," Alyce said.

"So I'll look like a tourist."

"You look like a tourist from Festus," Alyce said.

Today Josie wore sensible flat shoes, a blue polyester pantsuit and a short gray grandma wig that added twenty years to her age. Alyce, in her suburban matron suit of beige cashmere and blond hair, looked young enough to be Josie's daughter. Cheryl didn't pay them the slightest attention. No one did.

Click. Click. More photos of Cheryl at the slots.

"Her mother knows Cheryl gambles," Alyce said.

"It's one thing to hear her daughter gambles," Josie

said. "It's another to see her sitting at the slots like a zombie."

"Zombie is right," Alyce said. "Cheryl lost again, but there's no expression on her face."

Yesterday, the slots had magically spewed out money for Cheryl. Today, the fickle machines gulped it down, ten dollars at a time. By eleven thirty, Cheryl had lost five hundred dollars.

"Game's over," Josie said. "She'll have to sit out till the next session."

"Maybe she'll get some lunch," Alyce said. "I'm hungry."

But Cheryl went outside, making calls on her cell. She talked quickly as she walked with small, swift steps to the valet parking area. Then she turned flirtatious, laughing and smiling into the phone. She seemed dressed to meet a lover. On this gray November morning, Cheryl wore a tight black suit with a flirty skirt, black stockings and high patent heels with ankle straps.

"I thought you weren't supposed to wear patent leather after Labor Day," Alyce said.

"Better call the fashion police," Josie said.

"No, I think it's odd, that's all. It wouldn't mean anything if I wore patent leather. But someone like Cheryl pays attention to those things," Alyce said.

They watched Cheryl snap her cell phone shut and tap her foot, waiting for the valet.

"We'd better hike to the parking lot," Josie said. "We don't want to lose her."

They virtually ran to Alyce's car—or rather, the car Alyce was using—an ancient 1980 Ford she'd borrowed from her housekeeper. The car had patches of gray Bondo, like mange, and a rumbling muffler, but it started right up.

"This car is more embarrassing than yesterday's wig," Alyce said.

"You're smart to drive it," Josie said. "Cheryl might notice your SUV the third day in a row."

Cheryl's car arrived. She tipped the valet and headed for the highway exit.

"Must be motel time," Josie said.

"At least we have the right car for that sleazy place," Alyce said.

But Cheryl didn't go to the no-tell motel. They followed her SUV to a turn-off near the airport. Billboards for cheap long-term-parking lots dotted the road.

"She's going on a trip?" Alyce said. "She wouldn't leave her baby with a sitter overnight."

Without signaling, Cheryl swung into a residential street lined with neat, boxy apartments, anonymous places rented mostly by pilots and flight attendants. Airplanes roared overhead, low enough that Josie could see their landing gear. The noise was deafening.

"How can anyone live here—or sleep here?" Alyce said.

"I had an aunt who lived near the airport. You get used to it," Josie said. "After a while, you don't even hear the airplanes."

Cheryl turned into an apartment complex lot and parked in a resident's space. She pattered inside on her patent-leather heels. Alyce and Josie circled the block, then drove back to the lot and parked at the opposite end in a guest spot.

"This is weird. Does Cheryl have an apartment here?" Josie said. "Why? These are mostly studios and one-bedrooms."

"Maybe someone else has the apartment," Alyce said.

Josie waited five minutes, then entered the lobby. Like the building itself, it was neat and anonymous. "The elevator stopped on the fourth floor," she said.

They watched through the glass lobby doors as a man about forty swung a sleek black Lexus into the lot. As he climbed out, Alyce said, "Omigod, it's Hal Orrin Winfrey."

"You know him?"

"He lives in our subdivision. His wife and I are on the Christmas party committee. I can't let him see me here."

Alyce pushed Josie through the fire stairs door. She cracked the door and watched the lobby.

"Don't get excited," Josie said. "Hal could be here for a perfectly legitimate reason."

"Name one," Alyce said. "That slimeball. His wife is home with two kids and he's fooling around with Cheryl. I knew I never liked that woman."

Hal entered the building whistling. He was about six feet tall and well tailored. His face was round and open. His eyes were an innocent baby blue. As Hal punched the elevator button, Josie snapped his picture through the crack in the door. They could still hear him whistling as the doors closed.

"The elevator stopped on the fourth floor," Josie said.

"We've got him," Alyce said. "He's meeting Cheryl. I know he is."

"No, you don't," Josie said. "He could be taking a nap or doing some work."

"You don't whistle when you go to take a nap. Hal has no business here. He belongs in West County with his wife and children, or in Clayton at his office."

Alyce's floaty hair stood almost straight out and her face was red with indignation. She was angry, Josie thought, not just for her friend, but for all duped wives. Including, perhaps, herself.

"I can't wait for that snake to slither on down again. Mr. Hal Winfrey is going to tell us all about his love nest."

They waited for nearly an hour. Josie found a newspaper in the lobby and brought it back to the stairwell. She and Alyce paged through it, but neither was in a mood to read. The Mel murder story had slipped off the pages.

"I'm glad I brought my camera. This rendezvous will make for primo photos," Josie said. "I'll show Cheryl these photos later on, and she'll talk or else."

They watched a mail carrier fill the lobby boxes. A cable TV repairman went to the third floor. Alyce's stomach growled.

"I'm starving," she said.

Josie ransacked her purse for a pack of peanuts. They ate them, then took turns drinking from the lobby water fountain. Finally, the elevator hummed, the doors opened, and Cheryl stepped out.

Sinning—if that's what she'd been up to—had no more effect on her than winning. Cheryl looked exactly the same as when she'd pressed the elevator button an hour ago. She did not have a hair out of place or a wrinkle in her sleek black suit. Her makeup was perfect. Her pale skin was not flushed with pleasure or anything else.

Josie snapped Cheryl's photo as she opened the lobby door and clicked outside in her high heels.

"That's weird," Josie said. "She's wearing black heels, but not the patent-leather ones."

"Do we want to follow her?" Alyce said.

"I'll bet everything I own she's going back to that casino," Josie said. "Let's brace Hal before he leaves."

"You mean go up to his apartment and surprise him?" Alyce said. "I'd like that." Alyce smiled, but it wasn't pleasant. Josie's large blond friend looked like a Valkyrie going to war. Josie had good reasons to dislike Cheryl. Alyce seemed to have developed an instant hate-on for the woman.

"My guess is he's waiting fifteen minutes so he isn't seen leaving the building with his love muffin," Josie said.

"His what?" Alyce said. "Cheryl's more like a stale cupcake."

"Meow," Josie said.

There were two white doors on the fourth floor. One had a twig wreath decorated with orange ribbons and yellow silk flowers. "Someone lives in that apartment. Hal's love nest is the one with the blank door," Alyce whispered.

Josie nodded her agreement, then knocked.

"Are you back for more, Muffin?" a man's voice called through the door.

"I told you," Josie mouthed. Alyce wrinkled her nose in disgust.

Hal threw open the door wearing a towel and a smile. Josie shot him with her camera. The smile slid off. The towel stayed.

At first, Hal's face was blank with shock. Then it was

creased with rage. "Alyce Bohannon, what are you doing here? Why are you spying on me?" Hal tried to gather his dignity, but it was gone.

"Bluster won't work, Hal," Alyce said. "Explain yourself or your wife Mattie gets that photo."

Hal seemed to shrink before their eyes. He'd just stepped out of the shower. His wet hair, plastered to his head, looked thin. He must have had a good tailor. Seminaked, Hal had narrow shoulders, nice legs and too much belly fat.

"Can I put on a robe?" he said.

"Where is it?" Josie said. "I'll get it for you." She wasn't going to let him escape out the back way.

"On a hook in the bathroom."

The apartment must have been rented furnished. It was hard to imagine anyone deliberately choosing the plain beige furniture and no-color carpet.

Josie threw Hal a blue velvet robe. He shrugged it on, then sat down heavily in a square beige chair.

"It's not what you think. I swear I never slept with her," he said. Despite his recent shower and the November cold, sweat poured off his forehead.

Alyce looked at the tousled bed. "I believe you, Hal. There wasn't any sleeping going on in that bed."

Josie took a picture of the rumpled sheets.

"No!" shrieked Hal. "You don't understand. There was no sex. She won't do sex."

"So what will she do?" Alyce asked.

Hal said nothing. His face was dangerously red.

"Tell me or tell your wife," Alyce said. It was the voice of judgment and justice.

Hal looked at his bare feet. "I paid her to walk on me in patent-leather heels," he said.

Josie bit the inside of her mouth to keep from laughing. Alyce looked like grim fury.

The silence made Hal even more frightened. "Here, I'll show you," he said.

He opened a closet in the living room. Women's shoes, all size seven, were stacked on six shelves. Some were red, others were clear plastic, most were black. All had outrageously high, skinny heels and needle toes.

Hal pointed to a pair of four-inch patent heels with ankle straps.

"You're one of Mel's shoe freaks," Josie said.

"Please," Hal said. "I'm not a freak. I have special needs."

Chapter 20

"How can Hal go home to his wife with another woman's footprints on him?" Alyce said.

Josie started giggling. Then she was laughing and couldn't stop. She sat in the housekeeper's beat-up car in the dreary apartment lot and laughed until she had tears on her face.

"What's so funny?" Alyce demanded. She was still furious and hopped up on adrenaline after her encounter with the half-naked Hal.

"Everything," Josie said. "Hal in a towel. Hal's closet full of high heels. The fact that he pays Cheryl to walk on him. It's all funny."

"I'll walk on him," Alyce said. "I'd like to kick him in his—" A low-flying jet drowned out the rest of her words.

"He'd probably enjoy it," Josie said. "He might even pay extra. This is so bizarre. Hal looks like a normal executive. He lives in your subdivision. You had no idea he was into anything weird, right?"

"None," Alyce said. "He's like all the other husbands. He plays golf and tennis at the club. He buys furnace filters at the Home Depot. He chaired the pumpkin fund-raiser for our church. Now I wonder what he did with those innocent Halloween pumpkins."

"Nothing, unless they wore Pradas," Josie said. "I can see why Mr. Suburban Dad would have a secret shoe-freak apartment out by the airport: None of his set lives there. If anyone he knows should spot him on these roads, they'll think he's parked in some long-term lot.

But here's what I don't get: Why is he paying Cheryl—someone from his own world—instead of a hooker or a woman he picked up in a bar?"

"Oh, I can answer that question," Alyce said. "A hooker could blackmail him, especially if she saw his picture in the paper as Businessman of the Year. A single woman might make demands. She'd be dangerous, unpredictable. She might pressure him to leave his wife and get a divorce. She'd probably see him as a rich target and want to break up his marriage.

"But if Cheryl is from his own set, she has as much to lose as he does. If anyone knew about Cheryl stepping out with—or on—Hal, she would lose her house, her husband and maybe her child."

Alyce was really wound up on the subject. "Cheryl's protected, too," she said. "Hal's going to keep his mouth shut. He won't brag to the boys in the locker room. He'd be laughed out of the country club. None of his golf buddies would share a locker with a spike-heel lover. They might slap him on the back if he was having an ordinary affair, but this is the Saturday-morning missionary crowd. They don't like anything strange.

"His wife, Mattie, certainly wouldn't stand for it. She'd give Hal the boot and tie him up with an expensive, career-damaging divorce."

Josie snorted.

"Now what's so funny?" Alyce said.

"Giving Hal the boot and tying him up sound pretty kinky," Josie said.

"Guess I have a one-track mind." Alyce laughed, but there was no joy in it.

"Did Jake ever ask you to walk on him?" Josie said.

"My husband? No way," Alyce said. "We never did anything exotic with shoes, handcuffs, knotted handkerchiefs or silk scarves tied to the headboards. We didn't need them. Jake and I had nonstop sex on every surface in the house, from the hall floor to the kitchen counter."

Had. Josie heard that word, as if their hot sex was in the past.

"I mean, have," Alyce corrected quickly. She turned a deep red. "Jake works late now. And things are different with a baby and a nanny. But we made up for lost time on our cruise to the islands."

Josie could hear her friend's sadness and longing. She was sure none of Alyce's Williams-Sonoma gadgets would be swept off the kitchen counter in a fit of passion anytime soon. She was sorry she'd asked such a nosy question.

"Hey, I sure don't know," Josie said. "My sixty-eight-year-old mother gets more romance than I do."

Alyce started the car's engine and the old brown bomber rumbled into life. "I wish today never happened. How am I going to face Hal? I see him at the supermarket. He goes to our church."

"He should be worried, Alyce. He's the one who's done something wrong, not you."

"But I'm embarrassed," Alyce said. "I feel sorry for his wife. What am I going to do?"

"Nothing. Believe me, Mattie doesn't want to know. Maybe he asked her to walk on him and she said no."

"I wonder what I'd do if Jake asked me," Alyce said. "Some days, I'd like to stomp him into the ground. Other days, I love him to death."

"Most women feel that way about the men they love," Josie said. "Hal may be doing the smart thing, paying Cheryl. At least it's nothing personal."

Alyce laughed, and this time it was genuine. "Thanks, Josie. I feel better. But I want to go home and take a long hot bubble bath. I've had enough of Cheryl and her freaky friends."

"I need to think about what we've learned," Josie said. "Some of it is starting to make sense. At first, I didn't think we had any suspects. Now I see them everywhere. Maybe I can put together something to help Cheryl, so Mom can get her precious committees."

"I bet some coffee will help you think better," Alyce said, and winked.

It was three o'clock when Josie got to Has Beans. Josh was pulling out of the lot in his battered Datsun Z. He slammed on his brakes beside Josie's car and leaned out his window.

"Hi," Josie said. "Want to go for a cup of coffee?"

"Too much like work," Josh said. "How about a beer at Blueberry Hill?"

"Sold," Josie said. "But I have to be home by five."

"No prob," Josh said. "Meet you there."

Josie loved the old University City restaurant, although she hadn't been to Blueberry Hill in a while. In college, she'd spent many an afternoon playing darts there, many a night listening to the bands, and more than a few drunken moments contemplating the philosophy on the bathroom walls. After a few beers, sayings like "You can't get away from me—I've tried" and "Time is nature's way of keeping everything from happening at once" seemed profound.

Josh found a booth in the bar area. Their waiter was impossibly thin, pale and pierced. Blueberry Hill had hip waiters. Josie felt like she had to order something the server would approve, to maintain the restaurant standards.

Josh asked for a Pilsner Urquell and an order of toasted ravioli. "You'll split it with me, right?"

"Absolutely," Josie said. "I'll have a Heineken."

"Glass?" the waiter said.

"Bottle's fine," Josie said.

"Real women don't use glasses," the waiter said.

When the waiter left, Josh said, "The first time we went out, you ordered a beer. I loved it. Any man ever tell you how sexy it is when a woman drinks beer out of the bottle?"

"Mostly they tell me I'll look a lot sexier after they have two or three bottles," Josie said.

Josh reached for her hand. "You don't see how special you are, do you?"

Josie was glad the bar was dark. Her face was flaming. She wasn't used to compliments from men as handsome as Josh. She was average in every way: height, looks, weight. Even her brown hair was average. She was relieved when the waiter brought their drinks and toasted ravioli.

"Wonder why St. Louisans call these things toasted when they're really deep-fat-fried ravioli?" she said.

"Fewer calories in toasted," Josh said, popping a whole one.

"Ouch. You must have an asbestos mouth," Josie said. "Those babies are hot."

"So am I." Josh waggled his eyebrows, Groucho style.

Josie dragged a ravioli through the dish of red sauce and bit into it to keep from answering. Josh got the hint and cooled the conversation. "How's the Cheryl clearance project? Any suspects yet?" he asked.

"Tons," Josie said. "All of a sudden, I have more than I can handle."

"I told you they'd show up," he said.

"One showed up today wearing only a towel."

"Whoa," Josh said. "Do I have competition?"

"Nope. He should save that sight for his loving wife. Alyce and I encountered Towel Boy out by the airport." She told Josh the story while he sipped his beer.

"So do you think Towel Boy did it? Maybe Mel was blackmailing him," Josh said.

"He swears he wasn't being blackmailed," Josie said. "We asked him straight out. I'm not sure I believe him. An adulterer is a natural liar."

"Maybe," Josh said. "But maybe he's just a guy who got bored with home cooking and home loving."

Josie didn't like that answer, but she didn't want to get into a discussion of men who cheat. "The others have been around," she said. "I've finally realized their potential. There's the pastor who has the pay-per-view *Pretty Woman*. The man is prime blackmail material, going into sleazy motels with women in red heels. He could have sent Mel to his reward because the shoe salesman was squeezing him for collection-plate cash."

"Ditto for Towel Boy, Hal Orrin Winfrey.

"There are the other two women we know of who worked for Mel. I got their names from the housekeeper, Zinnia. One is a high-powered female executive. The other is one more perfect homemaker. Both have a lot to lose if their secret comes out. Mel could have been blackmailing them. Alyce and I found the homemaker, and I think I can get the executive's phone number from her."

"The police haven't charged any of these people yet?"

Josh said. He chomped another toasted ravioli. Josie dredged one more through the red sauce. She wished those tasty meat-stuffed pillows weren't so good with cold beer.

"Nope," Josie said. "The police questioned Cheryl at her house. They asked for her fingerprints and permission to search the place, but she refused. Then they arrested her on some trumped-up charge so they could get her fingerprints."

"That means she's probably their main suspect," he said. "They just don't have enough to charge her yet. They have to be a lot more careful with a respectable homemaker than some low-life drug dealer."

"How can you be so sure?" Josie said.

Josh hesitated, then said, "If I tell you, you may never want to see me again."

Josie's heart was beating faster in the dark bar. "How bad was it?" she asked.

"Bad enough."

"Did you kill someone?" she said.

Josh laughed. "Me? No, it wasn't that bad. I was mostly guilty of being young and stupid. I was twenty."

"I made my share of mistakes at that age," Josie said.

"Not like mine," Josh said. "Oh, hell, I might as well tell you. I got caught selling something a little stronger than coffee. It was strictly recreational, for my friends who needed to relax. I got probation and community service because it was a first offense. But I learned more than I wanted about how the police work."

I sure know how to pick them, Josie thought. My perfect man has a past. But then, so do I. Maybe someday I'll get the courage to tell him my story.

"That was kids' stuff, Josh. You're pushing caffeine these days."

"Talk about serious drugs. Coffee fiends are worse than heroin addicts." Josh took a long drink of beer. Josie watched the muscles move in his throat. Everything about him—the way he walked, the way he ate, even the way he drank a beer—was graceful and controlled.

"What are you planning to do next?" Josh said.

"Following Cheryl is getting me nowhere," Josie said.

"I took some photos of her at the casino and the motel, but I'm not sure I'll use them. What's my big threat: 'I'll tell your mother'?"

"From what you say about Mrs. Mueller, that's a powerful weapon."

"I'm not ready to use it," Josie said. "I need to talk to the other suspects, and soon. Like tomorrow."

"Good idea," Josh said. "If the police arrest someone, this story will be a hot one. It will be all over the media. You won't be able to get near them."

"That's what I thought. I'm going to be busy for the next few days. I'm doing this around my mystery shopping," Josie said.

"But I'll get to see you on Saturday? You haven't changed those plans?" Josh said.

Josie liked the way he sounded. She was important to him. "Saturday night is still Amelia's sleepover. The Barrington School world would end if it was canceled. And my mom has a date that night, too. I am a free woman."

"We'll have lots to celebrate. I leave for New York that Monday. I have interviews with three agents."

"Josh! Your big break. Where did you get the money for the trip?" Josie said.

"From my father," Josh said. "He spent my childhood at his office. He owes me something after all these years."

Josh's eyes were hard with hurt. Josie wondered if baby Ben would talk the same way about his hardworking father in twenty years.

Chapter 21

Josie was buying one of the most expensive candles in the world. The Jo Malone Luxury Candle cost $345.

The perfect gift for people with money to burn, Josie thought. The seven-inch candle melted at the rate of fifty bucks an inch. Josie didn't even like holding it. What if the pricey candle slipped and cracked on the shop's marble floor? Or melted in her car before she could return it to the next Extravagant Luxuries store?

Josie would have to pay for it. Suttin Services didn't shell out money for careless mystery shoppers.

"That's a lovely candle." The saleswoman smiled, approving Josie's good taste. The woman's hair was pulled back into such a tight knot, Josie wondered how she could move her lips without hurting herself.

"The bouquet is exquisite," the saleswoman said. "It's for someone with sophisticated tastes." She managed another smile, which strained the lines around her eyes.

Josie gave her a half smile. No need to say anything. If she was truly sophisticated, she wouldn't need a clerk to tell her. Her camel pants (Ralph Lauren seconds) and cashmere sweater (garage sale, slightly pilled under the arms) must have passed inspection.

"The candle has four wicks for even burning," the saleswoman said, as if she was describing an exotic invention.

Even unopened, the amber-and-sweet-orange candle smelled, well . . . rich. There was no other way to describe it. Josie didn't encounter this perfume when she mystery-shopped the popcorn-scented stores of the poor.

Josie had a wild impulse to take the candle for her date with Josh. For just one crazy evening, she wanted to quit worrying about money and responsibility. She'd love to set fire to all that lovely money. Ten years ago, she would have done it without a second thought.

But you already know about burning candles, don't you? she told herself. You burned the candle at both ends with Amelia's father and look what that got you.

The most beautiful daughter in the world, she answered defiantly. Amelia had her father's noble nose and straight hair, quick intelligence and courage. All of his good qualities, and none of the bad, or so Josie hoped. She didn't want her daughter to end up like her father— or her mother.

Josie was born to the world of Porthault sheets and $345 candles. Her father was a corporate lawyer. Jane was a clubwoman and a homemaker. Their life in the wealthy suburb of Ladue was her mother's idea of heaven, and Jane could have spent eternity there, going to lunch and serving on committees. But Josie's father left Jane for another woman and another city.

The divorce stripped Jane of her home, her social standing, and her income. Her ex-husband gave her a two-family flat in low-rent Maplewood. Jane took a job at the bank and rarely saw her old friends. Josie never knew if they abandoned her mother, or if Jane was too ashamed of her dreary life to keep up the old friendships.

Josie was seven when her father left. He seemed to forget her, as if she was something else he left behind in St. Louis, along with his second-best driving gloves and his tennis racket that needed restringing.

Josie told herself she didn't care. She liked Maplewood better than Ladue. She brushed off her mother's constant reminders that "it was just as easy to love a rich man as a poor one." Jane had one goal: Josie had to go to college, find the right man and recapture her lost dream.

Josie wasn't sure how it happened, but in her junior year at college, she was engaged to a man her mother adored, a future accountant named Andy. Andy had big

brown eyes and a brain filled with business clichés.
When Andy proposed, he looked at Josie with burning
intensity and said, "With you by my side, I will achieve
excellence in all aspects of my life." Josie believed him.
She had an "investment diamond" on her finger and a
restlessness her heart didn't understand.

Josie's engagement was the happiest day of Jane's life.
"Andy has a brilliant future," she told her daughter.
"He'll get a job in a top firm. Where will you live in
West County? Do you think you'll buy an older house
in Ballwin or Chesterfield? Or move to one of the new
subdivisions near St. Albans? I prefer St. Albans, if
Andy can afford it. It has a good country club. I can
steer you to the right committees, the ones that will help
Andy's career. Have you decided how many children
you want? I always think two, a boy and a girl, make
the perfect gentleman's family. But you don't have to
decide right away. You and Andy have your whole life
ahead of you."

For some reason, that prospect didn't thrill Josie. Her
engagement left her feeling oddly passive, while her
mother and Andy planned her future.

One afternoon, Josie and Andy were having a TGIF
lunch at O'Connell's Pub with some friends. Andy was
discussing bottom-line benefits when Josie saw Nathan
standing by the dark wood door. His hair was the color
of wild honey. He walked with a confidence Andy would
never have, even when he became managing partner.

A woman at Josie's table waved Nathan over. He sat
next to Josie, stole her french fries, and talked about
flying. "I'm a helicopter pilot, a good one," he said. "I
have to be. One wrong move, and I'm flying a piano."

Josie thought that was funny. She didn't remember
when she left O'Connell's with Nate, but she never forgot their moonlit helicopter ride over the Mississippi
River that night. It was a romantic dream.

Josie gave Andy back his investment diamond in the
same dreamlike trance. She skipped classes to fly with
Nathan to New York for lunch at the Four Seasons.
They hopped over to Breckenridge for snowboarding,
then flew down to Florida for sailing and stone crabs.

Nate took her everywhere, except on the trips to his hometown, Toronto. The Canada trips were business, he said.

Josie thought the helicopter business must pay well, because Nate had a Porsche, a Harley and an Infinity sound system, along with an insatiable desire for exotic places.

School seemed dull after her adventures with Nate. Josie shrugged off the concerned questions from her teachers and the frantic warnings from her mother. They meant nothing when she was with her high-flying lover. Nathan never talked about "supporting strategic business objectives."

With Nate, she was a different woman, passionate and inventive. Her old life seemed gray and dull. She could hardly stand her cramped student apartment with its tired curtains and paint the color of dirty teeth. She invited Nate for dinner, then realized she had to do something to brighten her place.

Josie bought a hundred candles. She would have done better to spend the money on curtains, couch covers, and throw pillows, but she came home with more than three hundred dollars' worth of tall tapers, tiny votives, and fat pillar candles. She borrowed every candleholder her friends had, then used all the saucers, wineglasses and plates in her apartment. She lined the windowsills, the coffee table, the kitchen table, and the fireplace with candles.

Nate arrived as she was lighting the last one. Her drab little room was transformed into something glowing and mysterious. "Why are you wasting your time burning candles, when you can set me on fire?" he said as he kissed her.

"I'm burning down my old world," she said.

"Welcome to our world," he said. "We made ourselves—all the fire and all the shadows."

They made glorious love by candle glow.

In the harsh morning light, Josie saw the box of condoms by the bed had never been opened. She spent a week scraping dripped wax off the tables, floors and chairs. She wondered why her apartment didn't burn down, but she knew. She and Nate were children of the gods—rich, beautiful and infinitely lucky.

Josie discovered she was pregnant about the time Nate was arrested for drug smuggling in Canada. Nate went to prison and was barred from entering the United States. Josie never told him he had a daughter. She never talked with him again. It hurt too much to think that her glamorous lover was a common drug dealer.

Amelia thought her father had been killed in a crash. It was true, Josie thought. My life crashed the day Nate was arrested.

Josie refused to give up her daughter, the product of her wild love. Amelia was a flawless child, born of a perfect time in Josie's life. Andy would have taken her back and married her, but Josie had lost her desire for a bottom-line boy. A house in the burbs seemed tame after all she'd almost had.

To Jane's horror, Josie dropped out of college. After Amelia was born, she became a mystery shopper so she'd have time to be with her daughter. Josie paid a high price for her reckless romance, but she wasn't unhappy with her life. She just didn't trust herself with men. They were either dull and sweet like Stan, or wild and crazy like Nate.

Josh was the first man who'd sent sparks flying since Nate. Now she worried that Josh and Nate were too much alike.

They're not, she told herself. They have nothing in common. Nate was a pilot. Josh is a writer.

With a drug-dealing past, whispered a voice.

A past he's paid for, she told herself. Just as I've paid for mine.

"And how will you pay for this?" the saleswoman said. Josie looked startled, then realized the clerk was talking about the candle.

"MasterCard," Josie said.

"Could I interest you in some Jo Malone potpourri?" the saleswoman said. "It's only forty-eight dollars."

For a brief snick in time, Josie almost said yes. Forty-eight dollars sounded reasonable after $345 candles. That was the trap of mystery-shopping the exclusive stores. Josie could easily lose track of reality and blow a day's pay on frivolities.

"Not today," Josie said. Or tomorrow, either. She'd made her choices nearly a decade ago and she couldn't change them now.

After Josie safely returned the candle to the Plaza Frontenac store, she checked the time, then made an appointment by cell phone. Next she called her friend, Alyce.

"What sleazy place are we visiting today?" Alyce said. "Should I wear a Hazmat suit?"

"We've had enough casinos and no-tell motels," Josie said. "It's time for spiritual enlightenment. I've made an appointment for pastoral counseling."

"What? Have you lost it?" Alyce never raised her voice, but she was almost shouting into her phone.

"I've found it," Josie said. "We have an appointment to see Cheryl's good friend, the pastor of the Hillwood Heights Evangelical Church. But I don't think the Reverend Zebediah Smithson is interested in the shoes of the fisherman."

"Oh, him," Alyce said. "The man who's saving the wrong kind of soles."

Hillwood Heights church was a flat brick building with a stubby white spire. A sign announced the pastor's Sunday sermon: LET WIVES BE SUBJECT TO THEIR HUSBANDS—FOLLOWING GOD'S WORD IN THE MODERN WORLD.

The church's sanctuary was a sunny room with tall windows and light wood. The pastor's office was at the end of a dark hallway that smelled of cooked coffee from countless meetings.

"Good thing this is a church," Alyce said. "Otherwise I wouldn't go down this hall without my pepper spray."

Josie knocked on the office door. "Come in," an orotund voice said.

The pastor was wearing another sober suit and a matching expression. He wasn't handsome, but that somehow made him seem trustworthy.

The Reverend Zebediah Smithson sat behind a big wooden desk, like the Lord's CEO. Josie saw his eyes flick downward to her shoes, and was glad she wore her dullest rich-lady flats. She lowered her eyes modestly and hoped Alyce didn't start giggling. She'd lose it for sure.

"I called you for spiritual advice," Josie said, sitting in one of the visitors' chairs. Alyce glided to the other. "I've brought my friend with me. I prefer she accompany me when I'm going someplace I don't know."

"A woman's virtue is a pearl above price," the pastor said, his voice growing deeper and rounder. "Chaperones have fallen out of favor with the modern woman, but I'm a preacher of the old school. I tell my flock what they need to hear, not what they want to hear. Women's libbers try to stop me, but I know that wives should be subject to their husbands. It says so in the Bible. And a woman's virtue should be protected, for her sake and his."

"Is that why you met a married woman in that nasty motel by the airport?" Josie said.

She heard a sharp intake of breath from Alyce, but she didn't dare look at her friend.

The Reverend Zebediah started choking as if he'd swallowed a peanut down the wrong pipe. His eyes bulged and his face turned a devilish red.

"Whoa, there, Reverend," Josie said, slapping him on his broad worsted back. "I don't want you clocking out on us now, especially since you haven't had time to ask the Lord for forgiveness for your sins."

"I—I committed no sin. It was your evil woman's mind that saw my Lord's work as a sin."

Josie pulled out her camera. "I was there, Reverend. In the parking lot. Would you like me to show your congregation the photos of you entering a motel room with a blonde in red high heels? I think they'd jump to the same conclusions I did. It didn't look like any pastoral counseling session I've ever seen. By the way, where did you get the money to pay that woman?"

"The pastorate's discretionary fund," he gasped. His color had faded from stroke red to flamingo pink.

"Going to motels doesn't show much discretion, Reverend," Josie said. "But I don't care what you were doing with the blonde or her red shoes."

"We watched a movie together," he said. "A PG-13. That's all. I'll swear on the Lord's holy altar."

"I wouldn't want to risk a lightning strike in your church," Josie said. "We passed a TV and a VCR in your fellowship hall. You could have watched the movie there, if it was such a virtuous activity. But you didn't, did you? You wanted to get Mrs. Red Heels off alone. When the Lord said to follow in his footsteps, I don't think that's what he meant."

"I swear—"

"Don't," Josie said. "I don't want to know what happened in that motel room, Reverend. I only need to know one thing: What were you doing the night Mel Poulaine was murdered?"

"You think I'm a killer?" The orotund voice shrank to a sibilant squeak.

"That's what I'm trying to find out," Josie said.

"This is outrageous! You are accusing a servant of the Lord, woman. I don't have to tell you anything."

"No, you don't." Josie held up the camera. "It's me or the church board, Reverend. I'll e-mail them the photos. Your choice."

The Reverend Zebediah was sweating now, just as he had on the afternoon at the motel. "I didn't. I— When was he killed?"

Josie noticed he didn't ask who Mel Poulaine was. Guilty, guilty, guilty. "Last Monday evening, between seven and nine," she said.

The reverend seemed to relax slightly. "I was at the Ladies' Auxiliary meeting from seven until eight in the fellowship hall. Then there was a board meeting in the same place starting at eight. It was supposed to be over at ten thirty, but it became quite heated. We were discussing the contract for the new roof, and one board member thought it should go to his brother-in-law. The meeting lasted until twelve thirty. I have the minutes here. My secretary just typed them."

He rummaged around on his desk and pulled out some typewritten sheets.

"Let me see," Josie said.

"You don't trust me?" he said. Some of the thunder was back in his voice.

"No," Josie said, grabbing the paper out of his hand. She skimmed the minutes, checking the date. It was the right night. Then she found the crucial sentence: "The meeting was called to order at eight o'clock. Present at the meeting were the Reverend Zebediah Smithson . . ."

"You're innocent of this crime, anyway," Josie said. "Go and sin no more."

The Reverend Zebediah bristled, then looked relieved. His color was now a lobster pink.

Josie looked at his red, sweating face. "Better get right with God, Reverend," she said. "I'm not sure you're long for this world."

Alyce didn't say a word. She glided out of the room with her odd, floating walk. She unlocked the SUV in silence. It was only after she pulled out of the parking lot that Alyce and Josie erupted into ungodly howls of laughter.

"I can't believe you told the reverend he wasn't long for this world," Alyce said.

"That guy's going to have a stroke any day now with his stupid sneaking around," Josie said. "Miserable hypocrite. I'm sorry he didn't kill Mel. I'd love to see him sweating in a cell."

"Josie, you're a bigger bluffer than any poker player. You never took a photo of Cheryl and the minister," Alyce said.

"No, I didn't. The Reverend Zebediah was blinded by his guilty conscience," Josie said. "The Lord didn't send him enough enlightenment to ask to see those photos."

Chapter 22

"It's barely noon, and we've already ruined the Reverend Zebediah," Alyce said. "Who do we destroy next?"

"Let's go for a perfect homemaker," Josie said. "Fiona Christie—the woman who took in Ben when Cheryl was on a winning streak."

"Oh, good, we get to see the Christie mailbox again," Alyce said. "I may personally rip off that stray apostrophe."

"And make the world a better place," Josie said.

Except for the errant apostrophe, the Christies' home could have been on a real estate calendar. The paint gleamed, the rubbery zoysia grass was raked, and the windows shone in the cold November sun.

Fiona, the foot fetishist's delight, answered the door wearing a fleece sweat suit and pink flip-flops. Josie thought she had exceptionally small, dainty feet. Each toe was painted shell pink.

A baby was crying, and Fiona had that harassed look peculiar to mothers of toddlers. Josie could see a large entrance hall with crayon scribbles on the wallpaper. A baby gate blocked the pale beige living room, which was two shades darker than Cheryl's showcase. Fiona's signed oil paintings were full-rigged ships. Otherwise, the rooms were identical.

The dining room had a gigantic lighted china cabinet. Josie wondered what those tender toes had done to get it.

"I thought you weren't coming until tomorrow," Fiona said.

Alyce and Josie looked at each other, nonplussed.

"If you give me a moment, I'll collect the rummage sale items from the basement," Fiona said.

"Oh, we're not here for that," Josie said. "We wanted to talk about Mel and his ten little friends."

The color drained from Fiona's face as if someone had pulled a plug. "I don't know what you're talking about." Her voice quavered.

Josie held up her camera. "I have the photos right here," she said.

Fiona never said, "What photos?" Josie feared she might faint on the spot.

"I—I can't tell you. I—I—" she stopped, too frightened to continue.

Josie patted the camera. "I think you better. Unless you want your husband to see these."

"No!" Fiona said.

"Why don't we come in, so you can sit down?" Alyce said, and pushed forward.

Fiona stepped back and the two women were inside. All three automatically headed for the kitchen, where a fat baby was crying herself into a red-faced frenzy in her high chair. A toddler was chewing on something.

"Adam," Fiona said to the toddler, "what do you have?"

Adam said nothing.

"Spit it out," his mother commanded. "Right now."

Adam spit a rubber-coated paper clip into her hand.

"Bad boy," she said.

Adam joined his little sister in a crying chorus. It took soothing talk and animal crackers before both children calmed down. At last, there was silence. Adam began rolling a truck over his animal crackers. The baby drooled contentedly in her padded chair.

"Coffee?" Fiona said, as if she was hosting a kaffeeklatsch.

Josie saw it was ready on the warmer. "Yes, thanks," she said. She watched Fiona carefully, just in case she slipped something into the cups.

"About Mel," Alyce said.

"Please. I don't have much money," Fiona said. Her

voice shook slightly. "We just moved here a year ago. Trip is doing well in the public-relations department at the insurance company, but—"

"We don't want money," Josie said. "We want information. We're looking into Mel's death."

"Are you with the police?" Fiona asked.

"No, we're trying to help Cheryl," Josie said. "We know you were one of three women who worked for Mel, and we know what you did for him."

Fiona blushed scarlet and looked down at her hands. She started chipping the pale pink polish off one nail.

"We're mothers, too," Alyce said. "We'd never tell anyone. We know it could cause problems with your husband. But we need your help. Cheryl needs your help."

Alyce's soft voice and large, calm presence seemed to reassure Fiona. She stopped chipping at her nail. "Cheryl's in trouble, isn't she?"

"Why do you say that?" Josie asked.

"Because Mel was pressuring her into doing something she didn't want to do," Fiona said. "He did that to all of us. He started out saying we wouldn't have to do anything except spend some time with men who appreciated pretty feet. They would pay for our company, just to watch us walk around. We couldn't believe it. But it was true, at first, anyway. We both needed money and it seemed so easy and so harmless.

"But Mel asked us to do a little more each time. Would I wear patent-leather heels? Would I wear fishnet stockings? Garter belt and hose? Ankle-wrap stilettoes?" She stopped, as if afraid to say what she did next.

"Then you worked in his fantasy room," Alyce said. It was the right guess.

"You know about that, too?" Fiona said.

"I was in it," Josie said. "It didn't look so bad."

Fiona looked relieved. Now the words came spilling out. She talked as if her confessional flood would wash away all she'd done. "It wasn't. All we had to do was play customer. Mel wanted us to wear garter belts and stockings, or sometimes plain white cotton underwear."

Josie remembered sitting on that footstool. Mel and

his kinky pals could look right up the women's skirts. Josie wondered if Fiona knew that.

"We pretended we were shopping for shoes," Fiona said. "The men would take turns playing salesman. It was so childish, I couldn't take it seriously. We got paid for our time and we got to keep some of the shoes. All Mel's friends liked the shoe salesman game."

"There were other games?" Josie asked.

"Sometimes we'd play valet parking. We'd have to drive up in front of Mel's house in a car he let us have for the evening. It was always a sports car. Once he used a classic E-type Jaguar from the 1960s. A silver one with a long nose and the most beautiful purr. Another time it was a new red Corvette. Then a black Ferrari."

All low-slung cars, Josie thought. All difficult for women in skirts to crawl out of.

"Mel's friends would pretend to be the valet car parkers. They'd hold the door while we scooted out of the car. They wore khaki uniforms with their names embroidered on the pockets. Mel would tell us what to wear at those, too. Sometimes it was full skirts and white panties. Other times it was tight slit skirts, fishnet stockings and patent-leather heels. Once it was clear plastic shoes, the kind you can see through, with rhinestones on the heels. I hated those. They looked cheap."

"Did Mel have any other requirements?" Josie said.

"All the women had to be blond and wear a size seven shoe. Mel thought that was the perfect size. He said women's feet were getting bigger and bigger. He complained young women's feet looked like skis, they were so huge. I hope I'm not insulting you."

"I wear a size seven," Josie said.

"I wear a ten," Alyce said.

"He also wanted women with no bunions, corns or calluses on their feet. We're hard to find," she said proudly.

Leaves me out, Josie thought. Her toes had been tortured walking the malls.

"I didn't mind the games at all. But then Mel talked me into walking on men. It's called trampling. Sometimes I wore heels. Other times I wore boots. I had a lot of requests for Mary Janes. There was a pair of Joan & David Mary Janes that really drove the men wild. Some wanted me to get rough. I didn't like to hurt the men, but they begged me." She was as wide-eyed as her son.

"And they paid you?" Alyce said.

"Well, yes." She lowered her eyes. "It seemed so silly, but it made them happy. I thought we could stop there, but then Cheryl and I made that video—"

"What video?" Josie said.

"I'm too embarrassed to talk about it," Fiona said. "If my husband found out, he'd kill me. But I wasn't unfaithful. It wasn't a dirty movie. It's not sex. Not sex as we know it, anyway. Cheryl and I refused to do the serious sex stuff. That paid the most. Paladia Henderson-Harrison did that."

"Paladia is the executive?" Josie said.

"Yes. She needed money really bad. She'd made a lot of bad investments. She was going to lose everything: her house, her BMW, her kids' college funds, maybe even her job. She was afraid her children would have to go to public school. Mel's shoe business was the fastest way to recoup her losses. Cheryl and I weren't that desperate. I wanted some nice furniture and Cheryl had a little gambling problem."

"What's serious sex?" Alyce said.

"She actually . . . you know . . . would . . . you know . . . get them excited with her . . . you know . . . toes and then they'd . . . you know."

Josie thought she knew.

"I wouldn't do that," Fiona said righteously. "Cheryl wouldn't, either. But Mel kept making more and more demands and they got stranger and stranger. Cheryl started meeting this preacher in motel rooms to watch shoe movies."

"What are shoe movies?" Josie said.

"There are certain movies that have special appeal to foot freaks. They love *Pretty Woman*—all those scenes of Julia Roberts in high heels and boots. They go crazy every time they see her in the thigh-high patent-leather boots. That Marilyn Monroe movie, *The Seven Year Itch,* where she gets her toe stuck in the bathtub faucet is another secret foot-fetish movie. And old episodes of *Sheena, Queen of the Jungle.*

"The best part for the shoe freaks is it's perfectly acceptable to watch those movies, but they see all sorts of secret stuff regular people don't. Mel's friends also watch lots of MTV. There's a Sheryl Crow video where she wears Mary Janes and then takes them off and goes barefoot. Drives foot freaks crazy."

"So that's why Cheryl was meeting the preacher at the motel," Josie said. "He was watching the shoe-freak special."

"I wouldn't do it," Fiona said. "I was afraid someone I knew would see me going into that horrible motel with another man. There's no way I could explain it. Cheryl said I worried too much. Nobody from West County went to those motels, and if they did, they couldn't talk about it. But her Tom isn't jealous like my husband, Trip. I couldn't risk it.

"Mel's requests were getting odder. I wasn't sure how Cheryl and I were going to get out of this, especially after we made that video. He told us it was for his private enjoyment, but then he found a distributor. He was going to sell it on the Internet and in adult stores. Cheryl and I were so upset. You can't see our faces in the video, not really, but you'd recognize us if you knew us. I wanted to quit right then, but I couldn't. Mel said he'd show Trip the video.

"I don't care if I never get a new sectional sofa," Fiona burst out. "I'm glad Mel is dead. I hope he died slowly and painfully."

There was an uncomfortable silence. Josie, Alyce and Fiona suddenly realized the house was too quiet. The baby was contentedly sucking on a pacifier, but Adam was no longer crushing cookies with his trucks.

"Adam! Where are you?"

Fiona padded off through the first floor on a search. She found the little boy in the guest bathroom. "Get out of that toilet! What are you doing unwinding the toilet paper? Look at that. A whole roll all over the floor. It's time-out for you, Adam. You've been warned."

A whining Adam was plopped on a pint-sized chair in a corner of the kitchen. This set the baby crying.

"I really can't talk anymore," Fiona said.

"Just one more request, then we'll go," Josie said. "We need Paladia's phone number and office address."

Fiona ripped some paper from a pad on the kitchen counter and pulled a pen out of a cup. She thumbed through the phone book, then recited the information while Josie wrote it down.

"We'll find our own way out," Josie said.

"And we promise to keep quiet," Alyce said.

A frantic Fiona could only nod as she struggled to comfort the bawling baby. Adam was peeling the paper off the wall by his time-out chair.

Back in the SUV, Alyce said, "Forget the sectional sofa. I would have spent the money on a nanny. That little guy, Adam, is a terror, and the baby has the lungs of an opera singer."

"It's only one o'clock and we've terrorized two people. Shall we go for three?" Josie asked.

"Better do it today before I lose my nerve," Alyce said.

Josie opened her cell phone and dialed Paladia's number. "Hi," she said. "Fiona gave me your name. I have a little money to invest, and she said you could help me. I know it's short notice, but I'm going to be in Clayton this afternoon and wondered if you could see me for a few minutes? In half an hour? Thank you so much. No, no, I'll have to leave by two o'clock. I have a daughter to pick up at school. I promise I won't take more than half an hour."

Paladia worked in one of those huge glass towers in suburban Clayton. A receptionist showed Josie and Alyce into Paladia's corner office.

Josie looked around at the vast dark desk and the sweeping view of downtown Clayton. Tasteful but dull flower prints lined the wall. Photos of Paladia's children decorated her desk: a dark, skinny teenage boy with an engaging grin and a chunky girl with braces. There was no man in any photo. Paladia's coffee mug said, WORLD'S BEST MOM.

Paladia's office was perfect and perfectly lifeless, a model for any executive.

I could have had an office like this if I'd finished college, Josie thought, and was glad she didn't. It would be like living in a cage. She enjoyed her freedom too much, even if her feet were sore at the end of the day.

Paladia did not seem like the stuff of fetish fantasies. She was a fortyish woman with generous hips, a matronly bosom and short, sensible brown hair. Her dark suit was well cut and professional. Josie sneaked a peek at Paladia's shoes. She wore prim black pumps with two-inch heels. Josie would lose her in any crowd waiting for the elevator. Paladia was Ms. Middle Management.

Suddenly, Josie realized Paladia's attraction. Men who dreamed of doing bizarre and humiliating things to their hated female bosses could take out their fantasies on this woman. Poor Paladia. She earned her money the hard way.

Paladia folded her hands and put on a professional smile. "Now," she said, "how can I help you, ladies?"

"You can tell us about Mel Poulaine," Josie said.

Paladia was smarter and tougher than Fiona and the preacher man. Her face didn't lose color. The only sign that she was under stress was that one eye twitched.

"I don't know who you're talking about," Paladia said.

Josie held up her camera. "Sure you do. I have the photos of you and one of Mel's pals."

"Fine. Let me see them," Paladia said. She was cool as January in Iceland.

"Uh," Josie said. She was caught. This time, her bluff didn't work.

"Exactly what I thought," Paladia said. "There are no photos. I suggest you leave immediately, before I call security."

They left in an embarrassed silence.

Tough woman, Josie decided, and quite capable of murdering Mel.

Chapter 23

"She's guilty," Josie said.

"Of what?" Alyce said.

"I'm not sure," Josie said. "But Paladia didn't act innocent. She never said, 'What photos?' Or 'Why are you threatening me? I'll sue your socks off.' She knew there were no photos. I bet Paladia searched the guys before she had sex with them."

"She probably took the men somewhere she knew was free of cameras," Alyce said. "Someplace where she felt secure. A version of Hal's nest by the airport."

Alyce unlocked her SUV with a little chirp, and Josie climbed up into the big vehicle and settled herself wearily in the soft leather seat. She watched a soda can bounce off their tire. The lot had seemed clean when they parked and rushed in to see Paladia. Now Josie noticed wind-blown plastic bags clinging to the shrubs, small clusters of trash and a broken beer bottle.

Josie felt squirmy-embarrassed over the scene in Paladia's office. She'd learned something from that awful visit, but she didn't know what.

Mostly, she felt sorry for the woman. Paladia was a high-powered executive. What had she done to get herself into such a mess? What did she have to do to get out of it? Josie couldn't imagine being at the mercy of Mel. She could hardly stand to have him touch her foot, much less anything else.

Alyce must have been thinking the same thing. "Paladia had to be desperate to get mixed up with Mel," she said.

A man in a black BMW cut her off in traffic, and Alyce laid on the horn. The Beemer driver laughed.

"She's a woman with a lot to lose," Josie said. "She has a major career with a corner office. Her desk photos showed two nice kids."

"She'd kill for them," Alyce said. "I'd kill anyone who threatened my Justin. If Mel was planning to go public, she'd kill him to keep her kids from becoming laughingstocks at school. Any mother would."

"I don't know," Josie said. "She's tough enough to murder Mel. But why would she? According to Fiona, Paladia was desperate for money. Mel was an easy source. He wasn't going to rat her out. He wanted money and so did she."

Alyce poured on the gas at the next light, whipped in front of the BMW and slammed on her brakes. The Beemer driver stood on his brakes, then screamed something out his window. Josie was glad she didn't know what it was.

"Paladia seemed surprised by our visit," Alyce said.

"Yeah. Her eye twitched," Josie said. "That's equal to shrieking and leaping into the air for ordinary humans."

"You'd think Fiona would have warned her about us," Alyce said. She was now driving sedately toward Josie's home in Maplewood.

"The queen of denial? Fiona is too busy pretending she didn't really have sex with Mel and his freaky friends."

"That's the other thing that got me," Alyce said. "Mel convinced Fiona that prancing around in high heels wasn't really sex. How did he do that?"

"He was one heck of a salesman, God rest his soul," Josie said. "His housekeeper was right about that part. That's how he trapped those women. He listened to them when they tried on shoes. He knew they were lonely. He could tell who needed money and how desperate they were."

"How did he find the male clients?" Alyce said.

"Probably the same way you find any freak these days," Josie said. "On the Internet."

"Wish we could find Mel's killer that way," Alyce

said. "Which woman do you think murdered Mel—Cheryl, Fiona or Paladia?"

"Any one of them could have done it," Josie said. "They're all about the same height, nearly as tall as Mel. They're all strong. Fiona may look delicate, but she lugs those heavy babies around. Ditto for Cheryl. Paladia has arms like a weight lifter under that tailored suit.

"They all had good motives. Fiona said they wanted to leave but Mel wouldn't let them. They made an embarrassing video for what they thought was his private use, then Mel double-crossed them and wanted to give it wide distribution. I'd kill him for that alone."

"Maybe all three of them did it, like that movie *Murder on the Orient Express,*" Alyce said.

"Maybe it wasn't any of them," Josie said. "Fiona said if her husband knew about that foot video, he would kill her. What if he killed Mel, instead?"

"Hmm. Possible. I like it, actually," Alyce said. "His name's Trip, right? What insurance company does Fiona's husband work for?"

"Probably this one," Josie said. She held up a green plastic pen with a company name printed on it.

"You stole that from Fiona?" Alyce asked.

"Not on purpose," Josie said. "Pens stick to my fingers."

"What are we going to do next?" Alyce said. "Go to his office and ask Trip if he knows his wife works for a foot-fetish ring? He'd divorce her in a heartbeat. She doesn't deserve that. Neither do her kids. We can't ruin a woman because she wanted a china cabinet."

"I'm not going to ask Trip directly," Josie said. "Give me some credit. I want to test him. Drop a few hints. See by his reaction if he knows what his wife has been doing."

"Just how are you going to do that?" Alyce said.

"I'm going to do a little soliciting myself," Josie said.

Josie was home before her mother picked up Amelia at school. She had at least an hour to herself, an unexpected luxury for a mom. She wrote her mystery-shopping reports and faxed them to Suttin. Then she fired up her computer and created a letterhead for a bogus charity she called Extraordinary Addictions: "Helping ordinary people with extraordinary problems."

You gotta love computers, Josie thought. In the old days, I'd have to pay a printer to make this stationery. Now I can design my own in two minutes.

Josie also wrote up a mission statement for her make-believe organization, six letters of recommendation from prominent St. Louisans, including Senator Harry Palmidge. She added a few case histories and a pretty decent brochure. It was a simple black-and-white trifold on plain white paper. Josie thought the charity shouldn't seem too rich or too slick.

She made some business cards for Harriet Hilliard Nelson, then popped the packet into one of Amelia's double-pocket school folders. She chose a dignified dark blue.

After Josie admired her handiwork, she made a phone call, then dialed Alyce. "I have an appointment to see Fiona's husband, Trip, at ten in the morning," she said. "I've put together a letterhead and mission statement on my home computer. I doubt he'll ever look at our information packet, but I'm prepared. I hope it was okay to put you on the board of directors."

"Is this one of those boards that pays its directors half a million a year?" Alyce said.

"No, I'm sorry to say," Josie said.

"Figures," Alyce said. "That's the kind I always get."

"Can I try out my pitch on your husband?" Josie said.

"Jake? Sure, as long as you don't tell him what we're doing," Alyce said. "He thinks I've been mystery-shopping with you."

"Of course not." Josie was glad she didn't have to answer to a husband. Her mother was bad enough. "I'll tell Jake it's a real organization and I need a corporate type to hear my pitch."

"Call him at work," Alyce said. "He should be in all afternoon. But be careful. He sounds half asleep, but he's got a mind like a bear trap."

Jake treated Josie with the same respect as a million-dollar client. "Sure, I'll listen," he said. "Try me right now."

Josie liked his voice. It was smooth without being oily.
She read her prepared pitch. The deeper Josie got into
it, the stupider it sounded. What was she thinking? She
stumbled a bit toward the end, then finally finished. Now
he's going to tell me what's wrong and I'll feel like an
idiot.

"Sounds good to me," Jake said. "Very sincere. That's
important. Just one point I can think of. Whoever you're
pitching to will ask if you're 501(c)(3). He'll want to
know if his company can get a tax write-off. I'm assuming you are or you wouldn't be doing this."

"Right," Josie lied.

"Also, ask him if there are any grants for community outreach."

"Outreach," Josie repeated. She could make good use
of that word.

The next morning, Josie and Alyce showed up at Trip
Christie's insurance office in Clayton. Josie did the driving in her car. She figured it was safe. They weren't
going near Cheryl.

Trip turned out to be two streets away from Paladia's
building. Josie prayed they wouldn't meet the outraged
executive. When a matron in a dark suit got off the
lobby elevator, Josie stepped behind a pillar until she
was sure the woman wasn't Paladia.

"What's the matter with you?" Alyce said. "You're
so jumpy."

"I'm afraid we'll run into Paladia," she said.

"We can do her more damage than she can do us,"
Alyce said.

"You didn't notice those arms," Josie said.

They were dressed for their own form of success. Both
wore their suburban-clubwoman outfits. Alyce's was
real. Josie's was a disguise, put together from sale racks
and secondhand stores. She hoped she'd pass, sitting
next to the genuine article.

Trip's assistant took them straight into his office. It
wasn't as high up as Paladia's, and the view had more
parking lot than skyline. Trip was about thirty-five and
had "good provider" written all over him—pink skin,

power tie, pudgy little gut. His brown hair was thinning, and he combed it over, which Josie thought looked more pathetic than honest baldness. Trip might have been handsome before he put on weight and lost his hair. Josie wondered if it helped his career to lose his looks.

Trip's walls were covered with plaques and certificates of appreciation. He kept a framed photo of Fiona and their two blond babies on his desk, but the picture wasn't where he could see his photogenic family. It faced the guest chairs. Josie found it unnerving to make this pitch with Fiona smiling at her. She was glad Fiona's shoes didn't show in the photo.

"Call me Trip," he said, when he shook hands with them. His handshake was firm, but he didn't feel the need for a macho bone-crushing grip.

"I'm Harriet Hilliard Nelson," Josie said. "This is my associate, Betty Joan Perske." She felt Alyce give a little jump at that introduction.

"Your company has a reputation for being very generous to our community," Josie said.

"We think your sponsorship of our program will help you reach your target audience of upper-income West County adults," Alyce said. With her legs crossed at the ankles and her manicured hands folded in her lap, she seemed a model of that very audience.

Trip relaxed on his padded executive throne. He was familiar with these women and their words. "Can you tell me about your goals and mission statement?" he said.

"Extraordinary Addictions is a community outreach program to help ordinary women with extraordinary problems," Josie said. "We find that many naive women can get themselves into trouble and into various addictions, then are too embarrassed to seek help."

"We are aimed at the upper-middle and middle-class suburban woman," Alyce said in her undeniably upper drawl. "We find these women are often overlooked by programs which cater to the underprivileged. Our goal is to help these women recover and resume productive and useful lives."

"What kinds of addictions do you deal with?" Trip said. "We don't fund AIDS programs or drug rehabilitation."

"Oh, no," Josie said. "There are many excellent organizations to take care of those people. We serve other needs, often unrecognized. For instance, we have a program to help women who are involved with foot fetishists."

Trip turned beet red all the way up and over his extended hairline.

Bingo! Josie thought. He knows about his wife. "It's a big problem in West County," Josie said, widening her eyes and trying to sound as sincere as possible. "We have photographs we can show you."

"Photographs," he repeated. Steam seemed to come out his ears.

"Yes," Josie said. "To help you understand the importance of this need."

"Let me guess," Trip said through gritted teeth. "You're looking for a special outreach grant. How much do you want? For your . . . charity." His anger was scathing.

Josie could feel Alyce tense beside her. "Fifty thousand dollars," Josie said.

"And would this be a one-time grant?" Trip could barely keep his temper under control. Josie thought he might start shouting.

"Ongoing," Josie said and swallowed. "Renewable annually."

"I'll. Get. Back. With. You." Trip bit off each word. "I think you'd better leave now. So I can consider your proposal."

Tension flickered through the room like lightning. Josie stood up, feeling wobbly.

"Thank you," Alyce said sweetly.

She took Josie by the elbow and practically threw her out the door.

Chapter 24

"He knows," Josie said, when she flopped into her car. "Trip knows what his sweet little wife is up to." Her clothes were damp with fear sweat. She wanted to get away. She was weaving quickly in and out of the downtown Clayton streets, trying to put as much distance as possible between them and Trip.

"He thinks we're trying to blackmail him," Alyce said. "I feel really slimy."

"You shouldn't. I wanted him to think that," Josie said. "It was the only way I could get him to admit it, unless I asked him straight out about his wife and that wouldn't do any good. He'd deny it. We aren't the cops. We can't make him answer our questions."

"I wish we were," Alyce said. "Cops have guns. That man would have killed us both if his assistant wasn't next door. What are you going to do when he calls you?"

Josie ran a red light to angry honks and upthrust fingers. Now she wished they were in Alyce's tanklike SUV. Josie's Honda seemed much smaller and more fragile. She checked the rearview mirror. No traffic-cop lights. Any passenger but Alyce would have protested her reckless driving.

"He can't," Josie said. "I made up all the phone numbers and addresses in that packet. He doesn't even know my real name."

"You put my name on the fake board of directors," Alyce said. "This is a mess. How am I going to explain it to Jake? What if a crazed Trip kicks down our door?"

Josie was going fifty in a thirty-mile zone. They were

going to be arrested for sure if she didn't slow down. Worse, she'd taken them way off course. What was she doing on McKnight Road?

"Trip won't do that. Besides, I didn't use your real name," Josie said. "You're on the stationery as Betty Joan Perske, the same name I gave when I introduced you. I wish you'd relax. There's nothing to connect us to this."

"Except Fiona," Alyce said.

Josie made an illegal U-turn and headed toward Highway 40. If she was going to drive that fast, she'd do better on the highway than wandering residential back roads. "Do you really think Fiona will tell her husband how she got that china cabinet?" she said. "She'll go to her grave keeping that quiet. She's certainly not going to discuss our visit to her house."

"What about Mr. Wonderful?" Alyce said. "What if Trip goes home and takes it out on her?"

"I wouldn't worry," Josie said. "He's no wife beater. Fiona wasn't wearing any cover-up makeup. We'd have seen bruises on that fair skin."

"A divorce might hurt her more," Alyce said.

Josie didn't think that deserved a comment. Alyce just said it because she was upset.

"I was careful to never mention Fiona's name," Josie said. "Trip won't have to face the truth if he doesn't want to—and believe me, he doesn't. When he doesn't hear from us, and there's no demand for money, he'll convince himself we were a couple of crackpots. He won't say anything to his wife. He'd have to take down that pretty blond picture on his desk. It would be bad for business."

"You're so cynical," Alyce said.

"I'm a realist. Trip and Fiona are experts at pretending nothing is wrong. I bet they'd kill anyone who tried to open their eyes."

Josie skimmed through a yellow light and turned onto Highway 40. That was a mistake. There was a four-car accident just past the McKnight exit. A delivery truck and two cars blocked all the eastbound traffic lanes. One car had flipped and landed in the oncoming traffic. From

the number of lights and sirens, the crash had to be
serious.

"We're stuck," Josie said. "The highway is a parking
lot. I can't go forward or back."

Considering the way I've been driving, maybe that
wasn't such a bad thing, Josie decided. She needed time
to calm down. Both women opened their cell phones
and called their homes. Jane didn't answer. Alyce talked
to the nanny about Justin's cough, which was definitely
getting better. They were trapped in the traffic almost
forty-five minutes while the ambulances and fire trucks
arrived, and the tow trucks cleared the smoking wreckage. Car parts were scattered across six lanes.

"I should have taken the side streets," Josie said.

"If you did that, the accident would have blocked
Manchester Road instead of the highway." Alyce took
traffic tie-ups personally. "Who's Betty Joan Perske?"

"Huh?" Josie said.

"The name you introduced me as in Trip's office.
Where did you get it? Is she someone you went to high
school with?"

"I wish. That's Lauren Bacall's original name," Josie
said.

"Good thing Trip isn't a movie buff. Who's Harriet
Hilliard Nelson?" Alyce said. "Sounds like a state
representative."

"She's the Harriet of *Ozzie and Harriet,* that old 1950s
TV show. It was my mom's favorite sitcom. I put Harriet
and Betty both on the fake letterhead. I gave you the
better name. You got the bombshell. I got the boring
housewife."

"I'm due for some excitement," Alyce said.

Traffic was moving now. "Finally, we're off the highway," Josie said. "I can't believe we sat for almost an
hour. I can practically see my house from here. We could
have walked home faster."

"You must be really rattled by Trip," Alyce said. "I'm
usually the one who complains about the traffic."

"He doesn't scare me," Josie said. "I'm used to men
like Trip. I've dealt with hundreds of them in my mystery-
shopping job. They're the petty department heads and

store managers who bluster and threaten Suttin Services, swearing their stores could not possibly have been as disorganized and dirty as I said in my report. You face them down and they melt like snow on a sunny day."

Alyce seemed to be relaxing now. Josie wanted to say that Trip would never come after them. But she wasn't sure. Had Trip killed Mel? He had a temper and a lot of hidden anger. If Mel made the man confront the ugly realities of his marriage, Trip could be dangerous indeed.

Finally, Josie reached her Maplewood street. She thought it looked like Mayberry this afternoon. An older woman was trundling a wire handcart full of groceries. Kids' bicycles were neatly parked by the porches, waiting for their riders to come home from school. Kitchen curtains were starched, concrete steps were scrubbed, shutters seemed freshly painted.

Alyce's elephant of an SUV was parked outside Josie's home. Her mother still wasn't home. Amelia was at school. Even Mrs. Mueller's curtains weren't twitching.

"You want to come in for coffee?" Josie said.

"Maybe just a cup," Alyce said. "Let the accident traffic die down a bit."

As they approached Josie's home, they saw a box on the front porch. Damn, Josie thought. Mom's ordering things from the Home Shopping Network again. A hot bolt of anger shot through her. Jane had promised she'd stop. Then Josie felt sad. Her mother had been doing so well since she started seeing her counselor. The pressure of dealing with Mrs. Mueller had caused this. Mom was allowed a setback.

"Hey, it's for you," Alyce said.

The box, wrapped in plain brown paper, was addressed TO JOSIE MARCUS in neat block letters.

"What do you think it is?" Alyce said.

"I don't know," Josie said. "I didn't order anything. At least, I don't think I did. It's a surprise."

She carried it into the kitchen, set it on the table and started the coffee.

Alyce shook the box. "Hurry up," she said. "It sounds interesting. I want to see what's inside."

Josie ripped off the brown paper. Inside was a shiny pink Soft Shoe box.

Alyce squinted at the shoe size printed on the box. "Seven," she said. "Too small for me. My feet got bigger during my pregnancy."

"Seven is definitely my size. Maybe it's a bonus," Josie said. "I wonder which style it is. I've tried on practically every size seven in the store. I never saw a pair I didn't like."

Josie had that Christmas-morning feeling as she lifted the lid. She loved good shoes. Inside was a cloud of pink tissue paper. Josie lifted one side to reveal a high-heeled black suede evening sandal.

"Wow," Josie said.

Alyce whistled. "Sexy," she said. "You'll look hot in those on your date with Josh." She peered closer at the shoe. "Look. It's fur-lined. That's really kinky."

"Kind of ratty-looking fur." Josie lifted the rest of the paper for a closer inspection. The fur was ratty indeed. Curled inside the left sandal was a dead rat. It had evil red eyes and long yellow teeth.

Josie dropped the box and the rat rolled out onto her kitchen table, landing in the bowl of apples. Alyce ran for the john, retching.

"Omigod," Josie said. "Someone's sending me a message. Like in *The Godfather*."

"I'd take a horse's head in my bed over a dead rat on my table," Alyce said in a shaky voice. She looked nearly green when she emerged from the bathroom.

Josie pulled the wastebasket over to the table and used the crumb brush to sweep the rat and the shoes into the trash. Then she threw away the brush. She found a pair of tongs in the kitchen drawer and used them to pick up the wrapping paper and the shoe box. Then she tossed in the tongs, along with the apples and the bowl.

"Ugh. Yuck. Ick," Josie said. She had goose bumps.

"Are you saving that bag of evidence for the police?" Alyce asked.

"Evidence of what? It's not against the law to send someone a dead rat and a new pair of shoes. Besides, what would I tell the cops? I've been messing in their murder investigation. They wouldn't appreciate it."

"They should at least see it for themselves," Alyce said.

"There's nothing to show them," Josie said. "There's no note. My name was printed in capitals with a cheap pen. The package wasn't sent by mail or a delivery service. I want this mess out of my house and out of my life."

Josie carried the rat bag outside and threw it in Mrs. Mueller's trash can. The old busybody deserved it. The curtains still weren't moving at Mrs. M's window. Where was she?

That woman spied on me for more than fifteen years, Josie thought. The one time I wanted her to watch my house, she wasn't home. There's never a snoop around when you need one.

She found Alyce huddled by the kitchen door, halfway outside. "Josie, what if that rat had fleas? It's not a lab animal. It's a nasty old city rat. How did it die? I didn't see any marks on it. Do you think that rat died of natural causes?"

"It could have had some disease," Josie said. She scrubbed her hands in hot water and soap until they were red and raw.

Alyce and Josie put on rubber gloves and washed the kitchen table with Lysol, then threw away their rags. They wiped everything with Windex next, and threw away those rags. They used bleach for the third treatment. They could perform brain surgery on that table, it was so clean.

Next they scrubbed down the chairs, cabinets and appliances with Lysol. They mopped the floor twice. Josie threw the kitchen curtains in the washer, along with all the dish towels and pot holders. Every time she thought of that rat on her table, she wanted to gag.

When Alyce and Josie finished cleaning, the kitchen gleamed like a floor wax commercial. But they couldn't bring themselves to drink coffee at the rat table.

"Let's go sit in the living room," Josie said. She still saw the rat's long yellow teeth.

Alyce looked relieved to be out of the ratless kitchen. "Who do you think sent it?"

"Cheryl," Josie said. "She goes to sleazy motels. I bet she found a dead rat in a parking lot and did this on the spur of the moment. She has plenty of shoes and Soft Shoe boxes. She knows where I live."

"Fiona has shoes, too," Alyce said. "She must feel just as threatened."

"I can't see Fiona loading two kids into the car, hunting for a dead rat, then driving all the way here."

"What about Paladia? She threw us out of her office," Alyce said.

"She's my second choice," Josie said. "Clayton is a city. There are always rats around. Maybe she found a dead one in her office parking lot and decided to scare me."

"How'd she get your address?" Alyce said.

"Can't be too difficult," Josie said. "She could call Cheryl."

"It could be Fiona's husband, Trip," Alyce said. "He looked ready to strangle us. He'd have time to get here, too. We got stuck in traffic. He could have taken the side roads and beat you home."

"It's possible," Josie said. "Although I'm not sure how he'd know my address."

"He's in the insurance business," Alyce said. "He could get someone to run your license plate easy enough. His office window overlooked the parking lot. He could have written it down when we left."

Josie didn't like what Alyce said, but she knew it could be true. She wasn't as smart as she thought. Trip could have gotten her license plate.

"There's one good thing about this rat," Josie said. "Somebody's upset. That means we're making progress. I wish I knew what it was."

"It means the killer knows where you live," Alyce said.

Chapter 25

"How can you say that?" Josie said. She slammed her cup down on the end table so hard hot coffee sloshed on the wood. A dark brown pool spread across the table and dripped onto the carpet.

"How do you know the killer left that rat? It's bad enough I found a diseased rodent in my house without my best friend acting like a—" Josie stopped suddenly.

"A rat?" Alyce raised one eyebrow.

"A fraidy cat," Josie finished. She knew it was the wrong word. So did Alyce.

"Are you mad at me or mad at what happened?" Alyce asked.

"I—I don't know," Josie said.

"Let's get you another cup of coffee," Alyce said. "Then we'll talk like the friends we are."

Josie stood up. "I should wipe up the mess on the end table. It will ruin the finish."

"No, you sit right there. You've had a bad shock." Alyce came back with a fresh cup of coffee for Josie. Then she mopped up the mess. Josie found it oddly soothing to watch her. Alyce was a good housewife, in the old sense of the word, a woman who could run a household. She knew how to restore the table's finish and get the stain out of the carpet.

"There," she said. "I think it will be okay." Alyce went to the kitchen for a fresh cup for herself, then sat down opposite Josie.

"I'm not trying to scare you," she said. "I'm trying to make you see what we've done. We've intruded into the lives of six people—three men and three women. Some of them are very well connected. We've discovered their deepest secrets. We've learned something important, but we're too dumb to know what it is. How can we? We're not police officers. We're blundering around in the dark. No, it's worse than that. We're running across a minefield on a moonless night. Something is bound to blow up in our faces."

"It's nice of you to say 'we,' " Josie said. "I'm the one who got us into this. I don't know how it got so out of control. All I had to do was follow Cheryl for three days so Mom could get her precious flower committee."

"It's just a committee," Alyce said. "I can get her on a hundred."

"She's wanted this one all her life. I want Mom to be happy," Josie said.

"How happy will she be if you're dead?"

"Nobody's going to kill me," Josie said.

"Someone sent you a dead rat," Alyce said. "Don't you get it?"

"It's not a death threat," Josie said. "Besides, the so-called secret isn't that bad. So what if Cheryl and Fiona played footsies with some guys? They don't even consider it real sex."

"A man was murdered," Alyce said. "He paid them lots of money. Cheryl had more cash than most people make in a year stuffed in her closet. That's a good reason to kill. And what about Paladia? Who knows what she did for Mel. This is St. Louis, not San Francisco. People are very conservative here. They have more to lose.

"Hal is so embarrassed he'll probably never look at me again. He's terrified we'll tell his wife. And don't forget Trip, Fiona's husband. He could have killed Mel because the man tormented his wife."

"That's five people," Josie said. "Who's the sixth?"

"The Reverend Zebediah. He paid a prostitute out of church funds."

"He was at a church meeting the night Mel was murdered," Josie said. "He's cleared."

"He could have stepped out for half an hour between

the Ladies' Auxiliary and the board meeting," Alyce said. "No one would miss him in the confusion. For that matter, who typed those minutes? Maybe he made them up as an alibi."

"Look, I know we stepped on a lot of toes—" Josie said.

"Puns like that hurt," Alyce said.

"I didn't mean it that way," Josie said. "But if someone wants me dead, there are plenty of chances to kill me. I was at the mall. They could have run me down in a parking lot. They could have put a bomb in that shoe box instead of a rat. They didn't. They just want me to stop investigating."

"You will, won't you?" Alyce said.

"Yes. No. It depends on Mrs. Mueller. I'm no coward," Josie said.

"I never said you were. You have to think about your mother and your daughter," Alyce said. "They could be in danger. Why don't you three stay with me until the police make an arrest?"

"They may never make an arrest," Josie said. "What am I supposed to do then? Move in with you? I can take care of myself. I have good locks on the doors and pepper spray by my bedside."

"You don't have an alarm system," Alyce said.

"Yes, I do," Josie said.

"Show me the keypad."

"I don't have a keypad. It's an analog system," Josie said. "Follow me." Josie headed for the kitchen. The cleaning fumes hit them like a slap. Josie opened the basement door, and a musty smell boiled up from the stairway. It was almost refreshing after the Lysol and Windex.

Josie pulled on a string. The single lightbulb showed a set of battleship gray stairs. The two women clip-clopped down the wooden steps. The basement had white-stone-and-concrete walls and a cement floor, like many old homes in the area. There was a washer-dryer, boxes of baby clothes and Christmas decorations, and an overhead clothesline. The windowsills were lined with dead geraniums in clay pots and aluminum pie pans.

"That's my home alarm system," Josie said, pointing

to the windows. "Those pie pans would make a heck of a racket if anyone tried to open the basement windows. When I lock up for the night, I put these at the top of the stairs, propped against the door." She held up four battered pots and an ancient turkey roaster.

"Plus, I have these in front of all the doors." She held up a sturdy metal folding chair. "Guaranteed to trip any intruder."

"Josie, that's not an alarm system," Alyce said.

"It is. It's as old as the city and nearly fail-safe."

"Sure it is," Alyce said. "That's why they sell your system in the Yellow Pages."

"Modern burglars can override keypads, but they don't know to look for my system. My pots, pans and chairs will catch them by surprise. They can't cut the phone wires on this. My system will never have a power failure. I admit I don't use it much, but I'll activate it tonight. I promise."

"Have it your way," Alyce said and sighed. But Josie could see she was only half convinced. "Are we going to follow Cheryl tomorrow?"

Josie headed back up the basement steps and Alyce followed. At the top, she put the pots on the top step, turned out the lights and locked the door. "I don't know," Josie said. "I need to see if Mrs. Mueller wants to spend any more time and money on this."

"Has that old bat paid you yet?"

"Not a dime," Josie said. "Not even the fifty-five dollars she owes me for the babysitter. Can I get you more coffee?"

"No, thanks. I have to get home. You should get some money from that woman before you do any more work," Alyce said. "She won't appreciate you otherwise."

"Good idea," Josie said. "I keep thinking about what I'm doing for Mom and forget what's in it for me."

"I swear, you need an agent. Or a keeper. I bet you haven't thought about this, either," Alyce said. "We've followed Cheryl all over the metro area. We've seen her gambling and meeting men in motels and strange apartments."

"Yep," Josie said. "So?"

"If we're doing this, the police probably are, too," Alyce said. "The cops have already taken her in for questioning, arrested her on some trumped-up charge to get her fingerprints, and searched her house for a murder weapon. Cheryl has to be a serious suspect. What do you bet the police are tailing her?"

"I didn't notice a tail," Josie said.

"If they were any good, you wouldn't. We didn't follow her every minute. How do we know the police aren't watching her right now?"

"They may not have to," Josie said. "All the cops have to do is get her cell phone records. Cheryl's whole life is in those numbers. They'll find the shoe freaks, the babysitter, the friend who picks up the baby at Bonnie's."

"Everything but the casinos," Alyce said. "She doesn't call them."

"I don't know if the cops are following her or not, but there's no point in us tailing Cheryl for another day," Josie said. "We know where she goes. It may be a different man or another casino, but it's the same old thing."

"Cheryl's wild life is duller than my domestic one," Alyce said.

"Her mother won't think so. Mrs. Mueller will faint dead away when she finds out. You know what the hardest part of this job is? Figuring out how much to tell Cheryl's mother."

"Why not tell her everything?" Alyce said. "That's why she's paying you."

"I can't do it," Josie said. "Mrs. Mueller is a mean old witch, but I still can't break her heart."

"She doesn't have one," Alyce said.

"She does when it comes to Cheryl. Her mantel is a shrine to her daughter. She worships Cheryl."

"Don't you think she'd rather hear it from you than the police?" Alyce said. "Isn't that why she really hired you? Mrs. Mueller doesn't like you. She never has. She wants you to tell her what she doesn't want to hear—so she can keep on hating you."

Chapter 26

Might as well give Mrs. Mueller a good reason to hate me, Josie thought. Alyce is right. I'll tell her everything about Cheryl. But if she doesn't like it, she's not killing this messenger.

Josie waved good-bye to Alyce from the porch, then went inside and called Mrs. Mueller. There was no answer. Mrs. Mueller's voice mail ordered Josie to leave a message and she obeyed.

Josie had another hour before her mother came home with Amelia. She cleaned the house so her mother wouldn't wonder why the kitchen smelled like a pine forest and the rest of the flat was closer to an old gym shoe.

By the time Jane came home with Amelia at three thirty, Josie's flat was a welter of lemon polish, floor wax, cleanser and ammonia.

"Pee-yew," her daughter said. "Gross. What have you been doing, Mom?"

Josie was slightly put out that Amelia didn't recognize the perfume of household cleaning products.

Jane, still in her Stepford Mom role, smiled like her heroine, Harriet Hilliard Nelson. "The house looks lovely, dear, so fresh and clean," she said. "You must be exhausted. I have a nice pot roast for your dinner, with new potatoes, baby carrots and little peas."

"Sounds like you invaded a nursery," Josie said, then caught her mother's hurt look.

"GBH," Josie said, and gave her mother a hug. "I'm thrilled you're fixing me dinner again."

Jane put on her ruffled apron. Josie wished she
wouldn't. It made her nervous. She wanted her old life
back. She wanted to spend her days at the malls, then
pick up her daughter at school. She missed her conversations in the car with Amelia.

She missed her mother, for that matter. Lately, Jane
did seem like a robot sometimes. On the other hand,
the pot roast was fork tender and the carrots and potatoes roasted just the way Josie liked. The lemon meringue pie was nearly six inches tall and lightly browned
on top.

Best of all, the good cooking smells wiped away all
memory of the yellow-toothed rat. Well, almost all.

"Didn't we used to have some apples on the table?"
Amelia said.

"I ate them," Josie lied.

"Mom, that was a dozen apples."

"An apple a day keeps the doctor away," Josie said.
"I'm almost two weeks ahead."

"Oh, Mom, I can't get a sensible conversation out of
you," Amelia said.

"Dessert, my dears." Jane carried the massive pie like
a glass sculpture. The meringue wobbled slightly.

"Yum," Amelia said.

The phone rang. For once, Josie beat her mother and
her daughter to the phone, and the call was actually for
her. Josie recognized the voice instantly. The hysteria
was new.

"Cheryl has been arrested," Mrs. Mueller said. "You
were supposed to help her, Josie Marcus. Now my little
girl is in jail and it's all your fault."

"What?" Josie said.

"You heard me," Mrs. Mueller screamed into the
phone. "Cheryl's been arrested. Quit standing there like
an idiot and do something."

How did she know I was standing? Josie wondered.
"I'll be right over," she said, and hung up the phone.

"What's wrong?" Jane placed the pie carefully on the
table, as if she couldn't trust herself to hold it in the
event of bad news.

"Cheryl's been arrested," Josie said. "I'm going next door to Mrs. Mueller's."

"I should go with you," Jane said, untying her apron.

"No, stay here with Amelia, Mom. Mrs. Mueller will talk more freely around me."

That was the polite way to put it, Josie thought, as she threw on her jacket. Mrs. Mueller never saved her words, especially the harsh ones.

It was a cold night and Josie shivered as she crunched across the frost-slick grass. She was giving up fresh pie and coffee for a tongue-lashing from Mrs. Mueller. If that old biddy didn't come through with Jane's committees, Josie would take her apart bone by brittle bone.

Mrs. Mueller was waiting at the front door. Josie didn't even have to knock.

"Come in. We can't waste time," she said, and led Josie to her kitchen. Josie liked the ancient Mixmaster and the Magic Chef stove, which must have been purchased when Mrs. M was a bride.

"Sit," Mrs. Mueller said.

Josie sat at the heavy oak table. Mrs. Mueller had a coffee cup at her place, but she didn't offer Josie any.

Mrs. Mueller paced. She was angry, but Josie couldn't tell who or what put her in that state.

"What happened? Why did they arrest Cheryl?" Josie said.

"The police found her shoes," Mrs. Mueller said. Pace. Pace.

"What shoes?" Josie said. Cheryl had tons of shoes. This wasn't making any sense.

"Cheryl's Bruno Maglis. They have her DNA inside the shoes, so the police know she wore them. His blood is on the soles—that Mel person. The police are saying Cheryl killed him."

Mrs. Mueller was pacing faster now, growing so agitated Josie thought she might wear a hole in the linoleum.

"Where did the police get the shoes? I thought they'd already searched her house," Josie said.

"They did. The police say they found these shoes at

some sort of love nest. They got a search warrant. They say my Cheryl went there with a married man. She didn't."

She did, Josie thought. Should I tell her mother about the closet full of shoes? Mrs. Mueller might be happier with garden-variety adultery.

"Um, was the apartment out by the airport?" Josie said.

"Yes," Mrs. Mueller said. She stopped pacing and stared at Josie. "How did you know?"

"I followed Cheryl there," Josie said.

Mrs. Mueller shut her mouth like a trap and went back to pacing. She knows, Josie thought, but she doesn't want to.

"Tell me about the bloody shoes," Josie said.

Pace. Pace. Pace. "The police did some sort of test on the floor at that Mel person's house and some shoe prints showed up."

"Luminol, probably," Josie said. She was a big *CSI* fan. Mrs. Mueller's words hit her. Cheryl had walked in the dead man's blood. Josie's stomach lurched. This was wretched. Had some kinky game gone wrong?

Josie realized Mrs. Mueller was still pacing and talking. "Someone tried to wipe up the bloody shoe prints with Windex," Mrs. M said. "The prints weren't visible to the naked eye, but they showed up faintly after this test."

"And Cheryl's shoes matched the ones in the prints," Josie said.

"It doesn't work that way," Mrs. Mueller said. "The prints aren't all nice and clear, like on *CSI*. But they found Mel's blood on her soul."

Josie almost said, "How can they do that?" when she realized Mrs. Mueller meant "sole" as in "shoe sole."

"They also found a partial bloody shoe print under the body. They're saying Cheryl rolled the body over, then put it back, and that's how her shoe print got under it."

"Oh, boy," Josie said.

"She didn't kill him," Mrs. Mueller said fiercely. She stood her ground and faced Josie. "She didn't do the other things they say, either. Cheryl swears she was never unfaithful to Tom."

Depends on your definition of adultery, Josie thought. She couldn't imagine standing at the altar and promising to "love, honor and never walk on another man till death do us part."

"But she's changed her story a little," Mrs. Mueller said. "My Cheryl didn't lie to the police. Not really. But she did hold back a little bit of information. Cheryl admits she was at that Mel person's house. She had a glass of wine and she passed out. She wasn't drunk. Cheryl wouldn't get drunk. She thinks he drugged her wine.

"When she woke up, Mel was lying at the foot of the steps in a pool of blood. She ran over to him. That awful man was dead. She checked to make sure. That must have been when her shoe print got under his body. Cheryl must have stepped in his blood."

Josie saw Mel in the shoe store, with his jaunty boutonniere, then imagined stepping in his blood wearing $250 shoes.

"There was blood everywhere," Mrs. Mueller said. "Head wounds bleed a lot. Cheryl admits she tracked some blood on the hall floor. She noticed her bloody shoe prints, went out to the kitchen and found some Windex to wipe them up. She took the wineglasses to the sink, emptied and rinsed them. But she left a partial print on one. The police found traces of some sleeping drug in one glass. That proves she was telling the truth, doesn't it?"

"Maybe," Josie said. "They could also say that Cheryl drugged Mel, then killed him. What does Cheryl say happened next?"

"She got out of there. She couldn't help Mel. He was definitely dead. She was afraid. She ran. I know it looks bad, but she wasn't thinking clearly," Mrs. Mueller said. "She was woozy from the drugs. She was a married woman alone in a man's house."

A dead man's house. "What was she doing there in the first place?" Josie said.

"She won't tell me," Mrs. Mueller said. "But her reaction was perfectly natural. She was confused. She saw all that blood and panicked."

A panicked woman wouldn't stop to rinse the wineglasses and scrub the floor. She'd run as fast as she could. Head wounds do bleed a lot, but only if the person is alive, Josie thought. Did Cheryl abandon a dying man? Did she watch him bleed out? She didn't bother calling 911 to give an anonymous tip.

At best, she was coldhearted. To Josie, she sounded guilty.

"You've got to find out what really happened," Mrs. Mueller said. "There's more to her story, but she won't tell it to me. You've got to help her. I'm begging you. I'll double your pay. I know my little girl is innocent."

Chapter 27

Josie winced when she saw the morning paper. Even Cheryl didn't deserve this headline:

HOUSEWIFE HOOKER: POLICE SAY DESPERATE HOUSEWIFE MURDERED HER WAY OUT OF KINKY SEX RING.

There was a photo of a smiling Cheryl in a sweet pink suit and matching heels. Josie couldn't imagine her using anything more dangerous than silver sugar tongs.

The story concentrated on the bloody footwear. The paper called them the "murder shoes." Cheryl was involved in a sex ring for foot fetishists, the story "alleged." Josie thought that was newspaperese for "we're covering our behinds so we don't get sued."

The murder shoes had been discovered "at an apartment rented by a client." Hal's name wasn't mentioned. Josie wondered if he had enough pull to keep it out of the paper.

Cheryl's fellow foot soldiers, Paladia and Fiona, weren't in the story, either. Josie felt a pang of pity for both women. She could see Fiona barricaded behind her china cabinet with her two babies. She wondered if Paladia had called in sick at her office. Josie flashed on the family photos on Paladia's desk. What would happen to the vulnerable little girl with the braces if her mother was pilloried in the press? How would it affect the teenage boy with the shy smile?

This was awful. How was Cheryl's poor family taking this public humiliation? Was hardworking Tom at home with the baby this morning? Josie couldn't see him going to work. Not with that headline.

Josie heard a rumbling noise and peeked out her front window. Another news van was rolling down the street. Stan the Man Next Door was on his lawn, shaking his head at a TV reporter, refusing to be interviewed. Stan was too decent.

But there was plenty of temptation for less noble neighbors. The street was packed with media vehicles. A few bold ones parked on Mrs. Mueller's lawn. Fifteen or twenty reporters were jammed on her porch. Mrs. Mueller's shades were down for the first time in Maplewood history. Josie almost felt sorry for the old snoop.

Josie put her sunglasses on and her head down and charged to her car, dodging reporters with the magic words "No comment. No comment." She was on a mission from Mrs. Mueller. A paid mission. "Just try to talk to her one more time," Cheryl's mother had begged her last night. "She won't listen to me. She won't cooperate fully with her lawyer. She's innocent, but she's hiding something. I know it. I'm her mother. I can tell. I'll pay you double if you find out what it is."

Cheryl was in the county jail, her bail denied. She was considered a flight risk. The police had told her not to leave the state and she'd gone to Illinois to gamble. Her trumped-up arrest also counted against her. The world had turned against Cheryl. It no longer did what she wanted.

Mrs. Mueller wanted Josie at the county jail for the morning visiting hours. Cheryl was behind a Plexiglas shield, like a creature in some enlightened zoo. She didn't look anything like the pink-suited woman in the newspaper photo. Her dirty blond hair hung loose, her skin was oily, and she had a zit on her right cheekbone.

But her lifelong arrogance survived. Josie picked up the phone, just like in the movies. Cheryl reached for hers. "My lawyer told me not to talk to anyone," she said. "You're the last person I'd talk to. Go away."

So why didn't you refuse to see me? Josie thought. That's your right, even in jail. She nearly slammed down the phone. But she remembered Mrs. Mueller's desperate plea. Josie had Mrs. Mueller's postdated check in her purse, ready for the bank Monday morning. For that kind of money, Josie could put up with a few harsh words.

"Your lawyer thinks you are guilty," Josie said.

Cheryl said nothing.

"Your mother thinks you're innocent," Josie said. "She doesn't even think you had an affair with Hal Orrin Winfrey. She's the only person in the world who believes that."

Cheryl's lower lip trembled.

"I'm here because your mother asked me," Josie said. "She thinks I can help you."

Cheryl started sniffling. Please don't cry, Josie thought. I can handle anything but real tears.

"I want out of here," Cheryl said, her voice ragged. "Can you get me out of here? I have to get out of here. I can't sleep. It's noisy. It's dirty. It smells bad. There are people here with tattoos and knife scars. The woman in my cell twitches and mumbles to herself. I think she's on drugs. She's weird."

Josie almost laughed. Cheryl walked on men for money, but she had the nerve to call someone else weird. She never mentioned the hurt she'd inflicted on her family. Only Cheryl's pain was real.

"Cheryl, you're hiding something, and it's going to hurt you. You can talk to me," Josie said. "I've been in trouble, too. I know what it feels like. I won't judge you."

"How much is she paying you?" Cheryl said, her eyes narrowing. "My mother. How much money is she giving you?"

"Nothing, yet," Josie said. She'd had enough. It was time to get nasty. "I have something to show you."

She pulled out three photos she'd printed on her computer that morning. Josie held the first one up to the Plexiglas. "These photos are a little different from the one in the paper. This one shows you entering the Prince's Palace. Here you are sitting at the slot machines, feeding them ten-dollar bills. But here's my personal favorite. I call it the Housewife Hooker. You're on a service call to Hal, dressed for success. Nice high heels."

Cheryl stared at the photos, but said nothing. Her face was white and drained of life, a death mask.

"How do you think these would look on the front page of the *City Gazette*? A lot different from the photo there today. I'd make far more money selling these to the paper than I'll get from your mother. But your mother, God knows why, wants to help you and I promised I'd try.

"Here's the deal: You can help me or you can hang up on me. I don't care. But I am your last chance. Your attorney's too busy talking to the TV reporters. He's supposed to be the best, but he couldn't even get you bail."

Cheryl's head snapped back and she nearly dropped the phone. Josie knew she'd hit a nerve.

"You're right," Cheryl said. "My lawyer thinks I'm a housewife hooker. He loves the headlines, but he doesn't care about me. At least you seem to believe me."

Her face froze into the death mask again and she shut up.

"So tell me, Cheryl," Josie said, her voice soft. "How bad can it be? Whatever it is, it can't be worse than this. Keep quiet and you'll never go home. You'll be here forever."

Josie waited. Other conversations seeped into their silence, each one a little sliver of hell:

"I done tole you, bitch, I need money—"

"And who's gonna watch my children? Your sister, the crack whore?"

"Mama's selling her mobile home, but it's still not enough to pay the lawyer. If I hock the car, how am I gonna get to work? The buses don't run—"

Josie watched Cheryl take a deep breath. Then the death mask came to life. A few words trickled out, raw and rusty, and then a great gush, as if she were relieved to be talking. "Mel had some women who did things for money. It wasn't sex; not really. Not for Fiona and me."

Cheryl stopped and looked at Josie, daring her to deny this. Josie kept silent.

"There were three of us. Fiona and I did the easy stuff. We catered to the guys who liked shoes, who had a thing for fishnet stockings, patent leather or bare feet.

The variations are endless. Paladia—you know about Paladia, right?"

Josie nodded.

"Paladia did the hard-core stuff."

Josie knew this already. Cheryl had passed the first test. She was telling the truth.

"We bought shoes from Mel. That's how it started. We all had financial problems. I was in debt from the casinos. Paladia had some stock market losses, and she tried to fix them by taking money from client accounts. She had to replace it before she was found out. Fiona wanted to furnish her house, but she knew it would be years before she could have what she wanted. Then Mel came along, offering us money to do things we couldn't take seriously as sex."

"Would your husband?" Josie said, then wished she'd kept her mouth shut. She didn't want Cheryl to stop talking.

"Tom?" Cheryl said bitterly. "He doesn't know I'm alive. I kept my figure after the baby, but I have no idea why. It's been so long since we've had sex, I'd have to look at the pictures to figure out how it's done. Tom's too tired. I've spent a fortune on negligees and perfume, trying to seduce my own husband.

"The last time I tried, I wore black lace from Victoria's Secret. I lit candles all over the bedroom. Do you know what he said? 'That reminds me. We need citronella candles for the back deck. Can you pick some up at Home Depot?' Then he rolled over and went to sleep. Tom's not interested in me. He only cares about making money."

Oh, boy. This was way out of my league, Josie thought. Was this whole sad saga about Tom? If he'd romanced his wife, would she have stayed away from the casinos? Did she get involved with Mel to prove she was sexy to other men? Maybe foot sex was her twisted way of staying faithful to Tom. Maybe Krafft-Ebing could answer those questions. They were too complicated for Josie.

"What did Tom say when you were . . . uh, taken in?" Josie said.

"He said he'd get me the best possible lawyer. This guy is supposed to be a wizard. He owed Tom's firm a favor. Tom never asked me if I killed Mel."

"Did you?" Josie said.

"Of course not," Cheryl said.

"Why were you at Mel's house the night he was murdered?"

"I made a video with Fiona," she said. "Actually, it's a DVD. Mel was using it to blackmail us. He didn't want money. He wanted us to keep working or he said he'd sell it on the Net. I was desperate to quit. Fiona was, too, but she wouldn't do anything to help herself. I went to Mel's house to try to get the DVD back."

"What kind of DVD?"

"An embarrassing one," Cheryl said. Fiona had used those same words.

"It's pretty hard to embarrass me," Josie said. "Did you have most of your clothes on?"

"All of them," Cheryl said.

"What about your shoes?"

"Those, too," Cheryl said.

"Were they kinky shoes?"

"No."

"Was there another man?"

"No!" Cheryl almost shouted.

"Another woman?"

"What do you take me for?" Cheryl said.

"If you were fully dressed and you didn't have sex, then what's so bad?" Josie asked.

"I was—" Cheryl took a deep breath, and the words rushed out like air from a deflating balloon. "I was pedal pumping."

"Huh?" Josie said.

"It's one of the more benign foot fetishes. A lot of fetishes are fantasies of female helplessness. That's why so many fetish men love women in spike heels. They're difficult for women to walk in. Others go for Mary Janes, little-girl shoes. Pedal pumping carries female helplessness a step further."

No pun intended, Josie thought. "I'm sorry. I've never heard of it," she said.

"They are videos of women in cars," Cheryl said. "The cars are usually on a deserted road or in a dangerous neighborhood. The cars won't start, so the women pump and pump the gas pedal. The women wear sexy stockings and high heels. That's a real turn-on for a certain kind of man.

"I made the DVD with Fiona. You can't see our faces clearly, but our husbands would recognize us. Fiona wore Trip's favorite black dress. My husband will know it's me when he sees the mole on my ankle."

"Lots of women have moles on their ankles."

"Not like mine," Cheryl said. "It's a perfect red heart. It's very distinctive."

Of course, Josie thought sourly, even her imperfections would be uniquely perfect.

"He can't see that mole," Cheryl said. "I don't want him to know I did this."

"Where is this DVD? Do the police have it?" Josie asked.

"I don't know," Cheryl said. "I don't think so. That's why I was at Mel's the night he died. I drugged his drink. I was going to search his house when he passed out. Instead, I was the one who blacked out. I think Mel saw me slipping something in his wine and switched glasses."

"What were you using to drug him?" Josie said.

"Sleeping pills. They're legal. The doctor prescribed them for me."

"In your name?" Josie asked.

"Of course," Cheryl said. "Oh. I see. That doesn't look good, does it?"

Josie said nothing. She didn't have to.

"I had to get that DVD," Cheryl said. "I wasn't going to hurt him. I wanted to steal it and destroy it. Mel lied to us. He blackmailed us. That scumbag! I'm glad he's dead."

Josie hoped the jury never saw the look on Cheryl's face. They'd convict her for sure.

"I ground up the pills in my Cuisinart so they'd dissolve. I put the powder in a Ziploc bag," Cheryl said. "Afterward, I threw the bag away. The police never found that."

That was one bit of luck, Josie thought. Cheryl was a terrible criminal.

"So you had some wine with Mel," Josie prompted. "You think he switched the glasses so you got the drugged one?"

"Yes. Probably when I went to the bathroom. I was so nervous, I had to go. I came back and gulped down my wine. I wanted to get it over with. He wouldn't drink his wine unless I drank mine. When I woke up he was on the floor at the foot of the stairs, dead. There was blood everywhere. I did a quick search, but I didn't find the DVD."

"What time did you wake up?" Josie said.

"It was about ten till nine o'clock."

"Did you look in his pretend shoe store?" Josie said.

"That was the first place. It wasn't there. I checked his bedroom, too."

Josie longed to ask what Mel's bedroom looked like, but she didn't dare.

"I couldn't spend too much time searching," Cheryl said. "When I first woke up, I was woozy and not thinking clearly. I thought Mel had fallen down the stairs and hit his head. Then I saw that the house had been ransacked and realized someone had probably killed him."

"Ransacked how?" Josie said. The killer's search had been kept out of the news. Zinnia hadn't mentioned it, either.

"The place was a mess. Chairs were overturned, drawers pulled out, shoes tossed everywhere. Mel's shoe boxes were open and scattered over the floor. I looked in a few more possible hiding places, but I had to get out of there."

"Why did you run?"

"There was nothing I could do for Mel. I was afraid I'd get blamed somehow. No one would believe I'd passed out and found him dead. I saw my bloody footprints on the floor and cleaned them up. Then I ran out of there. I was in a total panic."

"Who do you think killed Mel?"

"Not Fiona. She's too scared to do anything. She's terrified her husband Trip will find out. She says he has an awful temper. Paladia might have. Mel was really pressuring her, worse than either of us. But the killer could have been one of Mel's foot friends. They fought about things."

"What things?"

"Prices. What we did. Hal wanted more fantasy nights. Hal was like an addict for those fantasy nights. He almost punched out Mel once when Mel said he couldn't risk them because of the nosy lady next door."

"What nosy lady?" Josie said.

"The neighbor to the east," Cheryl said. "She hated Mel. She thought he was holding drug parties. She kept some kind of diary to show the homeowners association all the cars at Mel's place. Mel was afraid of her."

"Do you think the neighbor woman killed Mel?"

"I wish," Cheryl said. "She's eighty if she's a day. She can barely hobble to her front door."

"So you have no idea?" Josie said.

"Everyone keeps asking me who killed Mel. If I knew, I'd tell them and make this go away. The cops aren't going to look for the real killer now. They think I did it."

That was the sad truth. They both knew it. Josie sneaked a glance at her watch. Visiting hours were over in five minutes. Josie had nothing more to say to Cheryl, and nothing to lose. She might as well ask the one question that nagged at her.

"Cheryl, why did you keep the shoes?" Josie said.

"Which shoes?"

"The ones with Mel's blood on the soles. The murder shoes. If you'd tossed them, the cops might never have connected you to his death."

"Oh, I couldn't throw them away," Cheryl said. "They were brand-new Bruno Maglis."

Chapter 28

We have an amazing ability to transform ourselves from swans into ugly ducklings—a real genius for ruin.

I did a pretty good number on myself, Josie thought. But Cheryl does everything better. She's the grand winner in the screw-up sweepstakes. The perfect wife and mother transformed herself into a gambler, a housewife hooker, and murder suspect. No way I could beat that.

Cheryl's destruction frightened Josie. She fled the county jail as if hounds were after her heart. Once outside the Justice Center, she breathed in the cold November air, great gulps of it, even if it was tinged with carbon monoxide fumes from the downtown Clayton traffic.

Cheryl had talked. She gave Josie the information her mother wanted so desperately. But what good was it? How would it help Cheryl? If anything, it made her seem even guiltier.

Mrs. Mueller believed her daughter was innocent, but Josie hadn't seen any evidence to support that theory. So what did she do now?

Josie needed to think. She needed coffee. She needed to see Josh. That man was a bigger addiction than caffeine. She positively craved him. Her car seemed to drive itself to Has Beans.

When she pulled into the coffeehouse lot, her heart slipped. There was no sign of his car. She'd have to do without her Josh fix today. Well, she'd come this far. Might as well get some coffee.

Josh was not only at the store, he was alone.

"Where's your car?" Josie said. "I didn't see it. I thought you weren't here."

"So that's why you stopped in," he said. "You don't really want me, just my coffee."

"I want you both," she said. "I need your brew and I admire your brain."

"Too bad you like my fine mind," he said. "I have other awesome attributes."

Josh bounded over the counter with that one-handed pirate leap and gave her a deep kiss, running his fingers through her hair. He makes me feel like an actress with a long, gorgeous mane, Josie thought, instead of a working mom with plain brown hair.

"Harrrumph!"

The man cleared his throat like he'd swallowed a Roto-Rooter. But when he spoke, his voice was as small and prissy as he was. "I can always go to Starbucks if you're too busy to wait on me," he said.

Josie pulled away from Josh, her face flaming. She'd never heard the guy walk in. She blundered to the lumpy couch, hiding her red face in the paper. This time, she read Cheryl's news more carefully. Sure enough, where it jumped to the inside page, there was a short interview with Mel's neighbor, Adela Quimby Hodges, who'd lived in Olympia Park all of her eighty-three years.

"I knew something improper was going on next door," she told the reporter. "I warned the homeowners association about that man. They thought I was an old crank. Now we have a murder, the first one in Olympia Park history. What's that going to do to property values, I ask you?"

"Your mocha java, sir," Josh said.

"Thank you," the man said and slammed the door behind him.

"I have something hot for you, too, ma'am," Josh said. He started to leap the counter again.

"Whoa. Saturday's only two days away," Josie said. "Maybe we'd better wait."

"I wish you weren't right all the time," Josh said. "Your espresso is ready. How hot is the murder investigation?"

While she sipped her coffee, Josie told him about her talk with Cheryl. "Did you ask her if she left the dead rat on your porch?" Josh asked.

"What good would that do?" Josie said. "She'd clam up and never tell me anything."

"I think she did it," Josh said.

"The murder or the rat?" Josie said.

"Both," he said.

"You're probably right," she said. "But I promised her mother I'd try to find a way to exonerate her. You were telling me about your car."

Josh seemed confused. "Uh, right. My car. My car's at the body shop. I'm having the rust fixed and the body painted midnight black. It's a classic Z. Should be ready by Saturday night. *Vroom. Vroom.*"

The bell rang and a young man called, "Yo, Josh, I need what you got!"

"I need to go," Josie said, leaving her cup on the counter. "See you Saturday night."

Outside in her car, she opened her cell and called Alyce.

"I saw the morning paper," Alyce said. "Looks like we don't need to do surveillance on Cheryl. We know where she is."

"What a mess," Josie said. "I feel sorry for her. I never thought I'd say that. Her life is ruined."

"How's her mother?" Alyce said.

"Mrs. Mueller is convinced Cheryl is innocent. She wants me to find some way to prove it. I've got an idea."

"It better be a good one," Alyce said. "Cheryl looks beyond help to me."

"I'd like to know exactly who was at Mel's house the night of the murder," Josie said.

"And the cops are going to tell you?" Alyce asked.

"Not a chance," Josie said. "But Mel's nosy neighbor will. Adela Quimby Hodges was in the morning paper. She kept a diary of the goings-on at Mel's. Disapproved of them deeply."

"You called her for an appointment?" Alyce said.

"No, her line is busy. I've tried several times. I figure she'd hang up on me, anyway," Josie said. "You don't get to be eighty-three by talking to strangers. But she might talk to one of her own kind."

"Who?"

"You," Josie said.

"Josie, I'm not in the Olympia Park circles," Alyce said.

"Sure you are. You belong to the Junior League. You talk the talk and walk the walk. I can sort of dress like your crowd, but Adela will know I'm not one of you. Please, please come with me."

"How are you going to get past the guards at the gate without an appointment?" Alyce said.

"Charm?" Josie said.

"Not after a murder. Not when Adela's shot off her mouth in the newspaper. We'll take my husband's electronic pass. He goes there all the time on business. He has a gate card for preferred visitors."

"And he'll lend it to you?"

"No, but he keeps it in his car. I'll just swing by his office and borrow it, then put it back," Alyce said. "He'll never know it's gone."

The guards waved benignly when Alyce breezed through the "residents only" side of the gate. Why shouldn't they? Big, blond and utterly at ease, Alyce seemed to belong.

Mrs. Adela Quimby Hodges welcomed her, too. Mrs. Hodges was a tiny woman with a shining mass of white hair and a pronounced dowager's hump, partly concealed by tailoring. She leaned on a black cane with an elegant silver heron's head.

"Did you say Junior League?" she said.

"Yes, I did," Alyce said. "I'm sorry I wasn't able to get through to you. There seems to be something wrong with your phone. You probably knew my mother, Katheryn Hellespond."

"She was your mother? Oh, my, yes. Very active in the community. Very active indeed. Her death was a great loss. There's nothing wrong with my phone. I had to take it off the hook ever since I talked to that young reporter. It's been a nuisance, but it was my civic duty. Follow me into the parlor."

They passed large framed bird prints, delicately drawn yet vibrantly colored.

"Nice birds," Josie said.

Mrs. Hodges looked at her oddly, then said, "Those are Audubons, dear."

Josie felt like an idiot.

"My late husband was a birder. He left me those, as well as an excellent pair of field glasses. I use them for my hobby."

"You're a birder, too?" Alyce said.

"I watched the odd birds who turned up at Mel Poulaine's house. No one would listen to me, but I was right about that young man."

The living room was furnished in a stiff forties style, with flowered curtains, piecrust tables, huge silver bowls of cigarettes and bulbous lighters. There was even a long-handled silver silent butler to empty the ashtrays into. Josie hadn't seen one in years.

Alyce and Josie sat across from Mrs. Hodges on one of the oddly rectangular couches.

"I'll ring for tea." Mrs. Hodges gave orders to a woman nearly as old as she was in an honest-to-God maid's uniform. "Now, what was I saying? I'm little forgetful these days. And a tad tired. This is too much for an old lady."

"You're much too sharp to call yourself old," Alyce said. "You were telling us about your neighbor, Mr. Poulaine."

Adela's face turned pink with excitement. "It was disgraceful what went on in that house," she said. "Women and men, in and out all hours of the day and night. Drugs, I thought. But it was prostitution, which was just as bad. And now, murder. I don't understand why Zinnia stayed on there as housekeeper. She is a respectable woman."

"Did you ask her?" Josie said.

"I don't associate with servants," Mrs. Hodges said sharply.

Josie resolved to let Alyce do the rest of the talking.

"My housekeeper, Mrs. Simmons, told Zinnia she was endangering her reputation and any future employment.

Zinnia became quite defensive and said her employer didn't do anything while she was there. That was quite true, quite true. Mel held his most outrageous parties on Zinnia's days off."

"Did he have a party the night he was killed?" Alyce said.

"No. But he had several visitors. I kept a diary. The police took it, though," she said.

"Oh." Josie couldn't keep the disappointment out of her voice.

"But I kept a copy on my computer. My great-grandson, Trey, told me to always have a backup."

Adela stumped over to a dark wood secretary with gold oval handles and took out a leather folder. Josie and Alyce waited impatiently while the old woman made her slow progress back. Just as she settled in, the ancient maid arrived with a tea cart and there was more fussing.

Alyce offered to pour, which speeded things up somewhat. After the great issues of sugar, milk or lemon were decided, Adela was finally ready to talk.

She opened the folder and proudly showed Josie the detailed list of cars, license-plate numbers, times of arrival and departure, and descriptions of Mel's visitors. "Man 5 feet 8 with gray suit and red suspenders, drives black Lexus. Man, bald, overweight, with yellow tie, black Lincoln Towncar. Driver is Judge Summers Harlan."

"Amazing," Alyce said.

"That list reads like a who's who of St. Louis business," Josie said. "Look. There's the head copywriter at a major ad agency. Three surgeons and an ENT specialist. A big brewery executive. Enough lawyers to start a white shoe firm. Oh, dear. There's a bishop."

"Not from our church," Adela said. "I rejoice in the knowledge that no clergy from the Episcopal church were involved in Mel Poulaine's antics. My great-grandson tracked down the plates from the state. He can do that on the computer. Very clever boy.

"I complained to the board of Olympia Park, but it did no good. One of those license plates belongs to an Olympia Park trustee, I'm sorry to say. He told the

board I was an old busybody. That's why I couldn't get
the board to do anything about the shenanigans at that
house. Melvin's mother must be turning in her grave.
She was a Veiled Prophet maid of honor."

"What year?" Alyce asked.

"I believe it was 1938. Or was it '39? No. I think it
was 19 and 37. Somewhere in the late thirties. When it
was still an honor instead of a farce."

"May I see your diary for the night Mel died?"
Josie asked.

Josie looked at the list of names. Mel had been busy
on his last night on earth. Paladia had been there. So
had a prominent surgeon, "silver hair with bald spot in
back, green scrubs." Josie wondered if he'd met Paladia
for fun and games in the pretend shoe store. Fiona—or
at least her car—had stopped by for forty-five minutes.
Did Fiona tell her hubby she was running to the grocery
store? Cheryl had been there the longest, Josie noted.

"You say Cheryl arrived at seven p.m. and stayed until
nine thirty," Josie said.

"She kept her car hidden in the garage, but I saw her
drive in and I saw her leave," Adela said.

Mel was long dead by then, if the coroner was right,
Josie thought.

There was one more notation: "Black car. 8:17 to
9:01."

"No license plate on the black car?" Josie said.

"It was covered with mud. Deliberately, I think."

"No make?" Josie said.

"It was hidden behind the bushes in the driveway. I
couldn't see it clearly. All those modern cars look alike
to me, I'm afraid. I'm not as good at distinguishing them
as my great-grandson. When I was young, you could tell
an Oldsmobile from a Buick. Cars had character."

"Did you see the driver? Male or female?" Josie said.

"No. I dozed off. I do that a lot these days. The noise
of the car engine woke me up. I saw the brake lights as
it turned out of the driveway."

"You're sure it wasn't Cheryl's car?"

"Positive. She left at nine thirty-two. I was awake and

I saw her. She was running and she left very fast. She had on a dark dress. Blue, I think. And black shoes."

Adela put up a blue-veined hand to stifle a yawn. "If you don't mind, my dears, I'm a little weary. It's past my nap time." Adela suddenly seemed very old and frail. The pink color was gone. Now her skin was white and papery.

"Would you like us to call your maid?" Alyce said.

"That would be very kind, thank you."

"Mrs. Hodges, you need your rest," the maid said, when she arrived. "Here, let me help you upstairs."

"Don't fuss," Adela Hodges said.

"We'll let ourselves out," Josie said.

She watched the two tiny women totter up the stairs. It was hard to say who was helping whom.

"What now?" Alyce said when they were outside.

"I'm going to pick up my daughter at school," Josie said. "I've hardly seen her all week."

"I mean, where do we go from here?"

"You've got me," Josie said. "Nothing we learned from Adela will clear Cheryl. The mystery car could be the killer, or simply someone who came for fun and games, saw Mel and bolted. We had nothing before we saw Adela. Now we have less than nothing. Maybe if we found that pedal-pumping video it would help. Except I haven't a clue where it is. I'm quitting for the day."

Josie picked up Amelia at school. "Hi, Mom," she said, and bounced on the seat. "I thought Grandma was getting me."

"Nope. I've kidnapped you. We're doing a guerrilla gorilla visit. We haven't had one in ages."

"Yayyy!" Amelia said.

The St. Louis Zoo was practically in their backyard. Josie couldn't often spare a whole day for a field trip, so she and Amelia would stop by for quick visits. Josie preferred the penguins. Amelia was drawn to the apes.

Tonight, Josie was distracted. She kept trying to put together the puzzle of Cheryl without success. Fortunately, she didn't need to be much company. Amelia was fascinated by a family of chimps.

"Look at the mama with the baby," Amelia said. "She really takes care of him. And the dad, too. It's all about the baby."

"That's nice," Josie said vaguely.

She should have listened. Amelia had just given her the key to her unsolvable puzzle.

Chapter 29

Night's long fingers stretched across the zoo grounds, clutching what was left of the day in its cold grasp. The zoo was closing. It was time for Josie and Amelia to head home. Amelia skipped to the car. Josie moved at a slower pace. She felt suddenly low.

"What's wrong, Mom?" Amelia said. "We were having fun and now you're quiet."

"I hate winter days," Josie said. "They're too short and dark."

"I like them," Amelia said. "I like the cold. It's invigorating. Makes me—" She stopped abruptly when the car turned down their street. "Mom, what are all those people doing at our house?"

Josie peered into the gathering gloom and saw the horde of media vans and news cars. "Those are reporters," she said. "They're at Mrs. Mueller's house, not ours."

"Because Cheryl got in trouble?"

"That's right," Josie said.

"Do you think she's a hooker?"

"Amelia! I wish you wouldn't use that word."

"The paper said she was in a foot-fetish ring. Zoe found a bunch of stuff on the Internet about foot fetishes," Amelia said. "It's really gross."

"Yes, it is," Josie said. Now what did she say?

"Do people really do that stuff with their feet?"

"I think so," Josie said. "Some people. I don't."

Josie was starting to sweat and it had nothing to do with the car heater. Was there a self-help book to tell you what to do when your neighbor's daughter had a toehold in the sex industry? She braced herself for Amelia's next question. *I will try to be open and honest and give her an answer appropriate for her age and experience, which I hope to heaven is none.*

Josie swung the car in front of their darkened flat, and a swarm of reporters surrounded it like ants on a candy bar. They shouted questions: "Did you know Cheryl? Did you know what she did for a living? How does this affect—"

Amelia looked terrified. "Mom, do we have to answer?"

"No, we don't," Josie said. She cracked her window an inch and shouted, "Excuse me. Excuse me, please. My daughter and I are not going to talk about our neighbors. Please go away."

A thin woman with bad skin and a sharp nose tried to shove a mike through the window opening. "How did you feel when the woman you went to school with was arrested for murder? What did—"

More reporters crowded around, waving notepads, tape recorders and mikes. Josie didn't recognize any of them. The Cheryl story must be attracting the national media.

Amelia whimpered. "Mom, make them go away. I can't open my door."

"Relax," she told her daughter. "This is no worse than an August white sale. I'll have us out of here in no time."

Josie reached for her heavy purse. She might have to slam a few heads while Amelia ran for it.

Stan's front door flew open. "Let them alone," he said. His voice sounded high and reedy in the cold air. Josie's savior wore a cheap knit shirt that clung to his flabby chest, giving him prominent breasts. His pants sagged at the knees. Stan the Man Next Door looked more like an irritated retiree than a white knight.

"Let them alone," he repeated, his voice rising higher still. "Or I'll call the police."

The reporters ignored him.

He held up a video camera. "Let them alone or I'll

give this video to their lawyer. This is clear-cut harassment. I have that woman on tape saying she doesn't want to talk. Now back off."

The reporters backed away from Josie's car as if they were vampires and it had been doused in garlic juice.

Josie waved her thanks to Stan, while Amelia ran across the yard and into the house. Inside, Josie tripped on Amelia's backpack. Her daughter had dropped it in the hall. She found Amelia in the kitchen, opening a soda, something she wasn't supposed to do before dinner. Josie decided she'd make an exception tonight. She needed a drink after that encounter. No doubt the kid did, too.

Josie put her arms around Amelia and hugged her. "It's okay," she said. "I know you were scared, but the reporters weren't going to hurt you. They were just doing their job. They have to ask questions."

"They were so rude, Mom."

"Yes, they were. They're paid to be rude."

"Stan's a hero. He saved us."

"I wish our hero didn't wear baggy pants," she said.

"You're so superficial, Mom," Amelia said.

Josie wondered where her daughter got that. "You're right," she said. "But I can't help it."

"Aren't you at least going to call him and thank him?"

"Yes, I am," Josie said.

Her conversation with Stan was awkward. She kept imagining what she would have said to Josh. She would have batted her eyes and said, "My hero" in a jokey voice, but Josh would have known she meant it. Except Josh didn't save her. Stan did. Solid, stolid Stan, who had such a crush on her that it would be cruel to encourage it.

"I wanted to thank you, Stan, for rescuing us," Josie said.

"No problem," he said. She could almost see him shrug in that awful shirt.

I should invite him for dinner, she thought. But I can't. "Well, that's all I wanted to say," she said. "Thanks."

"You're welcome," he said.

She hung up with relief.

"You should have invited him to dinner, Mom," Amelia said. "It's only polite when someone rescues us."

"Bad idea, Amelia. He likes me and I don't like him the same way. It would be wrong. What would you like for dinner? Cheeseburgers?"

It was a bribe. Amelia took it. "With onions and ketchup? And no salad?"

"You've got it," Josie said.

But if she thought this treat would placate her daughter, she was mistaken. Amelia was in a mood. She slammed the plates down on the table and forgot the silverware and napkins. They were finishing dinner, when Amelia said, "Justin is an ass."

The ass game again. Amelia was still going for the Barrington School record of how many times she could use the a-word in a sentence.

"I don't want to hear that word," Josie said. "You know how I feel about curse words."

"I'm not cursing, Mom. I looked 'ass' up in the dictionary. 'Ass' is a perfectly good word. A donkey is an ass."

"Then say 'donkey' if that's what you mean," Josie said.

" 'Ass' also means a stupid or a silly person," Amelia said. "Jason is an ass twice. Once because he's stupid and once because he's silly. In my ass-ssessment, he's an ass times two. A double-assed ass. An ass—"

"Amelia?" Josie said.

"Yes?"

"Shut the fuck up," Josie said.

Amelia fled to her room in tears.

What's wrong with me? Josie thought as she rinsed and stacked the plates in the dishwasher. I can't believe I lost my temper over something so stupid. What kind of example am I? Using the f-word won't stop my daughter from using the a-word.

There was no excuse for her behavior. Josie owed her daughter an apology. She went down the hall toward Amelia's room. Josie heard it long before she saw it.

Green Day was playing on the radio so loud the hall walls vibrated. Josie knocked on her daughter's door.

There was no answer.

Josie knocked harder. "Amelia?" she said.

She cracked the door slightly and saw her daughter sliding a paper into the top of the chintz-covered footstool. Amelia looked up guiltily. Josie caught a quick glimpse before she slammed the lid shut on the stool. It was a list of ass words.

Josie bit her lip to keep from smiling. Like mother, like daughter. Josie had used that same footstool as a hiding place when she was Amelia's age. She'd reupholstered it in Laura Ashley chintz for her daughter's eighth birthday.

"Amelia, I know it's hard—"

Josie stopped short. Hard. Hiding place. That's it. That's where it was.

"Mom, what's wrong?" Amelia asked.

Josie picked her daughter up and kissed her. "I came in to say I'm sorry for using the f-word. That was wrong and I apologize. Now I have to say thank you. You've solved everything for me. I know where he hid it."

"Hid what?" Amelia said. "Solved what? Mom, you're weird."

"I'll explain tomorrow. I have to call Alyce."

Josie ran out of the room and dialed her best friend. When Alyce answered, Josie said, "I know where the DVD is."

Alyce said, "Hello, this is Josie. I know you don't usually take calls during family time, Alyce, but are you available to talk now?"

"Alyce, this is major," Josie said. "The DVD is in Mel's fantasy room. I know where. I'll call Zinnia and ask her if we can look around in there tomorrow."

"Are you going to tell her why?"

"No. She may not believe Cheryl is innocent anymore. I'll ask her if we can come over. You can go with me, can't you?"

"Tomorrow is the nanny's day off. I'll have to take the baby with me."

"Fine," Josie said.

"You won't say that when Justin gets cranky at nap time. I'll pick you up at ten."

"Good. And bring Jake's electronic pass, just in case." There was a loud knock at the door. "Alyce, I've got to go. Someone's at the back door."

Josie hoped it wasn't a reporter. She listened again for the knock. A woman's voice said, "Josie, open up. It's Verena."

Verena? Josie didn't know any Verena.

She parted the curtain for a look. Mrs. Mueller was on Josie's doorstep. She had no idea the woman had a first name. Verena Mueller. It seemed oddly indecent, like seeing her in a skimpy nightgown.

Mrs. Mueller didn't wait for an invitation. She sat down at the kitchen table. "I had to sneak in the back way," she said. "I didn't want any reporters to see me. What did you find out?"

"Cheryl made a DVD with Mel."

"Oh." Mrs. Mueller's face went flat. "How bad?" she said carefully.

"It's about pedal pumping," Josie said, and explained what that was.

"That's all?" Mrs. Mueller said. "See, my little girl is so innocent. She's worried about that harmless DVD."

"It's not harmless," Josie said. "Mel blackmailed her with it. He was murdered for it."

"I don't understand," Mrs. Mueller said.

"I don't, either. Not completely. But there's something in there worth killing for. Cheryl thinks the killer searched the house for it the night Mel was murdered. He didn't find it. I think I know where it is. I'm going there tomorrow."

"Good," Mrs. Mueller said briskly. "I'll tell Tom and—"

"No, don't," Josie said. "I don't want the housekeeper tipped off. Let's keep it between ourselves for now. Cheryl's freedom may depend on it."

"Well, in that case." Mrs. Mueller rose to leave. "You did good work today, Josie. Thank you."

My Lord, Josie thought. She'd learned Mrs. Mueller's

first name and been complimented, all on the same visit. Josie went back down the hall to check on her daughter. The music was still blasting, but Amelia was in the deep, heavy sleep of childhood. Josie spent a moment admiring her daughter's flawless skin with the sweet sprinkling of freckles, the long dark hair, the small curled hands.

Then she pulled off Amelia's shoes and covered her up. She switched off the radio and the lights. "Good night," she whispered, as she kissed her daughter on the forehead. Amelia never stirred.

Josie was shutting her bedroom door when the phone rang. She ran to pick it up before it woke up Amelia. A rushed voice said, "Josie, it's me. Fiona. Mrs. Mueller said you know where the DVD is."

Oh, no, Josie thought. I told that woman to keep her mouth shut. Mrs. M was barely out of the house before she blabbed.

"How did you find out?" Josie said.

"I called Mrs. Mueller to find out how Cheryl was, and she gave me the good news. Where is it? Do you have it?"

"I think it may be at Mel's house," Josie said. "I'm going there tomorrow to look for it. But please don't say anything. I don't want to alarm the housekeeper."

"Where do you think it is?" Fiona said.

"Not sure," Josie lied. "It's just a hunch. It may not work out."

"But you'll let me know as soon as you find it," Fiona said.

For a DVD with nothing on it, a lot of people were interested, Josie thought.

"I called for another reason," Fiona said. "You should have a talk with the babysitter. She knows a lot about Cheryl. Things you should know."

"Like what?" Josie said.

"It's better if you hear them from Bonnie," Fiona said, and hung up before Josie could ask for more.

This was getting twisted, she decided. She'd better call Mel's housekeeper before it was too late.

"Yes, you can come tomorrow," Zinnia said. "I'm still staying at the house. I'll help any way I can. I think it's terrible what those reporter people are doing to that poor girl. Nothing went on here. Nothing. I wouldn't work at such a place. How am I going to get decent work with the hoo-ha over poor Mr. Mel? Answer me that."

But Josie couldn't.

It was a sunny morning with only a few scattered reporters when Alyce pulled up at Josie's house. Baby Justin was safely strapped into his car seat, cooing softly.

"He'll be good for another hour or so," Alyce said. "Then you're going to hear some serious yelling. Where do you think this DVD is at Mel's?"

"In the pretend shoe store," Josie said.

"That's been searched by the police and the killer."

"They didn't have my advantage," Josie said. "They're not a mom. And speaking of moms, you're lucky Justin is too young to ask questions. Amelia asked me about foot fetishes last night."

"What did you tell her?"

"I skated around the issue in an open and adult manner and hoped she'd never bring it up again."

"That's how I'd handle it," Alyce said. "I have a hard time believing this shoe-freak club exists in St. Louis. It belongs in New York."

"Why?" Josie said. "Do you think New Yorkers invented sin? We have more time for it here and there's less to do."

"So New Yorkers say, 'Hey, honey, want to go to a Broadway show tonight or would you rather walk on me'?" Alyce said.

"No, it's not like that," Josie said. "I think we have more pervs here, but they're hidden. St. Louis isn't exactly an open culture. Not when you have Mrs. Mueller and Adela watching everything."

"And taking notes," Alyce said. "New Yorkers couldn't keep a diary like Adela did. What would they write down? Cab numbers?"

Once again, Alyce breezed past the gate guards in Olympia Park. She parked in Mel's circular drive. Some houses seemed forlorn after the owner's death. Mel's looked the same. Josie rang the doorbell, but there was no answer.

Josie tried again. The baby stirred restlessly in Alyce's arms. Alyce's Kate Spade diaper bag was crammed with baby paraphernalia. Arctic expeditions needed fewer supplies than Alyce and Justin.

"Are you sure Zinnia is expecting us?" Alyce said.

"Ten o'clock sharp," Josie said. "Maybe the doorbell is out of order." She knocked hard on the door and it swung open.

"Omigod. The door's not locked," Josie said.

"Of course it's not locked," Alyce said. "That's why you live in a gated community. I don't lock my door, either."

"Maybe she's in the back and can't hear us," Josie said. She stepped inside, calling, "Zinnia! Zin—"

Josie stopped abruptly. The sight was too awful for her to take in.

"What's wrong?" Alyce asked.

"Zinnia's here," Josie said. Her voice was somewhere between a croak and a whisper.

"Well, that's good," Alyce said.

"No, it's not. She's dead."

Chapter 30

Zinnia lay twisted on the white marble floor. A dark pool of blood bloomed under her head. No one was there, but Death was a powerful presence. Josie and Alyce stood on the threshold, awed, silent, afraid to enter the house.

Josie was the first to recover. "This is terrible," she said. "Zinnia worked so hard to clean up that floor. Now it's a mess again."

"Josie," Alyce said sharply. "You're not making sense. Are you sure there's no chance she's alive?"

"Look at her skin, Alyce. It's gray. Her neck's at a weird angle. The blood under her head is almost black. She's been dead a while."

"I don't want to look." Alyce sneaked a peek around Justin's carrier. "Her skirt's all bunched up. She wasn't—?"

"I don't think so," Josie said. "I think her skirt got rucked up in the fall."

"Poor Zinnia," Alyce said. "Death is so undignified. She'd be mortified to have strangers staring at her underwear."

"At least it's clean," Josie said.

Justin gave a cooing cry. "Omigod," Alyce said. "My baby. What am I doing? I can't go in there. I can't let my innocent child see a murder. He'll be warped for life."

"Go sit in the car," Josie said. "I'll get the DVD."

"Then what?" Alyce said.

"Then we'll get the hell out of here," Josie said.

"We can't cut and run," Alyce said. "What about

Adela, the nosy next-door neighbor? She's probably at the window with her field glasses, writing down my license plate right now."

"Damn, you're right," Josie said. "You stay here with Justin. As soon as I'm back with the DVD, we'll call 911. Meanwhile, you may want to call Jake."

"Are you kidding?" Alyce said. "He thinks we're mystery-shopping. I'd rather go to jail than let my husband know I'm at a murder scene. Besides, I've faked it as your attorney before. I can do it again."

"We have to get our stories straight," Josie said. "What are we doing here?"

"I wanted to see Adela about the Junior League," Alyce said. "We never finished our business yesterday."

"Yes, but why are we at Mel's? Wait. I know. I wanted to ask Zinnia about a church committee."

"Which one?" Alyce said. "Quick. It has to be a real committee. The cops will check."

Which one had Mrs. Mueller mentioned? "The bake-sale committee."

"Okay, here's what you do," Alyce said. "You don't talk unless I say so. You don't change your story no matter how stupid it starts to sound. Now go in there and get that DVD. If someone else shows up, we'll have an even bigger mess."

"I'll be quick. Is Justin okay?"

"Quiet as a little mouse," Alyce said. That's when the kid let out a full-throated howl that would have done Pavarotti proud.

"Go!" Alyce said.

"You have anything I can use to cover my hair? A scarf, maybe?" Josie said.

"There's a stocking cap in the glove box," Alyce said.

Josie shoved her brown hair under the cap. She pulled a plastic rain poncho out of her purse and put it over her clothes, then slipped on her leather gloves.

"What are you doing in that ridiculous getup?" Alyce shouted over the baby's furious yowls.

"It's a crime scene suit. I'm trying to minimize my hairs and fibers."

"You've been watching too much *CSI*," Alyce said.

"Oh, dear. I've found the cause of Master Justin's distress. It's diaper time."

At the front door, Josie stripped off her shoes and tiptoed through the hall in her socks. Josie thought she could see the black cotton fibers shedding from them.

She made a wide circle around Zinnia's body. That poor, foolish woman, Josie thought. The housekeeper had stubbornly refused to believe her beloved Mr. Mel could do anything wrong. Zinnia's blind faith had killed her.

As Josie passed the crumpled body, she saw the hall table had been overturned. Smashed china and glass littered the floor. The double parlor door was open to reveal more ruin. Chair cushions were ripped. Drawers were upended. A vase was broken, the flowers scattered on the floor. Even the portrait of Mel's mother had been slashed.

The kitchen was another wreck, but Josie didn't take time to survey the damage. She found the back steps and sprinted up five flights, careful not to touch the handrails. She arrived at the top breathless, and ran down the hall to Mel's special room. Her heart was pounding when she threw open the doors.

Mel's fantasy room was destroyed. Shards of broken mirror glittered everywhere. The pale pink carpet was torn up, exposing the bare pine floor. Upholstery stuffing poured out of cruel cuts in the pink chairs.

Josie found the slanted footstool lying on its side. The leather pad was unharmed. She prodded it with nervous fingers. It was harder in one section, an area the size of a DVD case. Josie had guessed right. But how was she going to get it out? She didn't have a knife.

Think. Mel had to get in there. How did he do it?

Josie poked and pulled on the leather pad, but nothing happened. Arrgh! The DVD was right there. She could feel it. She thought of stealing the whole footstool, but the police would know it was gone.

She heard a siren in the distance. The cops would be here any moment. Josie beat on the pad, but it wouldn't give. In frustration, she thumped the footstool on the floor. The pad slid upward on springs.

"That's it!" she said out loud. "I found it."

Mel must have designed this hidey-hole himself. The foam padding in the footstool had been cut out in a jagged rectangle. The DVD fitted into the hole. Josie pulled out a plain black plastic case hand-lettered TIP TOE THRU THE TWO LIPS.

Oh, yuck. No wonder someone had killed for this.

I've found it, Josie thought. I'm smarter than the cops and the killer combined. Josie nearly did a little dance of triumph around the room, except she'd cut her feet on the broken glass.

Now she had another problem: How was she going to get that DVD past the police?

The wailing siren sounded closer. Were the cops on their way so soon? Josie couldn't be caught inside the house wearing that outfit. She stuck the DVD in her waistband, then charged down the back steps, her socks slipping on the polished wood. On the second floor, she nearly took a header down the steps, and grabbed the railing with a gloved hand. Then she was out the front door, pulling the rain poncho over her head, folding it back into its pouch. She ripped off the stocking cap and slipped on her shoes.

"Did you get it?" Alyce said. She was changing Justin's diaper on the backseat.

"Yes!" Josie said. She kept the DVD hidden. She didn't want Adela Quimby Hodges, the alert octogenarian, to spot it.

Josie no longer heard the sirens. They must have been for another emergency. "We'd better call the cops," she said.

"Can you do that for us?" Alyce said. "Justin and I are busy."

Josie sat on the passenger seat and made the call. The 911 operator told her to remain calm and stay on the line. The police would be there in minutes. But Josie was close to panic. Time was running out. Where was she going to hide that DVD? She couldn't be caught with foot porn. The police would know she'd stolen it from Mel's home.

She couldn't put it in Alyce's SUV. That was the first

place they'd look. Her purse was equally bad. She heard more sirens. This time, they were coming to Olympia Park.

"The police are here," Josie told the 911 operator and hung up.

"Where's that diaper?" Josie said.

"What?" Alyce said.

"The diaper. Give it to me. No, not the clean one."

As the first police car pulled into the circular drive, Josie shoved the DVD into the reeking diaper.

Josie and Alyce didn't have to act upset. They were both shocked and horrified. The uniformed officers asked them some simple questions. They were sad and slightly teary and gave honest answers. Well, semi-honest. They fudged why they were at Mel's house.

Then the two homicide detectives pulled up, and the day unraveled like an old sweater. Detective Kate Causeman looked fresh from the pie-baking contest at the state fair. She seemed fairly cheerful for someone at a murder scene. Then she saw Josie, and her face screwed up like she'd swallowed a bad gooseberry. The other detective was Knob Ears, the man mountain who had stonewalled Cheryl. Neither one said a word to Josie.

The two detectives went inside Mel's house for a short eternity. Baby Justin was becoming fretful. His mother sang to him.

"It's nap time," she told Josie. "He's getting cranky. Those detectives are about to get an earful."

Finally Detectives Causeman and Knob Ears came over to talk to Alyce and Josie. If a smile was Causeman's umbrella, Josie was getting a poke in the eye.

"Josie Marcus," she said. "This is a surprise. When I interviewed you before, you said you didn't know Mr. Poulaine. You told me you'd only met him when you were in the store trying on shoes."

"That's right," Josie said.

"What are you doing at his house now?" she said.

"Excuse me, Officer. I'm Alyce Bohannon, representing Ms. Marcus."

Josie's friend had morphed into a different woman. Alyce was still blond, but she was no longer soft. She seemed tougher, more alert, all business, even with a fussy baby on one hip.

"Do you always bring your attorney to your murders?" Detective Causeman said.

"Ms. Marcus and I were here on business," Alyce said.

"If you don't mind, we'd like Ms. Marcus to answer," Detective Causeman said.

"I'm sorry," Alyce said. "But I have to be with my client."

"How do I know you two didn't kill Mrs. Ellis?" Detective Causeman said. Her partner stayed silent. All he had to do was stand there and he looked scary.

"Zinnia appears to have been dead several hours, Detective," Alyce said. "We couldn't have killed her."

"Oh, so you're a forensic expert, as well as an attorney," the detective said.

"Why don't you ask the woman next door, Adela Quimby Hodges, what time we got here?" Alyce said. "You know she writes down every license plate, along with a car and visitor description."

"A detective, a forensic expert, and an attorney," the detective said. "I'd like a talk with such a multitalented woman. Why don't you come with us to headquarters for a chat?"

"What about my baby?" Alyce said.

"He'll be well cared for." Detective Knob Ears spoke for the first time. "We'll have Family and Children's Services take your boy into custody."

"You can't do that." The panic on Alyce's face was painful.

"We can, Counselor," he said. "We most certainly can. What kind of woman takes a baby along on a B and E? You're not a fit mother."

"We weren't breaking and entering," Alyce said. Her voice trembled. She hugged Justin closer to her. He squirmed and whimpered.

"The victim's house was broken into," Detective Causeman said. "The gate guard said you entered Olympia Park

about twenty minutes ago. The security company confirms
that a pass registered to one Jake Bohannon went through
the entrance twenty-one minutes ago. That would give you
enough time to turn this house upside down."

"We didn't!" Alyce said. "Ask Adela Hodges."

"We want to ask you."

Baby Justin burst into full-throated cries.

Alyce's terror was more than Josie could bear. "This
woman is not my lawyer," she said.

"Josie!" Alyce said.

"I'm refusing counsel," Josie said. "I'll talk on one
condition: Ask Mrs. Hodges if Alyce went inside the
Poulaine house today. Go ahead, ask. Then ask her if
we came by yesterday to discuss Junior League business.
If you get the right answers, let Alyce go home and I'll
talk to you."

"And if we don't?" Detective Knob Ears took a step
forward. That small action seemed like a big threat.

Josie shrugged. "Then I'll shut up until another lawyer
shows up, and you won't get a thing."

"I don't make deals," Detective Causeman said.

"Fine," Josie said. "Then I don't talk."

On cue, Justin let out another furious roar. Alyce
clutched him tighter to her chest, which made him cry
harder.

Detective Causeman went into a huddle with Knob
Ears, then both disappeared. Alyce rocked Justin, but
the little boy refused to be comforted. He switched to
hiccuping sobs. Alyce tried to talk to Josie, but a uniformed officer stepped between them.

After several geologic aeons, Detectives Causeman
and Knob Ears returned.

"Okay," Detective Causeman said. "Mrs. Bohannon
can go. Mrs. Hodges next door confirms her story. She
says Mrs. Bohannon was outside in the driveway the
whole time, changing the baby's diaper."

Alyce looked faint with relief.

Detective Causeman turned to Josie. "You're another
story. You disappeared into the victim's house wearing
a plastic rain cape and a stocking cap. You're going to
headquarters and explain yourself."

Alyce looked stricken.

"It's okay," Josie mouthed.

"Josie, call me when you get free," Alyce said.

"Mrs. Bohannon, don't press your luck," Detective Knob Ears said.

Alyce pulled out of the circular drive, her baby wailing like a lost soul.

Olympia Park police headquarters looked like a mini-castle in a small English park. The inside was closer to a dungeon. The place was built more than a hundred years ago and the citizens hadn't lavished much money on refurbishing the interior. The interrogation room was small and beat-up. Josie sat a table that looked like it had been used for drum practice. The two detectives were across from her. Detective Causeman did most of the talking. Knob Ears sat like an Easter Island statue, silent, menacing, mysterious.

"How did you get into Mr. Poulaine's house?" Detective Causeman said.

"The door was open," Josie said. "I knocked and it swung open. I saw Zinnia on the floor."

"Did you go inside?"

Adela next door had seen her enter. Better tell the truth. "Yes," Josie said.

"Were you fibbing about your prior relationship with the deceased?"

"No. I met him at the store that day for the first time. I mystery-shopped Soft Shoe."

"Then why are you here?"

"I knew the housekeeper, Zinnia Ellis," Josie said. "She goes to my church."

"Which church?"

"St. Philomena's in Maplewood. She goes to nine o'clock Mass on Sundays and works the bake sales."

"Why didn't you mention your relationship with the housekeeper in the prior interview?"

"I didn't think it was important," Josie said.

"Not important. Then why are you here? Why were you dressed in a rain cape and stocking cap?"

Josie decided it was safer to answer the second question. "I didn't want to contaminate the crime scene."

"Very thoughtful. But what were you doing inside for twenty minutes? You searched the house, didn't you? Were you looking for something? Or looking to take something?"

"Yes. No!" Josie said.

"Did the deceased have something with which he was blackmailing *you* and you were looking for it? Had you been there before and were you looking for something you left behind? Is that why you killed the house-keeper?"

"No," Josie said. She was trembling. Her words were getting all twisted. It was time to tell the truth, if not the whole truth.

"Cheryl's mother is my next-door neighbor," she said. "Mel had a DVD that Cheryl thought would exonerate her and prove someone else had a good reason to kill Mel. Her mother wanted me to look for it."

"Cheryl and her mother never told us about this DVD," Detective Causeman said.

"Why should they?" Josie said. "You don't seem too interested in her innocence. Mrs. Mueller is convinced Cheryl didn't kill Mel. She begged me to find the DVD."

"So you tore the house apart," Detective Causeman said.

"No," Josie said. "The house looked like that when I got there. I took off my shoes and walked up the back steps in my black socks." Josie held out her foot. "See? You can have your crime scene people check for black cotton fibers. They'll find them going up the stairs to Mel's fantasy room and nowhere else."

"You've been watching too much *CSI*, Ms. Marcus."

"That's what everyone says."

Detective Knob Ears stood up suddenly, a moving mass of muscle. "I'm glad you find this murder amusing, Ms. Marcus. We can also arrest you for burglary and trespassing. Now, why don't you tell us why you were at the Poulaine house and what you found."

"I called Zinnia yesterday," Josie said. "I asked her if I could come over and take another look at Mr. Mel's fantasy room. She said it was okay. She thought Cheryl was innocent, too. She was right. Cheryl did not murder the housekeeper. Mel's killer did."

The detectives said nothing.

"I wasn't trespassing. Zinnia invited me. We had an appointment for ten o'clock."

"Too bad the only person who can confirm that is dead," Detective Knob Ears said.

"Yes, it is," Josie said. "She was a good woman."

"So what did you do with the DVD when you found it?" Detective Causeman was back asking questions.

Slick, Josie thought. "Detective," she said wearily. "I can't prove a negative. But I swear to you on my daughter's life that I do not have that DVD."

Her declaration had the ring of truth.

The DVD was in Justin's steaming diaper.

●

Chapter 31

Josie staggered out of the Olympia Park cop castle as if she'd been imprisoned for a decade. Even the weak winter sun hurt her eyes.

The two detectives had tortured Josie for another hour, but she stuck to her story. Finally, Detective Knob Ears had stepped out of the room. He came back a few minutes later and signaled Detective Kate Causeman for a quick conference. Josie wondered if the forensic team had found her trail of black sock fibers. For whatever reason, they let her go soon after that.

Josie walked to a nearby McDonald's, eager for modern light and sound. She called a cab from there. While she waited, she dialed Alyce.

"Omigod, I've been so worried," Alyce said. "I'm so sorry I abandoned you. Are you okay?"

"I'm fine. I'm free. How's the baby?"

"Good. Justin's asleep. I can ask my neighbor Joanie to watch him, and come pick you up."

"No, don't do that. I'm taking a cab. It's two thirty. I need to get home before my mother. If she asks why I'm in a cab instead of my car, I'm going to have to do a lot of explaining."

Alyce lowered her voice. "What about the—you know?" She didn't say "DVD."

"It's fine where it is," Josie said.

"Can I throw out the diaper you wrapped it in?"

"You'd better," Josie said. "I can't see you before Tuesday. Tomorrow I'm taking Amelia to the City Museum, then I have my date with Josh."

"Woo-hoo!" Alyce said.

Josie giggled.

"Josie," Alyce said in a small, serious voice. "Who do you think killed Zinnia?"

"We know it wasn't Cheryl," Josie said. "Other than that, I haven't a clue. I'll worry about it on Monday, when my normal life resumes."

All the way home in the cab, Josie asked herself Alyce's question: Who killed Zinnia?

Was someone trying to get the DVD before Josie found it? Only Mrs. Mueller and Fiona knew she was seeing the housekeeper this morning, unless they broke their promise and told someone. Or Zinnia talked.

Poor Zinnia. Josie saw her body again, lying in undignified death. Two tears escaped, but she wiped them away. Crying wouldn't help Zinnia. Asking questions might. Josie figured it was time for a little talk with her neighbor.

She got out of the cab in front of her house, paid the driver, and marched straight to Mrs. Mueller's door. There were no reporters today. Josie wondered if they'd heard about Zinnia's death.

Mrs. Mueller was in an imperious mood. She didn't invite Josie inside. She chastised her right on the front porch.

"Where have you been, Josie Marcus?" She had her arms crossed over her chest, as if to hold in her fury. Her chins quivered in indignation. "Your appointment with Zinnia was at ten this morning and you're just getting home now. You didn't have the decency to call me. I'm not paying you to be kept in the dark."

Josie let her have it. "You want information? Zinnia's dead. I found her body. The police have been questioning me ever since."

Mrs. Mueller sat down hard on the old metal porch swing. It creaked crazily.

"No," she said. "Dead? Someone killed her?"

"I think so," Josie said. "It looks like she was either hit on the head or pushed down the steps."

"But this—is terrible."

"Yes, it is," Josie said.

"Who would do such a thing?"

"Why don't you tell me, Mrs. Mueller? I asked you not to tell anyone about my visit to Zinnia, but you couldn't wait to blab the news to Fiona."

"Don't you dare suspect her," Mrs. Mueller said. "She's Cheryl's best friend, the only one who's bothered to keep in touch since her troubles started. Fiona was home all night with her family. She's as innocent as I am. I was here all evening with the hounds of the press guarding my door."

But Josie remembered Mrs. Mueller knocking on her back door. Verena knew how to give reporters the slip. "Did you tell your son-in-law, Tom, after I asked you not to?"

"I did nothing of the kind! I told you I wouldn't and I didn't." Mrs. Mueller asked with new humility, "Did you find the DVD?"

"Yes," Josie said.

"Thank God," Mrs. Mueller said.

"I didn't tell the police."

"No, no. That wouldn't be a good idea."

"I told them that you wanted me to find that DVD because it would exonerate your daughter," Josie said.

"That's exactly right," Mrs. Mueller said. She was an old clubwoman who knew how to read between the lines. "If they ask me, that's what I'll tell them."

"Good," Josie said.

"But I'd like to call Tom and tell him that you found the DVD," Mrs. Mueller said. "My son-in-law deserves some good news."

"Yes, he does," Josie said. "You can tell him."

"Where is the DVD?"

"I don't think you want to see it, Mrs. Mueller. I know Tom doesn't want to."

"I won't let him. Give it to me, and I'll make sure it's destroyed. Nothing will hurt those two precious girls."

I've already committed theft, Josie said. I've interfered with an official investigation. But I'm not sure I want to add destroying evidence to my sins. That's what will happen if I let Mrs. Mueller have that DVD. Should I give it to her? I'll worry about it later.

"You don't have that nasty thing in your house where your mother or Amelia could find it," Mrs. Mueller said.

"No. It's not here," Josie said. "It's hidden. I won't be able to get it until Monday."

"You will give it to me then?" Mrs. Mueller asked.

"We'll talk about that on Monday," Josie said.

"What are you doing this weekend while you keep me waiting?" Mrs. Mueller said.

"I'm going to get a life," Josie said.

Josie spent Friday evening shopping with Amelia for school supplies to take to Emma's birthday party "for the poor kids." Amelia's top pick was an outrageous pink feather–topped pen.

"This is sweet," she said. She looked so longingly at the pen, Josie bought her one, too.

She helped Amelia pack her clothes for the sleepover. Then she brought out her own dress for her Saturday-night date with Josh: a black scoop-necked number with a flirty ruffle at the hem. Josie did her nails and shaved her legs, then went to bed early. Tomorrow would be a busy day.

The next morning, Josie was at the City Museum with fifteen giggling, shrieking girls. She was one of five parents chaperoning the birthday girl's friends.

The museum was part artwork, part junkyard. Josie thought it looked like one of the dark, twisted Tim Burton *Batman* movies. It had undulating dragons at the doors and a yellow school bus hanging off the building.

Amelia and Emma loved the place. Their favorite section was MonstroCity, five stories of sky tunnels that led to real airplanes and fake castles. A joyous, shrieking chaos reverberated through the tunnels and twisting corridors.

Josie volunteered to take Courtney, Emma and Amelia to the museum's giant curved slide. This wasn't some lazy contraption that let you down easy. You had to achieve this slide.

Josie stood at the top of the curved slide. The kids had to run up it and grab the edge. All but the most athletic needed someone to pull them over the top. Josie was ready to grab a girl if she was having trouble making it over the edge. She was secretly pleased to see Amelia make it over the top without help. Her daughter was a natural athlete, like her father.

"Come on, Mom, you slide, too," Amelia called.

Most parents used their kids as an excuse to play at the museum. The dad hovering beside her seemed ready to jump down the slide any moment. Like most men there, he wore a Cardinals baseball cap, a polo shirt and jeans.

Josie thought he seemed familiar, but he looked like a lot of dads: nice, quiet, a bit of office pudge around the middle. A skinny boy, all arms and freckles, bumped into him. The man's baseball cap slid sideways, exposing his balding forehead.

Josie had seen that man—or at least his photos. "You're Cheryl's husband, Tom," she blurted.

The nice man turned on her. His mild face was gone, replaced by a snarling, threatening mask. "Where is it?" he said.

"What?" Josie had expected an introduction or an "Excuse me?" Not this rude demand.

"Don't play games," Tom said, his voice a crazy hiss. "I want it. Now."

Josie looked at his face, bright red with rage. Suddenly, pudgy Tom looked like he crunched more than numbers. What was wrong with him? He'd gone from dad to madman. The strain of Cheryl's ordeal must have sent him over the edge.

"I don't know what you're talking about," she said. She didn't, either.

"Sure you do," he said. "The DVD. Are you going to blackmail us like Mel did?"

Josie was shocked and hurt by his accusation. "Where did you get that idea?"

"My mother-in-law said you wouldn't give it to her."

"I said I'd have to think about it. I'd be breaking the law if I let her destroy it."

"So what's it going to cost me?" His voice was a snarl, but it was weary, too. Tom looked old and drained. Cheryl had taken everything, and given him nothing.

"No," Josie said. "Tom, I'm not like that."

"Then give it to me." His flat, menacing tone was an odd contrast to the happy kids' high-pitched squeals.

"I don't have it. Not with me."

"Let's go get it." His hands, soft and slightly sweaty, were clamped down on her shoulders. "Now."

"I can't," Josie said, trying to break free. "I'm here with my daughter and her friends."

"If you want to see them alive, you'll come with me." He tried to drag her toward the exit.

"Help!" Josie cried. No one noticed. She was surrounded by tumbling, laughing children yelling, "Help! Stop! Oh, God, I'm going to die!" No one noticed her serious cries for help in the midst of the pretend ones.

"Scream again," he said in that hissing whisper, "and I'll go after your daughter next. She's the one with the dark hair, am I right?"

He was. "Tom, you've been under a lot of stress with Cheryl," Josie said. "We'll just forget about this."

She felt something hard poking her side. "I've got a gun. You're coming to my car," he said. "Then we're going to get that DVD."

"Tom, don't do this. I'm not going anywhere with you. There's no reason for you to carry on this way." She stopped. "Do you drive a black car?"

"So what?" he said.

She almost blurted out, "There was a black car parked outside Mel's place the night he died. You killed him for this DVD." But she caught herself just in time and said nothing.

It was too late. Tom had seen her freeze when she mentioned the car. He could read her thoughts and see her fear.

"You think I killed Mel for the DVD, don't you? You're out of your mind," Tom said.

He didn't deny it. He called Josie insane, the one insult that would make any woman crazy. Josie knew that her wild leap of logic was true. She looked over at her daughter. Amelia had no idea her mother was being threatened. She and her two friends were laughing themselves silly on the slide. Good. As long as they didn't know what Tom was up to, they were safe. She flashed them a wobbly smile.

"Come on, keep moving," Tom said. He hit her in the ribs with his weapon. "Cheryl always said—"

Right in midsentence, Josie kicked him hard in the knee. The shock and pain made him let go of her. Josie stepped back and fell down the slide, tumbling end over end. She landed at the bottom with a dazed thud.

Courtney and Emma cheered. Amelia clapped. "Sweet, Mom," she said.

Josie sat up woozily and saw Tom running through the crowd, pushing people out of his way. She charged up the curved slide, but fell back just as she reached the top.

"Mom!" Amelia said. "You're such a klutz. You've got to try again."

Josie was furious that Tom was getting away. She made another, harder run and threw herself over the top. This time she made it. She lay there, panting. She could hear Amelia and Courtney applauding. "Way to go, Mom!"

They still didn't know Tom was trying to get the DVD from her. As long as they didn't tumble to it, they were safe. She had to keep them that way. She pushed Amelia over the slide. "Your turn," she said, sending Emma and Courtney after her daughter. The girls laughed and cheered.

"Wait there," she called over her shoulder. "I'll be right back."

The girls were too busy playing to notice her leave. Good. Josie saw no sign of Tom in the shrieking welter of parents and kids. Then she spotted a little girl leaning against a wall, crying, "That mean man pushed me."

"Was he wearing a baseball cap?" Josie said.

The little girl nodded and wiped her tearstained face with her shirt.

"He's a bad man, honey," Josie said. "You stay here. Which way did he go?"

The girl pointed to a door marked EMPLOYEES ONLY. "In there."

Josie ran toward the door. "Gun!" she shouted, pointing at the figure disappearing through the open door.

That word cut through all the pretend cries and joking pleas. "Gun!" she cried again. "Guy in the baseball cap. He has a gun. He's a killer."

The room seemed to be roiling with men in baseball caps, all trying to look harmless. A woman screamed as a man in a Cardinals cap moved toward her. Someone yelled, "Call 911. Call security." Some parents grabbed their children. Others hauled out their cell phones. A few men removed their ball caps. No one went after Tom.

"He's in there," Josie screamed, and ran for the door. She couldn't let him escape. He'd threatened her daughter. He could hurt a child, or take one hostage. He'd already killed two people. Cheryl's husband was a killer. Museum security would be along soon. All she had to do was keep Tom in sight until they arrived. Then the folks with the guns could handle the rabid CPA.

The EMPLOYEES ONLY door opened onto an inside staircase. Josie heard footsteps running up the stairs. Tom. That had to be Tom. Anger made her take the stairs two at a time. She wasn't frightened. He couldn't shoot her in the stairway. His bullets would go wild, ricocheting on the steps.

Josie chased Tom to the top of the stairs, but he stayed just out of reach. She heard a door crash open. Had he kicked it? She came out on the roof at her favorite part, where the yellow school bus hung over the side of the building. That section was deserted.

Thank God, Josie thought. He can't hurt anyone else up here.

"Don't come any closer." Tom's voice came in jagged rasps. He was standing on the edge of the roof, one leg over the protective railing. A gust of wind blew his baseball cap off. Josie tried not to watch it spin toward the street, far below. She couldn't let him jump. What if the children going into the museum saw his falling body? The sight would haunt them forever.

"I'm going to end it all," Tom said, his voice high and cracked by hysteria. "I'm insured. It pays even if I kill myself. It's the least I can do for my family."

"Tom, don't! I'll give you the DVD," she said.

"It's too late for that," Tom said. "I followed you here. I was going to kidnap you for the DVD. I didn't care if I killed you. I had to have that DVD."

"Why?" Josie asked. But she didn't wait for Tom to answer. "You went to Mel's house to make him give you Cheryl's DVD. You didn't mean to kill him. You wanted to save your wife."

"That's it!" Tom sounded desperate to convince her—and himself. "I'm no killer. I didn't even want to kill you. I'm glad I failed."

"Me, too," Josie said. He really wanted to kill her? Maybe she should let him jump. No, she had to think about all those kids on field trips down below.

"I'm a failure at everything," he wept. "I tried and tried to please Cheryl. Nothing worked."

Josie remembered the photos of Tom on the stairs of his house and felt a pang of pity. In each picture he was a little balder, a little heavier, and a lot more unhappy. Now he was a complete wreck, his armpits dark with sweat, his pants wrinkled, his bald scalp shining through the combed-over shreds of hair.

"Cheryl complained I didn't show my true feelings," Tom said. "She got me all these magazine articles about sensitivity and expressing my feelings. I'm not good at that. I flunked the quizzes. I'm not romantic. I'm a bean counter. But I knew how much she wanted new furniture, so I worked all those hours to get her what she wanted. She said I should be more romantic. I tried to give her that, too. But I was so tired, every time I hit the sack, I fell asleep.

"Then I found out she had hooked up with Mel and he was blackmailing her with that DVD. I couldn't believe what that creep made those women do."

Did Tom know about Cheryl's gambling? Josie wondered. She was afraid to interrupt.

"How did you find out about it?" Josie said.

"I'm more in touch with my feelings than she gives me credit for," Tom said. "Also, I listened in on the kitchen extension one night when she called Fiona. I knew I had to save my wife. I went to Mel's house to confront him."

"How did you get past the guards at the gate?" Josie asked.

"I have a number of clients in Olympia Park. I have a gate pass."

Of course. Josie remembered his mother-in-law bragging about his elite clientele.

"I didn't go there to kill him," Tom said. "I just wanted the DVD. But when Mel said those things about my wife, I hit him. Hard. Then I really got in touch with my feelings. I hit the bastard over the head with a paperweight again and again and he fell down the steps. He was dead and I felt good about it. I looked for the DVD, but I couldn't find it, so I got out of there."

"You didn't know Cheryl was in the house, drugged?" Josie said.

"No. The doors to the parlor were closed."

"What did Mel say that made you so angry?" Josie asked.

"He said he'd had my wife in ways I'd never dreamed."

Josie could see why a husband might kill the man who said that. But she couldn't understand why Tom let his wife go to jail.

"Why didn't you tell the police? You didn't plan the murder. It was extreme provocation."

"If I confessed, who would take care of Cheryl and Ben? If she was convicted, I'd come forward, but our lawyer thought she could beat the rap."

Beat the rap? The gangster words coming from domestic Tom made her want to laugh.

"You were going to put your wife through a trial?" Josie said.

"I didn't want to. I didn't know how to stop it. I never thought it would go this far. Then I tried to get the DVD back the other night and I made it worse."

"Zinnia," Josie said.

"That was an accident. I didn't mean to kill her. She fell down the steps trying to get away from me. I am such a screwup. I just wanted everything to go back the way it was. But it can't. It gets worse and worse. Now the housekeeper is dead, too. My family is better off if I'm dead."

Tom put his other leg over the barrier. He was teetering on the edge of the roof, holding on to the barrier with one hand. His shirt flapped up in the wind, exposing his fat white belly. He looked like a frightened, balding baby.

Josie felt sick with fear. She tried to keep her voice soft and calm. "Tom, please don't. We'll work it out. I won't say anything to the police. I'll forget about the gun you pulled on me."

"I don't really have a gun," he said. "I just pointed my BlackBerry at you."

"That's good," Josie said. "That was smart. See, you do lots of smart things. Now step back over the barrier and we'll find a way to free Cheryl. We'll work it out."

"You promise?"

"Absolutely," Josie said.

Tom put one leg over the railing, teetering slightly. Josie held her breath. Then the other leg was over. He was safe on the roof. Josie heaved a sigh. Cheryl wasn't going to be a widow. Ben wouldn't be an orphan.

"Tom, you did a brave thing," Josie said. "I'm proud of you."

"You are?" Tom stood straighter at her words. A passing cloud shadowed in his bald spot, and for just a moment Josie caught a glimpse of the handsome, confident man Cheryl had married.

Then two cops rushed out on the roof and arrested him for murder.

Chapter 32

Josie should have been exhausted after her adventures at the City Museum. Instead, she felt invigorated. Saving a man's life was a heady experience.

She had no idea if or when Cheryl would be released. That was Mrs. Mueller's problem. Josie had her own daughter to worry about. She made her statement to the police and avoided the press. A mystery shopper did not need her face flashed all over town.

"You were sweet, Mom, chasing that killer," Amelia said. "You didn't tell us, so we didn't get worried. And you ran after a guy with a gun. Nobody else's mother did that."

High praise indeed. Josie packed her daughter off to Emma's party. She saw Amelia greeted enthusiastically by her friends. She trailed a little of her mother's stardust.

Josie felt like she could leap tall buildings and lift them, too. Tonight was the night—her long-awaited date with Josh. She hummed as she got ready. Josie knew she looked smashing in her black dress.

Josh confirmed it when he picked her up at eight o'clock. "Wow. I'm supposed to say something sophisticated, but 'wow' is all I can manage. You look incredible."

"You look pretty hot yourself," Josie said. "Is that Armani you're wearing?"

"You must be a mystery shopper," he said. "Tonight

you will know all the secrets of my wardrobe." He kissed her lightly on the lips. "That was a butterfly kiss. It's my hint for where we're having dinner."

"Butterfly? You're taking me to Monarch?"

"Closest thing to New York in St. Louis," he said. "I won't have to think of anything sophisticated. The restaurant will say it for me."

They dined on duck confit served on flatbread, black bass rolled in hazelnuts, and risotto with truffle oil. Josh ordered an outrageously expensive wine.

"How was your day, honey?" he whispered in her ear.

"A killer tried to kidnap me, but I chased him down and talked him out of jumping off the roof. He confessed to two murders. That's all."

"Are you serious?" Josh looked delighted.

"Absolutely," she said.

"Josie, you're a freaking movie. You're better than a movie. You're a star, lady. Shine on!"

He looked so proud of her. He ordered champagne. They split dessert, a fabulous white chocolate blackberry pudding. Then Josh gave her a thin bracelet-sized box wrapped in blue paper.

"What's this?" she said.

"Open it and see," he said. His eyes glowed in the candlelight.

She ripped off the paper. Inside was a plane ticket.

"I'm going places," Josh said. "Come with me. Join me in New York next weekend. I'll have finished my agent interviews by then. We can celebrate. You believed in me, Josie. You're the only one who did. Be there for me."

I am in a movie, Josie told herself. It's an old plot: Girl meets guy, girl loses guy, girl spends a lonely decade without a guy, girl lives happily ever after.

She sighed as they clinked glasses. After ten hard years, she had it all. Some men were worth waiting for. She didn't have to settle for sweet, dull Stan the Man Next Door. She could have love *and* excitement.

"Josie," he said. "We've waited so long. Come home with me."

"Yes," she said. "Oh, yes."

He had a loft in an old city building. She saw only Josh, but she was aware of beautifully proportioned windows, hardwood floors, sleek black-and-silver furniture. In the bedroom, her dress slid away like an old regret. His Porthault sheets were softer than satin.

"You're so beautiful," he whispered. "You've taken my words again. I'm a writer, but I don't know what to say."

"Then don't talk," Josie said, and pulled him to her.

The next morning, Josie woke up in Josh's bed. He was in the kitchen whistling. Josie smiled and stretched luxuriantly.

"Is that coffee I smell?" she said.

Josh appeared in the doorway wearing a blue terry robe, his hair in wet spikes from the shower. He kissed her.

"Mmmm," he said. "That was good." Then they were in bed again and the coffee was forgotten.

Afterward Josie lay beside him, her head cradled in the crook of his arm. She felt loved and protected. Life would be perfect if she had a cup of coffee. Especially Josh's coffee. It smelled even better than what he served at Has Beans. She sniffed the air. That wasn't coffee.

"Josh, I know you're hot, but something else is burning."

"Omigod, the French toast." He leaped out of bed and ran for the kitchen. She heard the blare of a smoke alarm, then a hiss as he chucked the pan in the sink.

He was back in the doorway with a cup of hot coffee for her.

"Sorry about that," he said. "Have a drink while I put the kitchen back together. You can watch me and laugh."

"Sure. Do you have a robe?" she asked.

"In my closet," he said. "But I'd rather see you naked."

"Maybe in May. It's a little cold for that in November." She padded to the closet and rummaged for the robe. She found a red velvet one in the back. As she pulled it out, a box fell off the shelf. She tried to catch it and missed. It tumbled to the floor. Out came a gallon Ziploc bag of whitish powder.

"Oh, Josh," she said. A world of sorrow was in those two words.

Suddenly, it all made sense: Josh's new clothes, the car, the trip to New York, even the extravagant sheets on their bed.

Josh heard her heartsick cry. "Josie, what is it? What's wrong?" Then he saw the Ziploc bag.

"Josie, it's only coke. I needed some money to get back on my feet. I'll quit selling, I swear, as soon as I pay off my bills. Coke isn't serious. It's only recreational. Josie, wait. You can't do this. I'll give it up. I promise."

But Josie knew her lover was addicted to another drug—easy money. He would never give it up. Even if she wanted to stay with him, Josie couldn't. There was her daughter, and other daughters, too. Josie heard Amelia crying for the lost Celine, the "big kid" who was nice to her. Celine was only sixteen. She'd bought her death from someone like Josh.

Josie found her black bra and put it on, stuffed her pantyhose in her purse, and slid into her black dress. It looked dull and wrinkled in the bright morning. There was a stain on the hem.

"I'm sorry, Josh," she said, as she searched for her shoes. "You don't know how sorry I am."

"What about New York?" he said.

"What about it?" She found one shoe by the bed, another by the chair.

"You said you'd go with me. You believe in me. I need you, Josie."

Josie thought of Cheryl, Fiona and all the other women who needed things so badly they'd lost their souls.

"The trip's off, Josh." She slipped on her shoes and reached for her purse.

"Josie, you can't," he said. He was on his knees now, holding on to her hand, trying to make her stay.

Josie pulled herself free.

"I can," she said. "Good-bye."

* * *

There was no one home when Josie got back to her flat in Maplewood. Amelia was still at Emma's house. Her mom must be at Jimmy's. Josie was home alone.

I sure know how to pick men, she told herself. Not one, but two drug dealers. *"Josie, you're a freaking movie."* She mimicked Josh's voice. *"You're better than a movie. You're a star, lady."*

"And what shall we call this star vehicle?" she asked the room. *"The Two-Time Idiot? The Twice-Baked Fool?"* She fell to her knees weeping, rocking, holding herself because she could never trust another man to hold her.

When she cried herself out, Josie got up and dried her tears. She stripped off her dress and bra and threw them in the trash. The pantyhose followed. She kept the shoes.

Then she filled a bucket with hot water and squirted in a strong cleaner. She started scouring her house, stark naked.

She'd cleaned it a few days ago to get rid of the rat. Now she was scrubbing away another rat. She'd had another small-time drug dealer for a lover. What was she thinking? She'd seen all the signs. She just didn't want to look at them.

Scrubbing felt good. The hot water ruined her nail polish, but she didn't care. Her hands turned red and raw in the harsh water. She felt clean again.

The more she scrubbed, the more she thought. Gradually, her thoughts turned from Josh to another man and another failed relationship.

Why did Tom let his wife languish in jail?

He swore he loved Cheryl, that he did it to support her and the baby. He said he'd confess if she was convicted.

Josie didn't believe him. Oh, she knew Tom wanted that DVD. She knew he'd killed twice for it. But he didn't murder for Cheryl. He didn't love his wife. There was someone else in his life. Someone he would kill for.

Who was she? How did Tom know Josie was seeing Zinnia the next morning? Who told him?

Not Zinnia. And Mrs. Mueller swore she didn't say a word to Tom.

Who else had called her that night?

Fiona.

Then it all came clear.

Tom, who worked late nights at the office.

Tom, who couldn't be seduced by Cheryl, even when she wore her sexiest Victoria's Secret.

Tom, who never asked his wife why she sent Ben for late play dates at Fiona's house.

Fiona had been so eager to confess everything to Josie and Alyce—everything she wanted them to hear. Everything that would make her good friend Cheryl look even guiltier.

Josie poured the soapy water down the sink, dried her hands, dressed and drove to Fiona's house. It was still a model of suburban perfection, with an Indian corn wreath on the door. Josie knocked until the corn rustled.

No answer.

"Open up," Josie shouted. "Open up, Fiona, unless you want to talk about your part-time job here on your front porch."

The door opened. Fiona stood there in a dirty shirt and baggy pants. Her hair hung in long strands. Her nose and eyes were red. She had been weeping, but not for her good friend Cheryl.

"You told him, didn't you?" Josie said.

"Who?" Fiona said.

"Don't play games with me. How long have you been having an affair with Tom?"

Fiona whimpered.

"How long?" Josie shouted.

"Please, don't wake the baby," Fiona said. "I just got her down. Three months. Tom and I have been seeing each other three months. He found out about Cheryl's gambling. She was driving him to bankruptcy. He was slowly taking their assets and putting them in his name only, canceling his credit cards, severing his credit from hers. There are things you can do, if you're married to a gambling addict like Cheryl."

"Why didn't he insist she get help?"

"He—" Fiona burst out crying.

"He didn't care, did he? He wanted rid of her."

"Their marriage had been over for a long time," Fiona said, her voice wobbly with tears.

"When Cheryl called and asked you to pick up her baby, you loved it," Josie said. "You knew you'd have free time with Tom. He wasn't working late on those nights. He'd rush over to your house, wouldn't he?"

No answer from Fiona.

"I bet if I showed his picture to your neighbors they'd recognize him," Josie asked.

"All right, yes. My husband works until eight or nine every night. He's at work now, on Sunday. He's always at the office. When Cheryl would call and say she needed me to pick up Ben, I knew she wasn't at a meeting. She was in the casino. I could hear the slots in the background. I'd call Tom and he'd drop everything and come over. It wasn't just sex, although we had plenty of that. I'd fix him dinner. He'd give the kids horsie rides on his back. He's a terrific father. We were meant to be a family. Cheryl never understood what a good man she had."

"So why didn't you divorce? Cheryl would have let Tom go. She only cared about her slot machines."

"Tom had to have money to take care of us," Fiona said. "He needed his house. He had to have sole custody of Ben. Cheryl's mother would fight us if we wanted to keep Ben. Tom thought he could arrange it. It would take a little time, but he'd be free."

"To marry you," Josie said.

Fiona didn't answer. She was crying again.

"I could see why you love Ben," Josie said. "He's a sweet child."

"He gets along so well with my children." My children. Not our children. "He's like their brother. He practically lived here."

"It must have seemed like fate the night Tom walked into Mel's house and found Cheryl passed out on the couch," Josie said. "All he had to do was kill Mel and she'd take the blame."

"We thought so," Fiona said. "But he had to find that DVD. If my husband got his hands on it, I wouldn't get anything. No money, no children. Tom would have succeeded if that crazy Mrs. Mueller hadn't insisted Cheryl was innocent. She ruined everything."

Josie looked at the weeping, bedraggled woman. This was the femme fatale who wrecked two marriages and nearly sent an innocent woman to prison? "You are really something. You betrayed your husband and your best friend."

"All I wanted was a little happiness," Fiona sobbed. "I almost had it. You wouldn't understand."

Epilogue

"That miserable buzzard," Jane said. Josie's mother stood in the doorway, trembling with anger. Those were the strongest words Josie had ever heard her say.

"Who?" Josie put down her kitchen sponge. She'd been scrubbing the greasy furred dust at the bottom of the refrigerator. She'd come back from Fiona's and started frantically cleaning her house again, trying to wipe away all memory of Josh. It was working. Sometimes she didn't think about him for thirty or forty seconds.

"Mrs. Mueller double-crossed us," Jane said. "After all we did for that woman."

"What did she do, Mom?" Josie said.

"She's stopped payment on your check," Jane said. "She says she can't afford it now that Tom's in jail and she has to support Cheryl and her grandson. She's not going to make me Maplewood chair of the Flower Guild. The Altar Society is out, too."

"But, Mom, I saved her daughter. I did everything she asked."

"At the expense of her son-in-law," Jane said. "That's what Mrs. Mueller says. You won't believe how things have turned around, Josie. Cheryl is standing by her husband. She's thrilled that Tom killed Mel. She considers it the ultimate act of love. She's angry at you for exposing her husband."

"But I saved her from prison!" Josie said. "Her husband was going to run off with her best friend and take her baby."

"Cheryl doesn't believe a word of that. Mrs. Mueller

says you ruined her family. Her daughter and grandchild have lost their breadwinner. Cheryl has to go to work. She'll have a hard time finding a good job. She's thirty-one years old, she's never worked outside the home and she has a small child. She also has to find time to attend her Gamblers Anonymous meetings."

"She could be a mystery shopper, Mom," Josie said.

Jane took a deep breath and said, "Josie, I'm sorry I made you apologize to Mrs. Mueller when you put that flaming dog doo on her doorstep. I wish you'd do it again."

Josie laughed. "GBH, Mom," she said.

"I mean it," her mother said.

"I know you do," Josie said. As she hugged her mother, her outrage against Mrs. Mueller grew. Deep down, she'd never expected Mrs. Mueller to pay her. But the deal with her mother was sacred. Josie was not going to let Jane be cheated out of those committees. She'd lost too much in her life.

"I'll have to talk with her," Josie said. She threw her sponge down and wiped her hands. She was through cleaning up her life. It was time to go to war.

Josie knocked on Mrs. Mueller's door. The old woman opened it just enough to see who it was. Then she tried to slam it shut.

"Oh, no," Josie said, and pushed her way inside.

"I don't have time to see you," Mrs. M said. "I'm too busy coping with the wreckage of my family, thanks to you. I can't help your mother."

"You're not weaseling out of our agreement," Josie said. "Your son-in-law was going to let Cheryl rot in jail. He wanted to marry Fiona and take your grandson."

"He couldn't possibly do anything like that," Mrs. Mueller said. "Tom is not capable of such deception."

"Right," Josie said. "Keep deceiving yourself, if it makes you happy. But we had a deal and you will keep it."

"I haven't any money," Mrs. Mueller whined.

"I don't want your money. But you will make my mom Maplewood chair of the Flower Guild, or I'll put your daughter's pedal-pumping DVD for sale on eBay."

Mrs. Mueller looked thunderstruck. "You wouldn't dare," she said.

"Try me," Josie said. "And don't forget the Altar Society. You have forty-eight hours. I want an answer by Tuesday afternoon."

Mrs. Mueller's chins trembled, but her mouth was set in a stubborn line.

"What's it going to be?" Josie said. "I can make your daughter the Monica Lewinsky of Maplewood. I can make myself a nice chunk of change. Or you can make my mother chair of the two committees she wants. You have two days to make up your mind."

Jane got a call the next day, announcing her ascendancy to both chairs. She looked radiant, dancing around Josie's gleaming kitchen.

"I can't tell you what this means to me," she said. "I have so many plans, Josie. I've had years to think about what I would do. Now I can make it happen. I'm going to fix you the best dinner."

Jane pulled out her frilly white apron. But Josie couldn't take another night of Stepford Mom.

"Put down the apron," she said. "I'm taking you out to dinner. You're going to sit down, relax, and tell me your plans."

The next day, Josie sat down with Alyce at Spencer's Grill in Kirkwood for an early lunch. Josie loved the old restaurant with the historic clock sign. They sat in a big old booth and ate wonderfully greasy cheeseburgers and crisp salt-flecked fries.

"So how was your date?" Alyce asked.

Josie had prepared herself for this question. She'd gone over her answer in her mind a dozen times.

"It was—" All her words fled, drowned in a flood of tears. Josie tried to stop them, but she couldn't. At least they were quiet tears. Josie was grateful for that. She didn't want a scene in the restaurant. When the tear storm passed, she dried her eyes and took a quick look around the room. The other patrons were munching their meals. Nobody noticed her.

Alyce handed her another Kleenex. Then her friend

listened while Josie poured out her hurt, her disappointment and her loss.

"Josh was my dream lover," Josie said. "That was the problem. I was so wrapped up in the dreams of our future together, I never saw the real man."

Alyce let her talk. She had the gift of listening. She interrupted only once, at the very end, when Josie said, "What's wrong with me?"

"You mean, what's right with you?" Alyce said. "Do you know how many women stay with crooks like Josh because they're rich, hot and act like they'll go someplace? You had the courage to dump him. And don't kid yourself. That took courage. I can see the pain. It's real. But you'll get over him. I am so proud of you."

"You are?" Josie said.

"Yes."

"You don't think I was stupid for falling for him?"

"I'd think you were stupid if you didn't. But you were smart enough to see through him. You didn't let his drug money corrupt you. You did the right thing, Josie."

"You know the worst part?" Josie said. "I miss my coffee at Has Beans. I can't even drive by that place anymore."

"If you're missing the coffee more than the man, I'd say you're starting to recover."

Josie laughed for the first time since Sunday morning. It was time to change the subject. "I have news about your friendly neighborhood fetishist, Hal Orrin Winfrey."

"He's not my friend," Alyce said. "But I have news about him, too. You first."

"When I took Mom to see her counselor Monday morning, Hal Orrin Winfrey was coming out of the building."

"Anyone else in that office complex but shrinks and psychologists?" Alyce asked.

"Nope. I'd say Hal is taking a big step toward recovery."

Alyce leaned closer and lowered her voice. "Speaking of recovery, do you know that Hal dropped off six bags of nearly new items at the Saturday clothes drive for the poor?''

''That's very generous,'' Josie said.

''That's what I told him. It was especially generous to donate brand-new high heels.''

''No!'' Josie was laughing. ''You're making this up.''

''I swear,'' Alyce said. ''He never said a word about them, and neither did I. He had his wife with him, and they were all huggy and kissy.''

''What kind of shoes was she wearing?'' Josie said.

''Big honking running shoes. Ugliest footwear I've ever seen.''

''Good,'' Josie said.

Alyce chewed thoughtfully on a french fry and said, ''What do you think will happen to Hal and the other people in Mel's foot-fetish ring?''

''Nothing,'' Josie said. ''I've been watching the news. I haven't seen any stories about Fiona or Paladia being arrested. Those two women could implicate some highly placed men. You saw Adela's list of visitors to Mel's house—high-powered doctors, lawyers, even a bishop.''

''Not to mention a few Olympia Park bigwigs,'' Alyce said.

''We especially don't want to mention them,'' Josie said. ''I'm betting folks in Olympia Park pulled a few strings to hush the whole thing up. They wouldn't want any sole-baring.''

Alyce groaned at the awful pun. Josie laughed again. It felt good. Maybe it would become a habit.

''What good would it do?'' Josie said. ''Fiona and Paladia both have kids. They'd be destroyed if their mothers were arrested. Fiona's lost her lover and her dreams. And when I think what Paladia went through—'' Josie shuddered.

''So you think they'll just walk away flat?'' Alyce said.

''Probably in high heels,'' Josie said.

''Finished?'' the waitress asked.

''We've had enough puns, thank you,'' Josie said.

When the waitress removed their plates, Alyce dug into her purse and brought out the infamous DVD. ''Here. I cleaned it first,'' she said.

"I think Justin's diaper was an editorial comment," Josie said. "Did you watch it?"

"No, thanks. I have better things to do with my life. What are you going to do with it?"

"Keep it," Josie said, stowing the DVD in her bag. "It's Mom's insurance. I want her to have a productive year on those committees with no behind-the-scenes maneuvering by Mrs. Mueller."

"I'm sorry you didn't get your money. All that work for nothing," Alyce said.

"I got what I wanted," Josie said. "I'll never have to hear another Perfect Cheryl Report as long as I live. Mrs. Mueller's curtains will never twitch again when I go outside. It's worth it for that alone."

"I'd still like to know who put that rat on your porch," Alyce said.

"It was Cheryl," Josie said. "I'm sure of it, but I'll never prove it. She knew I was following her and she wanted me to stop. She had a closet full of shoes in the right size. She had the time. I live next door to her mother. I'm sure she stumbled across a rat in some grungy place and tried to scare me."

"What are you going to do about it?" Alyce asked.

"Nothing," Josie asked. "Cheryl has been punished enough. Her reputation is ruined, she has to work, and worst of all, she's staying with the husband who betrayed her.

"I'd rather have a rat in my shoe than one in my bed."

Alyce looked at her friend for a long moment. "Good for you," she said.

They were halfway through their pie and coffee when Josie's cell phone rang. It was her awful boss, Harry. "Are you ready to work or what?"

"What do you have for me?" Josie said.

"How do you feel about chocolate?" Harry said.

"I adore it," Josie said.

"I hope you like it for twelve stores. There's a chocolate chain that wants us to shop them. You gotta eat chocolate-covered strawberries, chocolate orange peel, white chocolate, dark chocolate, milk chocolate, chocolate up the wazoo. You like nuts?"

"Love them," Josie said.

"You gotta eat chocolate with nuts. Part of the assignment. Oh, and one more thing. They got a little customer service problem. Some of their women customers can't get waited on. Nobody knows why. Headquarters has been getting complaints. We're supposed to check it out. That sound good to you?"

"It's perfect," Josie said. "It's what I do."

"Then get your butt over here and pick up your assignment sheet," Harry said.

Josie hung up the phone. "I've got to go. Harry has a job for me."

"You haven't finished your pie," Alyce said.

"Won't need it. I'm shopping chocolate stores this afternoon."

Alyce groaned. "Life is so unfair. I have to attend the Wood Winds holiday decoration committee meeting to decide the burning issue of whether homeowners can put up colored lights or white twinkle lights only. I get serious boredom, stale cookies and bad coffee."

"Thanks, Alyce, for everything," Josie said.

"I didn't do anything," Alyce said.

"You listened when I needed it most."

"No big deal. Say hi to your sleazy boss for me," Alyce said.

Josie laughed and waved good-bye. Harry was a sleaze, but he was her sleaze. She wasn't a detective. She was a mystery shopper. Her job was to protect the American consumer, and she was proud of it.

She picked up her paperwork and was at Plaza Venetia by one o'clock, ready to visit the first chocolate store on her list.

Josie breathed in the mall's slightly over-oxygenated air and felt energized. She admired the great Venetian glass chandeliers hanging overhead, the Zen-like quiet of the fountains, the perfection of the shop windows.

This was where she belonged.

She smelled the chocolate store before she saw it. Its old-fashioned bowfront window had exquisitely decorated confections, each in a paper lace doily. Josie paused to admire them, and saw a trim woman in a blue turtleneck standing at the counter inside. Two sales clerks walked around her as if she were invisible.

"Excuse me," the woman said, "can someone help me?"

That would be me, ma'am, Josie thought.

Killer Information
About Shoes

Why do women like to shop for shoes?

Because they make us feel good.

Shopping for pants and dresses can be depressing. (Where did those pounds around my middle come from?) Buying a new swimsuit can be downright humiliating. (Who is that creature in the dressing-room mirror?)

But feet don't get fat, they don't have cellulite and they look good in any mirror.

Shoes are an affordable extravagance. You might never buy a $10,000 designer gown, but you can step out sometimes and treat yourself to designer shoes.

Shoes can suit your mood. The right shoes can turn you into an athlete, a cowgirl, a femme fatale, or a no-nonsense businesswoman. In hot weather, you can feel free in flirty little sandals. In cold winter, there's the hot fashion of soft sheepskin Ugg boots.

Here are some of Josie's favorite shopping tips on shoe fit, fashion and the best buys from coast to coast. Some were compiled from articles, shopping guides and frequent trips to New York. Others Josie got feet first, trudging through the malls.

Hard to fit: Josie's lucky enough to wear a size seven. I wear an eleven shoe. At most stores, I get my choice of two styles: plain pumps suitable for my grandmother or a gaudy number in gold and rhinestones, suitable for a female impersonator. There's rarely much in-between.

Two chains cater to hard-to-fit feet with a wide range

of sizes and designer names. My favorite is Marmi. Their stores have sizes four to thirteen, and width from super slim to wide. Designers include Rangoni, Vaneli and Sesto Meucci.

Marmi has almost thirty stores from California to Florida. The flagship is in midtown Manhattan at Madison Avenue and Fifty-fourth Street.

To find a Marmi near you, check out www.marmishoes. com. You can also shop online or ask for the mail-order catalog.

The shoe departments in Nordstrom department stores are another stylish place for the hard-to-fit. They carry sizes four to twenty and widths from AAAA to EEEE. There are more than 150 stores, including Nordstrom department stores and Nordstrom Racks. You can also buy online. Check out www.Nordstrom.com.

New York City shoes: The name says it all—Good Choice. Lexington Avenue is the place to shop for shoes, but many fashion mavens think Good Choice is the best choice. It's at 668 Lexington Avenue. For more information, call 212–813–9180.

The editors of *New York* magazine like Beverly Feldman, 7 W. Fifty-sixth Street, between Fifth and Sixth Avenues. They call them "giddy, colorful, there's-a-party-on-my-feet shoes."

For a real blowout, one of my favorite New Yorkers recommends Chuckie's Shoes, 1073 Third Avenue, between Sixty-third and Sixty-fourth Streets. She says it's "very high-end, very stylish, very expensive."

Planning a shopping trip to New York? Check out *New York* magazine's listing of daily sales at www.newyork metro.com. You'll find tips for sales of shoes, jewelry, clothes, household items, and luxuries big and small.

Rough up your new shoes: You may love leather-soled shoes, but they can be downright dangerous when they're new, slippery as an icy sidewalk. Run your slick shoes along a concrete sidewalk or driveway to rough up the soles a bit and give you some traction.

Designer shoes for $20 to $30: Target stores get top marks for style with their Isaac Mizrahi slings, slides, wedges and heels—all under $30. They look like shoes that cost ten times the price. But some shoppers say they buy Target's designer shoes only for special-occasion wear. They were disappointed in the shoes' staying power.

"If you are only looking for shoes to wear a few times to an event, then these are the shoes for you," one shopper wrote on www.target.com. "Adorable, comfortable, and easy to match with an outfit. But this shoe is not designed to become a staple in one's wardrobe, which is unfortunate as I truly love them."

Not sure your new shoes are keepers? Here's a trick the fashion models use. When they wear borrowed high-fashion shoes for a show, they cover the soles with masking tape to keep them clean and unscuffed. If you're not sure about a pair of shoes, tape the bottoms while you wear them around the house or try them on with your new outfit. Shoe stores may not take back the footwear if the soles look worn.

When flats fall flat: Flats have an undeserved dowdy reputation. They can look as stylish as heels if you wear them right. The trick is to have the right lengths with your flats. They're perfect with Capri pants. They look terrific with short skirts. But team them with long skirts or floor-sweeping pants and your flats go flat.

For chic flats, try www.frenchsoleshoes.com, or visit French Sole's New York store at 985 Lexington Avenue, 212–737–2859.

The permanent designer shoe sale: Many shoe lovers like the bargains at the DSW stores, which have name-brand and designer shoes for up to fifty percent off. DSW says a typical store has some thirty thousand pairs of shoes, including super-small and extra-large sizes and wide and narrow widths. The chain now has some two hundred stores, but if there isn't one near you, you're out of luck. DSW does not have online shopping or catalogs, nor will they locate or ship shoes to you.

They do have a cool free e-newsletter, if you like reading about shoes. Their Reward Your Style program gives you a $25 certificate for every $250 you spend at DSW.

For more information, check out www.dswshoe.com.

Shop your way to the top: You hate tennis and have a golf swing like a woodchopper. Drinking with the boys is fattening, not to mention dangerous. How are you going to advance your career?

Shop your way to the top.

Shoe shopping is the ultimate female bonding tool. Rather than barhopping with the old boys, go shoe shopping with the old girls. An after-work shoe-shopping expedition or a quick trip to the shoe shop on your lunch hour can do more for your career than a dozen memos.

If the shoe fits . . . You'll feel a lot better. Hobbling, as Josie will tell you, is not attractive. If your shoes hurt once you wear them at home, try these tips for a proper fit from the experts.

—Shop for your shoes at the end of the day. Your feet swell as the day goes on. Shoes bought in the morning, when feet feel fresh, are more likely to be too tight as the day wears on.

—Even if you think you know your shoe size, have your feet measured again. Shoe sizes may change. According to some foot experts, "The more we use our feet, the bigger they get from use in physical activity and at the end of the day . . . feet may increase in size by as much as ten percent as the result of physical activity."

Let your muscular feet grow in comfort.

—Ask the salesperson to measure both feet. It's not uncommon to have one foot larger than the other. Buy shoes to fit the larger foot and the other will follow in comfort.

—Make sure there's about a three-eighths-inch space

between your longest toe and the tip of your shoe. Note that's your *longest* toe. Some people's second toe is actually longer than their big toe. If you can't wiggle your toes, the shoes are too small.

—Try on the shoes with the socks or stockings you plan to wear with them.

—See if your local shoe repair shop can stretch those uncomfortable shoes. A good shoe repair shop can work wonders.

Let your mouse do the shopping: If you feel mauled by trips to the mall, or you'd rather save time and gasoline, shop for your shoes online. Zappos.com gets high marks from shoe lovers for their selection of styles, sizes and sales. You can find your favorite brands, from Birkenstock to Bruno Magli, from Aerosoles to Anne Klein. You'll see comfortable Clarks and hip Ugg boots. Last time I went online, there were ten thousand women's dress shoes. Zappos's couture section had more than two thousand women's shoes, including styles by Kate Spade, Kenzo, and Givenchy. Best of all, shipping and return shipping are free.

Killer heels: You want to remember your wedding, but not as the day your feet killed you. High heels really are murder if you're not used to them. Consider pretty, low-heeled sandals or ballerina slippers. These give you daylong comfort and a good look. Sexy kitten heels are another alternative.

Some brides wear their killer heels for the ceremony and as the reception wears on, bring out a stash of comfortable dancing shoes or sneakers decorated with ribbons and lace.

The hottest sales for summer sandals and shoes: The sales start Memorial Day weekend, and the prices go down as the temperatures go up. By June, you should get the hot discounts for summer shoes, sandals, swimwear and dresses. It's easy to plan your shopping expeditions. Many store chains, including Nordstrom, list the dates of their big sales online.

Nordstrom posts the June dates of its Half-Yearly Sale for Women and Kids and its Half-Yearly Sales for Men, as well as its July Anniversary Sale on www.nordstrom.com.

Hot fashion in a cold climate: The colder climes are not known for hot fashions. Witness the down jacket, which makes most women look like the Michelin Man.

Ugg boots are one winter fashion that's worn by everyone from Oprah to Paris Hilton. If you love the warm sheepskin boots, www.cozyboots.com has free shipping for online orders.

Shoe tip for men (and women, too): Looking for a good conversation starter or a safe way to compliment a woman?

Tell her you like her shoes.

Read on for a sneak peek at the next book in the Josie Marcus, Mystery Shopper series, by Agatha and Anthony Award–winning author Elaine Viets. . . .

ACCESSORY TO MURDER

On sale November 2008

"I can't believe anyone would pay a thousand dollars for a scarf," Alyce Bohannon said.

"Excuse me," Josie Marcus said, "but aren't you the woman who spent a thousand bucks for kitchen knives?"

"Those weren't kitchen knives," Alyce said. "Those were carbon-steel blades from Williams-Sonoma. They were works of art."

"And this scarf isn't?" Josie said. "Look at that color: Halley blue. It's three-dimensional. Feel it. It's Italian silk. The weight is perfect. It drapes beautifully."

Josie loved Halley blue. It was deeper than sky blue and richer than the color made famous by Maxfield Parrish. It was the blue of a bottomless lake. The color was magical with any skin tone from vanilla white to dark chocolate.

Josie held the scarf up to her face, reveling in its luxurious feel. Next to a Halley blue scarf, her plain brown hair had glamorous red highlights and her brown eyes were deep and exotic. Her ordinary looks were her fortune, or at least her living. Josie was the ideal mystery shopper, able to melt into any mall. She couldn't wear a scarf that made her stand out.

She traced the swirling bird-and-bluebell design with a manicured finger. Like all good designs, it was simple yet sophisticated.

"Josie, quit fondling that scarf before security picks us up," Alyce said. "It's pretty. But I could buy one almost as good at Target for thirty bucks."

"I could buy a whole drawer full of knives there for the same price," Josie said.

Alyce winced. "OK, so I'm conventional. I like my art in a frame."

Josie held the blue-and-white scarf against Alyce's

milk white skin. The fabulous scarf turned her eyes into sapphire smoke and her pale hair into platinum silk.

"When you wear something this beautiful," Josie said, "you are the frame for the art."

"Honey, I'm the whole exhibition." Alyce looked down at her generous curves. "I'm not built to be a clotheshorse, Josie. I'm too practical to spend money on something that isn't useful."

"Nothing in Pretty Things is useful," Josie said. "That's the whole point of this boutique. I wish I could afford this."

"You mean they don't give you a thousand bucks to spend here as a mystery shopper?"

"Not so loud," Josie said. "I'm supposed to be a *secret* shopper."

"We're housewives," Alyce said. "We're invisible. Those skinny sales associates are too busy being hip to notice us."

"Don't worry. I'll get them," Josie said. "I have thirty dollars to spend here, but it's not going to be easy to find something."

"How about those gold earrings?" Alice said.

"You have excellent taste. They're two hundred dollars," Josie said. "I may be able to buy a scarf ring for the scarf I can't afford. That's twenty-eight dollars."

"You know she lives on our street," Alyce said.

"Who?" Josie said.

"Halley. Her house is trimmed in Halley blue. That color is a little loud for shutters."

"Let me buy that scarf ring, and we can get out of here and talk," Josie said.

Only one sales associate was free. SABER, her name tag said. She had dark red hair and an air of chic exhaustion. Saber ignored Josie and stared straight ahead.

Josie recognized her type. Saber was a Captive Princess. The Captive Princess knew the universe had made a terrible mistake. She wasn't a salesclerk. She was royalty brought low. She did customers a favor by deigning to wait on them. They should be serving her. The Captive Princess took every opportunity to let the customers know they were inferior.

A lesser shopper would have begged, "Can anyone help me?"

Josie kept silent. She counted the minutes ticking off on her watch. One. Two. Three. At three minutes and fifty-two seconds, Saber finally said, "May I help you?"

"I'll take this," Josie said.

Saber picked up the inexpensive scarf ring with two fingers, as if it were a cockroach. "Anything else?" Saber was nearly paralyzed with ennui.

"This is enough." Josie smiled sweetly. She couldn't wait to write her report.

"You from New York?" Saber said.

"No," Josie said.

"I figured you didn't buy that here," she said, with a nod toward Josie's garage-sale Escada. "St. Louis is too Dutch and dumb."

"That's not fair," Alyce burst out. Josie was surprised. Alyce rarely spoke when she was mystery-shopping with Josie. But she was a fierce defender of St. Louis. She hated to admit her city had any flaws.

Saber stared at Alyce's blue silk pantsuit. "How old is that?" She didn't bother to hide her contempt.

"I buy classic styles," Alyce said. "It's five years old. OK, six."

"Old enough to start school," Saber said. "Too old to wear. That's why Halley is moving her business to New York. St. Louisans have no style. New Yorkers understand fashion. This cow town doesn't."

Saber slouched into the back room and slammed the door.

"Thank you for shopping at Pretty Things," Josie said to the air.

Alyce stood there, openmouthed. "Did you hear what that little snip said?"

"There goes her score for personal service," Josie said.

"How can she say that about St. Louis?" Alyce said.

"Uh, I hate to agree with Saber, but nobody would call us a fashion capital."

"Some of the richest women in the world live here," Alyce said.

"And buy their clothes in New York and Paris," Josie said. "Where do your rich friends get their clothes: Chico's, Ann Taylor and Talbots?"

"There's nothing wrong with those stores," Alyce said. "They give good value."

"Absolutely," Josie said. "But they aren't cutting-edge. Find one high-style woman in this mall."

"Right at the end of that counter." Alyce was too polite to point, but she radiated well-bred triumph. Josie followed her gaze to a classic type, the lady who lunched. The woman's ash blond hair was lacquered into impossible swirls. Her patrician nose was so heavily powdered, Josie wondered if she was hiding the telltale veins of a tippler. Some of those lunches were very wet.

"That's a designer suit, isn't it?" Alyce said. "That lumpy pink, green and yellow weave looks like oatmeal with sprinkles. She's wearing it with a mustard blouse. Those colors are so bizarre, she has to be rich."

"Her suit is Chanel," Josie said. "The bag is Kate Spade."

"What about the scarf?" Alyce said.

"What scarf?" Josie said.

"She had a Halley blue scarf in her hand a minute ago. She took it off the counter."

"Alyce, there were three scarves on that counter," Josie said. "I looked at one and put it back. You say she had the other. Now there are two. I bet she took it."

"Are you sure?"

"I think she stuffed it in her purse," Josie said.

"Tell someone. You're mystery-shopping this store."

"Don't have to. Security is already on the alert."

"Where?" Alyce said.

"See that woman pawing evening shawls by the door? Her hair is too short and black to be a customer here. Besides, her shoes are lace-ups."

"So she likes comfortable shoes," Alyce said. "She's wearing a nice suit."

"It's secondhand, like mine. The hem's been let down. I can see the line. She dresses like a cop. Her shoes tie so she can chase suspects. Slip-ons would slip off when she ran. Her hair is short so suspects can't grab it. She does her own hair color. No high-style salon would let a woman over forty walk out with coal-black hair. It drains the color from her skin and makes it look yellow."

"She's letting Ms. Chanel get away," Alyce said. "The shoplifter is heading for the exit."

"Security is playing it smart to avoid a false arrest," Josie said. "The suspect has to be out of the store, or she can say she meant to pay for the scarf. See the hard-faced blonde near the cash register? She's the other security person."

"How do you know this?" Alyce asked.

"Malls are my life," Josie said. "I can't tell you how many takedowns I've seen. Watch this one."

The two security women tailed Ms. Chanel out the door. Josie followed the trio into the mall and took a seat on a marble bench near a planter. Between the leaves, she had a prime view of Ms. Chanel. Alyce sat beside her. "What—"

"Shhh," Josie said. "The show's started."

The black-haired security woman flashed her ID at Ms. Chanel. "I'm with Pretty Things Enterprises, ma'am," she said. "I'd like to ask you about the Halley scarf you have in your bag."

"I am sure you are mistaken." Ice encrusted each perfectly enunciated word.

"Please return to the store, ma'am, so we can clear this matter up."

"I do not wish to return," Ms. Chanel said. "You are forcibly detaining me. I shall call my attorney. I have the receipt here."

She pulled a receipt from her purse. Josie thought the blond security woman turned a shade paler. But the black-haired one studied the receipt, then gave a small smile. "Your receipt was issued at nine ten today at our Clayton location, ma'am. It's eleven fifteen at the Dorchester Mall. You're using an old receipt with a new scarf. Step inside, please, so we can discuss it."

"I'm sure it's a problem with your cash register," Ms. Chanel said, but she didn't resist when security steered her inside the store and escorted her to a door behind a Japanese screen. The scene was conducted so quietly, the customers didn't notice.

"An old scam," Josie said. "Ms. Chanel buys an expensive item at one store in the chain and keeps the receipt in her purse. Then she goes to another store and shoplifts the same item. If she's caught, she tries to convince security it's a mistake. If she gets away with it, she'll return it for cash at a third store in the chain, or sell it on eBay."

"Do you think she's a pro?" Alyce asked.

"No, a professional would have spotted security closing in and dumped the scarf or paid for it. She's an amateur getting a thrill and a five-finger discount. I'll bet her mortified family will bail her out, and it won't be the first time they've had to deal with Mummy's hobby. She's pretty good, but security was alert."

Bass thumps from loud hip-hop vibrated down the corridor, drowning out the soft classical music on the mall's speakers.

Josie sighed. "I try to appreciate that music," she said. "It's supposed to be modern poetry."

"Yeah, a lot of words rhyme with 'bitch,' " Alyce said. "A store like the Gangsta Boyz Home is out of place at the Dorchester. Josie, you have to agree with that."

Three baggy-pantsed teens came out of the Gangsta Boyz Home and shoved their way through the mall crowd, leaving behind a trail of outraged glares.

"I'm sorry, but I don't want to shop with gangstas," Alyce said. "I don't feel safe. Jake would be furious if he knew I was at the Dorchester Mall. He made me promise I wouldn't go here anymore."

Statements like that made Josie glad she wasn't married. She didn't like making promises to a man—or sneaking around when she broke them.

"Jake's afraid you'll be attacked by the cane-and-walker crowd in Cissy's Tea Shoppe?"

"Don't be silly. Everyone knows crime is out of control at the Dorchester Mall, and it's the fault of the Gangsta Boyz Home. All the good stores are moving out. I don't know why it's here."

"Because the Dorchester invited them. The mall put in a gangsta clothes store and a video arcade. Those businesses aren't for the tea shop crowd."

"But why?" Alyce said. "Our crowd is so well behaved."

"And so tightfisted," Josie said. "The women who shop here buy one cashmere sweater at Lord & Taylor and wear it twenty years. You can't keep a mall open with that kind of spending. The mall wanted a younger crowd who spent money on clothes, sneakers and CDs."

"Instead, they brought in the people who shoplift them."

"Alyce!" Josie said.

"Well, it's true. Lucy Anne Hardesty's mother had her purse stolen when she left the tearoom. The young thug broke her elbow. Ruined her golf game. Another friend was held up in the Dorchester parking lot."

"I haven't seen anything about a crime wave in the papers," Josie said.

"Jake says that's because the Dorchester is a major advertiser in the *St. Louis City Gazette*. Jake says they're not going to report a rise in crime and risk the mall pulling its ads. Jake says . . ."

That was the other thing Josie hated about being married. The women quoted their husbands as if they didn't have a thought in their heads. Yet Josie knew Alyce put Jake through law school.

"Jake says . . ."

"Hey! You! Stop!"

Josie saw one of the tough teenagers racing down the marble concourse, clutching something in his huge hands. The security guard made a flying tackle and brought the kid down hard. They rolled on the floor while another guard jumped on top of the young man. A third yelled, "Call nine-one-one."

"Those security guards are good," Alyce said.

"They're stupid," Josie said. "Subduing a suspect like that is the best way to get slapped with a lawsuit. The kid's bleeding. The guards used excessive force. What did he take, anyway?"

"A biography of Donald Rumsfeld," Alyce said. "Why would he steal a book when he could get it free at the library?"

"He isn't going to read it," Josie said. "He's going to take it to another store in the chain and try to get a refund. If he can't get cash, he'll use the store credit to buy a CD. Where are his friends?"

"I don't see them anywhere," Alyce said. "I guess they took off."

"Unless he was supposed to create a diversion for the real action," Josie said. She heard a popping sound.

"Is that a car backfiring inside the mall?" Alyce said.

"It's a gunshot," Josie said, and pushed Alyce down under the bench. Two young men in short dreads were running for the stairs.

"Help me!" A young woman with wide dark eyes, four eyebrow rings and spiky pink hair staggered out of the athletic shoe store three doors away. Her face was bleached with shock. She could only talk in short gasps. "Two men. In dreads. They've got a gun. They held up our store."

Six shoppers with cell phones simultaneously punched in 911.

Josie ran to the young woman's side. Her name tag said COURTNEY.

"Are you OK, Courtney?"

"I'm fine," she said, but her teeth were chattering. Josie picked a sweatshirt off a display rack and wrapped it around her. Josie saw blue smoke and smelled cordite. "What happened? Did they try to shoot you?"

"They shot the cash register. Two guys in Crips clothes came in." Courtney stopped to catch her breath. "The tall one had a Glock nine. It looked like the ones on TV. He said he'd shoot me if I didn't open the cash register. My hands were shaking so bad, I couldn't hit the keys. He pushed me aside and blasted the register. He scooped up four hundred dollars. His friend grabbed three pairs of athletic shoes. The pair got away with a thousand dollars all together."

"But you're not hurt," Josie said.

"No," Courtney said. "Except my ears are ringing. Shit. I don't want to cry." Josie gave her a handful of tissues, and she dabbed angrily at her face, smearing her dark eye makeup. "I've never had a gun pointed at me before."

Alyce poured a cup of coffee at the courtesy counter. It was black as old motor oil. Courtney took a sip and made a face, but she drank it.

"I can't believe they'd hold up a mall shop in broad daylight," Alyce said.

"It's that freaking gangsta store," Courtney said. "I don't care if the manager did give me a raise. It's not worth it. Today's my last day." She tore off her name tag and threw it on the counter.

Mall security and uniformed cops rushed through the store door. Josie and Alyce faded out the side entrance. They hadn't seen the holdup and didn't want to be questioned by the police.

"I need some coffee," Alyce said. "Let's go downstairs."

They stopped at a kiosk for double lattes, then plopped down on the wrought-iron chairs in the mall's indoor garden. A pink froth of flowers poured from terra-cotta pots. Sunlight streamed through the skylights in shimmering shafts. The fountain's soft patter soothed them.

"This is such a beautiful mall," Alyce said. "It's a shame I'll never come back."

"Why? Because you saw two thefts? That goes on at every mall in America."

"Not where I shop," Alyce said.

"Yes, it does," Josie said. "One million Americans shoplift every day. They boost roughly twenty thousand dollars a minute. I know the gangsta kids looked scary, but what really happened? A white woman stole a thousand dollars and so did some black kids."

"No, you can't explain it away, Josie," Alyce said. "An old woman who shoplifts a scarf and an armed robbery are not the same. That holdup was frightening. Maybe I'm sheltered, but I like my life. I'll never come back here again, not even for you."

Josie shrugged. "OK, if that's how you feel."

"I do. My suburban neighbors can be crooks, but we don't shoot people in malls."

"You just hold them up on paper," Josie said.

"That isn't funny," Alyce said.

It wasn't. In another hour, more gunshots would shatter their lives. Nothing would ever be the same for Alyce and Josie.